Lucia's Masks

Lucia's Masks

Wendy MacIntyre

thistledown press

©Wendy MacIntyre, 2013
All rights reserved

No part of this publication may be reproduced or transmitted in any form or by any means, graphic, electronic or mechanical, including photocopying, recording, or any information storage and retrieval system, without permission in writing from the publisher or a licence from The Canadian Copyright Licensing Agency (Access Copyright). For an Access Copyright licence, visit www.accesscopyright.ca or call toll free to 1-800-893-5777.

Thistledown Press Ltd.
118 - 20th Street West
Saskatoon, Saskatchewan, S7M 0W6
www.thistledownpress.com

Library and Archives Canada Cataloguing in Publication

MacIntyre, Wendy, 1947-, author
Lucia's masks / Wendy MacIntyre.

Issued in print and electronic formats.
ISBN 978-1-927068-44-1 (pbk.).– ISBN 978-1-927068-54-0 (html).
ISBN 978-1-927068-78-6 (pdf)

I. Title.
PS8575.I68L92 2013   C813'.54   C2013-903935-X
                                   C2013-903936-8

Cover photograph, *The Masked Players,* by Teresa Yeh Photography/Shutterstock
Cover and book design by Jackie Forrie
Printed and bound in Canada

"A Rabbit as King of the Ghosts" from THE PALM AT THE END OF THE MIND by Wallace Stevens, edited by Holly Stevens, copyright © 1967, 1969, 1971 by Holly Stevens. Used by permission of Alfred A. Knopf, a division of Random House, Inc. Any third party use of this material, outside of this publication, is prohibited. Interested parties must apply directly to Random House, Inc. for permission.

Thistledown Press gratefully acknowledges the financial assistance of the Canada Council for the Arts, the Saskatchewan Arts Board, and the Government of Canada through the Canada Book Fund for its publishing program.

For John Stairs

Chapter One
Lucia

My deliverance came the day the vandals smashed my potter's wheel. I arrived home just before dawn, the acrid stench of bleach still in my nostrils. The door to my room was hanging askew from its hinges. My fingers trembled as I drew out my knife and entered the small, sky-lit space that had once been my sanctuary but was now violated and fouled.

I felt a sharp twist in my belly when I saw my wheel in pieces on the floor. It looked as if the interlopers had used a sledge hammer on it. I immediately knelt and groped under the bed, and cried out in relief to find the poet's life mask still intact in its box where I return it each evening before leaving for work. I bowed my head and thanked the household spirits of my ancestors that the vandals had not discovered the box. Was it the Chemical Head Children who had broken in? Whoever the intruders were, they had also pissed and shat upon my bed, as if the destruction of my wheel was not outrage enough for them.

For years now, it is only my beloved potter's wheel that has kept me here. It was simply too heavy an object to carry away with me if I decided at last to flee the City and escape through the forest to the north.

After my night's labour, scouring urinals, toilet bowls, and sinks in the washrooms of bleak office towers, my reward was to return home to my moist clay and my wheel. In my box-like room with its cracked skylight I felt completely free and secure through the early hours of morning, communing with the clay. It is a quick and responsive medium, with a binding truth of its own. A potter's hands and mind must be attentive — to the shaping powers of the imagination, and to the fluid form that thrives upon the wheel.

"What the Imagination seizes as Beauty must be Truth," Keats said. As I worked, I kept his life mask by me. I would glance up from my work and draw strength and calm from the noble forehead, the closed and dreaming eyes, the high cheekbones and the wide, tender mouth. If I wished, I could reach out and touch the shape of his features and the set of his expression, just as the young John Keats looked on a particular afternoon nearly three hundred years ago.

Now all my dear sustaining refuge was gone. The vandals had defiled it.

For some minutes I sat on the floor beside the shattered wheel, stunned and grieving. The realization came to me then that this desecration was my deliverance. I could have no surer sign. I had gone on too long, beset with anxiety that I would become like so many others in the City, either rancorous and sadistic like the worst of the street thugs, or numbed and dead of mind like the sky-screen addicts. I was becoming more and more terrified that the evil I witnessed each day would ultimately turn me into stone; that I would no longer understand or care what goodness is. Sometimes when I looked at the faces of the most depraved among us, I saw the head of Medusa — the one painted by Caravaggio, where her mouth yawns blackly. It is that hole of a mouth that transfixes you first. Only then do you see that her hair is a nest of writhing snakes.

With my wheel smashed, there was nothing to hold me back. I could discover for myself if there really was a place a thousand and more miles to the north where the EYE's surveillance did not reach, and where it was possible to practise a decent human kindness and serve one's craft or art freely.

I was seven years old when the EYE staged its coup. It happened on the cusp of night's stillest hour, a rupture that divided their time from everything we had known before. I was hurled from my bed and watched in panic the jagged light that pierced the curtains in time with the vast booming outside. My childish mind pictured a phalanx of one-eyed giants advancing, the entrails of their prey still hot and steaming in their mouths. The drums they beat in that ceaseless booming were made of the skins of all the lovely animals of the world. Soon these ogres would tear open our building and strip me of my skin and my sister and my parents of theirs. The giants would not care that we were still alive while they flayed us.

I saw the walls of my bedroom tremble in that ghastly light. Something was pummelling the soft tissue inside my head and chest. I had the urge to pee and vomit all at once, like a baby. That was how the EYE first imprinted fear in our bodies. They set a taper to our nerves to teach us what an unexcelled governance tool terror is. When the taper flared red-hot in our arms and legs, in our bellies and brains, we saw by its lurid light the crack the EYE had opened in all that once seemed solid and secure. We saw the mailed fist, without a face behind it, and how that fist could seize you by the neck and snap it and then toss your head to the dogs or worse.

It has taken me years to be able to articulate what happened that night when they burned their fear-brand deep into my core. These thoughts I keep within the confines of my skull. Concealment is self-preservation because the EYE's surveillance cameras are everywhere, and most of them cunningly hidden. Were I even to let the words "EYE equals terror" play upon my lips, they would spy me out. I would likely have my eyes and organs removed while I was still alive and semi-conscious and they were in optimum condition for sale. The remnants would be ground for fertilizer. The EYE is above all a "functional regime," as they never tire of telling us.

Do I exaggerate the regime's dedication to the "economic imperative?" Certainly, one hears rumours of such punishments, probably spread by the regime's own propaganda department. The EYE likes to keep our fear fresh.

I learned that first night a simple, decent way to make my terror smaller. In a splinter of silence between the explosions, I heard my sister wail. She was crouching on her bed and her tiny fingers plucked at her hair. Her rosebud lips had disappeared. In that part of her face there was only a little pink and white cavity from which issued the dreadful sound that roused me from myself. I ran to comfort her and gathered her in my arms as best I could to take her to our parents' bedroom. Thus my own fear dwindled by some small degree. Mama and Papa flew in at that instant, still pulling on their dressing gowns. They looked so unlike themselves, with their white faces and wild eyes, that for an instant I was afraid of this strange man and woman who snatched us up bodily. We fled down the two flights to the building's basement, Papa carrying me and Mama clutching Sophia to her breast. Under us the wooden stairs buckled. Papa gripped me in his arms so hard that it hurt. I focused on his familiar heat and the smell of his sweat and tried not to whimper.

In the cellar I recognized other families from our building. They sat holding hands, with their backs braced against the grey concrete wall. Papa guided us into a corner behind the big antique machine with its tubular tentacles that reached into snug holes in the wall. He had told me this machine was an "archaism" that belonged to a time when the world had a season called winter. I sat between my parents, clutching Papa's hand in my right and Mama's in my left. Mama had tucked Sophia's head inside the folds of her dressing gown so that my sister's eyes and ears were covered. I could see she was sucking her thumb. I strove to be brave. I wanted to ask for reassurance that it would soon be over; that everything would be all right. But it was impossible for anyone to hear me in any case.

When the silence fell upon us at last, I felt like someone had slapped my ears and made them tingle. Then came a great rush of relief and almost a joy, but undercut by wariness. I thought that if I had a mirror, I would see my ears had taken on the sharp triangular shape of a cat's when it is put on high alert. It was as well I stayed wary, because a siren lacerated the quiet. Sophia wailed. Then silence again. We sat waiting and on edge. Every face I could see looked wearied and strained.

Among the adults were those who plugged their ears with their fingers.

"Is it the all-clear signal?" someone asked.

"We should wait," Papa said. "Let us wait five minutes." But already he was on his feet.

The voice we heard next was a man's, hugely amplified, with a buzz of static.

"The EYE is triumphant," the voice proclaimed, a statement that made no sense to me whatsoever.

"We have made our country safe for our citizens," the voice declared. "Come out of your homes and look up at the night-sky."

All the adults were standing now, but no one moved.

"What if it is a trick?" asked Mrs. McPhilmey, who was a nurse and a particular friend of Mama's.

"Come out, citizens, and look up at the night sky." I heard the insistence in the command.

"I will go first," Papa said, "and come back to you with a report."

"No, Enzo," Mama told him. "Not alone."

And so we went up the stairs together as a family to meet whatever this new world had to offer. When we got outside, I was amazed to see every building intact. Through all those explosions, not a single stone was dislodged or window broken. The street was lined with people, all in their nightwear, so that a strange intimacy was forced upon us.

"Look up, citizens," the voice commanded. The blast of sound came from behind me. I turned to see a black loudspeaker the size of my face, covered in a dense mesh and mounted on the light standard. It was right outside our apartment building. Why had I never seen it before? I spotted several more at regular intervals down the length of the street. At a distance they looked nasty, like a smear of mould you wanted to clean away if only you could reach that high.

"Look up."

I was holding Papa's hand close as I tilted my chin upward, following his example. I saw how he had tightened his lips, so that his mouth looked like a crease in a sheet of white paper. I was frightened, but also excited. Because some of the people on the street wore clown-like pyjamas and fluffy slippers with pompoms on the toes, they looked like participants in a silly game whose rules were yet to be revealed. But it was fear that was the sharper of my two emotions, and as I stood beside my father, head thrown back and throat exposed, I pictured the rockets they might rain down on us or the liquid fire poured from great vats.

In fact, it was fire, or the illusion of fire, that we saw pricked out against the sky. Because the night was starless, the form they cast above us had no competition. Doubtless, they had planned it so. What we saw was a massive eye, its outline composed of countless dots of scarlet light. The eye was lidless. The centre of the iris was studded with a multi-rayed star. Under the image, an invisible hand began to write in a fluid script. I caught my breath, waiting to see what would emerge, what words the unseen writer would spell out.

At last, it was all there: a full sentence composed of reddest fire to match the outlined lidless eye. "The EYE will keep you safe."

We all stood staring up, children and adults both, caught by the crude power of the ugly, unsettling organ of vision arcing over us. It pinned us there, confused and small, and I shivered as I saw its scarlet darken.

"The EYE will keep you safe," the loudspeaker boomed. Then twice more: "The EYE will keep you safe."

When the amplified voice spoke again, we were instructed to return to our homes and watch the broadcast that would "explain the glorious liberation brought into effect on this historic night." Full attention to this broadcast was mandatory for all citizens. Parents were to explain the essence of the new regime change to their children based on the guide the EYE would supply.

"What is it, Papa?" I asked. "What is the EYE with capital letters?"

"Hush, Lucia," Mama told me. Papa did not carry me back upstairs. I wondered if he was angry with me. I had hoped I could sit with them to watch the broadcast that would tell us what had happened. Mama insisted I go to bed.

I listened hard in case I could make out any of the words of the broadcast myself. But all I heard was Papa talking in an angry tone I had never heard him use before: "There were no terrorists," he said. "They have staged this cataclysm themselves so that they could set themselves up as our saviours."

"But who are they, Enzo? Who is behind the EYE?"

"I don't know, Fiammetta. I don't know."

How sad he sounded. I wanted to go to him, but worried they would be annoyed with me. So I lay still, pondering what he had said to Mama. Of all the words he had spoken, it was "cataclysm" that hooked in my brain. I dared myself to try its harsh syllables silently upon my tongue. Although I did not understand its meaning, I sensed the steeliness grinding beneath the skin of the word; a sound like something snapped in half in the dark that could never be made whole again. No matter how often I repeated the syllables, the word remained a coarse and misshapen thing in my mouth that would not be softened. It seemed to fit all that had happened that night: the terror set alight and branded deep within me, and the sight of the lidless eye scored into the sky.

My body told me the EYE's promise to keep us safe was a lie. When I pictured the grim red image, the soles of my feet turned icy cold and the chill crept up my legs and lodged in my belly. I had felt this sick, numbed powerlessness once before — when Mama accidentally sliced through the base of her thumb with the sharpest of her kitchen knives and I saw the meaty texture of the flesh exposed and the white bone that lay beneath.

In school that week we began to learn by rote the "truths" by which the triumphant EYE would govern us. Our political instructor was Corporal Sweetman. He was a stocky, sparse-haired man in tight-fitting black uniform. Spittle flew from his mouth in a wide arc as he talked. Repeat after me, he began: "Pursuit of the economic imperative — which we hold above all other values — is why the EYE has taken charge, and consolidated the machinery of government under one strong arm." Eleven times we tried, our tongues encumbered and faltering, until at last he gave up and grimaced at us in disgust.

He handed each of us a pamphlet with a khaki cover bearing the official insignia of the lidless eye. Inside, printed in bold black type, were the questions and answers that contained the precious revelations of the new regime. Corporal Sweetman warned us that unless we got these truths perfectly to heart, he would have no choice but to discipline us with his rod. He showed us this tool, which dangled from his belt alongside the heavy gleaming baton we were soon to recognize as a prime identifier of the EYE's officials. The rod looked harmless enough, slim as a pen and with a pleasing silvery sheen.

Corporal Sweetman then asked if anyone in the class had ever been hurt by an electric shock. The trusting victim who put up his hand was Charles McPhilmey, whose lavish cap of auburn curls and milk-white skin seemed a marvel to me. Charles had his mother's good and giving nature and a rare beauty that made people like to look at him and smile.

So we were frozen in disbelief when Corporal Sweetman bore down upon him, seizing him by his bright hair and jerking his head back. The corporal thrust the silvery stick at the boy's chest. Charles's cry hooked into my brain, just like the cutting "cataclysm." This time though, the hook went deeper, tearing open a crevice into which a dreadful darkness rushed. For a moment it was as if I had gone blind. The interior of my skull went black except for two words, "Why?" and "Unfair" blazoned in an orange-red light. They ricocheted until I felt bruised inside by their battering.

My teeth were clenched. My hands gripped the sides of my desk. I wanted to leap up and protest. Fear kept me clamped in my seat, and I despised myself for it, although I could not then have defined that mixture of shame and deep unease that skirts self-hatred.

I looked to where Charles lay slumped on his desk, the fingers of his right hand twitching. I wished I could go to comfort him, but could not move.

"How do you like Mr. Rod?" Corporal Sweetman asked.

His eyes swept over us. I saw how protuberant and colourless they were, and I tightened, as hard as I could, the muscles that controlled my bladder.

This was our introduction to the pedagogical methods of the EYE.

I still have the EYE's repulsive catechism to heart and cannot think of these axioms without a sudden clench of cramp as I see again the slim shock-rod and blunt baton dangling from Corporal Sweetman's belt. At seven years of age, we students were at a loss to understand many of the words we parrotted. What was "acronym" or "innovative industry"? What did "inerrancy" mean? We were told just to mouth the sounds.

Papa squatted to speak to me face to face when I told him about the memory work and Mr. Rod. His eyes were wet. "You must be brave," he said. "This dark time will pass, and it will seem to us then like a bad dream."

I must remember the good household spirits of our ancestors, he counselled me, and draw courage from them. I must pretend obedience on the outside and memorize the questions and answers perfectly so that I did not suffer the pain inflicted by Mr. Rod. And I must remember, always, that the EYE's truths were really lies.

"Do you understand, Lucia?"

"No," I told them. "Why must I say these things, if they are untrue?"

"The people behind the EYE are ill," Mama explained. "They have a mania. They suffer a kind of madness or confusion in their brains so that they think foolish things, as people sometimes do when they are sick and feverish. We are unlucky that they have come to power. We live in an unlucky time, but this will pass, as Papa told you. And we will love each other and help each other through it. We will keep this secret: that we know the EYE's administrators are mad and that what they force us to learn is untrue and unkind. We must not let them know our secret. Do you understand, Lucia?"

"Yes." And so over the following months I learned to reel off the words embodying the "truths" of the EYE, beneath which moved a will denatured and without scruple.

THE EYE'S CITIZENS GUIDE

What do the letters of the acronym EYE stand for?
EYE stands for the Ever-Yielding Elite.

What is the Elite and how is it Ever-Yielding?
The individuals who make up the EYE are the Elite. This does not mean they are superior to the people. They are Elite only in terms of their special expertise, which will enable them to revivify our ailing economy. Pursuit of this economic imperative — which we hold above all other values — is why the EYE has taken charge, and consolidated the machinery of government under one strong arm. As the economy grows stronger and the people recover from their errors of selfishness, self-indulgence, profligacy, lassitude, and flagrant abuse of liberty, the EYE will yield its power to them. We say the EYE is Ever-Yielding because this process will be gradual.

What actions will the EYE take to make our economy strong?

The EYE's first step was to defeat the terrorists, who on the night of April 24, 2051 Old-Time, sought to destroy the infrastructure essential to the people's survival. As a second step, the EYE will utilize its exceptional expertise to harbour and build upon our essential resources of food, fuel, and raw materials. The EYE's third step will be to develop new innovative industries that make optimum use of our resources. These industries will generate profits for all the people.

What are these innovative industries?

To reveal the substance of these industries would jeopardize our economy's competitiveness.

How can ordinary citizens contribute to the EYE's vital work?

The EYE is aware that many of our citizens suffer from a sense of purposelessness. These citizens have been long unemployed in a stagnant economy and as a result, they find time lies heavy on their hands. Along with this sense of purposelessness, citizens often experience a sense of shame.

The EYE appreciates the suffering of the long-time unemployed. We have developed a program that will alleviate this suffering, and at the same time, enable these citizens to help strengthen the economy. This program, which is entirely voluntary, is called the Chrysalis State.

What happens in the Chrysalis State Program?
Citizens who opt to join the Chrysalis State Program will receive a scientifically designed support package. This package includes subsidized rent and a monthly pain-free injection that substantially reduces the quantity of food and drink an individual requires to sustain existence. By reducing their consumption, citizens in the Chrysalis State will directly contribute to cost savings for the economy.

What is the significance of the name Chrysalis State?
Citizens who opt for this program will be in a state of transition, like the chrysalis waiting for its transformation into a butterfly. Once the regime has the new innovative industries up and flourishing, there will plenty of jobs available for all citizens. Those in the Chrysalis State can then emerge to become active, productive members of the economy.

Is there a danger of lethargy in the Chrysalis State?
Citizens who opt into the program may initially feel more tired than usual. There will be some sacrifices entailed, for which the EYE will compensate these citizens.

How will the EYE compensate citizens in the Chrysalis State?
The EYE will provide free, non-stop entertainment to all those in the Chrysalis State. Gigantic sky-screens, now being erected over our cities, will offer exciting viewing to enliven the hours of these self-sacrificing citizens.

How should we regard the Chrysalis State?
There is no shame in the Chrysalis State. Those who opt into the program are vital contributors to the general well-being of all citizens.

What is the role of employed citizens in the new regime?
Employed citizens will henceforth be known as Survivalists. They will face their own challenges as some jobs are lost and new ones created in the EYE's restructuring of the economy. Survivalists will be expected to hone their skills of adaptability and self-reliance. These skills will be particularly useful as the EYE introduces essential cutbacks in social services, including reductions in the superfluous policing of our streets.

What is the role of the wealthy in the new regime?
The members of the Plutocracy are our exemplars. The Plutocracy's leading lights will be celebrated on the sky-screens. All citizens are encouraged to study and learn from the minutiae of their lives. The Plutocracy's glory is our glory. A prime function of the sky-screens is to cast that glory as widely as possible.

What is the main achievement of the EYE to date?
The EYE's main achievement to date is the founding of a regime that ensures our safety and security. We have removed the sting of anxiety that formerly plagued all citizens. As a result of the EYE's vigilance and consolidated communications, we have defeated, and will continue to defeat, all terrorist incursions on our soil or in our waters or airspace. Citizens are now bound

in one body, resilient and indestructible. We must all be firm of purpose. We will brook no undermining of our goals, from within or without.

What are the chief virtues of the EYE?
The chief virtues of the EYE are pragmatism, prescience, and inerrancy.

―

These opaque and rancid words we recited on command, some of us with the prodding help of Mr. Rod. Soon enough, they were to taste of blood and burnt flesh.

In the second half of the EYE-Year 1, the junta erected a ten-foot-high electric fence around the City. In the official nomenclature of the regime, this was the Safety Perimeter. In popular parlance, it became the "agony fence," because of the third-degree burns it inflicted on those reckless enough to try to cut their way out. An official decree went out forbidding the utterance of the phrase "agony fence." To use this heretical vulgarism was a treasonable offence.

EYE-Year 1 also saw the introduction of the "assimilation factories." Mrs. McPhilmey was one of the first inductees. When she came out she was unrecognizable, the light drained from her eyes. Her mouth hung open, like a fish. Under the terms of her release, she was made to wear a sign identifying her as "factory-complete" and to sit each day on a wooden chair outside our building. This was so that everyone who passed by might see the changes the assimilation factories wrought. Mrs. McPhilmey did not so much sit upon her chair, as hang upon it, like a rag doll that has been too many times through the wash.

In EYE-Year 2, the junta initiated its crackdown on all "frivolous pursuits." Held up for particular censure were written works of all kinds that focused on persons and places entirely fabricated. These were "time-wasters encouraging degenerate and immoral thoughts." The most heinous, in the EYE's assessment, were books that manipulated readers into shedding tears for "entities, whether human or animal, that had never actually existed." The shedding of tears, whether on behalf of flesh-and-blood or fabricated beings, impeded the regime's advance, as did every act of so-called comfort and kindness. If we all stopped to wipe away someone else's tears, or pick up those fallen by the wayside, how could we forge ahead as one body?

Because there were no resources available to sift through the mass of written material in the City, all books, with the exception of technical manuals and official documents, were to be yielded up for incineration.

In EYE-Year 5, the junta closed the public schools. Mama, who then lost her job as a teacher of mathematics, found work as a cleaner. Papa had already resigned from what had once been the Culture and Heritage Department to become a garbage collector.

In EYE-Year 11, officials shut down the workshop of Miss Spencer, the potter to whom I was apprenticed. In her shop we made clay pots for the preserves produced in the Agricultural Zone. Miss Spencer's crime was to give some of us instruction after work on sculpting the human face and form.

In EYE-Year 12, Sophia volunteered for work in the Agricultural Zone, seduced by the recruitment videos' innocent images of young people beaming over their honest labour. She was enraptured by the scenes of teenage girls, dressed in floral cotton gowns and crisp matching headscarves, who scythed the wheat with a sublime grace, moving through the golden field in sweet concert, singing as they went. Mama, Papa, and I waved her off on a bus packed with young men and women with shining eyes and hair. We heard from her sporadically. She was happy, she said, most especially working in the herb gardens, where the scent of basil reminded her of Mama. We rejoiced at the miracle of her release from the City's bondage.

In EYE-Year 13, Papa learned by chance the true name of our Zone. It was not the "Prime Zone," as the EYE had taught us, but the "Zone of Human Fodder." Papa was enlightened by one of the drivers responsible for trucking the bodies of the daily dead to depots outside the Safety Perimeter. Many of the deceased were Chrysalis State people, who expired quietly each day beneath the sky-screens.

Papa's face was contorted as he slammed his fist into the palm of his other hand.

"Do you understand, Fiammetta? It is not a metaphor. They use everything: eyes, skin, hair, internal organs, genetic material. When specimens are too poor to harvest, they rend them for fertilizer or for fuel.

"Human fodder," he repeated. And then he cried and Mama held him and told him to hush.

I retreated to my room to wrestle with the horror he had revealed. The dreadful thing was that I had sensed this all along. Papa had only spoken aloud the evil we all intuited beneath the obscurantist rhetoric of the EYE. They degraded us, even in death.

That night Mama took special pains with our family's ritual.

In EYE-Year 14, the junta introduced minuscule surveillance cameras that resembled buzzing insects. I began to notice how one of these sinister devices would zoom in on my face whenever I was forced to defend myself in some nasty street encounter with a hardened thug or a young gang member. If you tried to brush the thing away, you got a jolt-like sting, sharper than a hornet's.

"They are scrutinizing us for the Survivalists' spark," Mama conjectured, when I described the insect-cameras' fixation. "They want to capture what it is that keeps us going."

Then she laughed, which I found puzzling. "It is the one thing they cannot cut out of us and sell," she said. She smiled then in a way that was soft and warm and yet secret to herself. I had not seen such an expression on her face for many years.

In EYE-Year 19, I lost my parents in one of the epidemics that periodically swept through the Survivalist population. I was the last of my family left in the City.

In EYE-Year 20, the vandals violate my sanctuary and smash my wheel. I am twenty-seven, a year older than the poet when he died. If it is death toward which I will be walking today, I know that is preferable to staying. Without my wheel, I have nothing left here to keep me human.

I donned my thickest rubber gloves and gathered up the stinking bedclothes and thrust them in a garbage bag, which I sealed tightly and took outside to the huge metal waste container that serves the entire apartment building. I cleared up the pieces of my broken wheel as best I could, weeping all the while. Then I gathered only those clothes I would need, as well as the poet's life mask, a ball of clay, a washcloth, a bar of soap, a toothbrush and paste, salt, a box of matches, sun block, a bottle of water, and some dried fruit. At the last minute I remembered to tuck a little bag of pepper in my front hip pocket. I might need to brew some in hot water if I suffered from bad menstrual cramp. It was an old remedy of my mother's and a simple way for me to take something of her with me.

I was exhilarated to be leaving at last. I pictured myself as a pilgrim dedicated to the search for virtuous truth and beauty. If my feet faltered, if I grew afraid, I would think of Keats's brief, radiant life and take courage.

Just as I was finally ready to leave, I began to worry that in my haste and distress I might have forgotten to secure the lid of the waste container properly. I did not want anyone unnecessarily exposed to the stink of my fouled sheets, which the plastic bag did little to conceal. So I went back, on the last errand of my City life. And of course I found that all the bolts were securely set. I had closed the lid as automatically as I always did. As I bent down to pick up my backpack, I heard the scrape and scratch of claws on brick. Something was crouching behind the garbage container. I caught a whiff of it then, a stench that belonged to stagnant water and sewers. The thing began to chant. Its voice rasped cruelly, like the sound of splintered glass rubbing on glass.

"Beriberi," it sang. "Dengue fever. Dropsy. Cholera. Typhoid. Common syphilis. Lupus. Come to me, little ones, and taste my wares."

Suddenly the waste container started to tilt toward me. I spun round and ran out into the street before the thing was able to extricate itself from the narrow space between the container and the wall. Its nasty song played over and over in my head as I sped off. "Boils. Buboes. The pox." My legs felt rubbery — as if the taunting singer had indeed managed to inject me with an immediately enfeebling virus. Then my instincts took over and I began to run again, as fast and powerfully as ever. Within minutes I would be in the thick of the crowds in the city centre, weaving my way through the sprawled sky-screen addicts. Whatever it was, the being with the macabre chant would not follow me there.

Was the creature behind the waste container a Rat-Man? More than anything else in our cursed world, I have always feared an encounter with this hybrid abomination. Some of my co-workers scoffed at the idea they even existed. But I heard stories about the Rat-Men everywhere in the City and each fresh telling left me chilled to the bone and briefly paralyzed.

I have a horror of rats: of their ruthlessness and bloodlust and slimy coats. Surely these pitiless plague carriers are the most hateful of all living things? I try to reason with myself that none of the EYE's scientists would be so wicked or insane as to clone a human male and a rat. But when I think of the Chemical Head Children, or the sadistic young roller-blade gangs or the countless vacant faces upturned to the sky-screens, the Rat-Men seem far from improbable. Hadn't Papa said the EYE took genetic material from the "human fodder" they collected? What was to stop them splicing together the genes of a man and a rat? Such an evil seemed to me in keeping with the monstrous character of the regime.

Perhaps the EYE bred such aberrant hybrids for export, or to engage in perverse gladiatorial combat for the amusement of the Plutocracy.

According to the rumours, the Rat-Men specialize in spreading infections that cause maximum damage and pain. They want their victims' agony protracted. The disease takes hold the second they plunge a virus-laden syringe into your arm or sink their teeth into your throat, leaving deep puncture wounds into which they then decant a vial of infected blood. The thought of the Rat-Men is unbearable to me. I do not want to believe they are real. Yet I cannot help myself. More than anything else I dread the kind of lengthy, gruesome death they are said to inflict.

I watched my own parents die of the plague. It was the fourth major epidemic that year — Zeta 4 the EYE called it. From loudspeakers on every street, the EYE broadcast the usual warnings and paltry advice. Wash your hands thoroughly. Wear a gauze mask and cotton gloves when you go outside. At all costs, avoid contact with the sputum of coughers or the rheumy-eyed.

Until Zeta 4, our family had been lucky, protected perhaps by the genes of those sturdy peasant ancestors my father liked to boast of. He would laugh when he declared we were part soil; that the ancient dirt of Tuscany had made us what we were.

It was my mother who fell ill first. Each moment of that terrible day is scored as deep in me as a ploughshare cutting into earth.

Lucia's Masks

Mama was behaving strangely. She kept brushing her hands in front of her face and around her head. She let her knife fall from the cutting board where she was chopping garlic for the puttanesca. She began to pace back and forth in our narrow kitchen, beating at her chest and hips with her closed fists.

I felt wretchedly afraid and helpless, seeing her in this weird agitated state. I had no idea what was wrong or what to do. Papa was not due home for many hours. This was his week for the late shift.

I stood stupefied as Mama paced under some relentless compulsion, her hands flailing at the air.

"Mama? What is it? What are you doing?" I feared she had gone mad, broken finally by the changes in our lives. She had always been so strong for us through all the bad things that had happened: Papa resigning his job when the EYE made the department where he worked a propaganda ministry; and Mama losing hers when the regime closed the public schools. Children should be home-schooled, the EYE said. There was simply no money for any but the most essential services. Every penny had to be invested in keeping us safe from the terrorists of all stripes intent on destroying our economy.

"We must believe better times will come again," Mama always told us, even when she saw her former students running wild-eyed in packs through the streets, brandishing purloined kitchen knives. "Have the barbarians not been at our throats before? Did we not survive?"

She had developed a ritual she hoped would save us from despair. She would have me and Sophia and my father sit with her at the kitchen table; then she would bring out the treasure trove of picture postcards that had belonged to my great-aunts

Giulietta, Fontina, Nidia, and Claudia, the most ancient of our blood relations. These were women who had held fast to the tradition of black clothing once their men were dead, and who never ventured out-of-doors without their long, fringed shawls and head scarves.

Each of these old ladies had kept a personal shrine to Italy: her own album of photographs, dried flowers and grasses — and most cherished of all — the picture postcards, gone cloth-soft at the edges from being plucked so often from their paper brackets, held up to the closest light source for intense scrutiny and then pressed to the lips or to the heart. Together, these postcards made up a little map of paradise, eternally sunlit, sensuous, and above all, civilized to a degree I could hardly fathom.

At least once a week Mama would show Papa and Sophia and me the images she wanted us to take to heart: the piazzas of burnished cobbles; the marble fountains and statues. We looked together at the surging forms of Bernini's muscular river gods who daily come to life in the Piazza Navona; the rearing horses with their wild eyes; the flawless dolphin. I studied in wonder yet again the slender human figures of Canova, all suspended in the act of love or adoration or the dance. These graceful beings spoke to my own yearning for an enthralling passion that was also innocent. I looked at the wings of Canova's Cupid as he bent to caress Psyche and saw a substance like cloud vapour. I marvelled at how his delicate hand cupped Psyche's right breast, his touch as light as air itself.

These picture postcards were all I knew of sculpture and the milky stone Mama called *bianchi marmi*. The marble statuary that once graced our City's museums and public places was all locked away by the time I was eight years old. So for me, the greatest miracle was that these works of art were out in the open for everyone to see. They were a generous gift and testament to all that is worthy and yearning in humankind.

In this way, Mama helped us keep faith through the dark years of the EYE's tyranny. I barely recognized my gracious, steadfast mother in this woman with the contorted face screaming shrilly at me now: "Get rid of them, Lucia! Take them away!" She beat furiously at the air.

"Idiot girl!"

I cringed. She had never before called me such a name.

"The bats. The hideous little bats. Their wings are sharp as glass. They are cutting my face. How many are there? Lucia? Why aren't you helping me?"

She was shaking badly; her teeth were chattering. I tried putting my arms about her and she struck my face sharply, although I am sure she did not intend this. Even then I did not think "plague." I assumed she was hallucinating because she was overburdened. We were both working as office cleaners. At fifty-one, she found the job far harder and more draining than I.

And then the night before when we were coming home from work, we'd had one of those confrontations that left you feeling despondent and polluted. Mama spotted her first: an old woman, hunched over, moaning and rocking on the curb-edge. It was pitiful to see how she ground her knuckles into her temples. She smelled of damp wool and mouldy tea. When I touched the old lady's shoulder, I was surprised how hard it felt. Both Mama and I recoiled as the old woman stared up at us out of empty eye-sockets. Her wrinkled face dissolved. In its place was the tight flesh of a young man with fiendish eyes and a razored skull. I heard the ominous click of his flick knife and managed to pull Mama away after me, even before I saw the glint of the blade. I could hear Mama panting behind me. My legs are far longer and my lungs stronger than hers. But I kept tight hold of her wrist and she did her best to keep up, and so we escaped unharmed. Nevertheless, we both felt we had been touched by a contagion, as if his wickedness had seeped into our blood.

She sat heavily in her chair once we were home and began to cry. "Terrible," she said over and over. "How can we be compassionate, Lucia, and reach out to help, when nothing is as it seems? When a frail old woman isn't a woman at all, but just a cunning disguise a deranged young man puts on?"

I hated him even more then for making her weep. He had that semi-feral look, the eyes narrowed and set closer to the nose than is normal in the human face; the lips bloodless and no longer wide enough to cover his teeth.

Was it this incident that had made my mother break, or was it the EYE's "hygiene vans" we saw driving around in the small hours, collecting the dead and the near-dead from the streets like so much litter? There were new rumours that the corpses they gathered go into the making of "charnel pies" for which the rich with unholy palates are willing to pay dearly. Was what the EYE already did with human bodies not bad enough? Where did these unspeakable ideas come from? Sometimes I thought it must be the City itself that generated them, with its noxious air and heavy weight upon the earth.

Mama crumpled to the floor. At first I was relieved that her hallucinatory fit seemed to have passed. I knelt beside her and cradled her shoulders; put my cheek on hers and then instinctively retracted. She was burning and her breath smelled sickly. I managed to get her to her feet, and stumbling and awkward, we proceeded slowly to her and Papa's bedroom. She fell across the bed in a rigid diagonal; then began to shake again. I lay down beside her and put my arms around her. "Hush," I kept saying. "Hush." Just as she had said to me when I had nightmares as a child after Aunt Giulietta read to us from Dante's *Inferno*. Aunt Giulietta's voice had an uncanny penetrating power and her bowed spine and shrivelled face intensified the authority of the telling.

At nine years of age, I had taken every word of Dante's journey to the underworld as truth. I saw the damned in their torment, eternally suffocated, flayed, and eaten. In the nightmares a hundred devils stormed my bed, intent on roasting my girlish flesh and gnawing my heart. My mother comforted me, helping me to understand what allegory is and to grasp that in his *Inferno* Dante revealed to us the principles of conscience that prompt us to do good. Now, in the day-to-day life we witnessed in the City, the comforting notion of allegory had vanished. The squalid inhabitants of the Inferno had burst through the crust of Earth, so toxic and unregenerate that even to look at them imperilled one's soul.

"Hush, hush," I said to Mama, as she twisted on the bedcover. I wrung my hands helplessly and wished myself in her place so that she might suffer no longer. She began to scream, a sound curdled and unrecognizable as my mother's voice. I put my hand on her mouth to try to quiet her. I was afraid that the neighbours would hear and guess she was sick and report us; that one of the EYE's hygiene vans would come and that the disposal team, in their hermetic white overalls and goggle-helmets, would take her away.

Her lips were encrusted, and her teeth coated with a yellowish substance. She tried to bite me.

"Dirty slut," she called me. I couldn't believe what I was hearing. My mother knew I was a virgin. She knew how revolting I found the crude sexual displays and public intercourse we came upon on our way to and from work. She knew how disgusting I found the pornographic films the EYE had begun to show daily on the sky-screens.

"Filthy slut," she shouted at me again. Tears streamed down my face. I cursed the fact I had so few resources to help her: no potent painkillers or soporifics; no doctor on whom I could call. Only the wealthy had doctors. My sole chance of getting medical services would be to barter for them with one of my organs and I saw it was too late for that.

Whatever pathogen had taken hold inside my mother was working at demonic speed, consuming her from the inside out. She began to vomit up some putrid-smelling stuff. I held the basin for her, trying not to breathe in the stink. She asked for water. I ran to fetch it, but as soon as she drank she was immediately sick again.

She grew old and wizened before my eyes. I dreaded my father's return. He was a strong man still, with formidable powers of endurance but I feared that when he saw her he would be undone. When at last I heard him at the door, my heart flew to my mouth and stopped my speech. I had no words for what he must be told.

At first I thought he might be drunk because his face sagged and he slumped heavily against the door frame. Yet this didn't seem possible. My father always taught us that drunkenness is degrading. Then it occurred to me he already knew Mama was dying; that their infallible bond of love had given him a dire prescience. But he just went on staring at me glassily, and so at last I perceived the truth: that the plague had struck him too. He was too weak to get to the bedroom. With my help he managed to stagger to the couch where he lay down with his face turned away from me. Unlike Mama, he did not shake or cry out in his agony. It was as if he had willed himself to be granite-like and stoic, and to let death take him without a murmur of protest or rage.

I kept walking back and forth between Mama and Papa, checking to see if they moved or spoke. All the while, I prayed fervently for the kind of miracle the great Giotto painted: the omnipotent hand of God reaching out of the sky to heal them or the appearance of a blazing comet that would rewrite all our fates. I took from among the trove of postcards an image of the dome of Santa Maria del Fiore, which Brunelleschi and his artisans had laboured over three decades to raise into the air. I clutched it in my hands as a talisman. The thought of this astounding dome, topped by its stone lantern, summoned for me the very light of the *Rinascimento* and helped me to endure the worst hours of my life.

Sometimes I got down on my knees to pray. It was in that position that the functionaries of the EYE's hygiene unit found me when they burst through the door. They looked like grotesque parodies of angels in their glistening white protective suits and head coverings. It was impossible to tell what sex they were.

"Can you help them?" I cried. "Can I go with them?" They did not answer me. The peculiar nausea came upon me I always feel in the presence of the inhuman. I had clung to the hope I might reason with them or stir them to pity. I struggled to hold off the thick panic that began to coil round my brain. I had to keep my wits about me and do all I could to halt the "hygiene procedure." I could no longer delude myself about their intention. In the unconscionable inverted language of the EYE, "hygiene" always means extermination.

The three officers each produced a long zippered bag from an invisible pocket in their protective suits. These bags of olive green had the same repellent sheen as their white garb. I pictured each of these bags filled with a human body, like a horrific overblown pupa. I began to pull at my hair in a frenzy. I knew nothing would ever re-emerge from this accursed casing.

Two of the officers wrenched my father from the couch. I hurled myself at them and began to beat furiously at their backs and arms. But as soon as I touched the glistening material of their suits, an electric shock jolted my spine and I was flung back across the room. I saw them thrust Papa feet first into the zippered sack. I thought I heard him moan. I got to my feet and went at them again. Through a haze of tears and hot rage, I saw a white form looming over me. Something cold and steely pricked my forearm. Then I was plunging into a blackness so thick and wet and fretted with red veins, it seemed a thing alive.

When I came to, I was alone. I sat upon the floor in the thin morning light and rocked myself. A little child inside me wailed for her Mama and Papa who had been so cruelly torn away. I bit my own hand to quiet her.

I could not understand why the hygiene unit had not also taken me. I thought it would be better had they done so. When I struggled to stand, I saw a plastic disk dangling from a cord about my neck. I took it to the window to hold it to the light. Stamped on the disk was the sing word "Clean" above the EYE's imprimatur. So I came to understand that the needle they put in my arm was a viral check and not just a drug to knock me out.

"Why?" the child in me kept asking. "Why have I been spared? How am I to keep going alone, in this unbearable place?"

My survival seemed to me so totally undeserved, I felt I had committed a crime. The EYE, ever-brutal in its efficiency, soon obliterated any lingering hope I harboured that my parents might be cured and return home. Within an hour of my regaining consciousness I heard a sharply repetitive knock at the door. My first thought was that the hygiene unit had come back for me. Although I despised myself for the naked instinct, my flesh tightened in fear.

The functionary at the door was one of the EYE's messenger fleet. He was dressed in dull black and his face was obscured by a balaclava with slits for eyes and mouth. As he handed me a grainy grey envelope, I saw the truncheon swaying on his belt. He disappeared immediately into the gloom of the corridor. I glimpsed a neighbour's white face peering at me from behind her door. Her eyes were hard.

I could not bring myself to open the envelope right away. I set it on the table and then sat in Mama's chair so that I might draw on some of her strength. At last I tore the envelope open. How blunt the words were, and heartless. Only their names, the hour and minute of their respective deaths and the fact their bodies had been burned to control the infection. I was grateful for that small mercy: because they had died of plague, they were spared the crude violation of the "harvesting procedure." The communiqué also warned me I would soon be evicted because the size of the apartment exceeded my needs.

I lost track of time then. I let grief do with me what it would. Sometimes it made me dull and heavy as stone. Sometimes it tore at me with teeth so sharp, I had to put my fist in my mouth to stop myself screaming. Grief, I began to understand, has a killing power that can consume you whole. One morning I caught sight of my own image in the bathroom mirror and was appalled. My hair hung loose and tangled. My mouth was open in a silent howl. My skin was dry and salt-laden from the tears.

I heard my mother's voice then, as clearly as if she stood beside me. "*Laborare est orare,* Lucia. To work is to pray."

It was one of her favourite sayings, especially after the EYE's policies stripped her and Papa of their professions. "To work is to have dignity. Remember this, Lucia." In this way she imbued our toil as cleaners with a kind of nobility. Manual labour kept us human, Mama said. It was better to endure the petty humiliations of the itinerant cleaner than to live off the EYE's "support package" and enter the despicable Chrysalis State. *Laborare est orare*. I washed my face and brushed my hair until it gleamed. Then I plaited it carefully, ply over ply, as my mother had taught me when I was a girl.

I was most blessed that day that my first client was Mrs. Fancott, a gentle-spoken, cultured elderly woman who always treated me with a rare courtesy. When I had finished my cleaning in her apartment, she would offer me lemon-scented tea and speak to me about the young poet whose life mask had compelled my attention from the first time I saw it. The mask sat on its own shelf above the desk in her study. When I dusted and vacuumed in that room, I would always take some time to look at him.

I had never seen a face so beautiful or so calm. I was therefore amazed when Mrs. Fancott told me of the many misfortunes John Keats had suffered in his short life: the early and tragic loss of both his parents, and the painful wasting away of his beloved younger brother, struck down by the family curse of tuberculosis. In his devoted nursing of his brother, Keats caught the disease himself. During his last few years on earth, he had to battle not just the effects of his illness, but also a sometimes debilitating melancholy. Caustic critics reviled the sensuous language of his poetry and mocked him publicly for his lowly origins.

"I treasure not just his words, but the very example of his life," Mrs. Fancott often told me. "In his wonderful letters to his friends, he never loses sight of the moral and healing powers of the imagination. He goes on teaching all of us that there is a value and purpose to our suffering; that the testing by misfortune, this World of Pain and Troubles, is how we transform our intelligence into a soul."

That day I returned to the discipline of work, I wanted badly to look at the poet's life mask. Though it was just a copy of the original made hundreds of years ago, it projected for me the actual soul of the man: vast, empathetic, yearning, and selfless.

I did not tell Mrs. Fancott what had happened. I had no wish to burden her with my trouble. But she intuited my loss, I believe, and was even more sensitive and generous in her conversation with me than usual. She then astounded me by promising to leave me the life mask in her will. And so it came to pass into my keeping and my care.

It has always disturbed me that my parents had no proper burial place where I could go to pay my respects. But I strove each day to keep them in strong remembrance by living out the values they taught me: forbearance, kindness, and an unfaltering belief in the redemptive powers of art. Because it was my mother's voice I heard that morning rousing me from my despondency and back to discipline, I always felt it was she who sent me to Mrs. Fancott's apartment — at a time I most needed to hear of the poet's constancy and his unwavering faith in what the human imagination can achieve. Whatever trials I encountered on my journey north, I vowed I would hold fast to the idea of Keats's exemplary courage — a courage I saw even in the way he bore the ordeal of the mask-making process itself. His friend, the artist Benjamin Haydon, had wanted a plaster copy of the poet's face to help him paint a portrait. It always made me shudder to think of the wet slick of plaster gradually hardening over Keats's face until it became rigid, sealing shut his lips and eyes. He was able to breathe only through two straws inserted in his nostrils. I would try to imagine the long hours he had endured this potentially lethal casing, and the panic would rise from my chest to my throat, like something squirming and desperate to find its way out into the open air.

A longing to breathe the fresh air of the forest spurred me on now, for no quarter of the City stank worse than this congested area where the sky-screens proliferated. Many of the watchers were so sluggish they lay all day in their own filth. I did not like to look down at their faces, with their gaping mouths and the slobber streaking their cheeks. The worst were the ones who masturbated openly, so aroused by the scenes they watched that they had lost all sense of shame. Just one last time, I told myself, only once more did I have to pick my way through this sea of pitiful addicts. I have always feared these slug-like people would pull me down; that I would sink into their vice as if it were a living slime.

 I try to be charitable. There is a rumour that the sky-screens emit vapours which undo the capacity for clear thought and perhaps this accounts for the watchers' lethargy and lewd behaviour. Nevertheless, the core of the City devoted to the sky-screens always seems to me a circle of hell whose squalor not even Dante could have imagined. I averted my eyes from a woman baring her right breast so that the man lying beside her could fondle it. As I faltered, I swayed a little under the weight of my pack. From somewhere amidst the sprawled bodies at my feet, a hand locked on my ankle. I lurched forward and found myself staring down into the gulf of a leering mouth. I had no choice but to strike the man hard upon the brow.

He groaned and cursed me but loosened his grip. I sped away quickly — too quickly — for the blood rushed to my head and I had to stop a moment and close my eyes. When I opened them I was looking up, despite all my precautions, at the image on the screen above me. There I saw an act of sexual congress so violent I could not understand why it did not make the participants bleed. I went on, more wary than ever, and desperately wishing I could wash myself clean. I could not comprehend this compulsion for spying on lust's most extreme rampage. What good could there be in glorifying a desire tempered by neither spirit nor affection?

    I was familiar with the official EYE policy: that the screens provide free entertainment for the poor and all those who opt into the Chrysalis State. As with most of the EYE's propaganda, I knew the truth of the matter was far more insidious. The non-stop pornography the sky-screens projected was designed to keep the viewers stupefied and powerless.

    As I ran on I indulged in a little envy for the lot of the wealthy. With their armoured limousines, their gated and alarmed communities, their bodyguards and private armies, they alone can insulate themselves from the sickening daily spectacle of the sky-screen throngs, from the vicious children high on solvents, from the burnt and gnawed corpses in the alleyways, and the depredations of the semi-feral. But I reminded myself that the rich also pay a great price because, day and night, it is the images of the most celebrated and glamorous of these plutocrats that are projected on the City's many sky-screens. They are in some sense public property, co-opted by the EYE to perform in ways that are tawdry, if not disgusting.

I had several miles yet to cover before I came to the City boundary and the long-defunct rail track that would lead me to the forest where my real journey north would begin. This was the only opening left in the Safety Perimeter. The EYE assumed that only the foolhardy would attempt this exit, given the dangers of the forest beyond, not least the roaming packs of feral dogs.

The main threat I now faced was a possible encounter with one of the sadistic street gangs who give themselves names like the Vigilantes for Beauty, and Perfection on Wheels.

I find all these young men and women horrific. They have faces and physiques like Michelangelo's muscular angels. They flaunt their bodies in the skimpiest of clothing and wear necklaces hung with small, round mirrors. On their wheeled skates, they stream through the City in groups of up to twenty or thirty, often gazing at themselves in their little mirrors as they speed by. Their chief sport is baiting the infirm or anyone they find unattractive. They will surround a woman with a limp or a man with a bulbous nose, and then taunt and poke and prod their victim, until he or she breaks down. The sight of tears makes them laugh uproariously.

They are heartless and any time I saw them at their cruel business, I felt sick to my stomach. If they were not too many, I tried remonstrating with them. I have the advantage that I am taller than them all. Sometimes they listened to me and stopped tormenting their prey, probably because I had begun carrying two weapons. As well as the dagger strapped to my thigh, I had a machete in a leather case slung round my neck. It cost me a month's wages, and I hoped never to have to use it. But I knew I looked strong and determined enough to wield both weapons at once, and appearance is everything to these vapid, self-obsessed young people.

If there were twenty or more of them, they simply jeered, and called me a garlic-stinking wop woman or worse. When they were that many, I hated the fact I was powerless to stop their sick sport. The Vigilantes for Beauty are the most revolting of them all. Every day I would hear yet another report of them setting one of their victims on fire or kicking a street child to death, while videoing the murder for their later viewing pleasure.

As I strode on I began to wonder if it had been a mistake to leave the machete behind. But with the excess weight in my pack I was concerned that the heavy weapon, which was in any case mostly for show, would slow me badly.

I turned a corner and my stomach lurched. Barring my way, his chin titled upward in the arrogant pose he habitually assumed, was the Vigilante leader with whom I have had several vitriolic confrontations. He was the one who incited the Chemical Head Children to their worst mischief, getting them dangerously high on solvents and encouraging them to swarm their human targets to extract teeth and clumps of hair. His eyes are the colour of emeralds and he has a lean, cruel beauty that makes me think of Lucifer.

"Wop woman!" he said. "How very pleasant to meet you again. And just when I have a real craving for the reek of charred garlic." He kept his emerald eyes fixed on my face and his upper lip curled back over his perfect teeth. He assumed the loose-limbed, confident posture of one who is about to strike and knows he will not miss his target. I willed every muscle to be ready for him, whichever way he moved. How fluidly he slipped his hand into his back pocket to take out a lovely lacquered object in the shape of a canteen.

He twisted the cap off the ornate container to let loose the nauseating odour of gas. He was so preternaturally quick in his movements that he had a flaming fire-starter in his other hand before I had time to react.

Stupidly, I went on standing mesmerized, caught by the beam of triumph in his green eyes. Truly this was the power of Medusa. Under his malign gaze, my legs turned as heavy as my potter's wheel. What chance did I have now confronted by the gas and the flame? Within seconds my body would become a living candle, fed by my flesh and its natural oils. While I writhed and screamed, he would coolly film my death agony.

It is over, I told myself. It ends here. The City's evil has defeated me at last.

"No recourse now, Wop Woman," he sneered. I saw what deep pleasure he was taking from the terror I knew was all too visible in my eyes. I understood that was why he was waiting, prolonging the actual moment when he set me afire. He revelled in seeing me helpless. I was now a piece of meat caught in his snare, to do with what he would. It was a pitiful way to depart this world. One of the EYE's insect-cameras buzzed my cheekbone. I pictured a black-garbed official studying my final moments in his laboratory, noting the exact instant when my Survivalist's spark was extinguished. For comfort I thought then of my mother's face and as I did so, my fingers went automatically to the little bag of pepper in my hip pocket.

It was my only chance. He was still so fixed on my fear-filled face I was able to extract the bag and open it without his being aware.

Willing my hand steady and my aim true, I flung the pepper directly into his eyes. He fell upon his knees howling. I sped away, my determination to survive rejuvenated by my escape from this malevolent encounter. For some blocks I could still hear him wailing in pain. I wondered if I had irreparably damaged his vision. Perhaps his friends had already come to his aid. But then I wished to think of him no more.

At all costs I had to get out of this hellish place. Simply to make it beyond the City's confines would be a great relief.

It was only when I reached the farthest reaches of the Safety Perimeter that I remembered we were on the cusp of the cruel season. I had not seen a fall of red rain since I was a child. It is an experience absolutely unsettling and unforgettable. Red rain pelts down so thickly it can coat your flesh in an instant. It is always caustic. As a young girl, I saw red rain victims who looked as if someone had set a blowtorch to their faces, hands and arms. If they are still alive, they must be hiding themselves away.

We have been two decades now without red rain. But should it come again, I realized I would have no protection, no stout, solid buildings in which to cower while the skies poured down their searing blood. If the burning rains did come, surely I could find a cave in which to shelter? Or I could dig a hole in the earth and cover myself over with rocks.

I found the opening with the old rail track and walked a full day before I came to the forest. I had heard that once you are inside the woods you are no longer under the EYE's constant surveillance, which is a gift in itself. But there is still the threat of the wild dog packs, as well as the ever-present human predators — all the lost, mad ones who thrive on the blood of others. Then of course there are the Rat-Men, who do not confine their ravages to the City.

If you get through the forest alive, they say you emerge in a place of pure air, unsullied skies, deep, cool lakes, and purple mountains that give you reason to believe again in beneficent gods. I find this a most comforting idea even if it is untrue. The reality is I have no idea when I will get out of this thick fastness of trees. The branches above me are so entangled, they form a dense web. Although this has the advantage of shielding me from the sun, it makes for an oppressive atmosphere. The foliage at eye level is often black-edged and full of tiny holes. Sometimes I see barren trees whose shapes are so contorted they look like human figures in extreme attitudes of grief, prostrated and clawing at the earth. Others resemble the witches of my childhood nightmares, with hunched backs and long bony arms reaching out to seize me. You cannot escape us, they say. Or perhaps simply — you cannot escape.

But it serves no purpose to become down-hearted. I enjoy the ferns here, and the fact they still survive in this world renews my hope. I love their profusion and their intricate lacy forms. I like to kneel close to their spiny feathers, and sniff their peppery musk while the fronds brush my face.

Even so, there are times when I seem literally to see hope slipping away from me. When I am in these states of mind, hope takes the form of a graceful sea anemone, amorphous, the colour of a rosy pearl. This vision of shimmering grace keeps rising so speedily that soon it is out of sight altogether.

In these gloomy moods I picture myself sitting, hampered by the armature of my flesh and bones, on the bottom of the sea. I must make a tremendous effort to transcend the leaden despondency that invades my blood. I believe this depression is spawned by the evil I witnessed. Is it possible, I wonder, to look upon wickedness and not become contaminated? Yet of course I keep going. And then quite unexpectedly, as if the walking itself sets me to rights, I am once again in that state of grace where my flesh and bones seem filled with light, despite the surrounding sepulchral forest. The sea-flower is so close I am buoyed up by its breathtaking translucency and blithe ascent.

A lack of sleep was beginning to undermine my vigour and my pace. Even given my keen senses of hearing and smell, I spent much of the night tossing and wary, fearing I would fall into a deep and possibly dangerous slumber. I realized how helpful it would be to have a trustworthy companion with whom I could travel and take turns at a nightly fire-watch for our mutual protection.

Then yesterday I spied a woman with shoulder-length honey-blond hair several yards ahead of me. I stopped and hid myself so as to observe her carefully for some minutes. She appeared furtive, and walked with her shoulders bent as if to ward off a frontal attack. Every few seconds, she would stop to look behind her and into the trees that bounded the path. Her obvious anxiety reassured me she was not a living decoy for some murderous band waiting in ambush. I hallooed softly and she turned round, looking startled at first. Then she smiled at me, a smile so wide and white I was made just a little uneasy.

She rushed up to me exclaiming: "Oh, how wonderful to meet another woman travelling on her own. You are on your own, aren't you?" She peered anxiously again into the thickness of the foliage on our either side.

"Yes. I am journeying north alone. My name is Lucia."

She took a step back and regarded me frankly for a moment, as if assessing me according to a particular measure she had invented.

"Lucia! What an absolutely exquisite name! And mine is Candace. Isn't this our lucky day, Lucia? Isn't it simply a blessing that we've found each other and can forge on with our adventure together?"

I was uncomfortable with her gushiness but I had no choice in the matter. Now I had seen and spoken with her, I could not spurn her assumption that we would go on together. And I knew I had a moral obligation to give her what protection I could. There was no doubt I was far stronger and fitter than Candace. She then turned on me a smile so obviously manufactured I had an urge to look way. Already I was wishing myself alone again.

We set off and almost immediately Candace began to pry. She kept pressing me about why I fled the City and I had no desire to catalogue all those evils aloud. Finally I just told her the obvious: "It was because they stopped burying the dead. And then I knew for certain they would soon forget how to make pots."

That shut her up for a while and I was grateful for the silence. But Candace is never quelled for long, and she soon started up again. She seems compelled to expound upon her own boundless gifts and the happy community she plans to found once we reach the northern zone. "I will be its earnest beating heart," she tells me so repeatedly that I have begun to grimace secretly.

Yesterday, as we trudged onward, I glanced down at a particularly lacy bed of ferns. "Keep your head up when you walk," Candace boomed at me. "You'll look better and you'll feel better."

I was stunned. It would never occur to me to speak to someone I barely know in such a patronizing tone. The shameful thing was I wanted to retaliate with some mean retort about her plumpness or her unbecoming striped shorts. Of course I kept quiet. But I was upset by the intensity of my anger nonetheless.

And so now I long for some decent-hearted person to join us so that I might not always be listening to Candace. Most particularly, I would welcome someone who appreciates the blessings of silence. Together we might prevail on Candace to stop her self-obsessed chatter, if only for an hour or so each day.

Then too, I must admit that being alone with her sometimes makes me deeply uneasy. I know my vague suspicions of her are all likely unfounded, but the City left me with an ingrained, prickly mistrust. Is it possible Candace is not at all as she presents herself; that even her garrulousness is a guise to throw me off my guard? But what, then, could she be? A cannibal waiting until I let all my defences down so that she can murder me and feast on my flesh by moonlight? Is that why her teeth are so large?

These are tainted thoughts I struggle to control, just as I must the foolish idea that these words she spouts all day contain the spores of a pestilence that will gradually weaken my body and my will, and make me her slave.

So I stay wary. I walk. I wait. I hope. I am grateful for the profusion of ferns at my feet and for the wildflowers I sometimes see, like tiny blue cups a blessed spirit might drink from. We will meet like-hearted folk who will keep us company in our journey towards the north. I am sure of it.

Chapter Two
The Boy

AFTER THREE MONTHS ON THE ROAD, the boy still has a horror of the sky. Up until then he had never smelled or tasted the air of the real physical world. He had lived from birth under an opaque, impermeable, sealed dome located over one hundred miles from the nearest city. His father, who inherited great wealth, had built this fortress to insulate himself and wife and only child from the filth and greed of the world, and most especially kidnappers and other such predators.

He conceived the structure first in his mind: a white dome sitting upon the land like a glistening, new-laid egg. Like the World Egg of the ancient Orphic mysteries, he told himself, spun out of primeval Chaos and holding the perfect body of Eros. He became obsessed with this idea of his family's own World Egg, immaculate, self-contained, yet boundless. He spent a fortune on its self-operating climate control; robotics (for he could no longer put his trust in frail human servants); telemedicine; even telepsychiatry. He had a library — both paper and electronic — that rivalled the finest anywhere.

The only landscapes the boy knew growing up were the murals decorating the maze of corridors connecting the various functional areas inside the dome. He walked through the wet lushness and serpentine vines of a painted rain forest on the way to his bedroom. He saw the shimmer of a tranquil silver sea (outside his mother's dressing room); and the sharp visual clamour of granite cliffs thronged with gannets (the wall of his father's library). He knew too the melancholy stubble of a newly shorn hay field, the bales heaped and rounded, and rimmed with heat. He imagined their warmth when he traced the thick yellow of those bales with his fingertip. He touched the blue-painted swathe above the mown field and said "sky" to himself.

But "sky" remained an abstraction for the child. Until that fatal day when the dome of the fortress cracked like a fissure in a gigantic ice-floe, and he was flung into the world by the force of an enormous explosion. The Egg was built to withstand floods and all types of poison gas and germ warfare. Its entrances and exits were so well concealed that not even a master engineer or a genuinely gifted psychic could spy them out. But the boy's father had neglected to consider the brute force of dynamite. He was so besotted with the uncluttered form of his creation that the possibility of its wanton destruction never occurred to him.

Just before the blast, the boy was well into his morning run around the track built right inside the Egg's perimeter. He had the good fortune, or supreme misfortune as he often thought afterwards, to be much farther away from the main force of the explosion than were his parents. First he heard the wall beside him shatter. Next he was briefly aware of flying beyond the Egg's confines and up into the air. Then he plunged down into the lake whose waters had supplied the basic plumbing needs of the Egg. He immediately began to swim, using the strong breaststroke his father had taught him. His lungs felt like small bellows that had been set on fire. The smell and taste and look of the world — all so alien — dizzied and disoriented him.

He flew out of the smashed Egg and survived, brimful of knowledge. Over the course of his fourteen years, living in total seclusion with his parents in their fortress, he had absorbed vast amounts of fact and wisdom from his father's libraries. He held in his head much of the best that human beings had thought and written down over thousands of years. But at that instant on that dire morning, with his parents and the only home he had ever known blown to pieces, he could not even recall his own name.

In the lake, whose frigid cold assaulted his flesh, he kept swimming, urged on by his body's desperate need to survive, despite the ominous questions that throbbed in his head. What had happened? Where were his parents?

By the time he reached shore, he was exhausted and disoriented. He looked up, dazed. The sight of the endless blue vault above him made his gut coil in on itself. The boy saw the sky and vomited and then could look no more. He crawled on his belly. *I am Snake,* he thought. *Snake.*

Of all earth's species, the boy loved reptiles and amphibians best. He had virtually to heart all the volumes of his father's library devoted to lizards, snakes and tortoises. He had never seen an actual snake or a lizard or a tortoise. But he identified instinctively with a belly that constantly kissed the earth in what he saw as a holy embrace; and a hugging tight to the ground on which all human life began. *I am hugging tight,* he thought, as he propelled himself on his elbows and knees toward the open door of a rusted Quonset hut. *I am Snake*, he told himself. *Snake making his way toward his hole, where he can wrap himself in that soft, waiting gloom. The shadows will soothe my hurt. Snake will be healed in the darkness.*

He kept his eyes squeezed shut against the mass of hard sapphire above him. *Sky*, he thought. And then tried not to think. Sky still watched him, pinned him to the ground with its tack-sharp brightness. And tried to swallow him. Yes, swallow him with its boundless hunger. The boy had tasted infinity and found it vile. Later it was Snake who helped him cope with this aversion too. Or rather, an image of Snake that the boy pulled up from the deep well of story-pictures stored in his spine. Salvation came through Snake-as-Circle. Snake-with-his-tail-in-his-mouth. Snake had many marvellous shapes.

The boy slept some hours in the Quonset hut. He woke sporadically and felt his body swoop sickeningly. There were stars in his head and he understood these to be the close companions of his pain because they flashed simultaneously with the jabs and spasms along the edge of his nerves. Then he willed Sleep to come: sweet-faced Morpheus in his swirling cloak of scented smoke, who pressed crimson poppy petals to his lips and eyelids. Morpheus, who had never yet failed him, sent him drifting down into a yielding oblivion.

He did not know then that his power to summon mythic presences was rare. He was a chordate, and the mythic beings slumbered in his spine. He knew them to be that close. His father had taught him how to exploit this most human capacity and reach inward to draw on a source so deep it was infinite.

When he woke, sky was a trumpet. Someone, he thought, had set an orange ball on fire and rolled it across Sky. This blazing orange was trumpeting. A blast in his head harsh and fierce. An arrow in his eye. Sky, he saw, had many guises. Sky would always ambush him with some new and frightening face.

He crawled out of the Quonset hut on his belly, under a sky that was now a heaped and angry pyre concentrated in the east. *I will be thrown upon that pyre*, he thought. *I will be consumed. I will crumple like ash.* So he moved faster, still on his hands and knees, back toward the wrecked dome that had once been his home. The stench over the remains of the fortress burned his nostrils and made his eyes water. For this reason he did not at first recognize the clammy object his fingers brushed against as he groped through the rubble.

When his vision cleared he saw the white, once-living thing for what it was. The jolt that went through his body was every bit as brutal as when the blast had hurled him out of the Egg. He knew this thing and he did not know this thing. It was a severed human hand, ragged and red around the wrist, like bleeding meat. The top two joints of the middle finger were missing, the knuckle healed over in a puckered stump. This was the shape of his father's hand as the boy had always known it.

He retched as a sick fear swept from his belly to his brain. He put his head to his knees and dug into the hot earth. He flinched as his fingers encountered something hard and smooth and instinctively he gripped the thing and pulled it out of the debris. He studied the object in his hand, with its base of pale green stone mounted with a little metal paddle, and saw that it was streaked with blood. He realized the blood was his father's and that this was probably the last thing in life his father had touched. But the boy could no longer remember what this tool or instrument or artifact was. He could not fathom its purpose. He knew only that this thing belonged to his father and that he must keep it safe. So he thrust it deep in his pocket.

He forced himself to look again to his left, where the dismembered hand still lay. And in a spot where the reeking smoke had cleared, he saw what no child ought ever to see: the headless corpse of his father.

The shock left his mouth dry. He felt his testicles shrink and retract inside his body. Then his legs went numb. He was overcome by foolish, childish thoughts. *I will search for the pieces of his body and put them back together*, he told himself. *I will breathe new life into him.* A part of his brain recognized that these notions were completely mad. And then a new anxiety assailed him, that he might be driven insane by what he saw here. This had happened to his mother long ago, when her sanity had been undone by evil-doers in the world outside the Egg who hurt her so badly that parts of her froze inside. So his father had explained to him his mother's apparent coldness and self-absorption. In the Egg, she spent most of her time immersed in her Renaissance art books with their colour plates and tiny script. His mother could not touch him. She did not like him to touch her. His visits with her often left him unbearably sad. Was that why this awful thing had happened to them?

The boy was aware that the sight of his father's corpse had muddied and slowed his thoughts and that he was probably in the state known as "shock." His mind must be in turmoil, he told himself, compounded by grief and extreme fear. He was trying to be stoical and rational, as his father had taught him. The boy also knew he must seek his mother, regardless of what he found. She might still be alive, although he had no idea how he would cope or help her if she were badly wounded. He could strip off his clothes, he thought. He could make a tourniquet. He could call on Snake.

He got up slowly and quietly and surveyed the devastation to his right. What he saw brought him to his knees and shaped the word "horror" in his head. Only that single word, with its two vowels yawning like the gulfs of hell. In books in the Egg the boy had seen enough depictions of Hell's busy landscapes to know what the monsters did to their victims, the proddings and roastings and unholy meals. His father had reassured him that these visions were not real. But the boy knew his father lied. He had a natural gift for spying out the comforting untruth. He understood that such lies enable humans to endure what is unendurable.

In a space where the smoke cleared, the boy saw three beasts doing something to his mother's body that his mind simply could not bear. The sight sent a burning wire sizzling through his brain. Then a darkness mushroomed inside his skull. All he could see was a branching path in his head, flashing its urgent message. Fight or run. Could he fall upon the three monsters and save his mother? He was a slender boy of fourteen, only recently emerged from the Egg. He was unused to this world's air which drained the strength from his limbs. His nerves calculated his chances. He swallowed the vomit in his gorge and ran.

Then Snake was with him again, whispering his urgent counsel. "Go," Snake urged him. "Back to the hut!" The boy ran, a greedy self-love driving him on. In the rush of adrenalin that his lust for survival unleashed, the image of those dark figures at their foul work was for the moment obliterated.

Once again inside the Quonset hut, he collapsed and curled in on himself. He wanted oblivion and it eluded him. Part of him wanted death. He could not understand why he had been spared. Rational thought was agony but so too were the wounds that grief and wretchedness had torn open in his soul. He wanted to answer that sharp-toothed grief by tearing out his hair, and by wailing. Yes, he wanted to howl. Like the old king in Shakespeare's play, half-naked on the heath, cursing the very mould that made the human form. An adolescent boy just out of the Egg, he understood — as he had thought never to understand — why an absolute hatred for humankind was justified. This must, he thought, with mounting dread and self-loathing, include himself. To be human was to be complicit in the deeds of those murderers who now crept and poked through the ruin they had made. What option had he but to howl, or slash at his face and chest with his nails? But even as he parted his lips to wail (which was an effort, because already they were parched and sore), Snake was at his ear. "Be silent," Snake whispered. "Be silent, or you too will die."

There was a split second when the boy's decision hung in the balance. Why not embrace death? Why not join his mother and his father?

You still have me, foolish boy. Now do exactly as I say.

What Snake told him was to eat some clay from the dirt floor of the Quonset hut. The boy followed through, absurd and unsavoury as the instruction seemed. He dug into the earth with both hands and let the clammy substance ooze out between his fingers. Then he did as he was bid, squatting on his haunches in the half-dark. He ate of the clay, sparingly as instinct dictated, and the business of chewing and tasting soothed him and kept him silent. He fancied too, there was a power in the clay, telluric and mysterious, that steadied him and neutralized his rage and craven panic. Was it also a soporific? — for against all reason, he slept.

When he woke some hours later there was a bitter taste in his mouth and an unpleasant grittiness between his teeth. He got up and peered out the hut's one window. As he counted the columns of smoke, the boy understood what a filthy temple the evil-doers had made. While he slept the fire had reduced his entire known world to ash. A thin blood-red line kept pulsing in his brain as he tried to absorb the fact he was now an orphan, cut off forever from the roots of his own flesh. He fell to his knees, with his face pressed into the clay floor.

"Eat," Snake prompted him. So the boy chewed and spat, and chewed and spat, and the repetitive action comforted him a little. He began to weave himself a tale, to dispel fright and beguile time, as he had so often done in the Egg. He told himself he was new-made (for what other choice did he have?); that he was forged like the first man and first woman in stories of the world's beginnings. He knew he needed a life myth to drive him on, and to protect him from the brazenly cruel beings who would see him as tender and untried, ripe for tormenting, or for murder. I am new-made, he told himself, as he stripped off his clothes and coated his entire body and face with a layer of clay. Then he stood in the centre of the Quonset hut, arms stretched out and legs wide apart, letting his new skin dry.

He dressed again slowly, to keep his clay covering intact and because his hands were trembling. "Time to run," said Snake.

Sheer act of will got the boy to the hut door and beyond. Once outside, his eyes smarted. His knees buckled despite his best efforts. "Quickly," said Snake. "Hurry!" Snake's tongue lashed inside the boy's ear to spur him on, far from the demons who still rummaged amongst the ruins. Were they cannibals? The boy was unsure. Snake said, "Do not look. To look would drive you mad."

In this way the boy eluded madness and certain death. The wet clay of the earth and his loyal companion, Snake, were his saviours.

The boy ran for hours until at last he fell gasping at the foot of a massive oak, his small lungs aching, his breath like flame in his throat. As soon as he collapsed, the Hell-scape of the ruined Egg returned to torture him again. He saw his father's dear, severed hand, and the villains' obscene use of his mother's body. He answered this torment in the only way he knew how; by grinding his forehead into the bark of the oak, lacerating his cheeks, and rubbing his chin raw. He wanted to flay himself, send up a bloody prayer and expiate what he feared was his cowardice. He yearned to find a way to lament all he had lost, including his innocence.

The oak was the first tree of substance he had ever encountered, and he saw it as the instrument of his punishment. Later, as he made his way through the living forest, begging Night to smother the pictures in his head, he believed he loathed all these tree-things with their insidious whispering leaves and rocking boughs. Mocking him. Their mesh of branches raked and twisted, stirring the air to create a song that struck him as both cruel and deranged. He feared this mad song of swishing branches and air would undo his struggle to stay sane. He recognized the source of this song. It was the question that would have the power to torment him all his life. Was she already dead? Was his mother dead when those devil-men did those things to her?

He willed himself to walk rapidly through the swirling wood. All the while the blood oozing from his wounds congealed. By morning he made a piteous sight. A woman who saw him screamed. She was one of the nomadic People of the Silk who named themselves for the tents in which they lived, made of parachute silk. They cherished this silk. If ever it was ripped, they experienced the rent as a sharp pain under the breastbone. This was why the Seamstress was the chief of their tribe. Her stitching had the delicacy of a moth's wing. She healed wounds in silk.

The boy's first sight of the row of tents was at dawn. The sheer fabric drank down the sunrise's amber and ashes of roses. So tautly was the silk fastened to the frames and to the ground that the fabric vibrated in its confinement. He saw the triangular tents as live, pure forms, rimmed in palest fire. Briefly he was lifted aloft on their dazzling points. They danced in his mind's eye and he with them. The dance cleared a blessed space. There was, for a moment, no ruined Egg and no horrific spillage.

Until a woman screamed. What she saw was a refugee from that Hell-scape he had fled. He was white as paper, streaked with gore. The woman saw a death's head who came as a harbinger of plague.

A second woman appeared: Miriam, the camp's healer. With her was a huge man who made the boy think of the stories of Goliath and of Enkidu. This giant came at him, shaking his fists and growling. The boy had no strength to run. Kill me, he thought. I am emptied now of everything. Then he felt the woman's arms around him and he began to shake. He heard her shouting, but not at him. She was telling the giant to go away.

Miriam took the boy into her tent, where he still could not stop shaking. His teeth struck each other so sharply she feared he was having a fit. She lay down with him, and drew him in toward her so that his head was cradled between her soft breasts. She was happy to cradle him and bring him comfort.

In her City life, Miriam had been a midwife, and had forsaken her profession because twice she had to kill the life she helped to deliver. She had acted swiftly, pressing a cloth soaked in chloroform to what would have been a face, had the child (but was it a child?) had features. In both cases, there were no eyes, no ears, no nostrils. Miriam was a woman of finely honed compassion. She told herself it was mercy guiding her murderous hand. She imagined the life these beings would have, and knew she had no choice but to save them from their own futures. She buried the bodies with same dispatch she had extinguished their breath and told the mothers comforting lies of stillbirths. Then she turned her back on the City forever. She walked until her feet bled. Her guilt was a rancid stink that clung to her. She was distraught and near despair.

One morning she had come upon the clean array of the tents, with their luminous membrane-thin silk shuddering in the breeze. The flap of the central tent was pinned back. Miriam was drawn to the enfolding dusk of its interior. It was as if she were mesmerized by the heart of a jewel. In this tent the Seamstress was waiting. Miriam bowed at her feet. When the Seamstress's hands cupped her head, she felt the full force of a blessing that cancelled her guilt. When she stood up, she had no doubt as to her role. She would be the camp's healer. Her skills would flower among the People of the Silk.

She lanced boils, plucked out thorns and slivers and leeches, made herbal potions to ease aching bellies, heads and backs. The first time she attended a birth, her hands shook. The sweat of fear was a runnel between her breasts. The baby was perfect. Miriam wept.

She wept again when she bathed the wounds of the adolescent boy who had stumbled into their camp, because he was so perfect; his slight ivory body, tender and trusting. His face (as though his mother had dreamed him) was one that often appears in the frescoes of Italy. He had a Renaissance face. Miriam was shaken by his beauty, which she discerned even through the wounds he had inflicted on himself. She locked her strong legs about his body to help stop his trembling. And so it came about, as she rocked him with her body and hummed softly in his ear, that his sex rose and hardened. Miriam lifted her skirt and took him inside her. The orgasm, she thought, would help him sleep. And besides, she desired him.

In this way, the boy found a mother and a lover simultaneously.

This situation could not last. Theirs was a relationship too purely archetypal and too fraught with pitfalls to last. One of those pitfalls came in the form of Vulcan, the giant. The People of the Silk called him their Maker, because this massive man fashioned their tent pegs and frames. He was equally adept working with wood or what little metal they had. He mended pots and carts and the palanquin on which they transported the ancient Seamstress when they moved camp.

Miriam had once taken the Maker to her bed — initially out of desire, and later out of pity. But she reached a point where she could no longer tolerate his idea of lovemaking: his body the hammer and hers the anvil. Although she had encouraged him, he seemed incapable of learning other ways. After a time she came to loathe his smell of metal and sour sweat. She put him off gently. She hoped his common sense would prevail. Strong passions, she cautioned him, other than reverence for the silk and the Seamstress, would tear apart the tissue of the group's bonding.

There was a resolute discipline amongst the Silk People, its rule not so much defined as absorbed from the Seamstress's example. Her slight form, spare and functional as one of her own treasured needles, radiated purpose. Her age was a mystery, as were her origins. The fact she grappled daily with excruciating pain was not. Every one of the Silk People recognized and reverenced the ferocious determination the Seamstress brought to boring a channel through her agony. There were times it hurt them to look at her hands, clenched against her breastbone like claws. They watched amazed and relieved as she applied the fire of her will to her disobedient nerves so that she could carry on, mending any tears in the tents' delicate fabric. Her fingers unknotted, flexed, then fluttered, became birds in the air. This was no legerdemain. The Silk People saw the Seamstress's breath catch and her cheek pale. They knew the wrench of self-discipline this miracle cost her.

The Seamstress was their icon, and even the Maker was awed by her powers. For her sake and for the sake of the group, he wrestled with his rampant lust for Miriam. But because the gangly boy Miriam had taken to her tent was not properly one of the People of the Silk, the Maker did not put up the least fight against his jealousy of this pale, mute adolescent. His hatred of the boy was absolute, as dense as the point of the blade he pressed one night to the base of the young interloper's spine. The Maker drew the knife over each of the boy's knobby vertebrae, leaving behind the barest crimson thread that culminated in an upward flick under his left ear lobe. It was the same ear lobe that Miriam had punctured at the boy's request so that she could insert one of her own cut-glass earrings.

This earring had come loose and fallen between her breasts on the third night she and the boy slept together. He had plucked it up and mimed his wish. Miriam whispered her promise and in the morning pierced the soft flesh of his lobe with a sterilized needle. The hole healed speedily, which delighted her. Within days, she was able to insert the hooked wire from which hung the lozenge-shaped prism. The boy tilted his chin, moved his head in a graceful arc, held his hand up to his face so that the refracted sunlight made a rainbow in his palm.

"Chandelier," he said, and in that instant gave himself a new name, one bound in some way to this lovely woman. "My name," he told her.

These were the first words he had spoken to Miriam. Her soul was pierced then. It was the sound of his voice did it, a timbre that had only just crossed into manhood. Miriam appreciated the primacy of voice in love. Idiosyncratic as fingerprints, with its origins deep in the body cavities, voice was, she believed, the soul of the person bodied forth. She had learned that you could not always trust the eyes.

But even as the sound of his voice pierced her being, even as she registered how absolutely she was smitten, Miriam saw the relationship must be severed. It was as if she watched herself and the boy on one of the disgusting sky-screens that had multiplied above the City streets. The hugely magnified images of the rich at their indecent play had hung heavy on her back, although she shielded her eyes from them.

Now her conscience forced her to confront in her mind's eye the projected images of Miriam and Chandelier. She saw the ludicrous disparity in their ages, her already crinkled skin against his translucent gleam. Above all she saw and smelled his untried nature. She guessed he had been shut away, cloistered somehow. That was why he flinched each morning when he left her tent, and was exposed to the sky. Chandelier-and Miriam. Miriam-and-Chandelier. On the sky-screen in her mind, they played at being mother and son, mother and lover, lover and lover. The truth of the matter was inescapable — and for Miriam — unbearable. Yet she realized she had no choice. Her love, profound and complex as it was, would cripple him. His wings would go untried.

So even before the Maker toppled Chandelier to the ground and scored the flesh over his spine, Miriam had been planning for the boy's departure. She had given him an amulet to wear around his neck: a tiny pouch stitched by the Seamstress herself, containing a lock of Miriam's hair and a drop of her blood dried on a square of silk. "Apotropaic," she said, as she slipped the stringed pouch over his head. He mouthed the word back at her silently and nodded. As if, she thought, he knew what it meant. Which in fact he did. Her earnest, silent wish had the force of a blessing. She willed the contents of the pouch to deflect the evil eye. Evil eyes rather, because wickedness walked these days in many forms. She prayed the boy would be wary.

She gave him as well, little packets of nuts and dried fruit, a light-weight plastic bowl to serve as a hat, and the compass she had used to guide her on her flight from the City. "Go only this way," she said, pointing to the north. "Promise me," she urged.

"Yes," he answered, although he was saddened and confused still as to why she was sending him away.

"Never to the South," she insisted, pointing again. "South is where the City lies and it is full of dangers. In the North you will find others like us."

He nodded, yet sensed an uncertainty in her, as if some full force of will was lacking in her words.

There was no mistaking the Maker's murderous intent, when he carved his warning on the boy's back. Chandelier fled the camp of the People of the Silk, with his left forefinger pressed into the tender crevice behind his left ear where the Maker's knife had dug deepest. In his right hand he clutched the Pouch of Miriam threaded about his throat. He travelled by night because he still had some fear of Sky and the dizzying effects of the unbounded firmament. Night's blackness also made it easier for him to hide. He knew that in these woods there was no chance he would meet bear, moose, or wolves — all species with which he was familiar from the books and videos in his father's library. These forest animals had either been murdered by men, his father taught him, or poisoned or immolated in the falls of red rain, a climatic disaster for which wicked, selfish humans were also responsible. So it was the beings on two legs from whom the boy shrank whenever he caught wind of their approach. Their smell announced their presence long before he either saw or heard them. He then curled up and made himself small as Snake had taught him. Or he crawled beneath a blanket of fallen leaves and became invisible.

Sometimes he was fooled. One night he had to brake hard when he nearly stumbled over a man wrapped in a blanket, who sat cross-legged beside a prickly bush. The man had made a circlet of thorns for his head. The stars were so thickly clustered that the boy could see the blood trickling down the man's cheeks from the piercing of the cruel crown. He was rocking and mumbling and seemed not to notice Chandelier at all. He had no smell. Afterwards, the boy wondered if this was because the man was good. But if that was the case, then why would he choose to hurt himself with the thorns?

The third night he was not so lucky. He was moving silently and fast, skills he had mastered on the Egg's running track. He was holding to true north, as the compass needle instructed, when the tree branches above him disgorged an unwelcome load, knocking him down. He was badly winded and the pain in his head was like serrated files, grinding one on another. He groaned and blinked and saw, sitting on his chest, a boy whose face was obscured by a spotted handkerchief. The boy had his hands clamped on Chandelier's shoulders, with a force disproportionate to his size. Chandelier tried to shift his legs, and found to his dismay that these too, were weighted down. Were there two assailants then, or more than two? He could neither sit up, nor turn his head to look.

Were they thieves or were they murderers? Would they kill and eat him?

"What you got, sweet stuff?"

Thieves, then. What did sweet stuff mean? Did they want his fruit? He was running through his options. How could he assert himself if he could not stand erect? Snake does not stand, he reminded himself, or at least not often. *Take a cue*, he hears Snake at his ear. *Try cunning*.

"Get up, curly-top. Show us what you've got in your pockets."

He stood, swaying a little as he did so. He saw that they were in fact only two. But although he was older and taller than them both, they had a lean hardness that made him feel slight and unfinished. More disturbing to him was their agitation, which he strove not to absorb lest it tangle his thoughts. They were each like little pots on the boil. Their wrists twitched, as did their fingers. They ran upon the spot, lifting their knees high. They cocked their heads in one direction and then the other.

They were listening for a call, Chandelier realized. They were tied to an invisible rope. They were someone's toys to pull at will.

"Move it, sweet stuff. Show us what you've got or we'll rip your eyes out."

Toys, he thought again, and these are children. They like to play with things that move and glitter. Of the three precious things he carried — the metal and stone object his father been clutching when he died, the Pouch of Miriam and the compass — he knew it was the compass that would galvanize the children's attention. He took the instrument out, laid it on his palm, and offered it to them like a holy relic.

"Gimme."

Chandelier held his breath while the two boys studied the compass.

"It moves. The little arrow thing shivers." They made a sound that might have been laughter.

" A compass. To tell which way you are going."

"Hah! We're all going to Hell. Everybody knows that."

"Think Ralph will like it?" the taller of the two asked the other.

"Yup. It's metal, innit?"

"What else you got, sweet stuff?"

Chandelier knew he must fight to the death to protect his last two precious belongings. He readied himself, feet planted firmly apart, and his fists as hard as he could make them.

At that instant a whistle rent the air, one blast, then two more.

"That's come-back call," said one.

"What about him . . . ?" The other pointed to Chandelier.

"Ralph'll skin us if we're last in again."

They spun round on the balls of their feet, and lifting their knees high, sped off in a peculiar loping run.

Chandelier sank to the ground, trying to slow his breathing and quiet the thunder in his head. Then he moved on, a good half-mile from the site of the assault, and took refuge under leaf cover. He called on Morpheus, but a sore question kept poking at him. What was Ralph to those boys? Was it only fear of Ralph tugged them back on that invisible line, or was love like sons' for their father twined there as well? The question hurt him, sounding out the depth of the void inside he recognized as his loneliness.

When he set off the next night, clutching the Pouch of Miriam, he did not have even the stars from which to take his bearings. They were blotted out by slate cloud cover, overlaid by a kind of gluey haze that sometimes showed a purplish sheen. He knew he was lost; had been so since the moment he handed the compass over to the two boys. Why had he been so foolish? They might have settled for the nuts and raisins. He realized this was unlikely, but the idea dispirited him all the same.

Keep going. Snake's tongue flicked at his ear.

Yes. But how tired he was and how leaden his feet. He had ceased running because the air was so heavy it clogged his lungs. He noticed that the trees around him were thinning and that sometimes they disappeared altogether. When that happened, the exposed ground looked grey and cracked.

There were fewer trees in the North, or they grew scraggly there. Was that not what he had learned in the Egg? The sullen air made it hard for him to think clearly and remember things.

What an amazing outcome, if he had indeed stumbled on the right track northward. Perhaps it was the Pouch of Miriam looking after him.

Was this already the North? Up ahead he saw a mesmerizing sight that made him sure this was so. Wonderful lights in different colours played across the sky, swooping in great arcs and crossing each other. Orange he saw and pink and a yellow that dazzled his eyes. Were these the Northern Lights? Yes, they must be. His heart quickened and he propelled himself through the pall of his fatigue.

As he came nearer, he was disappointed to see the lights become less, rather than more beautiful. The colours did not sparkle and shift their shapes as he had expected. There was no spectral emerald curtain shimmering like the pictures he had seen. Instead the light now looked coarse and even ugly, as if the night sky had been whipped and was showing its bloody welts. But if this was not the North, then where was he?

Half an hour later, he had his answer. He was on the border of Danger-land. The six-letter word was spelled out in bold red capitals on white signs fixed to a fence more than twice his height. Made of wire mesh, it stretched as far as he could see in either direction. The fence barrier hummed and thrummed, and then began to buzz and crackle, making the hair on his wrists stand on end.

He did not like this place. It was time to retreat to the woods, although it seemed there was nowhere outside the Egg — other than in Miriam's arms — that was not full of danger. As if to prove this thought, three black shadows glided toward him. He stood rigid, listening to their nails click against the hard ground. Their harsh panting, undercut by snarls, made him swallow hard.

"Stay still," Snake said.

The hair stood up all over his body as the three dogs circled him, bounding in close; and then away. Strings of saliva hung from their mouths. They showed him their teeth, which were long and sharp. I will be torn apart, the boy thought, just as my parents were, except that wild dogs will dismember me and not an explosion.

Wake up! What food do you have?

Nuts, dried fruit. Do dogs eat fruit?

Try it.

Chandelier dug in his pockets as one of the dogs leapt toward his chest. The boy stepped back before the animal could topple him. He tugged out four little bags of Miriam's food and tossed them so that they scattered as widely as possible.

The dogs' heads turned. Their nostrils twitched.

Will they? Yes. All three were tearing apart the little cloth bags, and bolting down the contents.

What now? Where?

"Hole," Snake said. "Do you see it?"

Yes. He had already seen it: about twenty feet to his right there was an opening in the earth, with a metal cover partly pulled away. As Chandelier sped toward the hole, the dogs took chase.

Go! Go!

He dropped inside and found himself clinging to the rung of a ladder. Dogs cannot climb ladders, can they? The chorus of howls from above confirmed this was so.

When he reached the bottom rung and turned round, he saw there was nowhere to go except forward into the mouth of a tunnel. Deeper and deeper he crawled into the cool dark. A sickening stench made him shrink back and retreat, bending as low and shuffling as quietly as he could manage. Then splat! He ran into an obstacle that had not been there when he entered the culvert. A blazing light shone in his face that made him wince. He blinked to adjust to the glare and saw before him a creature whose appearance made him feel ill because he was so unlike a man with his flat, deformed features and naked skull. A worm-man, Chandelier thought. Were there such things? This person was so ugly the boy almost pitied him. But fear far overwhelmed his pity. The inside of Chandelier's mouth was dry and sore. He could hear his own ragged breathing and this sound of his own distress made him more panicky. He knew he must try to escape from this ill-made being and the nasty destiny it had in store for him. He could read his own fate on the worm-man's face.

But as he tried to slide away, bony fingers grasped his elbows from behind. A worm-man behind him and the other one in front had caught him fast. He found himself the captive of a band of Under-dwellers who had a penchant for mutilation. Their chief delight was decorating their sewer home and their clothing with fresh body parts. They coveted Chandelier's ears, which were indeed exquisite: calyxes that might have been shaped by the hand of Cellini. Which of the five sewer butchers would secure the right to pin the severed ears to the shoulders of his jacket? "Ear-paulettes," they cheered in chorus, and then laughed uproariously.

One of them put the knife's tip to his throat and then to his earlobe and gave it a nick. "Tell us a story, pale fright," the worm-thing demanded, placing the knife across his windpipe. "Amuse us."

Chandelier was so afraid that he spilled out the story which was always uppermost in his mind: how the blindingly beautiful god of Love had stepped out of the Cosmic Egg at the beginning of Time. Revealing this sacred tale to such an audience left him feeling tawdry and ignoble. The myth of the Egg and Eros was one of the holiest things he held in his head, and he had given it carelessly away. Was this the kind of trade people had to make to save their lives, or at least delay having their ears cut off? He was not sure it was worth the tormenting guilt he felt at what he had done.

"Stooopid. What are you on, kid? Your old egg story stinks. Stinks, get it?" And they were so taken with their own wit that they become quite merry. So they decided to postpone Chandelier's operation and their battle over the spoils until they had sat down together and been convivial. In their case, this meant inhaling solvents.

Their addiction was Chandelier's salvation. As they grunted and dreamed, he slid past them on his belly. Snake was with him again. Together he and Snake found another metal stair, and started up. Unfortunately, the middle rungs were just loose enough that they clanged like a doleful bell in the echoing dark when he trod upon them. Chandelier froze. He was certain this metallic racket would have roused at least one of the Under-dwellers. He looked down and saw, barely three rungs below him, a hand with long filthy fingernails, reaching up to grab his ankle. He pulled away but not quite fast enough to avoid the long nails grazing his flesh. Up and up he climbed, hand over hand on the rungs, as fast as he could. He could hear the worm-man panting close behind him.

At last he spied just up above a disc-shaped piece of his old enemy Sky, and that too made him afraid. Yet he had no choice but to go on.

Then he was out, emerging in a wasteland of parched grass and hardy weeds. Sky, as usual, went on forever. Today Sky was a heartless cobalt. The boy fell to his knees under its enfeebling blow. He clutched at Miriam's pouch. It was then Snake slithered up to his ear and whispered his secret.

"I am Sky," he said. "I am infinity. Hold this idea," Snake told Chandelier. "I bind in the boundlessness. It's just me, with my tail in my mouth. Now take that precious image of me and run."

But it was too late for running for the worm-man loomed above him, his face even uglier in the daylight than it had been underground. Chandelier's stomach turned as he looked at the lipless mouth with the thread-like red cracks in its corners, and its nasty green teeth. In one hand the pallid worm-man held a rusty kitchen knife; in the other, a blood-stained cloth bag for the trophies he was determined to sever from either side of the boy's small head.

"Think I'll take your pretty little snout as well since you caused me so much extra trouble." The worm-man seized Chandelier round the throat. The boy saw the air turn sickly grey, then black, then red. Something wet sprayed across his face. Chandelier staggered back. When his vision cleared, he was astonished to see the worm-man sitting on the ground in a daze. There was blood all over his flat face. Chandelier could see it streaming from a wound on the top of his skull. Who and what had brought his attacker down? And in which direction should he run now?

Then he saw at some distance behind the worm-man a tall, narrow, dark-brown figure moving slowly and jerkily toward him. So stiff were this person's movements it was as if he was forced to manipulate joints of rusted metal. The way the man walked — for Chandelier could see now that it was indeed a man — reminded him of the angular, long-legged birds he had seen in his father's nature films in the Egg. Birds like the ibex, crane, and rosy flamingo.

"Duck!" the man cried out and for a moment Chandelier was confused. Had the man called out the name of the bird he resembled? But ducks were small and had no legs to speak of. Then he understood the man wanted him to get down, low to the ground, where a duck would be. He complied just in time, for the man immediately hurled a small rock that caught the worm-man, who was struggling to stand, solidly on the forehead. Down the worm-man went again, this time lying prone and moaning and cursing.

Chandelier sped to the side of his rescuer and discovered that the dark brown was the colour of the well-worn fabric of the man's jacket and pants. The pants were grimy, particularly at the cuffs and knees. He looked up at the man's face and saw eyes of pellucid blue set above lean cheeks, so scored with lines both thick and thin that the boy thought the man must have spent many years weeping, or perhaps working in harsh weather with scouring winds that bit into his flesh.

Then he realized — this man is old! He had seen aged faces pictured in books and on film, but never on a living being.

Had they lived, time would have transformed his father and mother's faces in this way. "It is written in our cells," his father had explained to him. "The very code of our human story is to run down. Entropy, my son. We humans grow so tired as we age that we anticipate death's coming as we would the visit of a friend. We must accept this, with courage and a quiet joy, because it is our destiny to grow old and die."

Not, the boy thought ruefully, his mother or his father's destiny. But this idea of the body's life-force gradually dissipating still perplexed him. Where, finally, did the residual energy go?

Now that he was actually standing beside a very old human being he understood even less, for he perceived in this person's long, gaunt frame no obvious decline other than his wrinkles and stiff joints. In fact the old man projected something of the hardy, honed vigour of the heroes of his story books. Like Odysseus, the great adventurer. Had this man not saved him from having his ears and nose lopped off; from bleeding to death alone on this parched and blighted ground?

"Thank you, saviour." The words were out of his mouth before he could consider if they were the right ones.

The old man laughed and slapped his own thigh. "Saviour! That's a good one. I learned to skip stones over water when I was a boy. I can still see far off and judge my distance well. That's all, boy. That's all."

"Did that ugly critter hurt you? Are you all right?" These questions he put to Chandelier most earnestly, bending down to peer into the boy's face, seeking the truth of the matter in his eyes and the set of his mouth.

No. Chandelier shook his head. The worm-man had not hurt him, unless of course you counted malign intent. He did not say this aloud.

"Are you alone, boy? Do you have family?"

Again Chandelier shook his head, more gravely this time, in heavy remembrance.

"My name is Harry," the old man said. "And yours?"

Chandelier found himself tongue-tied. His thoughts were all entangled. That simple question — "Do you have family?" — had put him back in the thick of that baleful morning. The stink of the blasted Egg was in his nostrils as he groped in the debris and found the severed hand and saw his father's body without its head. Then he saw his mother's body . . . Stop! Stop! He clenched his fists and looked down at his knuckles gone a ghostly white.

Stop! Who had said this inside his head? Had he told himself to desist? Because otherwise he would go mad. Or was it Snake who warned him? Wasn't Snake there in the form of the big curved "S" at the beginning of the word? Stop!

He looked up again at the old man — Harry — who continued to wait to hear his name. Chandelier still could not get the word out. So he pointed to the cut-glass bauble dangling from his ear lobe.

"Earring? Is that your name?"

This actually made Chandelier smile.

"Chandelier," he said.

"Oh," replied Harry. "Well . . . that's a new one on me. Chandelier it is then.

"Well, Chandelier, I'll tell you what I plan to do, shall I? I've had a bellyful of this poisonous hellhole. I'm going to make the trek north — toward the place where I was born. There's no way to get there except through the forest. It's a very long way, and I won't kid you it's going to be easy.

"But at least the air will be fresher and with any luck, there will be far fewer abominations like that one to watch out for." He gestured to the unconscious worm-man.

"Would you like to come with me, Chandelier, to a far healthier place than this? We can keep one another company."

Company. Chandelier tasted the word, rolled it on is tongue and around his head. He liked the sound of it. This word seemed to speak of warm arms about him, and a place where he could rest, in complete trust he would be safe.

"Yes," he said, prompted not just by these positive associations, but also a deeply rooted intuition that this was a "good man" in his father's sense of the word.

So they set off together, Chandelier soon learning how to keep pace with Harry's stiff and occasionally faltering steps. Almost immediately, the old man began to tell him stories to help them pass the time on their long trudge to the forest boundary.

The boy loves the rainbow-coloured lights that flow from the old man's mouth when he speaks. Most of all, he loves the Polar Spirit he can see standing erect inside Harry's spare frame; and the landscape over which this spirit flies, with its mountains of glistening ice, and the emerald secret at its heart.

Chapter Three
The Six

When I saw an old man in a dark-brown suit limping ahead of us on the forest path, I wanted to strike my breast and cry out "*O Fortuna!*" as my great-aunt Nidia used to at any startling occurrence. *O Fortuna.* And exceptionally good fortune in this case. I was so sick of Candace's constant chatter and boasting I had on occasion considered abandoning her and slipping off in the middle of the night. In reality, I would never have done so. But I swear I would willingly have given one of my back teeth just to hear a human voice other than hers.

My instinctive urge was therefore to run ahead and speak with the old man. Just in time I realized how foolish my impulsiveness was. Hadn't I been taken in before by someone who appeared to be old and vulnerable and was in fact a villainous young man in disguise? Why should this person ahead of us be any different? He might well be a decoy, his feigned slow gait a ploy to entice us into conversation. His cohorts would then spring out from their hiding places amidst the trees. Already I had a firm grip on the handle of my knife.

"Have you got a weapon?" The words were out of my mouth before I actually looked at Candace and saw the fear in her eyes. She had turned quite pale. Her obvious apprehension, as she stared fixedly at the back of the man who laboured slowly on ahead, intensified my own anxiety.

"A kitchen knife," she whispered. Her hands shook as she tried to unzip her backpack to extract it.

"You stay here and keep close watch," I told her firmly. I pointed to a tree with a trunk wide enough for her to hide behind. Of course if there were others secreted by the wayside, they had probably already spotted us and this precaution was pointless. But she was so frightened I wanted to do all I could to reassure and comfort her.

"I have pills . . . in case we need them."

I looked at her dumbfounded.

"If there are others with him . . . if they try to rape us," she explained. I could see how difficult it was for her to speak these words aloud.

"Instantaneous," she said. "We'd be dead before they managed even to lay a finger on us."

I did not know how to respond. So I simply shook my head, angry at myself for having been so often irritated with her while all the time she nursed this gnawing fear. I wondered if she had already been harmed in this way, and promised myself I would try to be more accepting of her irksome little habits in the future.

"Take courage," I urged her. "He may well be what he seems and quite harmless. But we cannot continue to linger behind him. Are we agreed?"

She nodded. But I noticed she had something clutched tightly in her hand.

"Stay calm," I said.

Then I went ahead, keeping a keen watch for any odd movement or shape in the tree-shadow. When I caught up to him, I saw that the old man had a companion who walked in front of him: a pale, slender, fine-boned boy, with a cut-glass earring dangling from his left lobe. He watched me warily out of huge eyes the colour of Parma violets.

I introduced myself, and the old man scanned my face for a good half-minute, all the while keeping his hand on the boy's shoulder. He then looked right and left and over my shoulder.

"Lucia," he repeated, and he smiled to himself, as if my name pleased him. I was surprised how strong his voice sounded; had my eyes been closed, I would have assumed I was in the presence of a far younger man.

"Harry," he said. "And this is my young friend, Chandelier. He doesn't talk much," he added. And then, in an undertone: "I helped him out of a tight spot in a City wasteland a few days ago. Poor little tyke. Looks like he's been through some things that have left him pretty well mute.

"He seems to trust me," Harry said. "He likes listening to my stories."

Indeed it was many years since I had seen a young person regard an elderly one with such tender concern. But the boy was clearly edgy too, on the old man's behalf. It was the boy's wariness, as much as Harry's honest face and manner that reassured me, and so I gestured to Candace to come and join us.

She came forward cautiously, and kept glancing to either side of the path so obsessively that twice she stumbled. When at last she stood by me, I smiled at her warmly and told her the two travellers' names. "Candace and I met five days ago," I told Harry and Chandelier. Meanwhile, the boy kept looking me and Candace up and down as if he were afraid we might hurt the old man. I took a step or two back and let my arms fall loose at my sides so that the boy could see I held nothing in my hands. The furrow in his brow vanished and his face looked less pinched.

"Are you travelling north?" I asked Harry.

He nodded. "We're headed for what people call the Sea Lake. Beyond the great Rock Shield. I was born not far from there. I want to at least get close enough to see a birch tree again."

"Is it true what they say," I asked him "that the air there is pure and that the EYE's power cannot penetrate the shield of rock?"

"We must hope so," he replied. "We must believe and keep faith."

I liked the simple frankness of his reply. And it was sheer delight for me to speak again with someone so elderly, who was quick of mind and who still managed to walk strongly albeit he sometimes leaned heavily upon his stick. The mere fact of this man's existence made him a rarity. By the time I turned twenty we seldom saw an old person on the streets of the City. There had for years been rumours that the EYE had a secret program of mass euthanasia to dispose of the aged, regardless of their state of health. But if I saw Harry as a living wonder, Candace took a completely opposite view.

"He reeks," she whispered in my ear, yet loud enough I feared for Harry and the boy to hear. "He's probably crawling with vermin. And the boy's white as a slug. He's obviously got some kind of wasting disease. And that earring! You're not thinking of inviting them to travel with us, are you?"

She stood back, planted her fists on her hips and put on one of her censorious little pouts. I didn't even bother to respond. We had an obvious moral obligation here for one thing. Old Harry and the boy stood a far better chance of survival if Candace and I travelled with them. We were all headed in the same general direction and four pairs of eyes and ears would be a distinct advantage as we got into the denser part of the forest. Besides, Harry knew where we were going. He had actually lived near the northern Sea Lake. I had only heard of this place. For me, it was like a dream of paradise and all I had was my inner compass, the guidance of the stars, my nose and my faith to guide me.

So I decided on the spot to override Candace's reservations and ask Harry if he and the boy wanted to join forces with us — or with me, as the case might be. If Candace wanted to strike off on her own, she was very welcome to do so.

When she heard me put the invitation to Harry, she stamped her foot and glared at me. Her furious round face, with her straight-cut bangs, made me think of pictures I had seen of grimacing gargoyles. I at once regretted this unkind thought.

"Candace wants to found a community north of the Shield." I blurted this out, in some vain attempt to bring her out of her petulance.

"One of those holier-than-thou places?" asked Harry. While I was sure he was teasing, I knew how offensive Candace would find this remark. Indeed she looked genuinely affronted.

"Absolutely not," she snapped. "And I consider your question both insulting and in extremely poor taste."

"It was a joke," he said. "What people used to call light-hearted banter." He winked at me.

"Harrumph," said Candace. She uses this expression whenever she is indignant, and it seems to involve the expulsion of a great deal of air from her lungs in a noisy rush. She has quite often been indignant with me, usually because I have not been listening closely enough to what she is telling me.

"We would be very pleased to travel with you. Thank you," said Harry, pointedly addressing us both. Candace took herself off in an apparent fit of pique, and began to pace back and forth on the path at some distance from us. Her hands were thrust deep in her pockets.

Harry looked at me with a keen sympathy, and we waited until we were sure Candace was out of earshot.

"She's a bit of an endurance test," he said with a mock glum face that made me laugh. The sound of my own laughter surprised and pleased me. It had been a long time since I had last laughed in any way except wryly. And even my wry laughter was many years ago. The boy stared at me closely for some seconds. Then he smiled at me, a smile I willingly returned. I saw then how beautiful his face was when he let go of his rigid anxiety. I did not want to speculate on the kind of horrific things he had gone through before Harry came upon him. The boy had such a fragile innocence about him. It made me equally enraged and despairing to think of anyone deliberately making him or any other child suffer.

I wanted to get moving again and shake off these poisonous thoughts with a good stride. I sensed Harry's impatience with

Candace and her sulky show of defiance, as he looked at her pacing back and forth, and then at me.

"It serves no purpose to be standing around like this," he said. I got his drift. Her rudeness had gone on long enough.

"Candace?" I called out. "Are you coming?"

I heard her make one of her harrumphing noises, as she shrugged her shoulders. I had actually decided to go on without her, when she approached us, frowning. She said nothing, only glared at each of us in turn, but longest at Harry. Then she officiously took the lead, and we set off in a queue, with me at the rear, watching and listening, and with my right hand always close to the handle of my knife. I wondered again if my decision to leave my machete behind in the City had been the right one.

We walked that day until just after sunset; then settled for the night in a small clearing about ten paces from the main path. I made sure I positioned the campfire so that whoever was on night watch could see in every direction, with no trees blocking their line of vision. Candace took the first watch and Harry and Chandelier together did the second. When I assumed my turn at midnight, the forest was absolutely still. All I could hear was someone discreetly breaking wind (Candace, I thought), the occasional sharp crack of a joint as Harry flexed his elbow or his knee and sometimes — so soft it might be mistaken for the hum of insects busy underground — the sound of the boy moaning in his sleep. I wished with all my heart that I could dispel the dream-images that drew this pitiful sound from him. Yet I was relieved as well to hear he had a voice.

These were the sounds my human companions made in the darkness that enclosed us and I found a strength and contentment in the fact we were together (yes, even Candace), travelling in the same direction. Four of us. Four square. I wondered if we might meet others who would want to join us, not imagining then just how soon that would come to pass.

Two days later, when I was out on a morning foraging expedition, I saw a flash and blur of colour ahead of me through the trees. It was as if the arc of a rainbow was spinning on its axis. I was mesmerized, and a little frightened, as one always is at the apparition of some strange new form of beauty. I held my breath and approached as silently as I could, walking on the balls of my feet. Then I spied a young woman whirling with her arms out-flung in the centre of a ring of fleshy, brown-flanged mushrooms. The rainbow effect was produced by the dazzling hues she wore: translucent tangerine leggings, purple slip-on shoes, a tiny frilled skirt in an abstract pattern of cornflower blue and primrose yellow barely long enough to cover her bottom, and a leotard top of the brightest emerald green I have ever seen. Her hair was fair and fine and the morning light caught in her silken curls as she twirled and hummed to herself. "E-pon-a" is what she seemed to sing. "E-pon-a." The same word, or perhaps just nonsense syllables, over and over.

It was that repetition, and the whirling round and round, that made me fear at first she might be mad. I was concerned too for her safety if she was travelling alone. She had the prettiness and slender grace that make one think automatically of fairy lands, and there are many men, and some women, who cannot see such delicacy without the urge to trample it.

"Hello," I called out.

She froze on the spot as if she was playing the old childhood game of statues. She stood balanced on her left foot, with her right just off the ground. She kept her outstretched arms absolutely still, right down to her fingertips. Then she turned her small head to look at me and in an instant was at my side with her hand extended in greeting.

"Hello," she said. "My name is Bird Girl." I barely had time to tell her mine when she asked abruptly: "Have you ever read a poem called 'A Rabbit as King of the Ghosts'?"

She did not wait for my reply but rattled on. "Part of it goes: 'And to feel the light is a rabbit-light / In which everything is meant for you / And nothing need be explained.'

"Do you think," she went on, speaking extremely rapidly, "that this is rabbit-light?" And she thrust her hand into the gold-white shaft that fell aslant through the treetops. I smiled at her. From the look she sent me in return, I saw that she was not only quite sane, but also astute.

"I get carried away sometimes," she said, "with thinking about the things I love best."

I told her this also happened to me, especially when I was working with my clay.

"I thought you looked like an artist," she said, which made me warm to her all the more.

She told me then she was travelling alone, searching for her mother who had disappeared from the warehouse in the City where she had lived.

"Have you heard of a women's vigilante group called The New Amazons?" she asked. "They ride motorcycles and do raids on pimps and pornographers. My mother is The New Amazons' leader," she said proudly. "Her name is Epona."

So I understood then it was her mother's name she was humming when I first saw her twirling about.

"And do you believe your mother is headed north?" I asked.

"I think it's likely," she replied. "My mother and her gang have made some very powerful enemies — people who are close to the EYE. She had found out some secrets about links between the innovative industries and the brothels and human trafficking.

"And then too . . . " she hesitated. "She maybe felt she was getting too old to go on waging war against evil, ugly men.

"They say," and her face was ecstatic as she spoke, "that one is free in the North. I mean, freer to be the person we really are. We won't always have to be fighting thought-control because there won't be any EYE. And the air won't be poisoned.

"They'd started to put chemicals in the air that made you feel stupid and confused, don't you think? And all those corpses everywhere, just left . . . Ugh!"

She made a little leap on the spot and shook herself.

'I think that in the North," she announced solemnly, "there will be no end to the rabbit-light."

I realized then she was one of those people of such abundant quick energy it must always be spilling over, in dart-like action or glittering chatter. Yet unlike Candace, Bird Girl also knew how to be silent. On instinct I liked her immensely.

Her mood seemed to switch abruptly and she looked troubled. "You haven't seen a man with one real eye and one made of marble, have you? I mean here, in the forest? Or a man with a misshapen nose? You can see it's been slit right down the middle and then healed badly. Have you seen either of them? You would tell me, wouldn't you?"

She had become most agitated and was hopping from foot to foot, while wringing her hands.

"No," I told her. "I've seen no one like that. No one at all. Are they your enemies?" I did not know how else to put it.

"The man with the marble eye is my enemy. The man with the nose is my mother's. But I suppose you could say he is also mine, since I am my mother's daughter and he would consider me a quite suitable object of vengeance, I think.

"Let's talk about something else altogether," she urged me. "I cannot stand the shadows those two throw upon my mind if I think of them too long.

She twirled round then, and fluttered her arms. "Have you ever held a real book, one kept safe from the burnings?" she asked when she came to a stop again.

"Yes." But before I could say anything more, she grasped my hand and said rapturously "Isn't it wonderful? I mean, there's nothing better on earth than to hold and read a real paper book. Don't you think?"

She jumped backward again and whirled about, then asked: "Have you heard about the Cyberspace Library?"

I nodded, although I have always thought this legend of a vast invisible net holding all knowledge was likely mere fantasy — something people dreamed up after the book burnings.

"They say it contained much untruth, as well as wisdom," she said. "And that you needed a good internal map to negotiate its windings or you might find yourself unawares in a horrid trap and never get free again. But the most wonderful thing about the vast net was that it contained whole books. You could sit and read every word upon a little screen."

Her round blue eyes widened even more. "What do you think happened to all those cyber-books after the viruses destroyed the net? Do you think they're still out there somewhere?" She gestured vaguely at the sky. "Out there as spectral books or ghost-books?

"But I'd rather hold a real, three-dimensional book, wouldn't you, and know the joy of touching and turning the pages and looking off into the middle distance as you picture what you just read? Real books are all so amazingly idiosyncratic. They even have their own smells."

Here she stopped, as if another kind of thought had struck her dumb. She took three quick steps to stand close by me and clasped my right hand tightly between her palms. How cold her hands were.

"You would tell me if you'd seen either of those men, wouldn't you? I mean, you wouldn't hold back information because you didn't want to frighten me?"

"I would always tell you the truth," I declared. "I've seen no one like the two you describe."

"Would you like to travel with us?" I asked her. I very much wanted her to have whatever protection we could offer.

"We are four so far." And I told her briefly about Candace, Chandelier, and Harry.

She frowned at my description of Candace even though I tried hard to keep any hint of distaste out of my voice.

"She sounds like a know-it-all," she remarked.

I laughed.

In fact, Candace began clucking and fussing over Bird Girl as soon as she saw her. Chandelier watched her warily, as he did everyone with the exception of Harry. But Bird Girl and Harry hit it off immediately and were soon making silly faces at each other behind Candace's back as she went on at length about why her great gifts as a social facilitator made her eminently suited for founding a community where fellowship would flow naturally . . . I had heard it all many times before.

Bird Girl's arrival meant that each of our turns at the night watch was considerably shorter, but I still took the last because I was accustomed to being wide awake in those last few hours before dawn.

"Five," I thought to myself that night and the wonder of it for me was how vastly different we were one from another. We had come across each other by chance and the simple crossing of paths. And chance would likewise rule how our journey went and what other human kind, well-intentioned or not, we met on our way north.

He did not appear that night, or the next — the one who was to become our sixth member, and the most mysterious of us all. It was on the third night after Bird Girl's arrival, deep into my watch, that I heard something approach behind me. I could hear no claws; nor could I pick up any scent of animal fur or flesh. I assumed that whatever approached was human and I prayed that he or she came alone. One of my worst fears was that we would one day or night be swarmed by many more assailants than three women, an old man, and an adolescent boy could fight off.

I already had my knife drawn when he knelt beside me. I could smell burlap, rubber, and a touch of fever. I felt the heat of his breath in my ear as he said: "I wish to serve you and your friends."

Of course the question why immediately sprang to my mind, and almost to my lips. He answered my unspoken query by walking around to the other side of the fire so that he was opposite me and illuminated by the flames. I knew a monk's garb when I saw it and I guessed as well, that his gown with its capacious hood, which he wore up obscuring his face, was likely purchased from a costume shop.

"I am doing penance," he said. The gravity of his tone conveyed this was no jest.

"I have shadowed your group for two days. You will benefit from having a strong man to watch out for you."

"Do we have a choice?" I asked him, and immediately regretted it lest he think me ungrateful. I could certainly appreciate the advantages of having such a man accompany us. He was exceptionally tall and from the sinews in his naked feet and hands (the only parts of him that were visible) I could see he was probably as strong as he claimed.

"Should you all accept my offer of service," he said most courteously, "there is only one proviso. And that is that I will keep my face hidden from you. To be faceless," he added, "is a part of my penance."

This struck me as somewhat odd, but who among us is not at least a little odd these days? In a time so fractured and blighted, it would be strange indeed to be normal.

I thanked him and told him I would introduce him to the others in the morning so that we could make our decision together.

"Prepare them well," he whispered. "I do not want to frighten the young ones." I gathered he meant Chandelier and Bird Girl but my chief concern was — as ever — Candace.

"Are you insane?" she exploded at me when I described my night-time visitor and his offer. "Don't you know how dangerous these people are who dress up? There's usually some severe mental slippage. They just flip and start swinging their axes, chopping off heads . . . "

"He doesn't have an axe," I said.

"You don't know that," she countered in her most patronizing tone. "He might have a whole box full of weapons you didn't see."

I didn't say anything, but I had to admit she had a point. Other than my intuitive trust of his voice and his intentions I was largely ignorant of both the man and his weaponry. As a result I was probably more anxious than any of the others as we waited for him. Candace, who sat cross-legged on the ground, had set her long serrated kitchen knife in full view in front of her. I had not even tried to dissuade her from this. Bird Girl paced and did a series of high kicks. Chandelier kept looking anxiously at Harry who would smile and nod reassuringly at him. In fact Harry was the only one of us who appeared totally at ease. I kept asking myself if I was deluded in putting my trust in a man without a face.

Despite my best efforts to prepare her, Candace screamed when he did appear. I suppose I readily associated the monk's garment with images I had seen of Saint Francis cradling a dove in his hands. What Candace saw, I presume, was something loathsome and unholy.

He made his case to the others in almost exactly the same words he had put it to me.

"What is your name?" asked Harry.

"You can call me the Outpacer," he said, "for I would always be a few steps behind you or ahead of you, or to your right or left. I will maintain a kind of invisible cordon around you."

Candace gave him one of her frostiest glares. "Speaking personally," she said, "I find your disguise really suspicious. What exactly are you hiding?"

"The hood is part of my penance."

"So you say. But how do we know we can trust you?" she challenged him. "What guarantee can you give us that your intentions are honourable?"

"None," he answered her. "I can only give you my word."

Candace heaved one of her overly dramatic sighs. "I'll be frank. I decline your offer. I can't accept the word of someone whose face I cannot see."

I looked at the others. Chandelier was staring up at Harry as if seeking to read his thoughts on his face.

"I think we each need to mull your offer over," Harry said. "And then discuss it as a group."

"I agree," said Bird Girl. "We'll have a parley. Isn't that a nice word?"

"Harrumph," said Candace.

"Can we speak with you again tomorrow?" I asked him.

The hooded man bowed his head. "I will be nearby," he said, "should you have need of me." He left us as silently as he had entered our midst, and we all began to make ready for the day's trek.

"I liked the sound of his voice," Bird Girl announced. "I really think he means what he says. He wants to help us."

Candace simply shook her head in disbelief. But as I was stamping out the last of the embers of our fire, she came close and whispered harshly in my ear. "You have some wonderful qualities, Lucia. But you are being dangerously naïve about this madman in his ridiculous costume. Naïve." She repeated the word with an emphasis that made her exasperation with me abundantly clear.

"Can we not just consider his offer as we walk, and then discuss it this evening?" It took me all my effort to put this question to her civilly.

"There's nothing to discuss," she snapped at me. "Accepting his offer would be madness. He'll murder us, one by one. And heaven knows what else."

We all set off, and Candace aggressively took the lead. She assumed an uncharacteristic quick-march step, with her shoulders thrown well back. Every so often she would glance behind as if we were a row of ducklings in her charge. How tedious I found her domineering ways. I decided to fall in behind Chandelier and Harry and be the last in the line so as to avoid as much of Candace's posturing as I could.

It was shortly after I moved to the end of the line that I caught a scent of rancid meat. At first, I thought it must be the carcass of an animal rotting on the forest floor. Then I saw a flash of sliver and black bearing down on Candace from the left out of the trees. She screamed as a dog with ragged fur and yellow eyes, sent her sprawling. I drew my knife out so quickly

I nicked my palm, and pushing past Harry and Chandelier, ran to her aid. My intention was to plunge my blade into the dog before it could harm her badly.

At that moment, a man's voice roared and there was a flash of fire. I looked on, the blood thundering in my ears, as the Outpacer thrust a blazing brand into the dog's jaw. The animal howled in such pain I could not help but pity it, especially when I saw the mange that had stripped the fur from its flanks and left exposed its sore, pink, swollen skin. The dog slumped on its side, stunned and whimpering. I foolishly yearned for it to run off, but understood why the Outpacer felt he had to come up behind the animal and slit its throat. I turned my face away from the wound and the gushing blood, but not before I saw that the dog's eyes were not in fact yellow, but ringed with a purulent matter.

Candace was still curled like a ball, her arms protecting her head. "It's all right now," I said. I touched her shoulder as gently as I could.

I helped her stand and tried to interpose my body between her and the dog. She insisted on looking at it. "Ugh!" she said.

"The Outpacer stopped it..." I began.

"Yes," she said. "I appreciate that."

He made her a silent bow.

"But we must still consider your offer," she told him. "It was obviously a sick dog after all."

I couldn't believe what I was hearing. Surely she realized the hooded man had put himself at some risk?

"We will speak with you again tomorrow." She addressed him in her best regal manner. I wanted badly to chide her for being so ungrateful and arrogant with him. But I knew from experience how pointless my efforts would be.

At the end of the day, we all sat together over a frugal meal of gruel mixed with the berries I had gathered along the way.

"Have any of you considered," Candace asked, "that the dog might have been his; that he set it upon me deliberately so that he could stage a rescue?"

"For God's sake!" Harry exclaimed.

Bird Girl managed to say politely what the rest of us were thinking: "That's really unlikely, don't you think, Candace?"

"Unlikely perhaps. But not impossible. However, I'll go along with the rest of you," she conceded. "But it is with misgivings. We may yet all live to rue the day we agreed to this."

I saw Harry roll his eyes. Then Bird Girl did the same in mimicry. I tried not to laugh.

And so we became six.

There is a great comfort in knowing you have an invisible protector and I found my night-watch and foraging missions the easier for it. Although I stayed as vigilantly alert as ever, I was not quite as tense as I had been. It lightened my own load to think that he was somewhere nearby keeping watch, and pacing out his invisible cordon in his sandals of rubber and rope.

I recalled how well cared for and shapely his feet were. Not at all like mine with their many calluses and disfiguring bunions. I wondered then about the others, and whether our feet were as distinctive as our respective characters.

Chapter Four
Their Feet

IN VENICE, HARRY HAD BEEN DRAWN each day to the window of a shop that specialized in exquisitely wrought terracotta mouldings and small-scale sculpture. His eye and soul delighted in the detail and imaginative span of the work. There were complete bestiaries, dominated by the Lion of Saint Mark, his admonishing human features shown full-face and in profile. He was painted the red sienna of his desert home, then outlined in indigo. Roman matrons, in headdresses rayed like a medieval sun, looked down on prospective purchasers with a bemused serenity. Children gambolled with lambs in recessed tablets that might have been openings to paradise.

But it was one particular moulded frieze, small enough to fit in his pocket, that captured Harry's full attention. Set against a background of sunburst yellow were two pairs of naked human feet, depicted in the act of walking. And what feet they were. Flawless, palest ivory, sturdy yet elegant. They were the feet of the young, as yet unblighted by corns or calluses, set upon some brisk and happy purpose.

In part, it was the surprise of the subject that charmed him. Who would have chosen to make feet the subject of an artwork? A part of the body so often despised, except, he supposed, by fetishists. Harry could not understand fetishists. And there was nothing at all unsavoury about these feet. They held a promise, he thought, an assurance that the act of walking could still be an innocent and splendid undertaking, and not a desecration.

He considered the word "footfall" and shuddered at its heaviness and the fateful shadows it cast. He was thinking, as always, of Antarctica, and of the damage tourists had done by their tread on her glistening floor. The perilous stuff they had brought in on the soles of their boots: bacteria, microbes, alien plant life. Thankfully, tourism anywhere in the continent had at last been banned by an international protocol. Harry had always made a point of purifying himself before he stepped out of his plane. The clothes he donned to step into the Antarctic air were sterilized, as was his footwear.

To set foot down and do no harm. To make a pilgrimage. To bring humanity to a better pass by the simple act of walking, barefoot and sprightly. This was the testament Harry read in the pocket-sized tablet in the Venice shop window.

For years afterwards, he had deeply regretted not buying the terracotta. He was not a man given to material possessions, and it would have grieved him sorely had he ever broken the tablet in his travels. But eventually, the fact he did not own the moulding of those innocent and blessed feet seemed to him both good and fitting. For in some deep and holy well of his mind, the sculpted feet became purer and more blessed. They were the feet of young gods, robust, primed by an energy that was boundless, fed by the very veins of the cosmos.

Now, as he leans upon his stick, dismayed by the jangling of nerve pain that makes a devil dance in his spine, it is the image of those god-feet that drives him on. Toward sundown, he often has to grip the boy's shoulder to steady himself. The boy is willing. The boy is habitually at his side. Harry speculates that beneath those bizarre windings of silk strips that serve Chandelier as shoes are feet innocent as young doves. Whereas his own are daily more cracked and brittle and grey, except for his toenails, which have the consistency of dense horn and have grown so long they are talon-like, tinged the brownish-yellow of bad teeth. As he struggles to stand erect each day-break, his joints resistant as rusted metal, he pictures himself as an aged heron, his first steps of the day tentative and rigid. He sees his own stick-thin figure superimposed against the sky: a hieroglyph of a heron-man, a silhouette as frail as hope making its way across the horizon.

Harry is wrong about Chandelier's feet. Underneath the windings of silk, the blood has begun to seep from blisters the size of pigeon eggs. It was Miriam who had wound the silk round his feet. But she had no leather or rubber with which to make him protective soles. Chandelier's fragile footwear had started to tatter a little during his trials in the City. Like Candace, he yearns for sturdy, supple boots and soft cotton socks. It is one of the few wishes he and Candace have in common.

There had once been a time — in her city life — when Candace took an unbridled pleasure in studying her feet's shapely perfection. She put great store in a daily recitation of her own best qualities and physical attributes. The ego needed healthy food to flourish. So, in the cloistered safety of her bedroom, she would begin each day with a series of luxurious stretches that culminated in the right foot, and then the left, held aloft. The gauzy light of dawn was an ideal medium for viewing the rosy flesh of toes that had — she told herself — the pleasing plumpness of grapes newly plucked. And so indeed she envisioned herself, in her morning's mental exercises. She was a plant, vigorous and fresh. She emerged from her morning shower and saw her own mirror image gleaming, as if just wetted by the freshest rain. She rejoiced in her own cleanliness. When she dried her feet, she patted a triangle of towelling between her toes. How soft and vulnerable were those little valleys of flesh. And how open to the inexorable creeping of dirt and fungal infections. Candace vowed she would never let such nastiness plague her.

Yet now, after nearly two weeks' solid march, in socks that have begun to whiff and laced boots just a little too tight and certainly too hot, Candace feels an infernal itch pricking at the balls of her feet and creeping up between her toes. So maddening is the itch that she longs to strip her feet and sit and scratch with animal abandon. Like a stinking baboon, she thinks, wrinkling her toes up and down, which brings no relief whatsoever. Then she banishes the baboon image, and raises up instead, stone by stone, the vision of a farmhouse they might find along their way, with inner whitewashed walls, and clothes drawers smelling of lavender, where paired socks snuggle, thick and comforting and clean.

The Outpacer is cursed with a high instep. Before his self-exile, it was a flaw he had easily accommodated with shoes of superlative leather moulded to his feet by a craftsman of Italian extraction. Antonio was that rarest of beings, an artisan who lived for his work. He studied a customer's foot with the same grave and tender regard that a new mother gave her naked infant. The shoes he wrought were a perfect marriage of elegance and comfort. Never in shoes made by Antonio did the Outpacer suffer the crippling pain that would often fell him after a game of squash. For Antonio refused to work with unyielding rubber and flimsy canvas.

To alleviate any cramp in his arches, the Outpacer had been able to call on the services of an expert and wickedly imaginative masseuse. She would oil his aching insteps, smoothing and kneading the flesh much as he imagined some primitive woman might knead bread. And if she happened to arouse, as she often did, his slumbering desire, then he would raise his finger in that silent signal the two of them had come to understand. In silence, she unbuttoned her blouse. Her breasts were miraculous globes. They were golden and flawless, like the magical fruit that adorned trees in some long-submerged tale read to him in childhood. There was the added wonder that the round, soft breasts fit perfectly the concavity of his insteps, as if his foot had served as their original mould. She would raise his feet and, holding his ankles in her firm grip, initiate a contact he could only describe as sublime. For she did not merely hold his naked feet against her naked chest. She shook, or rather, she vibrated. He was not certain exactly what she did. For at that point in the session, his eyes were shut in a bliss nothing could compromise.

The friction of her erect nipples against that vulnerable stretch of his sole caused him a spasm — and then another and another — that slid deliciously between pleasure and pain. He wanted to gorge himself on the sensation, and at the same time, retreat. "Leave off," a small child's voice called inside him. What memory was it the masseuse stirred? Of being tickled by a loving hand, of being led to the very edge of torment? And yet trusting. The innocent trust which renders the sensual pure.

There is no ready ease now for the Outpacer's aching arches. In preparation for his flight from the City, he had taken from his wardrobe the crudest footwear he possessed. These are rudimentary sandals, made of strips of discarded rubber tires. He had bought them in his other life in one of the small states that make up the world's Pleasure Zone. For those who could afford tourist jaunts to the Zone, the sex was cheap and of infinite variety, the beaches relatively unpolluted and the sun safe, provided one took extreme caution. He had purchased the sandals from a beach vendor who wandered the strand with his wares strung on a rope looped around his neck. The vendor, the Outpacer recalled, had very few teeth and those he did possess were quite black. The man's gums looked sore and inflamed. Was that why he had bought the sandals? Did he feel pity in those days, he wondered. Most likely he had bought them because he saw them as an oddity. They are undoubtedly ugly. But they are serviceable and will endure. As he himself will endure until somehow he has carried out his penance. Of what that penance consists, other than laborious walking and his protective service offered up to this motley band, the Outpacer is unsure. He is counting on a revelation. Is that not what they call such conclusions? When he has paid in full for his sin, he will surely have the revelation.

Like the Outpacer, Bird Girl has an unusually high instep. During one of her least wholesome assignments, she had twisted her ankle severely, posing in the ludicrous platform shoes once favoured by Venetian prostitutes. "Turn a little to your left," the photographer had said, "and thrust your pelvis forward." He had meant her bush, but he was uncharacteristically modest compared with most of the creeps in that line of business. Which was why, perhaps, she had later lain down behind the tacky props with him. Gratis. But the awkward position in the cruelly heavy shoes, coupled with his weight on her (for he was not a small man) had wrenched her ankle so badly she could not walk for a week. Odd how she had not noticed until she was out of the studio. It was as if those sessions anaesthetized her.

Her ankle had never entirely healed. Towards the end of a day's march, she notices its weakness, despite the solid support of her high-top lace-ups. What she yearns for when she imagines their finding an abandoned house on their way north is a medicine cabinet stocked with the basics — most especially a bottle of liniment, reeking, hot as mustard, good for humans and for horses. Had she not after all, felt like a Clydesdale in those foolish platforms?

Lucia's problem is bunions. They were a family curse. Her mother and her mother's sisters had all suffered from this deformity. Like them, Lucia had been afflicted when she was still quite young. She blamed ill-fitting shoes (she never had the money needed for good footwear) and the fact she spent hours labouring as a cleaner on her feet, or for variation, on her knees. Apartment blocks and industrial towers were her nemesis. She had a fear of elevators, based not so much on claustrophobia as on who or what might lurk in them. A favourite sport of the embittered and deranged was to spring out of the dark and jab passersby with infected hypodermic needles. Lucia knew of one woman who had died after such an attack in an elevator.

So in her work she trudged up and down the metal stairs, bearing bucket, mop and broom, and a satchel filled with polishing cloths and cleaners. She definitely felt safer clanging her way up stairways but it did her feet no good. Peeling off her shoes and socks at the end of her night shift, she looked aghast at the absurd bulges that ruined her feet, at least superficially. Bunions were undoubtedly ugly but, since she could afford no remedy, Lucia determined to learn to appreciate her feet's transformed shape.

She began, as she often did, with a plaster cast. Once she had her mould she was able to create her own foot of clay. As an artifact, her foot seemed less repulsive. She could discern an energy, a resilience, a compelling asymmetry. For a time, she slept with the clay foot on her bedside table. When she woke she would sit up and study its form, until it came fully to inhabit her mind. In this way she learned to be comfortable with the change that time, work, and poverty had wrought in her body.

The day the interlopers came and smashed her potter's wheel, they had also used their heavy instrument on the clay foot, which lay in shards upon the floor. In her new life on the road, she reflected every morning on how lucky she was that in their frenzied haste, the vandals had not looked under the bed and discovered the box where she kept the poet's life mask wrapped in a fine merino shawl that had once belonged to her Aunt Nidia.

Lucia's Masks

Lucia is not the first woman to fall in love with a long-dead English poet, nor will she be the last. When she grows weary, and her feet pain her badly, she envisions his dreaming mouth, recalls the holiness of his heart's affections, and keeps on.

Chapter Five
Lucia Finds a House

LAST NIGHT I HAD ANOTHER OF my Rat-Man dreams. I hope I didn't cry out, disturbing the others. In the dream, the monster's fanged jaw came so near my face I could feel its fetid breath on my cheek, and feared my skin would turn ulcerous. I was in caught in a frigid terror, waiting for the jab of the Rat-Man's poisoned syringe and the agonizing cramps in my bowel, belly, and muscles that would follow. I woke with the smell of ripe sweat in my armpits. I was clutching my midriff, terrified I was hemorrhaging.

Then I realized the dream-claw I had felt pressing on my throat was in fact thirst. That awareness shook me properly awake, back into my world of duty and service. Our water supply has dwindled to a few drops each in our personal flagons. If I do not find some soon we will all be in danger of muscle spasms and delirium. It distressed me how dizzy I felt when I stood up. If I was already affected by my body's craving for water, how must the others be feeling?

I decided to risk drinking the last of my personal supply, which was barely enough to wet my mouth and make my throat contract in longing for more.

Everyone in the group is supposed to be constantly on the lookout for safe food and water. But the principal foraging duty has devolved on me. Despite my willingness to serve, there are times when this responsibility weighs upon me. The two demons who so often invade my mind are already buzzing. These are the ones who mock my laboured breathing when I have run for miles and found nothing. I picture them as blackened skeletons. Starvation and Thirst. In their most extreme form — when they have achieved their ultimate desire — they unite in a marriage that is Death.

I do not tell any of the others about my demons. I know that silence and forbearance are prerequisites of the service I owe them. But I did not anticipate when I first set out from the City that the lives of five other people would depend on my ability to sniff out potable water.

I heard Candace's voice then and quietly spoke the wish I make every morning, "Gracious Maker of all forms, give me the strength to endure Candace." I have given up trying to put an end to the perturbing images that take hold of me whenever Candace deliberately plies her cheery organizational skills. There are times I cannot help but envision cloying Candace trussed up in a tree and blessedly gagged. Or chirping Candace thrust down a well whose lid is then firmly secured.

It is not that I wish the woman any real harm. I simply wish her silent.

It still amazes me that Candace seems incapable of enjoying the profundity of silence. She must always be filling it with little verbal goads and the platitudes she has in such abundance. Each morning we are subjected to her tedious exuberance. "Another brand-new day," she brays on waking.

"Rise up, rise up, companions!" Her smile fills the bottom half of her face. Candace has a particularly large mouth, which I sometimes think must contain more than the usual number of teeth.

"Smile, young man," she commands Chandelier. "I know you can. Such a handsome boy when you smile." When she puts her hand on his shoulder, Chandelier visibly winces. Yet Candace seems oblivious to his discomfort.

"Bird Girl, just looking at you makes me want to dance." Candace does not see the mocking grimace Bird Girl makes in response for she moves on immediately to Old Harry: "How is the arthritis today, Harry? Are you ready to soldier on? Yes, of course you are." Candace always answers her own questions of Harry. Is this because she is afraid of what he might say?

It is my turn next.

"Good morning, Lucia, our Lady of Light," Candace simpers. "And what will our superb forager find us today? Water, I hope. Surely you can find us water with your wonderful skills?"

I cannot help but welcome the undertone of dislike I am sure I hear in her voice. I very much want to keep Candace at a distance. And so I simply smile, but without showing my teeth. In reality, I would like to stick my fingers down my throat in a childish pantomime of gagging. But I take comfort in the escape I will make shortly in my quest for water and for food. I tell myself it is well worth braving possible encounters with wild dogs or worse simply to get away from Candace.

Just when I think she must surely have finished her morning greeting, Candace proposes that we compose a group song: "To bind us; to cheer us on our way."

We are all parched and already fatigued, though we have been up for barely an hour. I cannot believe she is so foolish as to suggest her cheery song idea now of all times.

"If we lost you, we'd be five. Why don't you just take a dive?" Harry's acerbic rhyme captures the frustration we all feel.

Candace looks so obviously hurt I feel some real pity for her. Bird Girl whispers something in Harry's ear that prompts him to say "Sorry," but without great conviction.

The Outpacer appears then from wherever he has secreted himself during the night. He seems to enjoy staging these abruptly dramatic entrances. It is as if he tears open a fissure in our field of vision. Whether this is a symbolic wound or a door that he opens, I am uncertain. What I do know is how much I would like to approach him quietly, then stand on tip-toe to flip back the hood of his monk's gown and uncover his face. And then? Stare in revulsion or in awe? I cannot imagine his revealed features causing anything other than an extreme reaction.

"An inner song may serve us best for a while, don't you think, Candace?" Candace merely stares. We all stare at the talking cowl. The Outpacer so seldom speaks. He has not uttered so many words at once since he first made us his offer of service. His voice puts me in mind of steely cold water. Put your hand in and it will freeze. I pictured this water moving down my spine, drop by drop. Why does this image come to me? Because I am so damnably thirsty? Then I feel both confused and ashamed because I realize I am imagining the touch of his mouth on my naked back. The Outpacer's mouth and teeth and tongue. A mouth I have never seen. I must take care, for these woods would be a foolish and most perilous place for the birth of desire.

Is it his voice that pulls at me so powerfully, I wonder, or the simple fact of his mystery? Even a full mask would suggest more of his features than does the engulfing hood.

In the City I learned well that some shadows can be protective. But not the shadow play I believe underlies desire. Such shadows shift and slide, and make a mockery of what is real. On the shadow-stage of desire, I know that gods can transform themselves into devils, ears to horns, noses to beaks, all in an eye-blink. Nothing is as it seems. Nothing is to be trusted. And certainly not the seductive resonance in the voice of a man whose face I have never seen.

"Shall I tell you," the Outpacer inquires formally, "my own inner song?" I see that every one of us is hanging on his words. Five people are fixed on the utterance of a mouth we can only imagine in a face we cannot see. I notice Candace run the tip of a pink tongue over her upper lip. It strikes me too, how uncommonly still Bird Girl is standing, in her little lilac skirt that barely covers her hips.

Old Harry leans forward, his left hand on Chandelier's shoulder. Harry's eyes have a glitter-hard brightness, like the eyes of birds I have seen in photographs. I have observed this almond-shaped glint in the eyes of all the old men I have met in my life, few as they were. I always supposed this was because their souls were preparing themselves for flight. It is their eyes that are ready first, piercing the void and mapping out likely channels for the passage.

Chandelier's lovely face is rapt. I wonder briefly what he sees in the Outpacer for I am quite certain Chandelier perceives far more than he lets on.

"These are the words of a song my grandmother taught me," the Outpacer begins. "I will not sing them because I am no singer. So I'll recite what I recall:

Old Mother Moon has lit the lamps
The stars that light us on our way
As we travel toward the Mortals' Hotel
Where sleep will be peaceful and morning gay."

There follows a silence so total it is worthy of Old Mother Moon herself. It amazes me how, with a few simple words in his deep bass, the Outpacer has succeeded in recasting our mood, dispelling the jangled, whirring state that Candace foists on us each morning. He has offered us an impossible storybook destination, a moonlit hotel where we might come together for a night of blissful rest. I realize he was trying to take the fear out of the night for us — no, he was doing something more. He was subtly challenging Candace's presumption of authority. He was offering himself as our leader. He was implying that he could be more than just our shadowy watcher, who tailed and circled our group and kept off the ravenous dogs with his flaming torch.

I glance at Candace to see if she has grasped the Outpacer's intent. Her mouth is turned down in a sullen arc. I hear her take one of her excessively dramatic deep breaths before advancing to stand directly in front of the Outpacer.

I offer up a silent request. Please do not let her say: "Thank you for sharing that with us."

"Thank you for sharing your song with us, Outpacer," Candace says. Her tone is thickly patronizing, much as it was when the silly woman told me to keep my head up when I walked.

Immediately she has finished speaking, Harry lets loose a howl that propels Chandelier to his knees. The old man then begins braying like a tormented donkey.

I am momentarily stunned. Then Bird Girl and I go to help Chandelier to his feet. His face is an unsettling white that makes me think of shattered eggshell. Yet it is Harry to whom the boy turns, touching the old man's face tentatively as if to reassure himself his aged friend has not been monstrously transformed.

Bird Girl sends me an enquiring look; then abruptly confronts Old Harry: "See how your foolishness has frightened him!" Her heart-shaped face is stern, and for the first time I see that Bird Girl may be considerably older than the adolescent image she projects.

Harry puts his arm round Chandelier's shoulders in an unsteady embrace. "I am sorry," he says.

"It seems to be your morning for being sorry, Harry," Candace chides him. "Maybe now is the time to talk over what exactly is troubling you." I am uncomfortable at just how heavily she weights the word "exactly," and worse, at the way her mouth is stretched wide in a painfully false smile.

We are all unprepared for the old man's reaction. Harry straightens his spine, squares his shoulders and thrusts out his chin. I sense the supreme effort this movement costs him, based on my Great-Aunt Fontina's description of the arthritis that blighted her last years. I wonder if Harry must daily master such pain. My aunt said it was like rats' teeth gnawing incessantly at the nerves of her already twisted limbs. To my enduring shame, I thought Fontina must be exaggerating at least a little. Then, at the age of fifteen, I was hit by a virus that caused me such cruel arthritic pain I had to bite my lips to stop myself crying out. It was a harsh lesson. But I learned then that courage assumes many forms — not least the quiet, resigned stoicism of the aged.

So when Harry raises his arm and points angrily at Candace, I watch him in a kind of awe. Behind that slow, deliberate motion, I read not just the physical pain he must bear but also the red-hot source of his fury.

"I'll tell you exactly what's wrong," Harry barks. "It's you. You and your infernal phony optimism. You are nasty and pushy and interfering, and you are coming very close to driving me mad."

Bird Girl splutters in a failed attempt to swallow a laugh. This is infectious, and I have to look down at my feet and concentrate on the soreness of my wretched bunions, in order to quell a fit of giggles.

I expected Candace to be indignant with Harry and then launch into one of her condescending homilies. To my astonishment and dismay, she looks terrified. Her eyes roll upward. Then she collapses.

Bird Girl is the first to reach her. She puts her finger under Candace's nose and feels for the pulse in her wrist. "She's all right," she announces. As City dwellers, we had all witnessed plenty of sudden and inexplicable deaths, even among the young and apparently vigorous. There is a collective sigh of relief, with Harry's exhalation the loudest.

Together, Bird Girl and I straighten Candace's legs. She is wearing Bermuda shorts that have fanned out above her knees. I tug the cloth down so as to preserve her dignity and feel a revulsion of which I am at once ashamed. Candace's knees are so fleshy, they are dimpled. I have never before touched anyone whose flesh was not spare. It crosses my mind that my reaction to Candace's plump form is basically aesthetic; that it somehow relates to the way I shape my clay. Then I tuck this thought away where it belongs and unknot my long-fringed, embroidered black shawl which I always wear now tied about my shoulders. I wind the shawl round my fist, making a bundle to serve Candace as a pillow. Bird Girl and I then gently raise her head and I slip the bundled shawl underneath.

Bird Girl tips the last drops of water from her own flagon into Candace's mouth. "Her lips are pretty parched," she tells me.

Bird Girl has hardly finished speaking when Candace vomits up the water. Then she sits up abruptly, her eyes wide and wild. "Devils," she cries out in a voice guttural and grating. "Devils." She falls back with a little sob and her whole body begins to convulse.

"Her pulse is racing," says Bird Girl, a touch of panic in her voice.

"The effects of the dehydration," I hear the Outpacer say. I am already kneeling to tighten my shoelaces when he asks me urgently, "Lucia, can you find us water now?" I nod, feigning a confidence I do not feel; then rapidly straighten my belt to which is attached my knife in its leather sheaf. I take several deep breaths, raise my right hand in farewell and set off.

As I run, I keep close watch for any signs of moisture that might indicate the presence of a spring. But this part of the forest strikes me as particularly unpromising. The huge trees are all so similar in height and girth they appear to be clones of one another. It is perhaps a forest originally raised up so that it could be hewn down and the logs sent to factories. I see no insect life whatsoever, and I wonder if the tree bark might be poisoning other life forms. This does not bode well. Grasshoppers, slugs, and shiny-backed beetles are all edible. We still have small reserves of the honeycomb that was my first lucky find. We also have some raisins and a little oatmeal left.

Three days before, I had crept up upon a noble brown hare. He looked glossily healthy. I grimaced as I slit his throat. When I got back to the group and took the bleeding carcass from my pack, Candace yelped in disgust.

"Don't eat it then," I snapped. Candace took a step back, and looked at me in consternation.

"Do you think I found it easy?" I had hurled the question at her. It was guilt, I suppose, at murdering the poor animal that made me lose my temper with her. But it was worse than that. In fact, I wanted to slap her. Slap her so hard she would yelp in pain. It disturbs me to think of this now.

It was the Outpacer who had interceded, for it was evening and he had already joined us by the fire.

"Thank you, Lucia," he said. "It is a fine offering. Shall I skin it for us, or will you?"

"I will," I answered. I had already taken out my knife because I had a great need to busy myself. The anger churned in me so wildly, I had to will my hand steady.

The Outpacer intervened judiciously that evening, just as he did this morning. The difference was the degree of light. I realize he has gradually been coming closer to us, and doing this so subtly I was almost unaware. But this morning was the first time since he joined us that he stood together with us in the daylight. I wonder if he will stay with us now in the daytime. And if so, how will he manage to have the hood always in place? Or will he eventually come so close he will at last forsake the disguise?

It occurs to me that under the obscuring cowl he might wear a full-face or half-mask as a double insurance of keeping himself hidden. What if he is terribly disfigured? What if he is absolutely prepossessing, with features I immediately wanted to copy in clay?

And if his revealed face initially disappoints, would his authority still stand? But surely that powerful voice would prevail? I have to shake off the memory of the disquieting effect his voice had on me. This is where physical desire leads, I chastize myself, for it dawns on me I have been oblivious to my surroundings for some seconds. Certainly long enough to put my life in peril from potential attackers. Rat-Men. Dogs with a taste for blood from a human throat. Or a solitary, disgruntled outrider from a murderous band who would take pleasure in cutting off my hands.

I run on, with my sense of purpose cleansed and cleaving the way before me. I must find water. I notice that the quality of the light is changing and that ahead, the forest appears to be thinning. I run toward, and then through, a purplish mist spangled with dew. Abruptly, the forest ends and I find myself at the edge of a field of long, yellowed grass. The field rises toward the horizon so that I am unable to see what lies beyond.

I begin to work my way cautiously through the waist-high grasses, but their dry rasping declares my presence at every step. I feel more and more exposed as I advance. The field continues to the limit of my vision. I keep scanning the surface of the grassy sea, alert for any tell-tale shudder or ripple. What predator might be slinking toward me, belly slicking the ground? Every few minutes, I stop and listen. The utter silence and stillness unnerve me. There is not the least breeze and already the sun is hot enough to scorch exposed flesh. I keep my hands in my pockets as I move on. A white head scarf, pulled low over my brow, protects the top of my head. My hair, wound in a thick knot, keeps the nape of my neck shaded.

I stop and pray for cloud cover.

At that moment the air stirs. A breeze comes, scythe-clean and fragrant, making my nostrils widen. What is this scent that swirls round me where I stand? I feel a sudden joy as I recognize its source as mown hay. I move forward again, made fearless (and probably foolishly so) by the recollection of one of those rare childhood times when the world seemed good and bountiful and all beings well-intentioned. I was six years old when my mother and younger sister and I spent a month on a dairy farm belonging to friends of my father. After we returned to the City I treasured that stay in the country as a kind of paradise. I would try to remember exactly the effects those honest pastoral scents had on me: the reassuring fug of the cattle's breath in the barn, and the full, round perfume of the cut hay that made me want to invent a dance in answer to its bracing scent.

By the time I reach the crest of the field I am still absolutely lost to reverie, and the vista before me snaps me back to the present. I am made aware again of my own vulnerability and instinctively duck down. I picture what my lapsed attention might have cost; my flesh speckled with blood, my throat and belly ripped open. And if I die because of my own stupidity, what will become of Candace, whose need for water is so desperate?

I move forward as quietly as I can, on my knees. Once again, the air is absolutely still. *Too* still, I think. In fact, the silence now is paralyzing. I realize I am waiting — every hair on my body erect — for someone or something to emerge from this unearthly quiet.

They stand up from where they have been squatting or kneeling, hidden by the long grass. There are three of them, dressed in black rags. Their faces and arms are newly bloodied, and there are fresh gashes of the crosses they have cut, probably earlier that morning, into their shaved skulls. I sometimes saw such women in the City. They are penitents who believe that by shaving their heads and slicing their flesh, they may secure God's forgiveness for our sins. The *piagnoni*, my mother used to call them, the weepers. These women wail and howl and beat their breasts in unison as they wander about in little knots of three or four. It is a frightening thing to witness when they stop moving, as if prompted by an unseen hand, and clutch each other's shoulders and sway together and start their cacophony. Whatever power possesses them at these junctures is not just unnerving but invasive. When I came upon them in the City, I always tried to avert my eyes and get away from them as quickly as possible before the reverberation of their wailing chorus caught in my throat. If I stayed and stared, the frightful sounds they made, and even their grotesque self-mutilation, began to cast a hypnotically persuasive spell. The *piagnoni* gave a living shape to the latent despair of my City life, which I strove each day to subdue. I had to protect myself from the threat they posed. I could not let them contaminate my disciplines, or my nourishing of hope.

These women had another kind of frenzied fit for which I always stayed alert, because in these moods they saw me as a chief offender. It was one of their peculiar beliefs that long or luxuriant hair was a mark of the devil. They carried with them barber's scissors and razors to cut off the long hair of anyone they were able to subdue physically. When this "shearing frenzy" was upon them their strength doubled. In the City I had sometimes noticed them eyeing my long braid in disgust. But I was fortunate never to have encountered the *piagnoni* when the shearing mania seized them.

Now I see that time has come, as the three who circle me in the field press in closer. The metal of their scissors and razors flash in the sunlight. My stomach churns. I upbraid myself again for my stupidity. If I had not been daydreaming, I would have smelt them, spied them, or heard them. I am now at a perilous disadvantage, with two of them advancing speedily toward me, their limbs powered by their obsession, and another coming up behind me.

I draw my dagger and whirl about with it, keeping it close to my body for I have no desire to harm them if I can avoid it. All I want is to appear violent enough to frighten them off. But they keep coming. So I begin making lunging motions in the air, miming a fatal strike with my knife.

"Kneel, sinner, and be shorn," the one behind me cries out in a voice so quavering and high-pitched it seems to come from the cutting instruments they brandish. The *piagnoni* are so close now I can see the multitude of tiny crosses incised on their noses and cheeks.

I do not want to hurt them but neither do I want them to overpower me, lop off my braid and shave my head raw. This is not just for vanity's sake but also because I am sure my hair still holds some remembrance of the warmth and shape of my mother's hands, brushing, smoothing, and plaiting the thick strands over the years. As if this thought conjures her up, I hear my mother's voice at the instant I must either act, or fall at the wailing women's feet and submit. "Feign madness," she instructs me. "Become the very devil they fear."

I drop my knife between my feet. I bare my teeth. I growl. I undo the knot of my shawl and lift my arms so that the cloth spreads about me like black wings. I swoop at them, all the while pumping my arms up and down. I begin to laugh, in the way I had heard hysterical women do: a spiral of sound that was sometimes a bitter song.

The one who was behind me comes round to join the other two. They back away and huddle together, murmuring. I shriek and swoop; yet still they hesitate.

What I do next astounds me, and I have no idea what prompts my action. Undoing the buttons of my blouse, I bare my breasts to them.

"Whore. Devil's spawn," they call me. And indeed I feel a hot rush of shame at exposing myself in this way.

But it works. I see them tremble and stumble as they flee through the long grass. I do up my blouse again, while keeping my eyes fixed on their receding figures until they have disappeared. They ran toward the west. And so I determine to go on straight ahead, but chastened and unfailingly cautious. I must never again let my guard down so carelessly.

While keeping low to the ground, I raise my head just enough to peer through the tips of the long grass. Directly ahead is a scene so unexpected I fear for a moment I am hallucinating.

Behind a low stone wall, inset with a metal gate, is a two-storey house of matching stone. I have little knowledge of stone. This one is a dark grey, verging on black, blended with a lighter shade people still call dove grey, even though no one I know has ever seen a dove. The stones themselves have been cut in large rectangular blocks, mortared one atop the other so that they appear knitted together, like a resilient fabric.

The house has two windows upstairs and two down, and a central wooden door which stands open above a stone slab that serves as a stoop. There is a narrow chimney on the right side of the pointed roof. I can easily imagine smoke rising from the chimney, making a union of roof and sky. I drew pictures of such houses as a child, with an adult suggesting the squared windows, a chimney, and a tail of smoke. These details, as indeed the shape of the snugly self-contained house itself, resembled nothing in my known reality. Yet I found making the drawing satisfying as if I had fashioned a place of safety that would help in some small way to protect us from all the wolves of the world.

Now, of course, I know the truth. There is nowhere that is safe.

I stand up slowly, keeping my right hand close to my knife. I whistle softly. Then I call out: "Hello?"

The sound of my voice rises and falls, swallowed up by the surrounding field.

The forlorn character of the house suggests it has been long abandoned. Nevertheless, I draw my knife and stride forward, pushing open the metal gate in the stone wall. It is off the latch and swings readily to let me through. I proceed, keeping my eyes fixed on the door which still stands open at exactly the same angle as when I first observed it. The smell of cut hay is much stronger now, and something else — a vinegary odour that makes my nostrils prickle.

I stand a moment on the stone stoop. With my knife raised, I enter the house with all the stealth I learned in my City life. Immediately, I check behind the door. Here there is only angled space, empty of everything but shadows and the balls of dirt some people call sluts' wool. To my right, I see a chaotic room, with chairs upturned and cushions awry. Every surface is covered with a fur of dust. And here I find the source of the scent of hay. There are six squared bundles of it, bound with twine and scattered about the room.

I move next to the kitchen. On the table top dust lies so thickly I am able to trace a visible *X* with my forefinger. I have to hold my nose when I come near a jug whose contents have sprouted a dense yellow fungus. Everywhere there are signs of deliberate damage or of hasty departure and abandonment. Broken dishes, shards of glass, and mouse droppings cover the floor and the wooden counter surrounding the sink.

I wonder if the *piagnoni* have been here and done this damage in one of their fits. Knife at the ready, I open the cupboards and a door that looks as if it might seal a pantry. My mood lifts, for inside the cupboards all is neatness and order and amazing bounty. Stacked in regimented rows are many more cans of food than I can readily count: kidney beans, chick peas, corn, tomatoes, even olives.

Next, I try the hand pump beside the sink. If it works and the water tastes sweet I can fill my bottle and flask and return to the others right away.

I push the handle up and down with a silent prayer on my lips. There is a whine, a hiss, and a gush of clean-smelling water issues from the spout. I roll a drop or two on my tongue, and find it good. I drink more and fill the bottle and the flask I have with me and put them carefully back in my pack.

There is no time to investigate the upper floor before I leave. The house seems weighted in its own silence. I can hear nothing but the steady thump of my own heart.

Would it ever be possible, I wonder, to bring life back to this old stone house, to lift its burden of sullen silence and see smoke rise from its chimney, uniting roof and sky? Personally, I hope the others will not elect to stay here, even for a short time. I sense something angry and surly haunting these rooms. Once Candace is recovered and we have renewed our supplies, we must press on to the North without delay. We must not falter. I have a great dread of what might happen if we linger here.

I shoulder my pack and go out into the yard, then stop to sniff the air. Nothing seems untoward in that sultry world, and so I decide to risk running through the field, following the track I made earlier when I crept on my hands and knees.

I have water with me to revive Candace and an apparently abundant source to which I can lead the others. I have found a house with plenty of food where we can rest a day or two. I have managed to repulse the wailing women without causing them physical harm. For the moment, I feel blessed by circumstance and I run along in the happy belief that chance has enabled me to do my duty well. I hope that when Candace recovers, she will have forgotten the panic she experienced before she fainted and the devils she saw in her delirious state. I hate the idea that we distressed her, and resolve to be kinder and more forbearing in future.

I picture as I run the poet's wise and dreaming face, and as ever, draw strength from the knowledge I carry his likeness in my pack. If he were one of our group, I do not doubt he would be far more tolerant and forgiving of Candace than I have been so far. His empathy was finely honed and well practised.

As I near our encampment, I recall his poem about the Lamia, with her glittering serpent's body and a woman's lips and feelings. The Lamia falls in love with a mortal man, and Keats describes her anguish in such a way that my heart moved for her. It occurs to me that John Keats, with his extraordinary empathy and magnanimous soul, would probably even feel sympathy for a Rat-Man. I know that if I ever have the misfortune to encounter one of these monsters face-to-face, and with no means of escape, I am unlikely to feel any pity for it whatsoever. But this is obviously not a situation I ever want put to the test.

As usual, the very idea of the Rat-Men and the revulsion they inspire in me sharpens my senses. I think too of the man with the marble eye whom Bird Girl fears, and the other one with the slit nose, which I imagine looks like a fungoid growth feeding on his face. I swear I will never lapse into oblivious reveries again. The encounter with the *piagnoni* was my harsh lesson that the City follows us — not just in nightmares and loathsome memories, but in the flesh.

I run on swiftly and soon I can smell the charred remnants of our campfire and a whiff of something noxious and perturbing. It comes to me that this is the lingering odour of Candace's panic attack. I send ahead my most earnest hope that she has now been purged of her fear, and has forgotten whatever unwitting part we five played in her distress.

Chapter Six
The Unveiling of Lola

THEY ALL WAIT SILENTLY FOR LUCIA, despite their prickling thirst. Candace has stopped convulsing, much to the Outpacer's relief. He curses the fact he is unable to remove his hood and examine her more closely for her lips still seem to him to have a blue cast. He is grateful Bird Girl continues to be so attentive to the stricken woman.

Harry appears to be napping, his beaked nose occasionally bumping between his drawn-up knees. He seems a resilient old chap, the Outpacer thinks admiringly. He knows he is unlikely to live so long himself. The boy as usual is at Harry's side, sometimes watching the old man's mouth, sometimes staring into space — not vacantly, but as if he shapes some kindly living forms that might augment their company.

The Outpacer chides himself. Is he becoming stupidly fanciful in his new guise? But it is so many years since his mind has run cleanly of its own accord, without artificial stimulants. He is continually surprised at the intense pleasure he derives from this quicksilver mental play with its unexpected turnings, cross-connections, and sudden tugs back to childhood scenes he had thought lost long ago. So long too, since he has considered the word "play" in anything but a lubricious sense: those things one did between silk sheets or against silk-covered walls; on top of or under tables; or in the crypts of abandoned churches (twice); or in rooms equipped with the devices and substances that ensured he was in a constant state of arousal, and his desire never quite sated.

This was the drawback to the mind's free-ranging. It inevitably returned him to the lewdest scenes of his personal sexual theatre. These are scenes that now make him flinch in self-disgust and yet can still arouse him, which makes him detest himself even more.

As Lucia arouses him when she bursts into their midst, breathless and so hot that a visible steam rises from her skin. She stops, panting deeply, her hands on her hips, and leans forward. For the merest instant, her open-necked blouse reveals her breasts, quite naked and absolutely unbound, swinging a little as she bends from the waist. He only just catches sight of her long, brown, pointed nipples. Like pyramids of chocolate. And despite his thirst, his tongue moves in his mouth with desire, and under the full skirt of his monk's gown his flesh yearns for the long-legged forager.

He has to turn away to stifle a moan. Yet is this a more natural lust than anything he has felt for many years? A lust free of perversion. Is it possible? And if possible, is it permissible that he entertain such feelings? Perhaps it is, although he will have to constrain his desire, which will be an arduous test of his resolve.

Every aspect of his present life seems to be a test. His bleeding feet. His hunger. Candace's cheery nostrums. And now the forager whose delectable nipples he longs to stroke and make hard with little jabs of his tongue. It comes to him with a jolt that he wants to give her pleasure. This is not a practice he has much cultivated. Rapacity, certainly. Whenever he had engaged in seduction, his object was solely to prolong his own anticipation. His appetite — his own engorging greed — was paramount. He had given little thought to his sensual partners, except to demand their adoration or worshipful attentiveness.

He'd had female partners in particular who abased themselves only too willingly. How soon he had tired of their fawning and their besotted looks. Their fixation became loathsome to him. As a result, he had no choice but to humiliate them so completely that their love turned acrid, the stone in a fruit they must spit out, or else choke.

He shudders to recall the details of the degrading scenarios he devised for them: orgies in which he scripted their every move, with partner after partner or several at a time, while he looked on, and most crucially, they saw him looking on. They must witness the entire gamut of his reactions, which at least had been genuine. His titillated curiosity soon turned to indifference, and finally to disgust. He would pointedly turn his back on them. It was imperative that they witness his departure, preferably through a slammed door. He left them to their fate, which was sometimes a hatred of him so extreme, he was forced to double his complement of bodyguards.

He cannot imagine the Lady Forager so debasing herself, even if love tormented her piercingly. She would never grovel or forsake her dignity. It strikes him, and not for the first time, that she is protected by some invisible armour. He has no idea what this armour might be — only that it seems to deflect any prurient thoughts. He is gripped by the notion that Lucia has some inevitable part to play in his fulfillment of his penance, but he cannot even begin to speculate how this might come to pass.

Lucia draws a glistening bottle from her pack. Even through the forest's gloom, he can see the water's silvery sheen and his saliva glands contract at the sight. In his former life, he would have seized the bottle from her and satisfied his own thirst first. Or would he? Is it possible he has begun to judge himself more harshly than even he deserves?

Bird Girl steps forward to grasp the bottle by its neck. She takes it to Candace, uncorks it, and lifts it to her patient's lips. They all avert their eyes as Candace splutters, drinks deeply, and makes a mewling sound that reminds him of a kitten someone had thrust into his arms when he was a boy. Involuntarily he shudders, recalling how the sponginess of its soft-boned body repulsed him, and how he had struggled with a distressing urge to crush the helpless creature between iron hands.

He observes that Bird Girl does not drink. She takes the bottle next to Old Harry, who seems barely to wet his mouth before giving the bottle back. Bird Girl passes it to Chandelier, who demurs, shaking his head so that his wonderful corkscrew curls seem to float and catch at what light there is. The boy goes into one of his fluid mime shows, his right index finger symbolically closing his lips, his left hand next covering his mouth. Finally, he makes Bird Girl a slight bow, his upturned open palms inviting her to drink. All this is accomplished in a second. The Outpacer wants to applaud but resists, for the harsh sound would spoil the lingering tracery of gesture Chandelier has written on the air.

And so Bird Girl drinks, and then Chandelier. The bottle passes again to Lucia, who is panting still. He drinks last, and sets the bottle down beside him. He marvels at how civil they all are. And wonders what it might take to smash that civility to bits. He thinks of how the bottle had moved — from weakest (for the moment) to strongest (likewise).

An image of startling clarity bursts upon his brain. He sees six glass beads, of various colours and sizes, strung on a wire. Here we are, he realizes, separate entities yet ready to slide and touch. Or indeed, to clash and crash, if tilting chaos sends us there. How long can they maintain this obliging separateness, he wonders. With the exception of Candace, they are still all so careful not to intrude on each other. They have somehow tumbled into a tolerant, resilient looseness. They are not tightly bound. He foresees this state cannot last.

Lucia is finally able to summon the breath to speak clearly. At first he cannot grasp her meaning. It is so long since he has heard the word she utters, it remains for some seconds an empty cage of sound.

"House," Lucia repeats. "I found an abandoned house.

"There is food there," she tells them. "And water."

"House," Chandelier repeats to Harry, who is apparently having problems hearing. "Food and water."

Is it a morning for miracles? The Outpacer has never heard the boy speak so many words consecutively.

Only Harry does not appear surprised. "Yes, boy," he says. "This is good."

Bird Girl has skipped up to Lucia, her skimpy skirt bouncing on her slender legs. The Outpacer makes himself look away until she stands still again, on her tiptoes, in order to whisper something in Lucia's ear.

How pleasing it is to gaze on these two women standing together. One blond. One dark. One sinewy and small. One strong-boned and muscular. His former self would have automatically imagined their heads touching on a pillow, their naked limbs tangled for his delectation. Now he finds the mere idea of their sexual juxtaposition distasteful. He decides this is a good indication of how far he has come.

He is curious, however, as to what Bird Girl has whispered to Lucia.

He sees Lucia slowly shake her head and Bird Girl take a step back, momentarily dejected. But not for long, for she is soon summoned to Candace's side.

Candace is obviously agitated. She struggles to sit up, plucking Lucia's bundled shawl from under her head impatiently, and tossing it at her feet. Candace's gracelessness irritates him. As the woman draws her knees up to her chest, readying herself to stand, he has to turn his head away. He has no wish to see her exposed upper thighs where her shorts bell out unbecomingly. He judges this aversion must have more to do with Candace's character than her physicality. At the height of his philandering, he had bedded plenty of well-rounded women.

Outside of his tormenting thoughts, Candace is undoubtedly one of his sorest trials to date. Her smugness seems to permeate her entire being so that even her retroussé nose (which in another woman he might have found charming), strikes him as repugnant. He notices that Lucia looks on glassy-eyed as Candace, now apparently fully recovered, hugs herself and hops about in a parody of childish delight. "Clean socks," she sings. "Are there socks, Lucia?"

"Oh, how wonderful! A house! A house! We can be a real community in our own house."

Harry launches a cannonade of coughs so harsh, Chandelier puts his fingers in his ears. Candace glares at him; then turns to the others: "Are we all ready, then?"

Lucia and Bird Girl exchange a look in which the Outpacer reads a much-tried forbearance.

"Are you well enough to travel?" Bird Girl asks Candace.

"Oh, yes. I am quite recovered. And much more than that. I am re-energized. A house. Abandoned, you said, Lucia? A house in which we can settle, let our tensions diffuse. Purify ourselves."

"Drop you down a cistern, perhaps." The Outpacer is close enough to make out Harry's muttered comment. Behind him, he hears Lucia's smothered laugh. He turns to see her bend from the waist to gather up her shawl; watches as she smoothes out the crushed bundle, folds the material corner to corner; then stretches it with her arms fully extended so that from the eyes down, her face and upper body are veiled by a triangle of black silk. Its deep fringe brushes her knees. Then a flick, a twist of black in the air, and the shawl settles again on her shoulders.

"The heat in the field is fierce," she warns them. "We must all keep our heads covered."

Harry tugs from his pocket the tubular toque that looks as if it might once have been a sock. Bird Girl pulls a man's ancient fedora rakishly over one eye. Candace puts on her hat of woven straw, with its clump of garish plastic cherries. Lucia sleeks down her head scarf and draws it tightly over her brow. Chandelier's headpiece is a battered plastic mixing bowl. What a marvel, the Outpacer thinks, to see this dull object transformed, once set upon the boy's pliant curls. Immediately it becomes the delicately moulded helmet of a young warrior god.

So they set off, with their heads protected, and their naked hands either thrust in their pockets or tucked up inside long sleeves.

Lucia takes the lead, followed by Bird Girl; then Chandelier with Old Harry, then Candace, and the Outpacer in the rear.

Once they leave the cover of the forest, it is as the Lady Forager warned: a heat so fiery, it would surely split open the flesh of an exposed infant. Even swathed in his burlap cowl, he cannot rid himself of the image of sizzling meat. Long afterwards, when he thinks of that fateful crossing of the field, it is the picture of a blazing hot grill that comes to him, and six bodies squirming on its murderous surface.

He silently curses again his smothering disguise as the sweat streams down his face and chest. His eyes sting. He sometimes stumbles blindly. When he can see clearly, it is Candace's ample backside that fills his gaze. The plump cheeks straining against striped fabric remind him of the inflated beach toys of his childhood. He recognizes at once how cheap and vicious is this projection and forces himself to examine the real roots of his own gnawing and growing unease. How can he properly protect these five beings when he can barely see? It was one thing to shadow them, to circle them silently at night, brandishing his torch at the odd scavenger mutt that crept up to their camp. It is quite another to be constantly in their company. It weighs on him so oppressively, this awareness of all their various frailties and of his own shortcomings as their champion.

Is it this vulnerability that feeds his concern they are being followed? He will catch some disconcerting rustle, or snap of twig behind him, and turn and see nothing. But the prickle at the back of his neck persists, as does the gluey sensation of unknown eyes watching their every move. There is no one there, he assures himself as he turns yet again, the damned hood always slightly obscuring his peripheral vision.

Someone shouts. He nearly collides with Candace who has stopped in her tracks.

"Oh, how darling!" he hears her gush.

Candace is jumping up and down, waving her straw hat in the air. "Our house! Our house!" she exclaims. She hops from one foot to the other.

"Hush!" This from Lucia, who raises her left arm in warning. He sees the forager's hand close on the handle of her knife. Automatically he manoeuvres his arm inside the bell of his gown to grasp his own dagger.

How inept our preparations are, he thinks. It is all merely gesture. We could not even make a decent show of force: three women, an aged man, an adolescent boy, and I. Without the cover of darkness I have neither stealth nor cunning. And I am boiling, blinded by this damn disguise. He wipes the sweat from his brow and studies the stone house. It is a dull, squat affair. No entrancing wooden gables here. He thinks the stone face looks clammy. He feels a chill in his spine, and then in his hands and feet.

He glances at Candace. Her eyes are round and glowing, her face flushed. She stands on tiptoe. Her fingers twitch. He reads her body's agitation as a naked wish to launch herself into the waiting house, and crown herself chief organizer. She will hold little morning colloquies or pep talks, try to thrust them all into roles she has elaborated in her ever-busy brain. The idea is so unbearable he almost groans aloud.

And if the group elects to stay? How can he maintain his duty as protective watcher on the boundary of this exposed, putrid farmyard? He is getting ahead of himself, he realizes. Who could tell what the group might yet choose to do?

"I'll go in first," Lucia calls back. He nods his assent, but moves quickly to follow in close behind her.

"It looks just the same," she tells him as they stand together inside the front door.

Indeed, it could look no worse. His spirit recoils at the putrid smell and chaotic mess of the place. Every surface offends his sensibility: the coarse upholstery, the synthetic lace curtains, the flung hay bales.

The others seem captivated, though. They crowd inside, heedless of danger. He sees Lucia's black eyes widen in alarm. Her arm jerks forward. For a second only, he thinks she may grab his hand. Instead, she draws her knife from its sheath. "We must check upstairs," she whispers.

"I will go first," he says. "Stay close behind me."

A tawdry schoolboy thought flits through his overheated brain: Oh, yes, to precede this lovely woman upstairs, usher her into a bedroom where he might gaze upon her nakedness, spread her muscular legs apart, and trace on the tender flesh of her inner thighs invisible messages of his desire. Until her back arcs in answer, and her dark eyes implore. First, he would use his tongue, entering and withdrawing from her dark, luxuriant nest in a rhythm she cannot anticipate. So that she would writhe and twist away from him in such a frenzy, he must hold her down with his hands on her shoulders. And her passionate shudders would reverberate through his arms. Oh, what pleasure he would give her. He is erect again, lost anew to this wonderland of lust for Lucia who is just behind him on the wooden stair. I must stop this, he urges himself. I must pull myself together. Who was it used to tell him that? It is not an expression he has thought of for many years.

As he mounts the last step before the landing, with its two closed doors, one straight ahead and one to his left, he freezes. For he is sure he has heard something. What? A deep intake of breath? And not from Lucia, but ahead, from behind one of the doors.

He starts to ask, "Did you hear that?" when he is silenced by an abrupt wail, a shrill, animal cry that seems to signal either impending death, or the basest possible despair. He turns to Lucia. "Cat?" she whispers.

"Perhaps." He smiles bravely even though she cannot see his face. He glances down and sees that the others have gathered at the bottom of the stair. From their widened eyes and opened mouths, he reads their fear. He knows he must make a move.

Only Harry appears unperturbed. He looks up, one hand on his stick, the other stroking the boy's cheek. Chandelier's face has turned the colour of sour milk.

The wail pollutes the air again, a curdled, strangled sound. The Outpacer grabs the door handle, pulls, then pushes. The door is apparently locked. Dagger gripped firmly in his right hand, he heaves at the door's central panel, using his left shoulder as a battering ram. There is a metallic snap, and a shudder of the wooden frame as the door gives way.

The wailing is unbroken now, a human siren so shrill he can hardly bear it. The siren's source is, if anything, more horrific than the sound, and he stands for a moment hypnotized by what he sees.

The creature on a narrow bed wails through an open mouth ringed with carmine. Its cheeks are daubed with a ghastly mauve pigment; the eyes so thickly outlined with kohl, it is impossible to see their true colour. This coarsely painted being is wizened, as fleshless and apparently brittle as a twig. As she wails (for it is a "she," he can see her shrunken dugs beneath a transparent blouse of gauzy stuff), her body writhes. Her gaunt arms are spread wide, and her fingers are laced through the tubular bars of the metal bedstead.

The old woman writhes and wails and the metal bed shakes. And still he stands frozen as if her grotesqueness has literally petrified him. She is a gargoyle, a fright, a nightmare come to life. Feel pity, he tells himself. He plumbs what he believes are his emotions and hits only revulsion.

Her feet twitch, making him all the more aware of their transparent spotted skin. Her skirt is calico, with a flounce at the hem. He has seen such skirts on the young whores in the Pleasure Zone; and such blouses too. You can pinch their nipples through the filmy gauze as you pass by, and those pleasure girls will smile at you alluringly. For a second, he wonders if this painted abomination on the bed is a chimera sprung from his own brain, intent on self-punishment. Is this what his lecherous past has conjured up? If so, he can imagine no more harrowing spectacle than the one before him.

The old woman is screaming now. The smudged eyes are fixed on him. He sees Lucia move to the bedside, softly touch the withered, gaudy face, and unpluck the crone's fingers, one by one, from their rigid grip on the bedstead. Lucia sits on the bed, stroking the old woman's hand. Her long ebony braid falls over her shoulder. The old woman reaches out, her gaunt hand trembling, to touch the glossy plait. Her gesture is so tentative, so civilized, that the Outpacer is encouraged to move closer to the bed.

The transformation is immediate. The crone is once again a gargoyle, her mouth a dark hole spouting curses at him. "Dirty, filthy priest-man. Keep away, you bugger. Burn in your own hell, nasty monk-man! I know what you're thinking and hatching under your robe."

She knows, he thinks; and so the idea comes again that this decrepit woman is a necessary aspect of his penance. Snarling, pathetic yet terrifying, like a skeleton rouged and dressed up for a dance, she is another ordeal he must undergo.

She lurches forward. Her long, sharp nails flash near his face. He fears for his eyes. As he jerks his head away from her assault, the hood of his robe falls backward. For the first time in many weeks, the Outpacer stands with his naked face exposed to another being. The crone is able to view his face in those few seconds before he can rearrange the folds of the shadowy hood over his eyes. Lucia does not see him because she is directly behind the old woman, arms gripped round her waist, attempting to pull her back down to the bed.

But someone else has seen him. He is aware, even as he tugs the hood back into place, that there is another person in the room. Not Candace, he implores whatever beneficent forces might still visit the world. Please, not Candace.

He turns to see Bird Girl standing just inside the bedroom door. She stares directly into the dark well of his hood. He knows that from now on she will see the actual features it hides. Bird Girl runs the tip of her tongue over the length of her upper lip. He has no time to ponder what this gesture might mean because the old woman is babbling, making little clucking sounds. Her cracked tones have softened, and it takes him some seconds to recognize this is her attempt at seduction. She is crooning to him, the honeyed words of some bed chamber of a century ago. "Boo-ti-ful man. Such a handsome man. Like a god, my dah-ling. Come lay your head between my breasts."

He steps back in disgust. His deepest wish is to flee. He ought to have stayed stock-still because his symbolic retreat sends the old woman into a frenzy. She wrenches herself from Lucia's circling arms, and reaches out to him, rising on her haunches.

"I know tricks to make you quake in pleasure, handsome man." He cringes inside his monk's habit as she raises her hips toward him. "I am the reincarnation of Lola Montez," she exclaims, "lover of kings and great composers. I have the secret knowledge of the courtesan."

She wriggles her hips under her flounced skirt, then draws up her knees.

Afterwards he tells himself that he ought to have anticipated her next move. He should at least have had the sense to turn his head away, and so spare himself the unwanted vision he will never be able to expunge from memory.

But this ancient woman wriggling obscenely on her metal bed exerts her own iron compulsions. He cannot look away. She is too horrific. She is her own vulgar carnival, and like a child, he must stand and gawp. So that when she flings up her skirt, exposing her spindly thighs and her bald pudendum, he must look. What he feels above all is a scalding shame — for her, for himself, and for the state of the world. At first, he does not fully understand how the world comes into it, and why this incident strikes him as so much more than it was: an old woman who has gone mad and forsaken her dignity.

In a right and proper world, this kind of unseemly behaviour would not occur. Aged women would sit with their knees decently covered, in long, warm skirts. They would hide the mystery between their legs and sometimes speak of the one in their breasts, telling stories droll and wise. A right and proper world — what does he know of such a world? He was born in a time in which the sun was already an enemy, when all birds — with the exception of tortured battery hens — were extinct, and all fish were hermaphrodites. Did the old girl eat too many poisoned fish, he wonders. Or sniff the wrong air of the wrong sky at the wrong moment? There are so many ways to be imperilled in this worst of all possible times.

Then something wondrous happens.

He hears an intake of breath, but whose? This is followed by a silence that seems somehow musical, and a subtle shift in the quality of the light. He has the notion that both space and time have been purified. For a moment the box-like bedroom is transformed into the green-gold pasture of some long-ago poem, a place where one obeys a beautiful compulsion to dance, or to make up a song of praise. It *is* a kind of dance that he witnesses, and he is filled with wonder at the way its simple gestures open another world inside this place they are.

There is only this: two young women gracefully attendant on an elderly one, both of them intent on restoring her dignity. Bird Girl stands on one side of the bed, Lucia on the other. Together, as if choreographed by an unseen hand and mind, they cover up the old woman's nakedness. Drawing the cloth of her skirt gently over her knees, they tuck it under her feet.

Why does this scene move him so? He watches as Bird Girl and Lucia stroke the old woman's hair and temples. Apparently soothed by their touch, she lies down again, her head on the pillow. Her eyes close.

With her face in repose the kohl-rimmed eyes and carmine-stained mouth are softened. This is no longer farce, he thinks, but tragedy. For a moment, he sees the pale, withered visage with its crudely daubed colours as a grieving mask. And beneath the glaze of grief is something else — a contradictory surging vitality, and absurdly, yes, hope. It is as if things have for the moment tumbled back into place. The plot of the tale is back on course, which is why the room seems to him to have burst its bounds and to float upon a sea of light.

The crystalline spell is shattered by a voice that could only belong to Candace.

"Ugh!" she says.

"What a fright!" she exclaims.

"It stinks in here," she says.

"There's always a fly in the ointment," she tells them.

Who has let this donkey into the cathedral, he wonders. He has no idea how this image has entered his head for outside of the vintage films he watched as a young man, he has never seen either a cathedral or a donkey.

"Someone should put her out of her misery," the donkey says.

"Well, she can hardly have much longer to go, can she?" it brays.

A quick glance at Lucia's and Bird Girl's faces confirms that he has indeed heard what he thought. They look as stunned as he feels.

He is amazed at himself when he raises his hand as if to strike Candace. Although he does not actually follow through, the gesture nakedly reveals how ragged is his fury.

Candace glares at him. He stands before her, face covered, unnerved by his own loss of control and by the image that now fills his mind. He sees himself upending the noxious Candace and paddling her fleshy buttocks with the sole of his rubber sandal. What he wants desperately is to humiliate and hurt her. He takes small comfort from the fact that this imagined scenario causes him not the least sexual thrill. Nevertheless he is frightened of his own rage, and beset by guilt. For has Candace not merely spoken aloud thoughts that have already passed through his own brain?

"I need air," he announces.

And so he leaves them all on the second floor of the stone house, for Harry and Chandelier are now also on the landing just outside the old woman's door. He leaves them but of course does not abandon them. He is their sworn Protector. They are his fate.

He seeks a temporary refuge from the human donkey and her unholy pragmatism in the property's wooden outbuilding. The wood is so old it has developed long fissures through which he can peer and maintain his watch. He decides that at some point during the night, he will go back inside the house and sleep in a chair with his feet against the door.

To his distress, he nods off. What wakes him is Candace's shout: "Socks!" he hears her cry out. "I've found socks."

He can all too easily picture her hopping from foot to foot. He groans aloud.

When he sleeps again (inside the house, with his feet against the door) he dreams of a donkey with Candace's face. Strapped to the beast's sides are panniers stuffed with pairs of thick woollen socks. He is also in the dream, as the donkey's master, driving her on with sharp goads to the flanks. The dream donkey howls. The Outpacer jerks awake, a cold sweat prickling his chest under the burlap of his gown.

He feels the silence of the house circle him like a noose. In his former life, he could have plucked from his personal pharmacopoeia some vial or pill to obliterate the day's vexations. He recalls one drug in particular that seemed to render him weightless, where he thought he floated above the stamen of a closed lotus. When the flower opened, he had no doubt he would look out through the eyes of some god or other, the cosmos swirling in a mesh of black and silver at his feet.

But how far indeed has he progressed from that voluptuary he once was? Is he not still shallow and vain?

Even today, had he not wondered how Bird Girl reacted to him when his hood fell away? It was seconds merely, but long enough for her to get a good view. The thought did cross his mind as he saw her eyes widen. Does she find me remarkably handsome? Irresistible even? And only then did the salient question strike him: Does she recognize me from my antics on those cursed sky-screens?

He had been famous once. Or "infamous," as he now realizes. He had belonged to the spoiled and feted elite whose images dominated the mammoth sky-screens spread above the City's crowded streets. The EYE's official line was that the sky-screens gave the rabble dreams to which to aspire: a cushioned, perfumed idyll where pleasures never cloy, where all faces and bodies are flawless and no one ever grows old. He saw through the sham. He knew the sky-screens' vacantly glossy productions were designed to keep the populace in a malleable, vegetative state. And why not, if it helped the indigent to endure their miserable existences? Why not?

Besides, it was foolhardy to turn down the EYE's invitation to join the sky-screen roster of scintillating celebrities. One never knew where a refusal might lead. A precipitous and inexplicable drop in one's financial holdings perhaps. Or a lethal microbe invading one's personal water supply.

So he had become one of those gods in the sky, sporting, diving, dancing, savouring delicacies, even making love for the arousal of the watching plebs below. Foolishly he had agreed to allow the boys from the EYE's propaganda department to bring their cameras into his bedroom. He had performed sexually for them only twice, slithering and panting with some particularly luscious Love-Girl on black silk sheets. But he had forgotten that the sky-screens also transmit smells. What is it about our own odours, even the stink of our shit, that makes us want to hug them to ourselves, keep them wholly intimate? An invisible tent of self.

So that he had felt plundered, raped even, when he found himself by chance one day on the street, staring up at a gigantic, three-dimensional image of himself. There was his brown-tipped cock entering the Love-Girl. There he was, teasing the rim of her hole with the glossy head of his prick. Teasing and teasing, so that she did genuinely moan and cry out and shudder. She was an exceptionally ripe girl, he remembered, full-breasted, the cheeks of her ass like cinnamon moons. She smelled of oranges and of cloves. She had a look of the Levant. Of course, he did not remember her name.On the screen in the sky, he saw his cock plunge into her, her buttocks tensing under his iron grasp. Then he smelt it, caught the potent whiff of that most personal of a man's scents. The salt pong of his semen wafted in the air around his head. He felt invaded, wronged, violated, and ashamed.

A voice cried out in a language he had not heard for many years: *Aidez-moi! Aidez-moi!*

It took him a full minute to realize the voice was his own. He was on his knees, his clipped fingernails scratching at the piss-encrusted pavement, and he wept as he had not done since he was a boy.

Yet even then he did not really see. That incident was not his revelation on the road to Damascus. Although he never again allowed their cameras into his bedroom. But in all other ways, he continued to live as he had always done, sealed off from the bestial happenings on the City's streets, chauffeured about in a silver-plated, armoured car.

His avowed hedonism, and the multifarious designer pharmaceuticals, conspired to hide from himself what he was. He particularly favoured chemicals that intensified the charge of every kind of erotic experience, and the hallucinogens that dissolved not only time and space and the structure of matter, but also his actual sense of a separate identity. And of course, his entire fortune was founded on illusion. Not smoke-and-mirrors or wearisome sleight of hand, but something far more insidious — the illusion that actually invaded human consciousness, and planted the spore that left its host moribund.

As a young man, he had watched the spread of this fungus with disdain. A virtual reality machine in every home; a compact model for the bedroom. Marketed first as "dream machines," and subsequently as "wraparound reality," the craze rapidly became a social addiction. Live your most secret fantasies. *Touch the breast and vulva of your preferred goddess. Put your finger inside her. Have her do your will. Taste her saliva and her sweat. Quake in pleasure.* The marketing goads were the old reliables: sex and violence. One highly vaunted product — popular with males of all ages — put the viewer inside the skin of a wolf. The scenario was in fact a thinly disguised vampire fantasy. The victim was invariably female and young.

Slick marketing exploited crass desires. At the age of twenty-two, he had railed against people's stupidity. He sees his young self standing on a table, left arm raised as he drunkenly harangued his equally drunken companions. "Who remembers the great masters — Kieslowski, Godard, Bertolucci, Tarkovsky? Who knows now the wonder of sitting in the dark, while the images spin out and around us, enlarging a world that is no longer dark, bringing a vision that satisfies what men once called god-hunger? Who now knows the catch of the breath as the last credit rolls away, and you grasp the fact that you have witnessed something infinitely mysterious — and proof absolute that we human beings do indeed have souls?"

Yes, he had once been that young and risibly idealistic. But he could not fault his own obsession. For obsession it had been. He would go without a meal in order to rent a rare video from the ever-dwindling number of outlets catering to "archaic tastes."

He would watch scenes that magnetized him over and over, running the film back and freezing the image, unplucking the disparate elements, marvelling at the composition, the use of colour, tonality, chiaroscuro. And so he remembers . . . an undulation of saffron silk as a banner is loosed from a dark parapet; a woman's sorrowing face reflected in a rain-beaded window pane. Or a gauntly elegant man in a dress suit, who wades hip-deep through a spa bath, cradling a lit candle between his palms, striving to keep the flame alive.

That had been his objective too, once upon a time. He had wanted to keep that flame of the great masters alive. But fate interfered. He had inherited wealth and it had been his undoing. He sees that clearly now.

His inheritance had come as an utter surprise; the lightning bolt that later made cinder of his dreams. He had had a lover — no, more a keeper — an older woman whom he serviced with his hard body and supple hands. He had not known she was dying. She had kept her secrets as meticulously as she did her person. In his case, the classic human irony had proven true: it was only when she had gone that he realized the depth of his affection for her.

She left him not just a substantial financial fortune, but also stocks in a company renowned for furthering the "exact mimesis potential" of virtual reality technologies; specifically, the digital spooks that stimulated human taste and touch receptors. He found himself on the company's board of directors, drawn into the lair of the monster he had once abhorred. Inevitably, he emerged transformed. Wealth corrupted him. Power corrupted him. He served the monster where once he had served the flame.

He discovered he had a gift for cunning scenarios. Because if the public taste for simulated gore and pillage and orgy was insatiable, so too was its thirst for plot. Climax was not enough in itself. There was still a deep human hunger for the sequence of steps that led to the climax. And then? And then? And then? In the beginning, when he still bothered to analyze what it was he did, he had thought this hunger for story a good sign. Here perhaps lay a seed for the possible redemption of humankind. Perhaps — just perhaps — people would at last tire of climaxes that were mere simulated explosions.

In those early, self-deluding days he had hoped the "virtual reality audience" might eventually hunger for Art, and for the transcendent joy one feels in the presence of mystery and symbol. He had even tried for a time to deploy in his scenarios visual images that had once conjured up so much more than they were: a fluted glass of ruby wine; a round loaf of crusty bread set on a scoured table; a house painted the shimmering green of poplar leaves in spring, with cut-out gables like lacework.

These feeble efforts came to nothing. His natural cynicism reasserted itself. The public did not want plot for story's sake. They did not care about symbols. They wanted a stuttering sequence of events, slippery stepping stones that prolonged their anticipation of the final debacle. "And then? And then?" was merely a kind of torturous foreplay, self-serving and self-indulgent.

The resonance of things greater than themselves — of wine and bread and gabled houses — had no place in the world where he now lived. So he had forsaken his dream of artistry and become a consummate hedonist. For many years, his only goal was to indulge his cravings for evermore intense and novel sensations, liberated from the burden of remorse.

Then he had found himself caught up in a wretched twist of fate. He heard about a study group dedicated to the work of the twentieth-century genius, Antonin Artaud. As a student, he had read about Artaud's Theatre of Cruelty, a kind of extreme staged drama, using gargantuan mannequins and masks, and all manner of outrageous sights and sounds. The goal was a deliberate derangement of theatre-goers' senses so as to unleash the full powers of the unconscious. This idea still intrigued him, intellectually at least. He wanted to experience those heady insights Artaud described as emerging from "dark matter," liberated by the "engine of cruelty" this idiosyncratic theatre celebrated.

When he applied for admission into the study group's tightly guarded circle, he found his looks an asset. At his interview, several of the women made their desire for him crudely evident. He had another distinct advantage — or disadvantage, he was to think later — that smoothed the way to his initiation. This was his physical resemblance to the French dramatist as a young man.

He sees again in his mind's eye the Man Ray portrait of Artaud in profile. The playwright looked like an ivory god-head floating in his primeval chaos. His eyebeam tunnelled through the generative smoke, fixed on the tempests and conflagrations of his own imaginings. An enlarged version of this portrait dominated each of the Theatre of Cruelty's meetings, except for that last fatal gathering when every wall was smothered in black.

In that room, he had been party to an act so nefarious it had etched itself on the tissues of his brain. No drug, no drink, no daunting physical risk, could erase the memory of what he had done. Remorse (or was it guilt?) gnawed at his gut. His dreams became torture rooms in which he was flayed alive and worse. He had thought he would go mad. At his worst moments, he had seriously considered self-murder. What stopped him was an atavistic fear of what lay beyond death. Did this make him a coward? He thought not, particularly as the form of penance he chose, pruned of all artificial supports, seemed often as punitive as any imagined afterlife could possibly be.

He had plunged into penance as a man might plunge into churning water so as to douse the flames consuming his body. He had not thought the consequences through.

Examining his conscience, now naked and vulnerable as a peeled egg, he realizes he had even taken a selfish, childish pleasure in his disguise. Readying himself for departure from the City, he had put on his gown (left over from some best-forgotten costumed orgy) and studied himself in several of his full-length mirrors.

He had thought himself a handsome penitent. Vanity had dogged him even then. Throughout his cosseted, mature adult life he had seen himself reflected in many mirrors: strikingly handsome still, lean and slightly louche. His features were those of a wolf who had mated with a particularly gorgeous woman. He had long recognized this and exploited his innate magnetism to the full. His dark-blue eyes took people aback. They were among the finest weapons in his arsenal of charm. As was the fleeting smile that both discomfited and fascinated his admirers. It set a fleeting twist upon his lips that might betoken irony, bemusement, or a penchant for cruelty.

He emanated danger and had learned by his early teens just how powerful an aphrodisiac this was. It had secured him plenty of sexual conquests, and that edge in the business world essential to survival. But there had been occasions — under the influence of especially potent hallucinogens, for example — when he looked in the mirror and was terrified by what he saw. The lineaments of the wolverine straining beneath the skin. A crown and cape of spiked flame around his head and shoulders. He had to turn away from his own image, and tell himself consoling tales about his flame-tipped charisma. This was true enough. He was charismatic. He did have abundant, erotically charged allure.

But that — he reminds himself yet again — was the man he *had* been, superficial, self-obsessed, and ripe for corruption. He is another being now: a server in a monk's garb who must do his penitential duty, if necessary onto the day of his death. Protecting these five — now six, if he counted the old woman — was his elected duty. He was their Outpacer.

He had croaked his wish that first night into Lucia's ear. She was on fire-watch duty, the only one of the five awake. What a hapless, mismatched crew he had thought them. The three women seemed the most competent, and resolute to survive. Although the boy Chandelier showed evidence of problem solving, prompted by instinct alone perhaps. They needed him more than he needed them. (Or did they? Was this assumption just his old arrogance at work? He must strive to keep this in check, along with so many other shortcomings in his far from exemplary character.)

Lucia had not flinched when he spoke into her ear. She was remarkable. He thought only a cat could have heard him approach. He had come up behind her, swift and silent on the balls of his feet. He moved with such stealth, he had time to count the vertebrae visible beneath her shirt. Her eyes widened when he bent down and spoke his name into her ear. That was her only reaction. Her eyes widened, pulling the night deeper into her soul. Her eyes were black as sloes.

He had stepped back two paces, and walked round the camp-fire, directly across from her, so that she could take in what he was. She raised her exquisitely moulded chin a little, looked at him and nodded. Her mind was quick. She grasped the meaning of the monk's gown right away.

He was lucky it was Lucia. Any of the others might have screamed at the sight of

him. His monk's habit could trigger nightmarish visions. What lay beneath the shadowy cowl? A face horribly disfigured, hacked at and badly healed? Or a sucking vortex to grind you bone by bone?

Lucia, with her swift intuition, had looked at him and seen the inexorable discipline of the monastic life: the rising before dawn, the prayers on one's knees on hard floors, the meagre repasts, the labour in garden, granary, or library. Above all, she saw his willingness to do penance. *It would be done. It would.* Somehow, he would compensate for the abhorrent sins of his past.

He knows the hateful animal still inhabits him, despite his monk's guise and honest desire to do penance. The animal's muzzle presses into his brain; its claws scrabble in his bones. The animal wants out. He must keep it in.

At these times, when the unrelenting guilt makes him quake, he wonders whatever possessed him to come into the midst of these innocents. Was it loneliness? Or the magnetism of Lucia? Had he simply wanted to hear the sound of his own voice? Or rather, hear himself speaking to beings who might respond and thus affirm his existence?

No, not his existence. His self. It is not a word to which he has given much thought over the past several years.

The hour is upon him again when he must seek out a landscape of pain. He will bear it in the understanding that it is only a minuscule part of his atonement. He will behave as the Outpacer must. He will keep the rapacious beast inside him at bay.

Chapter Seven
Which Circle of Hell?

I CANNOT RECALL IF DANTE HAD a Circle of Hell for the slothful. If he did not, it was probably because he knew sloth is its own punishment.

There is something about this old stone house, or perhaps the ground on which it stands, that induces a torpor in me. I see signs of this in the others: in Harry's increasingly long daytime naps, and in the way the Outpacer sleeps at night in the hallway with his feet against the door instead of maintaining his invisible cordon outside. I too am failing in my duties. I am neglecting my watch because we have fallen into the foolish assumption that if we are inside the house, we are safe. I go out foraging less and less — even though I know fresh berries would be more nourishing for us than the insipid canned pears in their viscous syrup.

Worst of all perhaps, I feel estranged from my clay. I moisten the small precious ball I brought with me and roll it again and again in my palm. But it generates no spark in me. I cannot feel the vital pulse of yearning, either in my fingers or in the clay itself.

I wish we were on the road again. I wish I had never found this house. I believe there may be some mephitic element in the atmosphere that is corroding my will. Every day I promise myself I will speak with the others about how we can solve our basic conundrum — this most pressing problem we leave largely unspoken. We cannot move on toward the north and leave the old woman behind. Yet how, in practical terms, can we take her with us? As far as I know, she can barely walk at all. How she coped on her own before our arrival will likely remain a mystery.

Like Candace, I am concerned that Bird Girl's relationship with Lola is becoming unhealthy. She hardly ever leaves the old woman's bedside. Bird Girl's complexion has lost its natural colour and she eats as sparingly these days as does the old lady. Whenever I go into their room to offer to sit with Lola in her stead, Bird Girl looks startled as if I have just roused her from a heavy dream. She always refuses my offer of help. I sense she is anxious for me to go so that she can be alone with Lola and her own thoughts.

I am perplexed and distressed too, at how Bird Girl and the Outpacer seem now deliberately to avoid each other. Whenever she does come down the stairs, either to get food or go outside to the privy, they do not speak to each other, not even to extend the barest greeting. If by chance the Outpacer happens to be sleeping when she comes down, she sends little furtive looks his way.

I am sure something has happened to make them uncomfortable with one another, but have no idea what it might be. I believe the Outpacer takes the fulfillment of his penance too gravely to have made sexual advances to her. And surely she would tell me if he had done so?

Chapter Eight
Bird Girl Spies a Rat

BIRD GIRL WAS AT ONCE ASTONISHED and thrilled when she glimpsed the Outpacer's naked face in those few seconds his hood slipped to his shoulders. She felt a burst of heat between her legs as well. There was no point denying he had that effect on her. She could think of more vulgar terms for describing his power, but in her new life as wanderer she was trying to eschew vulgarity. She liked the word "eschew." It sounded like an intellectual sneeze.

She recognized his face from the sky-screens right away: those thick, black, pointed eyebrows, and the lean, chiselled face that declared "I am a beautiful predator." He was gorgeous, without doubt. The old girl was right enough: a boo-ti-full man indeed.

Somehow his wicked magnetism had emanated right off the sky-screens. How did he do it? Was it his smile, so sensually inviting, and the gleaming eyeteeth just pointed enough to make your flesh quiver? Or the dark-blue eyes with their virtually hypnotic power? When Bird Girl's mother taught her the litany of all that's wrong with the male of the species, the Outpacer's type was high on the list. Born seducer. Cunning corrupter.

Barefaced, he had certainly succeeded in arousing poor old Lola on her brass bed, with her dollops of rouge the colour of canned tomatoes, black-ringed eyes and red slash of a mouth. A totally botched attempt to make herself attractive. Or was it a fright mask the old lady had intended, to scare off death? But what of the gauzy blouse that revealed her withered tits? In fact, Bird Girl was grateful that Lola had exposed her two sorry old dugs because a ludicrous fear had seized her when she first saw the old lady wailing on the bed. There was a moment when she really was afraid this person might be her mother, her flesh fallen away and prematurely aged as a result of some evil injection concocted by one of The New Amazons' countless enemies.

But logic prevailed and quieted Bird Girl's spinning brain. Epona had only one breast and this ancient woman had two. So relieved was Bird Girl that she kissed the old lady tenderly on the brow. "Lola," she heard the old woman whisper. "My name is Lola."

"I like the look of you, little chick," Lola confided. "You'll stay a while, won't you?"

Bird Girl was willing. How long had it been since anyone had extended her such spontaneous trust? The old woman needed company and a ready ear, and these were things Bird Girl was able to give.

Besides, the old lady's warnings made her laugh.

"You're a pretty one, little chick. Don't fall for a rogue."

"Always carry a rubber, little chick." How many centuries had it been, Bird Girl wondered, since people called condoms rubbers? And were they really made of rubber in Lola's day? Bird Girl knew Lola was right, of course, despite her antiquated vocabulary. Forsake the condom and embrace death.

Well before her decision to leave the City, Bird Girl had begun to question whether satisfying the sexual urge was worth the risk. There were more STDs around these days than she could count on her fingers and toes. Her admittedly scattered book learning confirmed her suspicion that sexual intercourse had always been one of the most dangerous human pursuits. In the eighteenth century, they had cures for syphilis and gonorrhea that were every bit as bad as the disease. Sip on a little mercury, my dears, and you'll get rid of those nasty chancres. Never mind that you'll destroy your brain and lungs in the process.

Was it ever safe to fuck without protection? And if there was such a time, was it paradise? Bird Girl often wondered if she had indulged in sex far too young, driven as much by the need to escape Epona's puritanical grip as by physical desire and curiosity. But no matter how frequently she did it, her sexual experiments always fell far short of her expectations. She often felt an excited pleasure, yes, and much less often had orgasms that totally engulfed her. A glut, a feast, a spiced drink from a jewelled goblet. And then? — A complete evaporation of the least remembered residue of the spice, the feast, the glut. Gone, and worse than gone. She was sometimes left with a taste on her tongue so bitter, she wanted to spit. And not because of self-disgust. Just massive disappointment.

Over her years as a sex trader, she had had plenty of opportunities to analyze what it was she did want from the carnal act. She wanted to bed someone, do the full physical, sensual gamut, including all the panting and stickiness, and rise up transfigured. She wanted to stand up and feel herself remade, as if in the act of bedding she had grown wings. She could almost see them, although admittedly her idea of wings was all based on images from books. She had never seen an actual bird in flight, or a real live bird of any kind. Nor did she imagine wings like angels', for as she understood it, angels had no sex organs. She found this idea disconcerting.

Her wings would be wide and weightless, with a proper fretwork of bones that glided together like a folded fan when at rest. They would be tinged the flawless blue of the sky in a healthy world, a blue she glimpsed one morning when she was harvesting potatoes with the Diggers.

And hadn't that dream of a transcendent winged love at least partly inspired her Bird Girl name? This silly, fluffy appellation was far more than just a ploy to put potential predators off their guard. The name was born of a genuine deep-down wish: to rush out through the letter "o" in "love" like a full-throated songbird on its way to paradise.

"Call me Bird Girl," she had told her new companions of the forest. She always felt a bit guilty about using such a derivative opening. But who would know these days, even as "Call me Bird Girl" spills off her lips, that she had thieved the basic phrase from poor old suffering Herman Melville? Who now has the stamina to read right through a book of more than six hundred pages about a mad man's obsession with a white whale?

She did. And the reading did not require patience. Only time. The kind of time that had a proper weight, or gravitas. Time with a stretch through space that allows for transformation. So that you look out through eyes other than your own. They used to call this astounding process "imagination" — yet another human gift, as far as she could see, that had got buried in the City's general slag-heap.

She told the others she left the City to look for her mother. In fact, Bird Girl honestly believes she is far more likely to find Epona if she does not deliberately seek her out. Her mother might just turn up, roaring into the forest one night on her bike with the whole gang in train. Then again, she might be dead.

Her father, as she'd never tired of telling people, was a test tube. "Well, actually," she would continue, with her practised ingénue smile, "he was the sperm inside a test tube that my mother and her cohorts stole from a eugenics laboratory. They decanted the semen carefully into a turkey baster . . . and so forth." Here she would lower her eyelids delicately, "Out of my mother's body I came."

My father was a test tube. She loves the subtle undertones in that statement. The phallic shape. The immaculate hygiene. The coolly clinical use of the male seed. But most of all, the wonderful naïvety of it. *My father was a test tube.* Spoken with a lisp, this was classic Bird Girl stuff. Poor, twittering little fool, people thought.

Yes, Bird Girl was one of her best guises ever. This cute little persona had helped get her out of a lot of scrapes. In the City, it seemed every second person was either a pimp or a sexual predator, men and women both. And there she was, looking on good days as if she was about twelve and a half. Fluffy cap of white-blond hair, rosebud lips, button nose, big blue eyes (fortunately not the least bit protuberant), small-boned body. She knew she looked new-hatched and crushable. She reinforced this image with vapid Bird Girl chatter. Adorable, feather-brained Bird Girl.

So that in her danger-filled City days they were all unprepared — the lust-filled older men with their horny wandering hands; the younger ones who smiled from behind hooded lids, their eye beams probing through to her nakedness (they might want her for themselves, or they might be pimping, or both) and worst, the white slavers — when she kneed them sharply in their nasty nuts, or delivered a wicked karate chop that left them groaning. Or gouged out their eyeballs with her thumbs. She had been forced to do that once and it made for a nasty sight. There'd been no pleasure in it. She cannot at all comprehend the pull of sadism for some people. But if her life depended on it (and what is rape, after all, but a living murder?) she would blind the buggers if she had to.

She still worried he would come after her — the man whose eye she'd removed. His name was Grimoire and he was a totally disgusting human being: one of the most sadistic minions ever to work for the sex slavers, who in turn worked for the EYE. So she'd felt no remorse at all for what she'd done. If she hadn't half-blinded him, he would have raped her, then chained her to a wall until she was submissive enough to be shipped off into bondage, heaven only knows where.

She heard he'd had the empty socket implanted with a carnelian — a white stone with red-orange streaks — and that he apparently relished the fact it made him look more sinister and of course unforgettable. But Bird Girl didn't buy this. He must hate her for what she had done and want to kill her — probably slowly, by infinitesimal degrees. And so she was always on guard, maintaining the mental and physical exercises that would keep her fighting acumen sharp.

It was her mother and her gang who taught Bird Girl these skills and imbued her with a certain ruthlessness. *Give no succour.* She could parrot this by the time she was four, and understood well enough what it meant. At that age, she would always watch from an upper window of the warehouse whenever The New Amazons set off on one of their raids, so that she could send them her best secret wishes. What she saw from her lookout was a phalanx of superbly fit women, straddling their motorbikes with a graceful confidence. Their proud backs bore the decal of the archetypal Amazon, holding her spear aloft. As they gunned the engines and proceeded up the alley-way, Bird Girl would focus hungrily on her mother's profile. The artificial lemony light from the window briefly illuminated Epona's shingled hair, and brushed over her broad, flat cheekbones, the hook of her strong nose. The way the light fell made a kind of cross on her mother's face, so that it looked as if she was wearing a visor.

As a child, whenever she heard the roar of their bikes in the distance, she thought her god-like mother and her cohorts were making thunder. They unfurled their invisible banners. They wielded their invisible swords. In reality, The New Amazons exacted vengeance with the slimmest stilettos and honed razor blades. They always left their mark, which was one reason they were so feared. Because pimps, child torturers, pornographers, and wife beaters are often physically vain men. They do not like the idea of having their precious skin slashed by several muscular and militant lesbians. They do not want to be stripped naked in front of twenty jeering women. Or have their noses slit.

Bird Girl's mother and her gang were legendary in the city. The most evil of men — even those with their own small armies — instinctively clutched their crotches when anyone mentioned The New Amazons.

It still hurt Bird Girl terribly that she and her mother had become so estranged. She tried to tell herself that perhaps it was inevitable. Her mother, after all, had no way of knowing all the traits that lay waiting in the semen she stole, other than a likely brilliant brain and basic good looks. She had not minded her daughter's smallness or her fine bones. But other qualities emerged she could not bear.

Epona was no fool. She knew that raising her daughter in a militant lesbian community was no guarantee for her child's ultimate sexuality. There was a world outside the warehouse that was their communal home and Armoury, and that world was sodden with sex of the hetero variety. In raising her daughter, Epona was therefore up against all the visible and invisible propaganda this new Dark Age could muster.

From her pubescence on, Bird Girl's mother kept the warnings coming thick and fast. Epona wanted desperately to keep her daughter in the fold, but it would have gone against her principles to confine her physically. So she turned on her own propaganda guns. And of all her mother's moralizing missiles, Bird Girl still regarded "The House of the Rising Sun" folly as the pièce de résistance. Epona would get Laura-of-the-Gashed-Cheek to sing her the old song. Laura had a voice like dark velvet that has been rent with a pair of shears.

Her rendition of the old ballad would send the ghost of that poor girl in the Louisiana brothel running up and down Bird Girl's spine. As Laura sang, Bird Girl could see the girl from that old whore house evermore clearly. She had hair that covered her face like a veil, and her skin was flushed and a little damp from the New Orleans heat. Her breasts were little buds; her thighs were narrow and smooth as glass.

"Ruin," Epona would intone in the excruciating hush that followed on Laura's last note. She would slice the air vertically with her forefinger, in a gesture suggesting both evisceration and doom.

"It's been the ruin of many a poor girl," Epona would growl, while Laura nodded her head solemnly.

"She's going back to wear that ball and chain." At this point, Epona would do her own pantomime walk across the floor, dragging her left foot.

"Ruin," she repeated. "Doom. Disease. Slavery. An early death."

Such was her mother's propaganda. Even early on, Bird Girl had judged it excessive. But as she grew older, and ventured more and more into the streets, she experienced exactly what her mother foretold: the compelling lure of corruption.

"It may be something perverse written in our DNA," her mother conjectured, "or the noxious fumes of *that*." Epona would jut her strong jaw toward the world outside the warehouse. What she meant was the thriving sex trade of the City. But there were times she could not bring herself to speak those words.

"It is young girls' foolishness," her mother warned, "to think the fallen woman is romantic. To yearn to be corrupted.

As if that was the road to bliss," she snorted. Epona was a consummate snorter.

Of course, Bird Girl had listened to her mother. She always listened to her mother. But not even her deepest, fiercest daughterly love and attention could hold off the fascination of the House of the Rising Sun and all it symbolized. The idea of that wicked, steaming brothel in New Orleans had conjured up an equally wicked and steaming lover in her pre-adolescent imagination. *Snuff out the candles, draw back the crimson curtain that makes a canopy round the bed.* The face that emerges from the carmine darkness, the hot breath that assaults your face and naked waiting body, is His — the one who will undo the hard knot of your virginity.

Bird Girl had thought about Him constantly in terms she now realized were ludicrous, lurid and clichéd. He had the searing passion, and the bag of tricks (by which she meant superb technique) to induct her into a world whose delights defied description. Her blood would sing of wild horses and of the sea. She would be utterly ravished and become in consequence the most beautiful person on earth.

This was the lure of the House Where Young Girls Are Ruined, and the magnetic pull of that temptation was just too strong. Bird Girl had to test it out for herself. And so she made the symbolic break to start freeing herself from the Armoury. She dropped her virgin status at age thirteen, only too willingly. Her lover had seemed remarkably mature to her at the time. He was twenty and good-looking. He had the kind of hot, falsely worshipful eyes that stripped a girl slowly where she stood. It was a look, as Bird Girl was now well aware, that pumps a young girl's self-esteem, and gives her an illusion of power she is sorely disabused of soon enough.

As for sore . . . well, yes indeed she was. She was surprised how much it hurt. She had found precious little sensuous pleasure in the deed once her partner finished stroking and licking her and got down to the actual penetration. Despite plentiful lubricants and a smooth-as-silk condom, it burned terribly when he thrust inside her. At that moment, she seriously doubted the wisdom of her decision. More power to The New Amazons, she thought, if they were smart enough to avoid this kind of pain.

Epona never found out about that first sexual liaison. But by that time, she was already in a fury about Bird Girl's wardrobe. "You look like a cheap whore," was the least vitriolic of her comments. What she meant was that her daughter's skirts were too short. The New Amazons did not wear anything but slacks, made of durable cloth or leather. Epona scorned the very idea of skirts.

"You're pandering to their filthy desires dressed like that," she warned her daughter. Bird Girl merely shrugged.

The last time she saw her mother, Bird Girl had on a flimsy see-through dress the colour of mint julep. Later she burned the dress in a foolish attempt to destroy her memories of that day, particularly the vicious things she had said. Those unconscionable words had precipitated the end between them as surely as if she had fired a bullet into Epona's remaining breast. She would never forget the look on her mother's face, gone granite-hard with hatred. Epona did not speak; only pointed to the Armoury door, which she then barred. When Bird Girl tried to return she found they had not only changed the locks, but also the password. Not one among The New Amazons would open up and let her in.

"Your mother's disowned you, kid." Bird Girl heard this from Mary Magnificat, whom she met by chance one night in the City's dockyard area. Mary was a wrestler. She had the strength of three men, but had always been kind to The New Amazons' only child. Mary had tried to give her money that night, which Bird Girl proudly refused.

"You shouldn't have called her a . . . ," Mary said bluntly. Bird Girl had plugged her ears with her fingers. As a wrestler, Mary had never had to cultivate much subtlety.

After that encounter, Bird Girl had leapt into the thick of the City's darkest places, testing her cunning in its labyrinths, where far worse threats than the Minotaur lurked. She became the thing that would most appall her mother: a highly selective and expensive sex trader. She told herself it was a business where she could hone her wits and her instinct for survival, and where she might, on occasion, meet cultivated individuals who would tell her some of the things she so longed to know about the world. Some of her clients, oh, glory of glories, might even give her books as payment or part payment.

Bird Girl was always on the lookout for books. By which she meant real books — literature. The contents of the City's libraries had all been burned when she was still a baby, but she knew you could find books if you were assiduous, and had a nose for them. She had found treasure troves stuffed under the floor boards of derelict houses. She had once yanked a copy of Dante's *Inferno* from the mouth of a dog. It was well gnawed but still quite readable. In refuse dumps she had uncovered books from which she had to pluck the maggots one by one;

books smeared with muck and maybe even shit. If you want to read these days, Bird Girl always told herself, you can't afford to be fastidious.

One day, after sobbing over Cordelia's death scene in *King Lear*, she found the courage to go back to the Armoury and seek a reconciliation with her mother. Awaiting her was the scene she had always dreaded. Something large and lethal had gouged through the Armoury's outer steel door. The inner door had been wrenched from its massive hinges. It lay flat on the concrete floor and because it was so completely out of place, she did not at first recognize what it was. She succumbed for a moment to the wrenching delusion that the door was a vast pit dug for the dumping of her mother's corpse.

Her legs were rubber; her stomach acid. Something hard and nasty stuck in her throat. She flung herself to her knees and was sick. She was aware of an ominous thunder gathering in the room, and of a slick wetness gathering at the back of her neck, in the crooks of her elbows, and behind her knees. It took her some seconds to realize that the thunder was the pounding of the blood in her head. She could remember thinking, because she has the kind of mind that never stops seeing things in words, that only one letter separated "dead" from "dread."

Even on her knees, rocking herself in anguish, she clung to the idea that The New Amazons had staged this assault on the Armoury themselves as one of their clever moves to disorient the hydra-headed enemy. There were rust stains on the concrete floor that might have been blood.

Bird Girl had made herself creep up the metal spiral staircase. Her legs trembled at every step. She could not recall ever before having to hang on to the handrail. Chilled and hot by turns, she forced herself upward and into every room on the two vast upper floors. There was some broken glass and more rusty stains on the floors, but absolutely nothing else. The Armoury had been stripped. Not a bike part, not a bed sheet, not a single sanitary tampon was left.

And that emptiness gave her hope. She believed, as she believes still, that The New Amazons had moved all their belongings out gradually so as not to attract notice; staged the raid on the Armoury doors themselves, and decamped. She clung to that belief, not least because she could not bear to think of the tortures the enemy would have inflicted on her mother and her warriors. She wished The New Amazons safe. She wished them well. She wished, with her heart's blood, that she had not uttered those poisonous final words to her mother.

It was then she decided to leave the City. She sensed Epona was out there somewhere beyond its confines, roaming free. Bird Girl was also convinced that once on the road, she might find somewhere a whole library still intact, in some sleepy town or village as yet untouched by the decay. She knew she would smell the library if she came close. It would smell as she imagines the sea smells, briny and sharp and full of promise.

In the absence of books, Bird Girl now strove to read the world; or rather, what was left of the world. Before joining up with Lucia and the others, she had dug potatoes for a while with the bunch of grimy, good-hearted folk who call themselves the Diggers. And so she had learned how to study and to read potatoes, and to dream away, with the cold clay soil freezing her fingers and wrists. She had seen a picture once in an old yellow-covered magazine of an Australian Aborigine. His naked body was completely covered in dried clay decorated with the most intricate spirals of colour, twining and twining, heading for some miraculous nub of power.

She had felt like him while she worked in the potato field. She had imagined herself to be long and lean and potent, simultaneously new-made and ancient, with the cold clay caking her arms.

The shapes of the potatoes were miracles in themselves. Some had a proboscis. Some had the huge flowing breasts and buttocks of the figurines people secreted thousands of years ago in caves. Yes, she had enjoyed her time with the Diggers. But there was one man among them who looked at her with such obvious lust, she grew more and more uncomfortable. One night she woke with his fetid breath on her face and had no choice but to knee him in the testicles. After that, she had gone on the move again until one lucky day, she met Lucia.

When Bird Girl first washed Lola (with the softest washcloth she could find, for the old lady winced when anything at all rough touched her skin), she wondered if the old girl had ever had to fend off a man with a well-aimed knee or her pointed nails. Or were all of Lola's sexual experiences pleasing, or even ecstatic? Did the old lady actually have the many lovers she boasted of? Was she ever really a seductress or courtesan?

Cleansed of its patches of lurid colour, the old woman's face was leadenly pallid, small as a child's, and so cross-hatched with lines Bird Girl could not imagine Lola young. It bothered her that she could not do so, as if this failure was somehow a betrayal of the old lady's growing attachment to her.

Initially, Bird Girl was extremely disappointed not to find the least scrap of reading material in the stone house. Then she realized that Lola's life was probably itself a book. She found herself wanting to make up a life story for the old woman but always managed to resist the impulse. Why did she stop? Because to impose an imagined story on Lola seemed disrespectful? Or because this urge reminded her uncomfortably of the machinations of the EYE? There was a rumour the EYE had machines that could suck your brain cells dry of all you ever were, and rewire your neurons so that another being walked about in your skin.

What an abomination! To be emptied and then filled, as if your essence was just stuffing for a sausage.

No, Bird Girl reasoned with herself. Her wish to make up a rambunctious past for Lola — even a happy, rambunctious past — in no way resembled the horrific manipulations of the EYE. The truth was she wanted to protect Lola from harm, the way she imagined some women had a natural urge to protect a baby, although Bird Girl had never actually held a baby, or even seen many. None of The New Amazons pursued the artificial pregnancy route in the time Bird Girl was with them. Not at least, with any success. Growing up as the only child in the Armoury accounted in part, she supposed, for her self-confidence. In a sense, she had had ten mothers. There were more than ten in the cohort, of course, but quite a few of The New Amazons merely tolerated her presence or remained stolidly indifferent to her. And why not? Bird Girl had no illusions about every woman having a soul-deep need to nurture something small and helpless, and often — or so she understood — wet and stinky.

Lola doesn't smell, whatever Candace might think. Does Candace think? Now, there was a question and not as cruel as it might appear on the surface.

As far as Bird Girl can see, Candace is a kind of puppet of her own making. Candace has apparently swallowed a line, an entire life-choreography in fact, and now simply jerks herself about to it. What amazes Bird Girl above all is that Candace seems quite oblivious to this, just as she seems unaware they all find her cheery homilies and intrusiveness so irritating. It is only Harry who habitually gives voice to that irritation, which endears him to Bird Girl all the more.

She likes to savour the irony of the situation: that while Candace simpers and chatters and thinks up insipid ways to bind them as a group, it is their shared contempt for her clumsy efforts that bring the five of them closer.

One had to feel sorry for her. Well, one didn't have to, but Bird Girl does. In fact, what she feels for Candace (apart from endless annoyance and sometimes fury), is pity rather than sympathy. And pity can exude some pretty nasty miasmas: condescension, smug superiority, noxious self-regard. All deeply flawed and dangerous.

Would Candace ever see how artificial her own devices were? And a cruel question — does Candace have eyes under those blinkers? And an even crueller one — is Candace bright enough to be truly introspective? With all her gabble about synergy and accommodation (sugary mental group gropes, Bird Girl always thinks), Candace is apparently incapable of empathy.

Had Candace ever read a good book? For what better way was there to learn how to look out of the eyes of people absolutely unlike you: pig-headed old kings or guileless young women like Miranda in her brave new world, or even murderers, whether they committed their frightful deed by accident or by design? As many beings as there were good novels and plays and poems.

Based on Candace's callous and despicable remarks about Lola, Bird Girl surmises she had never even tried to imagine herself inside the withered, spotted skin of a frail and elderly human being.

Well, as an imaginative act, it took courage. No doubt about it. Bird Girl finds Lola's fragility both oppressing and terrifying. She dreamt that Lola got up from the bed and danced: a bungled pirouette and some faltering kicks of her bony, old limbs. No, "limbs" was too robust a word for those twig-like, vein-scored appendages of Lola's. But a more accurate description, like "skin-covered bones" would sound disrespectful, if not doom-laden.

The most frightening part of her dream was when the dreaded thing happened and Lola fell. In the dream, Bird Girl felt the crack in her own bones, and Lola's sharp little cry seemed to issue from her own throat. Bird Girl woke, with a dry mouth and a racing heart, in fear of the bone-grinding pain that had beset her poor crumpled Lola. In the final dream image, seared on the back of her eye-lids before she woke, she saw Lola lying absolutely motionless on the wooden floor, curled in on herself like an embryo in a womb.

If Lola fell and injured her skull, it would be the end. Just as Bird Girl assumes it would be the end if someone dropped a baby on its fragile bulb of a head.

She does not like to dwell on how vulnerable human flesh and bone are, particularly at the beginning and end of life. This line of thought too often leads her to the conclusion that human beings must be a mistake. Or worse, that the human species is a deliberate joke perpetrated millennium after millennium by some hard-eyed soak in the sky, swilling down his ambrosia and having a good old belly laugh as he pulls human beings' strings and another one falls on its head, or rams a stiletto into a neighbour's kidney. Or...

Enough, Bird Girl, she tells herself. "Oh, that way madness lies," as King Lear said.

She must lift up her mind, and concentrate on the tiny pulsing light inside her she thinks must be her soul. Bird Girl does not doubt that Lola has a soul. And she is always delighted to witness the old woman's transporting joy as she meanders through the most cherished scenes from her past. Lola's memories (or are they imaginings?) are often just highly vivid, disconnected fragments that nevertheless tantalize Bird Girl by their brightness and illogic.

She has come to see that Lola fixes her flitting memories by focusing on what she wore. "I had on my apricot sheath," she will say. "When he slipped it over my head, there was a rustle of silk."

"The sound was like new leaves turning in the wind."

"He told me I looked as if I bathed in moonlight."

"He told me the word for 'brightness' in his language put together the signs for 'moon' and 'sun.'" (Bird Girl relishes this mysterious allusion, which Lola often repeats. It seems so unlikely that one of Lola's lovers was Chinese or Japanese.

And if Lola had travelled so widely and been so adored, how had she ended up in this remote stone farmhouse?)

"His hands were delicate as doves, his body as lean and supple a lion's." (The image of the dove-like hands makes Bird Girl shiver in delight. She thinks "dove" is a lovely word, like the slip of a satiny tongue round one's nipple.)

Sometimes Lola gets a bit more graphic. As in: "I wore my emerald-green ball gown. It was midsummer. Two beautiful young men came to me and waited upon me all night. Like moths to my green flame, he told me afterwards.

"They walked me to the riverside, where he was waiting and watching, in a rowboat just off the shore. He watched as they stripped me under a great spreading tree. And oh, I was willing, for them to do it, and for him to watch.

"Such pleasure to be had from two soft young mouths, two strong pairs of hands, and a single watcher offshore. Oh, the moans I sent out from under that spreading tree as I came and I came and I came.

"How often, he asked me afterward when we lay in bed together, how often did you orgasm? I was exploding in the little boat, he told me, exploding as I watched you with the two young men."

Bird Girl almost comes to orgasm spontaneously herself, listening to Lola and thinking of the two mouths, the four hands, and most especially, the exceptional, liberal-minded watcher.

Candace barges in on them.

"Ugh!" Candace says. "It's unfortunate when they get to this stage. Their wandering often turns foul-mouthed.

"You don't have to sacrifice yourself this way, you know," Candace says. She lays a moist hand on Bird Girl's shoulder.

"I admire your charity," Candace simpers, with extravagant insincerity. "I really do. But you must weigh your priorities."

Bird Girl turns to face her; puts on her very best round-eyed, innocent gaze. "Pardon?"

"We need you downstairs," Candace confides. "The group needs you."

"The dynamics are faltering," Candace adds; then immediately corrects herself: "Our centre needs strengthening."

Lola begins to wheeze, and then to cough, generating much flying spittle. Bird Girl knows this is a ploy, even if Candace doesn't.

"She doesn't have long to go from the sound of her chest," Candace remarks.

Lola rolls her eyes, and begins to make rude spluttering sounds, like eruptive farts. This is more than Candace can take.

"We'll hold a little airing session this evening," she says on her way out the door. "I'll call you when we're about to start, if you haven't already joined us." She bestows on Bird Girl one of her most painfully artificial smiles.

Bird Girl grimaces, amazed anew at how blind Candace is to her own manipulations. In the group's five days in the stone house, they have all, with the exception of fretting Candace, found ways to occupy their time. Bird Girl tends and listens to Lola; Old Harry huddles together with Chandelier, telling the boy tales of his past and drawing diagrams of some kind in the dirt just outside the front door; Lucia prepares their meals, and works at a ball of clay she must have found somewhere.

The Outpacer, around whom Bird Girl now feels a bit uncomfortable, is often busy splitting wood in the barn — to keep fit, she presumes. Only Candace is at loose ends.

Bird Girl takes this to mean that Candace has few inner resources, other than revising her tedious theories of group dynamics and cohesion exercises.

Lola lets out a great sigh. "Is that one gone?"

"Yes, for now."

"Where was I?" Lola asks. "What was I wearing, little chick?"

"An emerald gown. There was a man watching you from a row boat."

"Oh yes." Lola is silent a moment. Bird Girl finds herself wishing she might one day experience the bliss written on the old woman's face.

Oh my dove, Lola recites in apparent rapture, *thou art in the clefts of the rock, in the secret places of the stairs.*

"He was the finest," she continues. "He told me pleasure was a great wheel. It did not matter where you got on or off, so long as you ran no one over.

"*His left hand is under my neck, and his right hand doth embrace me.*"

Could there be such a man, Bird Girl wonders, watching from his Pleasure Wheel in a state of supreme arousal, while his beloved frolicked with other men? This sounded not at all like grubby voyeurism — of which she'd seen quite enough in her sex trade years — but exalted adoration.

He brought me to the banqueting house, and his banner over me was love, Lola says, her little face aglow. Bird Girl longs to know the source of these images. She has never been lucky enough to get her hands on many books of poetry, but she knows the genuine article when she hears it. She honestly believes she has an instinct for poetry, just as she has for smelling out books. Is this something gifted to her through her genes? Was her test-tube father a poet? She guesses that poetry has much in common with spells, and the old idea of working magic. Concentrated power, musical, sometimes resistant as a hard-shelled nut to your understanding. But with reading and rereading and mulling over, the meaning springs out at you and insight floods your brain at the speed of light. You feel a delicious pleasure then and it's as if you're floating.

She longs to know where Lola plucked the line about the banqueting house and the banner. She wants to know its provenance (another word she is fond of because it sounds like an intellectuals' palace.) It is not likely a word Lola would know. And Bird Girl's instinct tells her it is best to let Lola ramble and not to press her with questions, even if her own greedy curiosity makes her squirm.

She intervenes only when Lola is in her worst fits of incoherence, when she moans piteously or cries out as if she has cut herself on a barbed memory. In these distressed states, Lola can become quite literally blind to the present. She will emerge from the dark of her confusion only with the help of touch as Bird Girl strokes her hand, or caresses her cheek.

"You're a regular blessing, little chick," Lola will say, when she has shaken off whatever bad spell possessed her.

"A regular blessing," Bird Girl muses wryly to herself, was certainly not what her mother used to call her. As Lola sleeps, Bird Girl strives to push away punishing thoughts of her final confrontation with Epona. She is sure she still carries the damned words she uttered like razors buried in her flesh. Will her remorse always haunt her, a doleful presence she cannot shake off? Like the pitiable Raskolnikov, his soul racked in Russia's endless White Nights. Of course, she had committed no physical murder. But words can murder, can they not? Words can murder love.

Mother, she thinks, please forgive me my murderous words.

She hears a cry from somewhere outside that carries a searing anguish. Her first thought is Lucia, and a cold sluice of fear numbs her flesh.

She runs to the window. At first she sees only two of them. Then they seem to multiply so that a mass of dirty-grey fur appears to writhe upon the sparse grass. Within seconds she can make out details she would far rather not see — their huge size, and the flash of their long teeth in prodding snouts, the slit eyes adapted to sewer life, and the wire-like whiskers that pierce the air.

She pinches the flesh of her forearm. Maybe these disgusting creatures are part of a waking dream, or an ugly projection of the guilt she feels about her mother. She pinches herself hard enough to make her eyes water; blinks away the tears. When she opens her eyes, they are all still there — the Rat-Men she had always assumed were apocryphal. For years, she had dismissed the rumours as just the residue of people's nightmares, sprung from an instinctive unease about the monstrosities cloning might produce. Who does not fear waking one morning to find a seething, fetid rat on the pillow? And what worse chimera could there be than a man-sized rat, with human hands, legs, and arms?

These things ought not to exist, and just looking at them makes Bird Girl feel sick and despairing. For the first time in her young life, she sees the future of humankind as irretrievably damned. She pushes her closed fist against her lips as the monsters swarm closer to the house. She can smell them now. There is a taint of sulphur.

The thoughts that go through her head are these: *How do I save myself? How do I protect Lola?*

Later she will wish she had not put herself first, and that she had run downstairs to warn the others before the monsters stormed the house. But in these last moments she has left, she is obsessed with their pitiably few options for escape. Meanwhile, Lola sleeps her blissful sleep as if sated from bouts of robustly satisfying love-making. Very soon Bird Girl will have to rouse the old woman. And then what? Obviously exiting the window with Lola in tow is out of the question unless she wants to reduce the old woman to a literal bag of bones.

Bird Girl sees no choice but to stand her ground, make a weapon of her body, and fell as many Rat-Men as she can when they force in the door. She always has the advantage of surprise. No one expects the iron in her fists; the kicks that can rupture a man's spleen or break three ribs at once.

She begins to smell her own fear — never a pleasant scent — and sets about channelling her adrenalin rush. She paces from the door to the window, judging her distance, looking for possible impediments to the scythe her body must soon become.

She sees that the Rat-Men have now clustered together. She counts four snouts, four strong wide backs, four sets of shoulders that look as if they could easily repel the blow of an iron bar. She hates the fact that she cannot stop staring at them; that they exert their own perverse fascination.

As she peers down, hiding herself from view as best she can, one of the Rat-Men lifts his arm to scratch at the back of his neck. The skin of his hand is a deep olive and fully human.

Here is a most diabolic combination, she thinks, as she watches human fingers prodding matted rat's fur, slick with sewer slime. Then she sees something extremely odd, a visual illusion she initially attributes to her own agitated state. It looks as if the fur at which the Rat-Man scratches is lifting. Suddenly the whole monstrous head falls away. What Bird Girl sees next astonishes her as much as would a veritable miracle.

A god, from whose hand dangles a huge rat's mask looks up at her in the window where she stands in full view now, gap-mouthed in amazement.

The man smiling up at her belongs in one of the Italian Renaissance paintings she's seen in books. A muscular young Mars maybe, or Mercury, the messenger with the winged sandals and the caduceus wand that works wonders.

"You have to leave," the god-man shouts up at her. "There's a cloud of nerve gas drifting your way.

"We are doctors," he tells her. "Trust us, please. There is little time."

He points west. Bird Girl sees a fist-shaped orange mass grow larger even as she watches.

"How long have we got?" she asks, trying to work out how she can get Lola safely and speedily down the stairs, let alone out of the house and away.

"Less than an hour," he says firmly. "You must head north. How many are you?"

"Seven," she tells him. "We are seven."

"We have masks," he says, taking from his rat's pocket a filmy transparent disk. "You must put these on immediately if the air starts to take on an orange or yellow tinge.

"Don't risk coming back here" he warns, with a sternness that makes clear how grave their situation is. "The gas will permeate the ground around the house.

"There is a complication," he adds in a rush, "a meteorological complication. But I want to explain this to everyone at once. Are your companions all here?" he asks urgently.

She nods, although actually she is not at all sure where they are. Then she closes her eyes for a moment to try to absorb the full weight of his warnings, and to make the shuddering orange fist in the sky disappear, however briefly. It is ludicrous, she knows. But there are still times she indulges in the childish wish that she can obliterate the degenerate and besmirched things of the world simply by shutting her eyes.

When she opens them again, the Rat-Men have gone. She hears Candace's shrill squeal that tells her the doctors in their nightmare garb have entered the house.

Lola wakes with a panicked cry. "What was that?" she asks Bird Girl, who goes to her immediately and takes her hand.

"He's not back, is he?" Her frail spotted hand grips Bird Girl's so tightly, the young woman has to make an effort not to wince.

"Who, Lola?"

"The one with the stone eye." The old woman trembles and points to her right eye.

"Ouch! You're hurting me, little chick." Bird Girl removes her hand from Lola's in alarm.

"It's not him, is it? Tell me, little chick. Tell me."

"No," Bird Girl says. I must stay calm, she tells herself. "It's some men who are doctors, who are warning us we have to leave. There is a poison in the air coming our way."

Lola barely considers this remark before she begins shaking her head.

"Can't go," she declares.

"You have to, Lola. You'll die if you stay. I can't let you stay."

"Can't leave Charlie."

"Who is Charlie, Lola?" Is the old lady in one of her wandering states, Bird Girl wonders. And if this is the case, the man with the stone eye might be just a coincidence, a nightmare figure that has clung to Lola's waking consciousness.

Lola looks at Bird Girl as if she is being deliberately obtuse. "Charlie was my helpmeet. He was my lover once, little chick, but that was long ago. Haven't I told you about Charlie?"

"But where is he, Lola? Why haven't we seen him?"

Lola screws up her eyes. Her mouth twists round the words: "Dead . . . dead and buried. Behind the house. We had a garden there once, little chick, with green beans and hollyhocks. I buried him there. As best I could. Took my last strength from me."

Lola sinks back into her pillow as if newly exhausted from the effort of burying Charlie.

Bird Girl was beginning to feel frantic. Surely this couldn't all be happening at once — like a melodrama run amok, disaster piled on disaster, revelation on revelation.

Grimoire here. She shudders. And Charlie. And doctors masquerading as rats. Poison gas balls. I am spinning, she thinks. I must try to focus. I must speak with Lucia. She will help me make Lola see she must leave. But all the while, Bird Girl's mind is wincing away from the question she knows she must ask.

"How did Charlie die, Lola?"

Tears begin to course down Lola's face. "Tortured," she says. "By the barbarian with the stone eye and the orange hair. Out in the barn. Tortured.

"Couldn't save him. Couldn't."

Bird Girl embraces the old lady tenderly. She feels Lola's tears wet her own cheeks and chin.

"He said he was looking for a little whore. Wouldn't believe we hadn't seen her.

"I hope he never found her," Lola adds. "I hope he's sitting in Hell right now, with a burning ember up his ass.

"We tried to keep him out of the house with the hay, little chick. It was Charlie's idea. He noticed the brute's one good eye streaming and how he was fighting for breath whenever he was near the old hay bales we kept outside. So we brought them right into the front room.

"After a couple of days, we thought he'd gone. So Charlie went out to check. I had to listen to his screams, little chick.

"Poor Charlie. Oh my poor, poor Charlie. But how could I help him? How, little chick?"

Lola rocks on the bed and begins plucking at the little hair she has.

"Oh, Lola, Lola. There was nothing you could do. Nothing. He was an evil, evil man." Bird Girl strokes the old lady's fingers in the soothing way that usually brings her comfort.

"Don't think about it, Lola. Think about the day you wore your apricot sheath instead."

"Apricot," Lola repeats, smiling. She lies back like a good child, and closes her eyes.

Bird Girl speeds down the stairs just in time to hear the god-man deliver the same information he had given her. She observes her companions' successive states of disbelief, wariness, and final capitulation as they all observe the evidence — the blood-orange gas ball which now looks to her denser, and far more deadly.

"And something else," the doctor adds sternly, "it seems there is a new kind of red rain, which is not only more caustic but also highly flammable. Given the right conditions — and we are not entirely sure what these are, but certainly dry air and acid soil — the red rain will combust. In the worst cases, and this has already happened, the burning rain creates a gigantic fireball. These have the impact of an exploding meteor. They consume everything in their path, including human flesh and bone.

"If the red rain begins," he continues, "take cover immediately. The area through which you will be travelling most fortunately has a network of caves. Keep watch for these openings in case you need to take shelter. Inside the rock, you will be protected."

No one says a word. We are all too stunned to speak, thinks Bird Girl. Poison gas. Potential fireballs. How meagre are their chances for survival?

"Oh, we surely don't have to leave our little haven?" Candace wails.

"If you stay, you'll be a vegetable before nightfall," one of the masked Rat-Men informs her. His voice is muffled under his snout, but Bird Girl is sure she detects a note of pleasure in his baleful utterance. She wonders why three of the doctors have kept their masks on. It occurs to her that the reason is vanity; that they might not be as striking as their leader.

Chandelier is examining the rat mask which the god-man has put on the kitchen table. "Like the old plague doctors," he says. Chandelier speaks so rarely, Bird Girl always listens carefully when he does. This observation, however, is lost on her.

"That's right, kid," responds the doctor. "Except that the medieval plague doctors' masks were made to look like birds, with protruding beaks. Who knows birds these days? But we all know rats.

"See?" he says, showing them all the inside of his mask. "The snout's the right shape for a built-in gas mask. And so far, we're safe from the EYE because the regime's controllers don't believe we exist. They think we're nightmare figures; figments of the imagination; manifestations of people's dread."

He slips off his wide belt, and unrolls it. On the inner band are minuscule pockets, each containing tiny vials and packages of disposable syringes.

"We carry antidotes for specific plague and gas attacks," he explains, buckling his saviour-belt back in place. "But we have nothing for this nerve gas coming your way, crude as it is.

"We do know that the gas originated at one of the EYE's own plants. Whether it was released in error or deliberately, we are in the dark."

He frowns. "The EYE has developed a particular interest in the profit-making potential of the so-called cleansing sciences as a new focus of their 'innovative industries.' My colleagues and I do what we can to help those unfortunate enough to get in the way of their inhumane experiments.

"It is little enough," he adds quietly, as if admitting a complex truth to himself.

"You have fifty minutes," he presses them. "Please make haste."

"Due north?" asks the Outpacer.

"Due north," the lovely doctor confirms.

Already Bird Girl is imagining Lola's weight on her back, preparing herself for the burden she must carry. Surely she and Lucia can together persuade the old woman to co-operate? "Where is Lucia?" she asks.

"Here," comes the answer. Bird Girl is surprised to see Lucia emerge from the cramped space between the sink and the pantry. Had she been crouching down? Was she ill?

The Rat-Man's leader moves toward Lucia, who wards him off with a gesture that strikes Bird Girl as discourteous.

"You've warned us, and we thank you," Lucia tells him. "Now save yourselves."

The doctor nods curtly before donning his mask. Then he and his companions are gone.

"We must hurry," the Outpacer urges them.

"What if they're lying?" Candace whines. "What if they want the house for themselves?"

They all ignore her. And for once, she keeps silent.

Lucia begins filling their water containers from the pump. Harry makes himself ready by stretching one limb at a time, while Chandelier helps him to balance.

"How will we transport the old woman?" the Outpacer asks.

"I will carry her on my back," Bird Girl says. The Outpacer nods, and Bird Girl is close enough to hear him sigh. They both know why he cannot offer to help; that if he carries her, Lola will try to unmask him and so undo his dignity and her own.

"I will spell you off," says the generous Lucia.

Candace is already at the door, straw hat on her head. "You're both fools," she declares. "She will slow you terribly."

Bird Girl promptly turns around, and sticks out her tongue at Candace, before running up the stairs with Lucia to get Lola ready. When she tells Lucia Lola's story about Charlie and Grimoire, Lucia responds with a composure and strength on which Bird Girl feeds greedily.

"We will walk on together with courage," Lucia says, "and watch out for each other."

Chapter Nine
The Cry

DESPITE THE DANGERS WE FACE, I am so relieved to have left that squalid house. Relieved too, not to have to look out each day at the little wood where I did the most despicable thing I have ever done.

Did any of the others hear my cry, I wonder. The sound I made was born of a remorse that eats me to the bone. I ache to tell someone exactly what happened and so ease my burden in some small way. Bird Girl is too young to hear. Old Harry has cares enough of his own. As for the Outpacer, I cannot confess my sin to a person whose face is hidden from me.

If only Candace were more empathetic, or less judgmental, I might consider telling her. But Candace, alas, is Candace. I would probably fare better speaking to a tin can.

I will walk strongly. I will help Bird Girl carry Lola. I will think only of the haste we must make if we are to survive.

Chapter Ten
Candace Sees a Bird Fall

CANDACE IS IN A FURY. HER anger is like boiling fat. She can feel its searing-hot bubbles erupting under her skin, making her itch intolerably. She clomps rather than walks, the last in the line. She glowers at every back and bottom ahead of her in the procession.

Most especially, she glowers at ancient Lola's buttocks, their bony protrusions all too obvious through the taut cloth of her thin calico skirt. The way Lola clings to Bird Girl's back reminds Candace of some disgusting antediluvian spider. She shudders at the thought of this spider's bite.

Lola is just a parasite feeding on Bird Girl's innocent host. Surely it was obvious the old woman had more resources than she was choosing to reveal? How else had she survived before they stumbled upon the stone house? Candace had seen this kind of manipulation before. The old fastened on the young, feeding off their energy and life force. They had many cunning ways to keep firm hold on their youthful prey. Deliberately eliciting pity was a standard device — pity for their wobbling chins and slobber; for their palsied hands and buckling knees; for their failing faculties and apparently constant pain. Some of the old used tale-telling to keep the young in thrall: fantastic concoctions of times past when political monsters were slain before they could thrive and multiply, when the act of physical love was free and safe and transporting, and beauteous youth lay down together amidst flowers and wafting incense.

This was how the decrepit Lola had managed to sink her fangs into the gullible Bird Girl. Candace is sure of it. She has overheard enough of the woman's filthy prattle to grasp the prurient subject matter. Sex and nakedness and shameless display. Sex and nakedness and reckless self-indulgence. No wonder Lola is such a dirty, shrivelled, incapacitated hag. One reaps what one sows.

There is a way to age with dignity and grace, Candace is certain. She has twined this conviction into the goal she had so painstakingly mind-woven before departing (she does not like to use the phrase "running away from") the City. Her new community will nurture people of all ages. The elderly will be able to radiate their particular warmth and light. She will develop special workshops to draw out the best of their wisdom and experience. Every member, whatever their season of life, will benefit from the teachings of the aged.

She often pictures her resplendent community from above, as if she were an angelic presence floating over it. From this airy perspective, she sees its individual members quietly thriving, intent on the hour's set task. She floats over her imagined fellowship at breakfast and at supper, and sees them all joined in contented communion. She surveys her own workshop, a wide, high, spotless room with windows on every side. Here, she will practise her discipline and perfect her gifts, gluing and sealing the fractures and rifts that are inevitable in any group's interactions. She will map minds, absolve petty wrongs, and illuminate the correct, healthy channels for breathing, being, doing, forgiving, and creating. Her aerial view reveals her as the vibrant pulsing heart of a community she sustained by selfless love and sterling example. She treasures this metaphor which gives her much solace in the current bumpy passage of her life. I am, she tells herself repeatedly, a vibrant, beating heart. My potential to do good is unbounded.

She is beginning to understand that she has fallen in with a group who fails to appreciate all she has to offer. Of course, she is disappointed. More — she is hurt. From Lucia and the young Bird Girl, the two in the group she encountered first, she had expected much more. She had anticipated, if not full-bodied friendship, then at least respect and willing support of her efforts to help the group bond.

"Talk to me," she had encouraged each and every one of them, with the exception of disgusting Old Harry. What was the old adage about not casting your pearls before swine? And swine Old Harry certainly was. "Talk to me," she invited them. "Open the channels," she prompted. "Let me be your very heart." She willed this silent wish to enter their consciousness, and flower there.

Her beneficent overtures have met with youthful contempt (Bird Girl), indifference and irritation (Lucia), an apparently bemused toleration (the Outpacer), and absolute vacancy (the largely mute Chandelier).

Candace knows she had undermined herself badly by exposing her own vulnerability the morning Lucia discovered the stone house. She had offered them the binding tool of a group song. Old Harry had mocked her. The Outpacer had usurped her place. And then . . . what happened exactly? She had felt, rather than heard, a whisper creep up the back of her neck like a clammy worm. Or was it a look they seemed to transmit one to the other (although she could not actually see the Outpacer's expression) so that five cold-eyed beings confronted her?

Was that the reminder that undid her? Five pairs of eyes (the Outpacer's admittedly obscured) all empty of fellow-feeling. The glint-hard eyes of beasts intent on her humiliation. Of course, she now sees this viciousness was just illusory, merely a projection of her own irrational anxiety. Her travelling companions had failed to recognize her talents, granted. But sadists they are not. Even the repugnant Old Harry is more cranky than cruel.

Yes, it was her own lingering fear that transformed her five companions into the beast-people who laid their trap for her in the City. Harry's contemptuous mockery took her back to her ordeal in the boardroom, a vision so overwhelmingly real that her tormentors' stink made her gag. She thought she saw again the yellow eyes of Death fixed upon her.

How could she have known? How could she possibly have seen through their duplicity? She genuinely believed they had hired her as a living medium to help them resolve their differences, and she was elated at the prospect.

So much of her work in those bleak days in the City had left her drained and upset. Under her grief containment contract with the EYE, she sat in the drab kitchens of the newly bereaved, explaining the advantages of the regime's hygiene procedures for disposing of their dear ones' remains. *No, they would not be able to look at their loved one for a last time. They might, in any case, find such a sight upsetting. They would receive a commemorative photograph (she knew these images were doctored, and in some cases bore little resemblance to the deceased, other than sex and hair colour). No, there would be no grave to visit, or urn containing ashes. These old-fashioned practices were unhealthy in the extreme, and ran counter to the economic imperative. The EYE appreciated that family and friends' pre-eminent task must be the working through of their grief and the gathering up of precious memories. The regime's sensitive and respectful procedures made it possible for the bereaved to focus on this crucial work, unencumbered by practical concerns.*

Directly behind her chair had stood an EYE official whose threatening presence helped quash any objections or questions. She had on occasion made the mistake of veering off-script and felt in the small of her back the uncomfortable pressure of the official's blunt-nosed baton. At least, she assumed it was his baton.

She had detested this contract work, not least for the turbid untruths she sensed lurked beneath the rationale she spouted — only sensed; of course she had no evidence. Nonetheless, by the end of the day she would feel tainted and often had to wrestle with an invasive self-disgust. She comforted herself at night with fantasies of a love so fiercely hot and all-encompassing that it would blot out her sin, if sin it was. Her lover would lick her clean and in his mighty embrace, she would feel innocent as a child. But by morning, with the fantasies long faded, she would feel grubby and dispirited again.

This new job, though, with its tremendous promise of using her talents well, had roused her from bed extra early that day. She was ready and charged with the crackling energy that a new task and new faces inspire. She had primed herself by focusing on one of her favourite images. Her mind was like the hand of God smoothing out the nubs and crinkles in the fabric of life. She pictured the final length of snowy linen, unmarked and shining in the sun.

They tore it, stained it, smeared it. They dirtied her.

And how was she to know? That sumptuous boardroom, and the six of them so elegant in their expensive suits. The women too, which is perhaps what still torments her most. How could she have known what was to come? Their exquisite grooming and striking attractiveness beguiled her, as their setting beguiled her.

They ushered her into the circular room with its carpeting so thick and soft, she longed to take off her shoes and wriggle her toes in the plush. That wish was to mock her cruelly later, when she sat half-naked and bound before them, with the iron taste of blood in her mouth.

How could she have known? They invited her into a room whose walls gleamed. Real wood panelling, the colour of fine sherry decanted into crystal. In the centre was a polished table, as round as the room. The soft lighting cast a golden glow on their faces and hands, and on the wide watch bands of the three men. Neither of the women wore timepieces of any kind. Why had she noted that? Because she had been so besotted with their damned impeccable elegance, their finely tailored suits and silk shirts, that she had fed hungrily on the smallest detail.

She'd had an instant of self-doubt, as she settled herself at their invitation into an armchair covered in mauve brocade. Against her grain, against all her training, she had succumbed for some minutes to a perilous self-denigration, contrasting her own ample hips with the slim figures of the two women sitting opposite her. This negative self-appraisal soon fattened on itself, as such appraisals will. She fixed on the coarse weave in the sleeve of her suit jacket, the tawny down visible on her wrist. The skin of the two women, by contrast, seemed everywhere as smooth as porcelain.

It was at this point she came to her senses, and saw this reckless, irrational run of thought for the sham it was. She took a cleansing breath. She sat erect. Her self-esteem flowed warmly through her veins. She thought of the long-ago proud heritage from which her own blood flowed. A low land strongly diked against the sea. A land watered and fed by canals, a testament to both genius and honest toil. A civilization built on order and cleanliness, where proud housewives sluiced the door stoops each morning and did battle with dirt as if it were the devil himself.

In that boardroom in the sky, the spirit of Dutch Purity touched Candace on the brow, speaking in the low tones only she could hear: "Be proud of your cleanliness and your rosy flesh and your powers for dissolving discontent." Candace listened and raised up the imagined dikes against the unruly sea of self-doubt. She had her tools ready: her powers of persuasion, her optimism, her conviction, her smile, her readiness to listen. She laid her briefcase on the deep carpet beside the brocade-covered chair. She folded her hands neatly in her lap. She raised her chin just a little, tilted her head to the left and smiled widely at the two seated women, and the three men standing behind them.

"How can I help you?" she asked.

One of the women sniggered. Both women crossed their legs, and there was the unsettling sound of silk rubbing on silk. The man on Candace's far right raised one eyebrow quizzically. "Help?"

The sniggering woman sniggered again; then threw back her head and laughed. It was, Candace registered in fear, a remarkably fiendish laugh.

The savage laugh spread from one to another. Candace was finding it hard to breathe. On every face, she saw the same arched eyebrows, the same bold appraising stare, the same sneering upper lip pulled back over the teeth. An image flashed on her of horses rearing, their long white incisors caught in a bit. Was it then she realized these were beast-people and that she was in gravest danger?

Silently, she began praying that her life and her honour might be spared. And honour mattered to her intensely. In her sexuality, as in all elements of her life, she strove for a scrupulous cleanliness and a chasteness that set her apart. Only one man had enjoyed her body, a young man to whom she had been engaged. She was never entirely sure why he had called it off. She was optimistic ("Optimism is my spirit's food and drink," she liked to say), that she would one day meet a man worthy of her body and soul.

"Please spare my honour and my life," she prayed very hard indeed, so hard she unwittingly spoke aloud. Five malevolent laughs joined in a sound that cut at her ears like a stinging lash. They circled her, their dark shadows momentarily blinding her. One of the men took off his silk tie and used it to gag her. Another used his tie to bind her wrists. The women had lifted her skirt, and removed her underwear.

There was much jeering. Their faces were brutish. Their eyes were wild. Naked fear made Candace dizzy, nauseous, and cold. She saw her own grave, and her body laid in earth.

It was her victory that she did not show them her terror. She did not tremble or plead for mercy. Even when they brought the spray can and spread foam thickly between her legs and shaved her, she did not cry out. Inwardly, her panic was a live, writhing thing. Death, she saw, had yellow eyes.

What saved her? What held her up through their wicked game?

The long-ago world of her forebears saved her, for the most uplifting images came to her, so lifelike they carried her away into the sanctuary of the past. She saw women in white caps and tidy gowns folding freshly laundered sheets, corner to corner, edge to edge. She saw immaculate towers of starched linen inside cupboards scented with cedar and lavender. She felt the cooling touch of snow, and a froth of ice fly up from under a skate-blade and settle on her skin.

Cleanliness, she chanted to herself. *Sobriety. Moderation. Thrift. Comfort.* The lacy touch of imagined frost cooled her flesh where otherwise she might have burned with shame. Her heritage held her up, kept her unsoiled and immune from the evil of the beast-people. Had she pleaded or wept, she really believed they would have killed her. But she did not give them that satisfaction, and so they tired of their filthy game.

She found herself thrust roughly out the boardroom door. She fell on her knees. Someone wrenched off the ties that gagged and bound her. Candace gasped. She heard the door slam behind her. She turned her head too swiftly, and nearly fainted. She was alone in the oval waiting room. She found she was unable to walk. She had to crawl to the door leading to the hallway and the elevator that would afford her escape. She grasped the door handle with both hands and used it as a lever to pull herself up. The door sprang open so that she was propelled forward, stumbling into the hall. It was also empty, except for the hidden cameras. Yes, she thought, the EYE was doubtless documenting her frantic pressing of the elevator button, her brave attempts to subdue her disarray, smoothing down her skirt, examining her legs to see that she was not spattered with either shaving foam or with blood, for they had nicked her flesh several times.

Come, oh come. Did the EYE see her lips moving as she implored the elevator platform to rise up the glass funnel? She kept turning to check on the hateful office door. Her tormentors might still appear and pull her back for the kill. Come, oh come, she whispered to the glass tube, pressing her lips to its chill surface, willing what bodily warmth she had in reserve to spark the elevator into life.

She felt she was choking. She feared her heart would stop. She kept glancing back at the closed office door which might at any moment burst open. She, who had always regarded time as a friend (*Every hour with its bounteous gifts. Let us honour each minute like a cherished guest*) now saw its slow passing as odious. She squirmed inside its heartless grip. Finally, she heard the purr of the rising platform. She peered down into the depths of the funnel and saw the gloomy disk grow infinitesimally larger. At last, the funnel opened and she got in, managing to speak the word "ground" sufficiently clearly and loudly to activate the invisible mechanism. And down she went, her knees wobbling and chest heaving. She longed for a metal bar to grip, or a solid wall against which she could collapse. But there was nothing. This was a machine stripped to its function.

She succeeded in keeping her dignity and composure when she at last entered the lobby's pyramid of glass. She concentrated on the bath she would pour herself, the scented soap she would use to wash away their stink. Their breath and their flesh had smelled sickly when they came close to taunt her. She kept focusing on the ways she would make herself clean, and she raised up, again and again in her mind, the dike that preserved her from their pollution.

She was fortunate that her trip home was uneventful. No howling beggars exposing real or manufactured sores, no couples copulating amidst filth under subway stairs. Only when she closed her apartment door behind her and set its deadbolt fast, did she finally allow herself to give way. She hugged and rocked herself and cried scalding tears that seemed as much punishment as release. "I will mother poor suffering Candace," she told herself firmly as she rose up from this bout of weeping. "I will soothe and heal myself," she murmured as she filled her bath tub full and poured in oils of eucalyptus and chamomile.

It was while she lay immersed in water just a little too hot, soaping herself head to foot, that the vision came to her. A *gemeenschap*, a little community with its own dear soul, flowering from the values she had recited in her hour of deepest need: Thrift. Cleanliness. Order. She could, and would, preside over such a community. Far from the putrid abscess the City had become, she would help to build a new world of which her forebears would be proud. Like them, she would root out the wastrels and the evil-doers, the parasites and the sluggards. And she would cast them out.

She pictured the sign over the door to her community — for indeed, it would have a stout door and a wall to deflect corruption — "Only the cleanly may enter here." She was not entirely sure that "cleanly" was a word. But if it were not, she was happy enough to invent it. Clean in thought and in deed, she mused, and those who transgressed would be sacrificed. This last thought set off a trembling of her hands; her entire body shook as she tried clumsily to wrap herself in a towel.

"Honesty, Candace," she chided herself. "Honesty is the purest note in the sterling character. Open the floodgates of emotion," she counselled herself, as she had so often counselled her clients.

She had shocked herself, as she followed her own advice to the letter. The floodgates opened. They could go no wider. Twenty minutes later, she stood aghast amidst wreckage so total she had to push away the debris with her foot in order to clear a place to sit. Except for the damp towel, she was still naked from her bath. Her chest heaved. The air she forced into her lungs felt like tarred rope. She slumped down, with her back against the wall. Slowly she unlatched the fingers of her left hand, loosening her grip on the handle of her largest, sharpest kitchen knife. This was the weapon she had seized in blind obedience to her own instinctual urging that the floodgates be opened. Here was the hand, and she studied closely the trimmed cuticles of each pearly pink nail, that had wreaked such destruction.

She surveyed the chaos, amazed at the extent of her fury. She had slit and gutted all her upholstered furniture, including a new day bed covered in a sprig print, of which she had been particularly fond. Her mattress had suffered the most from her frenzied cuts. The cover was a ruin of deep scores and hatchings. Through the gapes, she saw the cruel, taut springs revealed. She was both appalled and elated at the chaos wrought by her furious knife hand. She had murdered each and every one of her tormentors symbolically, and knew it was well done.

An ingrained housewifery had prompted her to remove the sheets before her mad attack on the bed. These she used to wrap round her and make a nest in a corner of her living room. She curled up with a relic of her childhood, a soft-bodied doll with long legs, and rocked and hummed herself into a state resembling calm. She considered, and rejected, the idea of calling a friend to solicit comfort. The fact was she did not want anyone to know what had happened to her. In part, this was because humiliation still smarted rawly within her. In greater part, it was a matter of pride and self-preservation.

She did sleep, albeit fitfully, waking once in a panic because she seemed to have stopped breathing. "I am a rational person," she crooned to herself. "Reason is a straight and sun-lit path." She pressed the soft-bodied doll to her tight and aching chest, and pictured the air passages in her lungs filling freely. "Deep and even breathing is the royal road to calm and insightful action," she reassured herself.

Candace breathed deeply and evenly, hugging the pliant doll to her chest, so that it too seemed to inhale and exhale with her. Towards the onset of a murky dawn, she succumbed to a sleep deep enough to dream. In the dream, she saw the bodies of her five tormentors laid out in a marble-walled morgue. Under grey-white coverlets, only their rigid faces and naked feet were visible. Her dream-self strode the corridor between the two rows of mortuary slabs. In her right hand, she held a long, thin needle, like an ancient hatpin. She stabbed each corpse in the flesh of its left heel. This action left her feeling exuberant and free.

When Candace woke, she remembered something else: that each foot had been marked with a ring of black fungus. She understood this to be an indelible sign of evil. "It is good they have been sacrificed," she thought. "The world will be a better place for it."

This notion hit her with the full force of a natural law as she made ready to begin her new life. Now was the time for her to leave the City for good. The signs were clear. The corruption had gone too deep. The black fungus threatened everyone. Her skills and energy and optimism were wasted here. You cannot reclaim what is unredeemable, she told herself. Some people were beyond help. Beyond hope, even. It was folly to waste one's time on them.

She told herself she was ready for adventure, as few in this world are ever ready. She had her goal superbly well fixed. By the minute, her community-to-be took on a degree of detail that confirmed she had at last found a life-task matched to her abundant talents.

Destiny beckoned. And thus Candace was not surprised when her exit from the City passed without incident. Following the track of the ancient, defunct railway that led out from the urban enclosure, she was relieved to see a few other refugees like herself. Some laboured under the weight of what seemed to be all their worldly goods, staggering with misshapen bundles on their heads or backs.

One woman Candace passed was bent nearly double under a punishing load of sticks and twigs. From a distance, she resembled an animal with horns, a dangerously ill beast whose every step faltered. Close up, Candace shrank instinctively from the coarse, raddled texture of the woman's cheeks and bony nose, and the rotting cloth under her armpits. She vowed then she would always keep herself fresh and clean no matter what the travails to come. It was comforting nonetheless to know the woman with the poor hygiene was somewhere close behind on the trail, should she run into trouble. Candace focused all her positive thoughts on soon meeting someone simpatico with whom she could travel in greater safety.

Later that morning she overtook a person (man or woman, she could not tell), swathed in thick towelling despite the already scorching heat of the day. This walking bundle pulled behind it a thick plank of wood, studded with fragments of dishware. To what purpose, wondered practical Candace, for the stuck-on shards of china were of indifferent quality, in shades she associated with industrial plumbing fixtures. Broken Delftware Candace could have understood, although she doubted she would go so far as to fix even the most captivating blue and white pieces to a board to drag behind her through life. We each cling to what we consider most precious, she reflected.

Among the precious objects Candace had in her pack was a pendant of glass microscopically inscribed with the Ten Golden Rules for a Productive Life, and the cloth doll that embodied the most pleasing of her childhood memories. She took with her as well, the cherished thoughts that nourished her fortitude and positive outlook. She was endowed, above all, with a luminous sense of purpose and destiny's assurance that she had been born to lead.

Candace knew she had undermined her burgeoning leadership when she let her five travelling companions see her naked fear. But by the time they were all settled in the stone house, she had forgiven herself this lapse. She still cannot fathom the paradox: how dwelling together under one roof had driven them to their separate devices, rather than bring them together. But as she trudges on in their new exile, glaring at old Lola's bony backside, the answer becomes startlingly clear. It was the old woman who had poisoned the atmosphere and set them at odds.

Here is the one who should have been sacrificed, Candace determines with a grim satisfaction. This thought no sooner forms in her mind than the air around her is split by a piercing whistle. Candace looks on in numbed disbelief as Bird Girl rears abruptly, and Lola slides from her back.

"A hit! A hit!" comes a shrill demonic cry off to their left. The Outpacer immediately sets off in pursuit of the attacker, a figure dressed all in black.

Candace, Lucia, Chandelier, and Old Harry stand momentarily frozen at the sight of Bird Girl lying on the ground, her small face bleached and contorted, her fingers clawing at the air. A stout wooden arrow protrudes from her left breast. Lola is on her knees beside the girl, swaying and moaning.

"Pull it out," Bird Girl whispers. "Oh, please, pull it out." Her eyes are rolling.

Lucia kneels beside the distraught Lola, and looks toward the sky as if asking for blessing. She takes firm grasp on the arrow's shaft and pulls. It comes out whole. Bird Girl's yelp is so sharp, Candace feels her stomach lurch.

The girl's spine buckles and she goes rigid. Lola is beside her, rocking on her knees and moaning, plucking at her own scant hair.

The wound is unclean, the torn flesh already discoloured. "Poison," Candace announces, and they all see the greenish ooze still dripping from the arrow's point. Chandelier stares open-mouthed at Candace and the arrow; then speeds off after the Outpacer.

"I'll save you little chick," Lola cries. And before either Candace or Lucia can stop her, the old woman puts her mouth to the wound and sucks.

Candace has to look away. The sight of the old woman's mouth at Bird Girl's bare bud of a breast sickens her to the marrow. She cannot make the parts fit. How can an act so obviously obscene be the most profound act of love she has ever witnessed?

Chapter Eleven
Miracles

FOR ONE FOOLISH MOMENT AFTER I extracted the arrow, I stared transfixed at the red-black slit in the pale mound of Bird Girl's left breast. The wound seemed to me somehow sexual. I feared death hovered nearby, eager to penetrate it.

I immediately berated myself for this notion, as dangerous as it was unforgivable. I closed my eyes for a fraction of a second in a deliberate effort to cleanse my mind. That sliver of inattention was enough for the balance of life and death to swing abruptly.

Lola's mouth closes over the wound before I can stop her. She sucks and moans and sucks again. I grasp the old woman's shoulder to try to drag her away. It is all over even as I touch her. Lola lifts her head, utters a high-pitched cry and then lies quiet on the breast of her adored girl.

I am horrified as the old woman's skeletal frame goes rigid, and her thin skin tightens to transparency. Her naked gums are exposed in a rictus that could be either a grimace of agony, or a grin of triumph. I choose to believe it is triumph, but my eyes tear nonetheless. I know we have to work quickly and move Lola's body because even its slight weight is impeding the girl's laboured breathing. We must get on with the cleaning of the wound, although I have no doubt Lola has made a good start.

"Help me!" I urge them, for Candace and Harry are still standing spell-bound. I think we are all under the leaden net death casts. Candace is shaking her head back and forth in heavy wonderment. Harry drives his balled fist repeatedly into his chest.

"Help me!"

It is Harry who comes first to assist me. Together, we pull Lola as gently as we can to a spot well away from where the young girl lies.

Harry stays by Lola's body while I run back to Bird Girl. Candace has at last sprung to life and fetched water, gauze, and a clean T-shirt. As I swab and bathe the wound, I hear Harry say, "Well done, old woman."

The silence following on his words expands to make a vaulted dome above us. Protect her, I implore this sacred arc of space. Bird Girl's complexion already looks less opaquely white. As I sponge the girl's wound, words come to me that I hold briefly in my mind and speak silently.

Dignity is one. Altruism another. And again, sacrifice.

I remember Lola as I first saw her: a nightmarish vision, vulgar, crassly made-up, apparently senile. Love for Bird Girl steadied and transfigured the old woman. At the very end, that affection ennobled her.

The girl's breathing has become quieter, her pulse steadier. I feel oddly light-headed. Whether the cause is simple relief or awe, I do not know.

A little colour returns to Bird Girl's face. Candace is silent. These are miracles in themselves.

Chapter Twelve
Chandelier Heeds Snake's Counsel Again

CHANDELIER RUNS, SOON CATCHING UP TO the Outpacer who is hampered by the long skirt of his monk's habit and his flapping rubber sandals. Because the boy's soles have hardened, Miriam's boots fashioned from strips of silk have come to serve him well enough, and he is better equipped than the Outpacer for speeding over the forest floor. As perhaps Miriam intended, the strips of fabric have melded with the help of dirt and perspiration. Chandelier can, and does, slip his fabric boots off each evening to air before he lies down to sleep. It amuses him to see them standing so solidly when he recalls Miriam's repeated winding, round his foot, of floating silken lengths through which the light passed.

He thinks of Miriam as he runs, overtaking the Outpacer. But then he often thinks of Miriam. The protective pouch she gave him bobs on the string about his neck. Her cut-glass earring bounces against his cheek.

If Miriam were here, she could cure Bird Girl. The image of the crude shaft lodged in the girl's chest pierces him again. He winces to recall the way Bird Girl crumpled to the ground, her face so deathly white, her mouth open in a silent gasp.

Before he and the Outpacer took off in pursuit of the evil archer, Chandelier had paused long enough to see the ragged hole the arrow tip had made and the greenish toxin already discolouring the skin around the wound. "Poison," Candace said.

Candace always makes him uneasy. He dislikes her booming voice and her grand, empty gestures miming a warmth he senses she does not really feel. But he knows she is right about the poison.

Is that why he and the Outpacer are pursuing the dark, gliding shape of the archer? Do they want to seize him and make him spit out the name of the venom so that they might know how to heal Bird Girl? But the elusive attacker is soon swallowed up by the forest. Each tree seems to cast its own heavy spell, spinning shadows thickly out of its roots and branches. The boy is wary of trees still, of their towering indifference and secretive inner life. He cannot dissociate them from a hot anguish of mind and flesh, and the way he had scored and slashed and rubbed parts of his face raw, banging his head against tree bark on the day the Egg exploded.

The Egg. He has been thinking of the poison seeping into poor Bird Girl, and has come back to the Egg. This is always happening. He cannot stop it happening, except sometimes when he loses himself in the unbounded whiteness of Harry's tales of Antarctica. And sometimes too, if he pays close attention to Snake's whispered counsel; if he lets his friend curl round his throat like a necklace so that Snake's cool, bony mouth is close to his ear.

The effort of remembering his life in the Egg is an agonizing discipline, like prodding an open wound with a calloused thumb. Perhaps if he went into this pain deliberately now, he might remember something that would help Bird Girl. *Endure*, he sends out thoughts to her. *Persist*. With such injunctions, Snake has often kept him alive.

Inside the Egg, Chandelier is certain he and his father could have found the cure for Bird Girl. Together in the laboratory wing, they would have speedily analyzed the poison and just as speedily found the antidote. The best of the world's wisdom was preserved and protected in the Egg. So his father told him, and so Chandelier believed. He can still recall in sharpest detail the content of many of the Egg's countless videos, tapes and disks, and of the real books in its vast library. He had liked to sit with a book in his lap, turning its paper pages slowly or quickly, as the narrative demanded. It was in books that he found the human and animal company that sustained him when loneliness threatened to undo his selfhood.

Allein. That was a better word than lonely, he thought, with a keener, biting sound. For sometimes in the Egg the aching solitude had caught him and strung him up, like the rabbit in a snare he had seen once in a video and ached for. He knew himself then to be a flimsy thing, which would rattle if shaken. The rattle, he guessed, was the sound of his heart and other organs, gone hard and dry.

Of course, he knew his father loved him. And although she did not often show it, he believed, as he had to believe, that his mother cared for him deeply.

It still amazed him to recall how like his mother Bird Girl looked as she lay ashen and unmoving. Until the attack, he had never noticed this resemblance because Bird Girl was always in motion: fingers aflutter, head swivelling, chin tilted skyward, then lowered, elbows jutted out, then pumping up and down, as if she were making ready to fly. He thought she must be named for the hummingbird, which was a shimmering blur of purple and crimson when it hovered in the air.

In the Egg, he had liked to watch his nature films at regular speed, then replay them in slow motion so that he could study how each living being moved in its environment. Freeze the frame and there was the tiny bird, wings out-flung, ready for uplift.

Surely Bird Girl would not die? He has always given her quite a wide berth, mostly because he found her bright energy and quick speech unsettling. He marvelled at the ease with which she moved in the world: her "superb adaptation to her element." This was a phrase from one of the nature films, another of the oddments his brain had stored and that would pop up, in or out of context.

For fourteen years, the only element he had known was inside the Egg. The air was clean. Any fluctuations in temperature and light were regulated by sensors tuned to optimum conditions for the human life form. Of whom there were three in the Egg — Father, Mother, Son. And no others, as he had often mourned to himself in his echoing loneliness. No other life forms at all, not even a harmless spider.

He had regularly asked his father for a pet, most particularly a lizard or a snake. The answer was always no. Introducing such a life form into the Egg might compromise their immune systems, his father said.

He had absorbed enough of his father's stoical forbearance and self-control not to give way to fits of pique. He learned to subdue his disappointment by flinging himself into physical activity. He would plunge into the blue temperate water of the Egg's swimming pool and turn lap after lap under the watchful gaze of the robotic lifeguard. (Bird Girl would have liked the swimming pool, it occurs to him. She would have said something funny or rude about the lifeguard robot which had a face like a flattened pan.) Or he would apply himself to the punching bag, hurdles, and climbing wall of the Egg's gymnasium, which his father called Plato's Playroom. When his distress was most acute, when his yearning for company other than his father's and his books became a physical ache, he would run.

Running brought the added pleasure of the ineffable light. For the track circled inside the actual perimeter of the Egg. There, he was separated from the external world by a mere membrane of semi-translucent material. Until the day of the explosion, this was as close as Chandelier ever came to the polluted, corrupt world from which his father had sealed his family away. So it perturbed the boy that he found so pleasing this light that had so evil a source. Soft, diffuse, with a tinge of amethyst, its sheen on the track's air seemed a miraculous medium, buoying him up. He thought sometimes he floated, rather than ran.

How could this be, he asked his father. This was the kind of light that bathed the faces of the people in his mother's art books. How could it come from so impure a place?

Was it anger he read on his father's face as he instructed his son yet again on the dangers of illusion? The idea of danger had an instinctual appeal for the young Chandelier, who wisely said no more. But he was too much in awe of his father, too conditioned to life in the Egg, to try an assault on its confines. Besides, he had no reason to doubt his father's description of the crimes perpetrated minute by minute in the cursed world outside. Think of the Hell-scape of Hieronymus Bosch and multiply it ten times, his father said. These were images Chandelier could not bear to contemplate for long.

The time of the world's healing would come, his father assured him. Every day, his father monitored the signs, filtering through the news that came to him in encrypted messages from other members of the Arête. This was a group of intellectuals who had opted, like him, for total seclusion from the world, like the desert mystics of old. The Arête inhabited caves, eyries, underground bunkers, or manufactured fortresses like the Egg, keeping alive the imperilled sparks of disinterested knowledge, reason, clarity, the power of mythos, and virtues like probity, honour, courage, and empathy. They saw themselves as the guardians of what was best in humankind.

The demons they battled, each in their fastness, were pride (lest they succumb to the folly of elitism) and despair (lest they never see their own time emerge from darkness). Each morning brought the necessary demand that they renew their hope. In their separateness one from the other they fed the spirit in their respective ways, whether through ritual action and prayer, disciplines of attention, or multi-chambered silence. Through the encrypted messages, they offered each other solace, and a basis for faith. They shared their latest daily gleanings from a scrupulous sweep of readings meteorological, atmospheric, and astronomical. They were alert to the slightest cultural shift. Reports of a pen scratching words on paper, or of a clay figure baking in the sun, were cause for elation. They transmitted to each other that most rare sound of living voices mingled in song. Listening, Chandelier's father had believed the space inside the Egg transfigured. He seemed to stand directly beneath a star-clustered dome, and the current that moved through his veins was purest longing.

But the sign for which the Arête watched with keenest anticipation had so far eluded them. And that was birdsong. When the songbirds returned, Chandelier's father explained, it would be safe for them to leave the Egg.

Chandelier never told his father that he found this prospect terrifying. It was one thing to study sky, ocean, mountains, and savannah on film. It was quite another to visit them. Chandelier feared the real world might be too much for him. He feared he might fall down or go mad.

Of course, he strove to master his anxiety, and even before the explosion, it was to Snake he turned as his prime mentor who knew all about survival. Chandelier had encountered many gods and heroes and mythic beings in his books. But from their very first meeting, when Snake slithered from his secret underworld in the myths of Earth's beginnings, Chandelier was mesmerized. The fine hair on the boy's wrists and at the back of his neck stood erect. His entire body, his spine especially, was alert to Snake's majesty and supple energizing power.

Coiled. Circular. An emerald zigzag. A dark bolt distinguishing earth from sky. The boy marvelled at Snake's guile, his shape-shifting, his flickering tongue. He knew there was no situation from which Snake could not extricate himself, whether by stealth or hypnosis or darting venom. In story after story where Snake reigned, Chandelier saw a visceral truth confirmed. Here was his life's spirit guide. He knew he would never find a better one. He read of Snake as the founder of great cities, and of the Serpent as Time itself. He saw Snake make his sinewy belly a platform to support a dancing god with eyes of fire. He saw Snake as a healer, curled round a slender staff, a counsellor to physicians through the ages.

Snake, he implores as he runs, *please help Bird Girl.*

And he saw Snake maligned, his wisdom misconstrued in tales where he was cursed and miscast as the evil seducer of humankind. In this mistaken form, Snake was made demon and dragon, to be slain again and again by a warrior angel with trident and sword. Of course, the sinewy one did not die, no matter how often he was slain. He rose up again shining, because he was Snake.

Chandelier recognized that any willful defamations of Snake's character only proved the paradox his father had taught him: that the sacred was also the cursed, the two aspects so entwined they made a single shape, like the old skin Snake sloughed off in resurrection. The boy looked and saw only Snake's gleaming, benevolent, heroic self. What other being was so at ease underground, sliding along the earth's surface, or through water? Snake was a climber too, up poles, pinnacles, and cliffs; so heights were no obstacle.

Now, as Chandelier bends double, his breath spent in pursuit of the archer who shot Bird Girl, he wishes such a saviour hero for her. She cannot die. She simply cannot. His hands are balled in fists, one of them tight round the little slab of green stone with its metal paddle which he had seized from the ruins of the Egg. It perturbs him that he still cannot remember what this object is. He has kept it safe because it belonged to his father. This fact alone makes the thing precious.

He looks around and sees the Outpacer some distance behind him, striving to catch his breath. The cowl of the man's gown touches the earth.

"We have lost him," the Outpacer says. "See here." He points to a wide fissure in the earth that the boy must have passed moment ago, unseeing. "I believe this is the opening to a tunnel. There may be a whole network of channels under the earth, or perhaps this leads into the chambered caves the plague doctor spoke of."

"And there!" The Outpacer points to his left. Chandelier has to rub his eyes before he can properly make out a peculiar dark hump. He blinks and sees that the hump has a yawning black mouth. The boy has never before seen a cave. Immediately he thinks of bears, aurochs, ossuaries, and magical pigments.

"We must hurry back." Chandelier hears a catch in the man's voice. Like a tear in a purse, he thinks, through which a treasure is escaping.

Do we all love Bird Girl then, the boy wonders, as they speed back. The knot in his throat keeps tightening. As he runs, he tries to summon up images of hope. He remembers pictures from his mother's books of exquisite, flower-like faces turned skyward, and the miraculous sign that would appear, sometimes in the shape of a shaft of light or an angel. But these static images will not do for Bird Girl. He needs movement and sprightliness. He needs a landscape in which to picture her bounding and leaping about — flying even, in her exuberance.

The image that comes to him is of the hills that so often defined the horizon in the paintings of the Quattrocento his mother loved. His eye had always been drawn to those soft undulations that served to show how deep and wide the world was within the picture's frame. Sometimes bare; sometimes dotted with slim trees, the foremost hills were crowned with purple or burnt sienna — a name, once learned, he loved to roll upon his tongue. In all those images, he had thought he perceived a slight movement. He was certain that hills embodied an actual joy. They must, he told himself, be the laughter of earth.

Since he emerged from the Egg, Chandelier had seen no hills, only flatness and forest, and the wretched Cityscape and sewer land he would prefer to forget. Hills were a wonder yet to come. I will lift up my eyes, he promised himself, and there they will be. He pictures how he and Bird Girl would make their way up to the rounded peak toward the source of that vivid colour. She would run, skip, and leap up the yielding slope. Once they reached the top, they would breathe quietly, absorbing the plenitude of space. And perhaps there, the actual shining world of myth and story would reveal itself to both of them, and Snake would show himself and speak.

Where is Snake, he wonders anxiously, as he and Outpacer plunge through the last of the brush to the place where Lucia kneels, pressing a cloth to Bird Girl's wound. Candace stands sorrowful at Bird Girl's feet. Harry, leaning heavily on his stick, stares down at the girl's small face, almost unrecognizable in its waxen pallor. It seems to Chandelier that Harry's grizzled face has noticeably sagged since the arrow struck.

"We lost the bastard," the Outpacer whispers. Candace frowns. Harry's mouth twists over his lower teeth.

"We have cleaned the wound and put on some ointment," Lucia says. "Now we can only hope." Her brow furrows under the taut band of her kerchief.

"Lola is dead," she tells them. "She sucked out a lot of the venom before we could stop her . . . "

The Outpacer puts a hand to his hidden face. "My God! Who else among us would have made such a sacrifice?

"The boy and I will bury Lola."

Chandelier begins to summon his courage. He is afraid that when he touches Lola's corpse, he will feel again the clamminess of his father's severed hand. He wishes Snake would come, for isn't his friend a cool and wily fellow, well acquainted with death?

Help me.

It is then the rain begins to fall. At first the boy assumes the sizzling sound he hears behind him is the Outpacer lighting his torch. He turns round and sees a small crater in the earth from which a dense sulfurous smoke rises. He is reminded of the stink of the Egg's smoldering remnants. His eyes begin to water and so it is through a glaze that he sees a huge drop of rust-red rain fall directly ahead of him. The instant it touches the earth, the rain burns a hole and the stench catches in his throat despite his mask.

The Outpacer has picked up Bird Girl, and is shielding her body with the skirt of his gown which he has pulled up to cover her, leaving his legs bare. "Run," he yells. "We must take shelter. Follow me, and be quick."

Candace is screaming. Harry is gesturing wildly, urging the boy to speed ahead after the Outpacer. Chandelier shakes his head, and seizes Harry's hand, pulling him forward. The boy struggles to resist the terrible urge to look up. He knows that if he obeys this foolish compulsion, he may scald his face badly or even go blind. What or who is bleeding above them? Or is this Sky weeping for himself, his tears stained by the innards of the Sun?

"Go boy! Let's get a move on." Chandelier cannot recall Harry ever moving so quickly before, but they are still the last in the line. Lucia, who is just ahead of them, keeps looking back to make sure they have not stumbled.

The deadly drops are spaced far apart, and it is this that saves them. Plunk, the boy hears. Sizzle. Plunk and sizzle. This destructive percussion keeps them company as they run, but the sound is always a little to their left or to their right, or just behind or ahead.

Who is slowing down the rain, the boy wonders. Is it Snake? Or are his parents watching over him? This idea has never occurred to him before.

Once he and Harry reach the cave mouth and retreat inside with the others, the Sky-being of Chandelier's imagining begins to roar. Then Sky lets loose a curtain of blood.

"Farther back," calls the Outpacer, in a sharp tone the boy has never heard him use before. "Keep close to the wall."

The boy clutches Harry's hand tighter, and together they inch their way toward the Outpacer's voice, their backs grazing the damp cave wall. How dark it is, and how cold.

Even as he forms this thought, the cave mouth reveals itself as a crimson gash. An ear-shattering roaring invades the world. The boy's flesh contracts. There follows the sound of an explosion so massive that the stone behind their backs shifts and groans. "Courage," he hears Harry say. Or was it Snake who spoke? This is a new kind of pain, the boy thinks. They are all being tortured by the roaring and the booming. Chandelier begins to wonder if this is indeed the end of all things; if soon he will see his parents, made whole again and happy. He seeks comfort in this idea.

"Keep moving," the Outpacer cries out. "Carefully. Cautiously. Stay close to the wall. This is the fireball the doctor predicted. We will survive this."

The fireball. It will demolish everything in its path, the plague doctor said, including human flesh and bone. The boy's heart lurches in his chest as he pictures the fire consuming Lola's body. There will be nothing left of her now, not even ash. Not even that. Where then would she be?

Foolish boy. You know the answer to that. This is Snake again.

Yes, of course he knows the answer. Lola's story goes into the deep well of what we are.

At that instant the entire interior of the cave is briefly lit with a lurid glow. For a split-second only, just as long as the hellish light lasts, Chandelier sees a face he does not recognize. Plunged again into darkness, he reconstructs the image in his mind's eye as the group progresses onward into the heart of the rock. The unknown man, with the stern, lean face of a warrior angel, wears a monk's gown. In his arms he bears the slight, slumped figure of a young girl.

Chandelier is so amazed that he stops, and Harry's shoulder bumps his.

"Boy, what's wrong?"

He cannot say: I have seen the naked face of the Outpacer and he looks like a warrior angel; so he simply whispers, "Nothing, sorry." He and Harry inch forward once again.

A putrid smell makes the boy's nostrils prickle. Harry coughs.

"There is sweeter air ahead," the Outpacer calls out. "Keep moving."

How odd it is to hear the hooded man's voice and be able to picture his face.

"Speak your names, please." The Outpacer sounds anxious, and the echo intensifies his concern. "Let me know you are all here."

"Candace."

"Lucia."

"Harry."

"Chandelier."

But no one hears the boy speak his name. For at that moment, the toe of his fabric boot dislodges a stone that clatters and flies out from under his foot. He rights himself, squeezes Harry's hand, and listens to the intense hush in which they are all now immersed. Some ten full heartbeats later, they hear a splash.

"Oh, my God!" The boy thinks it was Lucia who spoke, yet the voice was so fear-filled, he cannot be certain.

"Stay calm, all of you," the Outpacer says. "Press your backs against the wall.

"Lucia, could you strike a match? Can you manage this?"

"Yes."

Ah, thinks the boy. It is all right. This is the Lucia he knows who is speaking.

They wait. Then they hear the rasp of the struck match. In the brief light Lucia makes, the boy sees first the gleaming wetness of the cave walls. We are inside the mouth of one of the old gods, he thinks, the first ones. He looks down and gasps, as they all do. They are standing on a ledge barely two feet wide. Far below them is a ravine whose ebony water, churning and alive, speaks of its deadly depth.

Now they are in the dark again. They all instinctively press back against walls that are wetter, slippier, and so much more inhospitable than when they first entered the cave.

A woman sobs. Is it Candace or Lucia? Or is it Bird Girl?

He hears Lucia speak in words he does not understand: "*Per me si va ne la città dolente . . . Lasciate ogni speranza, voi chi entrate.*"

He registers the raw fear in the words nonetheless, and some other emotion he cannot identify — something heavy that slows her speech and makes her sound unlike herself.

"Courage!" This from Harry.

"Take courage! Let us keep on." This is the Outpacer.

"*Speranza. Sì.*" Harry again.

"*Speranza,*" Lucia repeats.

"Another match, Lucia." As the match strikes, the boy concentrates this time on looking directly ahead, toward the back of the cave. At first he cannot believe his eyes. What appears to be a ring of dazzling white stones marks out the boundary of a solid platform of rock, wide and deep enough for them all to sit and rest; even to lie down and to sleep.

"It is quite solid and safe." Already the Outpacer is standing on the platform, encouraging them to join him. His hood is once again in place, the boy notes. He sees how carefully the man has laid Bird Girl down in the centre of the stone floor. The Outpacer stands above her still form, rummaging in the deep pockets of his habit.

Lucia's match goes out.

"I have a small flashlight," the Outpacer tells them. "I am sure it has several hours of power left." A small tube of light illuminates Bird Girl's prone figure. With the utmost care and caution, they all make their way along the remainder of the narrow ledge to the platform which seems to grow out of the roots of the cave, like a tongue in a mouth.

"Ugh!" Candace yelps. The Outpacer swings his torch to where she stands, her hand covering her mouth. Candace points to a hollow in the cave wall, from which a skull grins down at them. He then sweeps the slim beam around the perimeter of the platform, where his light discovers an assortment of gleaming bones: rib cages, clavicles, tibias, and many more skulls.

"We have been preceded," he says. "We will be protected by this circle," he tells them. Harry murmurs his agreement. What choice do they have but to believe this, the boy wonders.

"We will wait here," the Outpacer tells them, like a father speaking in stern reassurance to his children, "some eight to ten hours. Then I will make the first foray out to ensure it is safe for us to leave.

"For now we must conserve our strength. We have survived the firestorm. We have brought Bird Girl through this ordeal.

"We must persist; head north speedily as the doctor advised."

To Chandelier's great surprise, the Outpacer begins to sing. The boy is so weary he cannot take in all the words. Later he remembers "valour" and "constant be" or perhaps it was a "constant bee." The song's quietly thumping beat makes him think of a healthy heart in a great strong chest on which he might lay his head. Perhaps that is why, despite the day's harrowing event and tormenting worry, he falls asleep. When he wakes, his head is nestled against Harry's hip.

"The Outpacer went out about ten minutes ago," Harry whispers. "Soon we will have news of when we can leave this damp and wretched place."

"Bird Girl?" the boy asks. He cannot keep the apprehension out of his voice.

"She is still breathing, although a bit raggedly," Lucia answers. "There is hope," she adds. "*Speranza*."

"*Speranza*," the boy repeats. The sound of this word has a power to brighten and quicken his spirit when he speaks it quietly to himself.

"What's that?" Lucia asks. "Hush."

At that moment they hear the unmistakable slide of shoe soles on loose stone; and the rub of cloth against the slick stone wall. Someone has entered the cave.

"The Outpacer?" whispers Harry to Chandelier and Lucia, for they are the only three awake. Lucia shakes her head, even though they can barely see each other in the dark.

"He would have called out to us," she responds in a hush. She flicks on the flashlight, and sends the beam sweeping over the wall. A man with a shock of orange hair is making his way rapidly along the narrow ledge. He is dressed completely in black. Over his right shoulder is slung the strap of a quiver.

"I think it is the archer," she whispers to Harry and Chandelier, who flinches at the odd croaking quality of her voice. Immediately the boy is on his feet, positioning himself in front the unconscious Bird Girl. But his legs go weak when he hears a voice like an animal's snarl, "Grimoire's here to finish off the little whore." Chandelier thinks he has never heard a human being say anything more terrible. How can they stop him? How? What would Snake do? What weapons do they have to hand?

The answer comes from Harry. Calmly and quietly he tells Chandelier, "Fetch me a skull. Just go behind me and get me a whole one from the row of bones. Lucia will train the light so that you can see. Be quick and careful as you can, boy."

Chandelier homes in on an intact skull, which he scoops up with a scrupulous care and places in Harry's outstretched hands. "Good lad. Now stand behind me, boy. And pray if you wish."

"Put the beam on the bastard, Lucia," Harry instructs her. "Try to shine it right in his eyes."

Lucia does as she is bid. At once, a round creamy-white missile whirls through the beam of light. Grimoire moves his head just in time. The skull plunges off the ledge. They all wait with rigid nerves in a silence which pounds upon the boy's ears like a closed fist. Lucia's hand is shaking so much that the beam of light slips and they can see Grimoire no more.

The tension thickens the dark and the air around them. Where is the evil man now? Chandelier wonders. He considers throwing himself on top of Bird Girl. Would the arrow also penetrate her body or would it stop in his? His teeth are gritted and the silence still assaults his ears so painfully he does not at first hear Harry's urgent whisper. "Another one, boy. Fetch me another nice round skull."

"More light, Lucia, and keep it steady."

She sweeps the beam along the ledge and just as it catches Grimoire, they hear the cave echo with the sound of the first skull hitting the water below. In the cone of light they see that Grimoire has his back pressed tight against the wall. His mouth is open and his eyes wide. He knows now, thinks the boy. He knows how narrow is the ledge and how deep the watery cavern below. There is fear in the evil man now, a fear that will eat at his courage and his sense of balance.

"He has only one eye," Lucia says softly to Harry.

"Which one is missing, Lucia?" Harry sounds angry at her.

"The right, I think. I am not certain," she confesses.

"Hold the beam steady."

Lucia complies. In the beam, which she directs as Harry instructs, they see the orange-haired man still standing frozen against the cave wall, arms akimbo.

"Bastards!" he screams at them.

Harry hurls the second skull. This one strikes the man on his right temple and his head and shoulders jerk forward. As he tries desperately to regain his balance, he missteps so that his right foot is off the ledge. For a moment Grimoire appears to hang in mid-air. Then he plummets. So shrill is his scream, as he goes down and down, that Chandelier puts his fingers in his ears. The scream wakes Candace, but Bird Girl sleeps on.

"What happened?" Candace exclaims. "What? Tell me!"

"Harry stopped a killer," Lucia says, "the man who shot Bird Girl. Harry hurled a skull at his head and the archer fell into the chasm."

"Harry?" Candace keeps repeating in puzzlement. "Harry?"

"Harry." Chandelier confirms proudly. "Yes, Harry."

All four sit silently, their bodies trembling from the emotional aftershock. Chandelier senses some current of fear still moving among them, though the evil man must surely be dead. He keeps seeing the archer's look of utter surprise, round-mouthed, at the last instant before he began to fall. This picture causes a corkscrew of pain in his gut, and the feeling that he has swallowed a vast emptiness. Is this sensation pity, he wonders. And if so, why does he pity such a wicked being? He knows he will turn this question over and over in the years to come.

Some hours later they hear the Outpacer returning, humming to himself the tune with its thump-a-thump beat.

"How is the child?"

"She lives. She hangs on," Lucia tells him.

"But we had an interloper. The archer came into the cave, looking to kill her. Harry toppled him from the ledge by hurling one of the skulls."

"What!" The boy pictures the swift transformation on the warrior-angel's face, the shadow of alarm succeeded by relief. "And I was not here to protect you. But none of you are hurt?" he asks. His words sound high-strung, as if he walks a wire.

"Shaken and wary, but well enough," Lucia tells him.

"We are all in your debt, Harry," the Outpacer says.

"And here is an ironic consolation for us. When we go out again, we need not fear another ambush. That is one clear advantage of the destruction the fireball and red rain caused. There is such utter devastation out there, no one could find anywhere to hide for a covert attack."

"*Utter* devastation?" Lucia asks.

"Yes. You must prepare yourselves.

"But we will be safe, I think, if we wear the masks the doctor gave us, and if we make haste. If we hurry, we can reach terrain untouched by the fireball by nightfall perhaps.

"We must be resolute," he urges them. "Try not to be downhearted by what you see."

They stand and stretch. Chandelier helps to raise Bird Girl's head while Lucia slips the girl's gas mask gently over her face. Then she puts on her own.

The boy watches Candace put on hers. Then he and Harry help each other to fix the filmy masks carefully over their mouths and nostrils.

They set off with the Outpacer in the lead, bearing Bird Girl in his arms. Inch by inch, they make their way along the perilous ledge, trying to accustom themselves to breathing normally with the masks in place.

When at last they exit the cave, Chandelier's eyes begin to smart. He might as well cry, he thinks, and so blur to some degree the appalling ruin all around them. There is nothing left; not the least skeleton of a leaf. The air has a nasty orange tinge. They tread carefully, trying to avoid spots where the ash is still dangerously hot. Chandelier is especially cautious, not wanting to burn his woven silk boots.

It is a good thing that the masks make it so difficult for them to speak and hear each other clearly. For what could they say about this infinitely sad, immolated ground? To look at it, to think about it for any length of time, makes a hole in his brain into which twisted fiends rush, with faces he does not want to look upon.

"Be resolute and of good cheer." Whose voice does he hear? Harry's? The Outpacer's? Or is it Snake?

Who would say — "Be of good cheer"?

The boy begins to sing to himself under his mask as he walks, his hand beneath Harry's elbow. He makes up his song in which the words "*speranza*" and "good cheer" intertwine. It seems to him sometimes, on their long trudge northward, that Snake sings along with him.

Towards dusk, he hears the Outpacer cry out. "Just below us, in the valley — there, look. It is safe now. You can take off the masks."

Looking down where the Outpacer points, the boy sees his first fir trees. Their compelling shapes, like slope-shouldered beings with full bell-like skirts, make him want to laugh. This is the beginning of the north, he tells himself. He takes off his mask, wanting to speak this idea out loud and find out if he is right. But his lips are still numb, and he cannot make his mouth move properly. A wonderful scent fills his nostrils, which somehow makes the air brighter and wider. It is like an emerald song, he thinks. Essence of green. Snake will like this.

"Only a little further," the Outpacer encourages them. They move on, hungry and foot-sore, yet heartened by the sight of many more coniferous trees ahead. At last they reach a spot that the Outpacer judges to be safe and sheltered enough.

Together they scoop up cedar boughs on which to lay Bird Girl. She is so unlike herself the boy does not like to look at her for long. An unmoving and silent Bird Girl is like Nature undone. He thinks again of Snake, who had been present at the birth of time, and yearns for his guidance. But Snake does not come.

Nor does Snake return when Chandelier assumes his turn at the night watch, sitting cross-legged at the girl's side. Every few moments, he puts his ear near her mouth to assure himself she is still breathing. Whenever he hears a sound, he looks up, his muscles tensing, his hand ready to take up the thick cudgel that lies by him. He hears the Outpacer's soft whistle which reassures him it is only their protector making his circuit.

Chandelier feels the girl stir. She sits upright and looks about her wildly.

"Lola!" How sore her throat sounds, he thinks. He offers her water, but she pushes his hand away. "Where?" she demands.

He gets to his feet, intending to waken Lucia whom instinct tells him will be the better comforter. But Bird Girl grabs his wrist with a grip as forceful as it is unexpected. Her eyes lock on his and will not yield.

"Where is Lola?" He hears the animal urgency in the question, and is frightened by the invisible claw marks her other hand tears in the air. How can he refuse her an answer when she so burns to know? Then he thinks: what if the answer kills her? But such a truth did not kill me that fiendish morning, he reasons. And Bird Girl is stronger than I.

He kneels beside her and put his lips to her ear. He believes it will be less cruel to whisper Lola's fate. As he breathes the words through the tendrils of Bird Girl's hair, he feels her body stiffen. He is not ready for the inarticulate sounds that issue from some deep cavity inside the girl's body. "Oh. Oh." He recognizes his own voice weaving with hers in a plaintive song.

Her head strikes him repeatedly in the chest. She pummels his back with her fists. He puts his arm round her, and she writhes against this offer of comfort, writhes against him as he too grimaces, his jaw clenched and his eyes screwed shut. She writhes and coils and strikes inside his grip as Snake might writhe if he were caught.

And then he is there. "Kiss her," Snake hisses. "Kiss her full on the mouth as you would kiss me if I were in agony."

The boy grasps the girl hard in his arms and does as he is told. Her lips are so dry, they rasp against his. He manages to moisten her mouth with his tongue. His tongue touches hers, and there is Snake. Chandelier recognizes his mesmerizing electric charge.

And that is enough — Chandelier knows it was enough — to spell her into quietness for a time.

She gestures for water and he raises the bottle to her mouth. She asks him to hold her.

"Talk to me," she pleads, as he hugs her tightly. "Tell me a story to stop me thinking for a while." Chandelier tells her the story that is always foremost in his mind. He describes the Egg and why his father built it and what happened on that fateful morning.

Bird Girl listens and asks only: "Why did your father call it the Egg?"

And so Chandelier recounts the myth of origins that had captivated his father when he was himself a boy: "Night and the Wind made a cosmic egg, and out of that Egg came Eros, the god of Love, who carries the seeds of all things in his body."

Bird Girl does not laugh mockingly as the sewer people had when Chandelier told them this tale. They had held a knife to his ear lobe and throat. "Tell us a story, pale fright," they said. "Amuse us, or we'll cut you now."

He had told them and immediately felt unclean. Now the story seems to have found its right shape again. There is a gleaming place in his mind where it lives.

"And the god's wings?" Bird Girl prompts. "What were his wings like?"

"They were as glorious as the tail feathers of the male peacock and as wide as world," he tells her.

She nods, as if this response makes perfect sense and is exactly what she expected. And she sleeps, her hand still clutching his.

Chapter Thirteen
Harry Finds a Theatre Box

HARRY SLEPT BADLY, A WEIGHT OF doom upon his chest that was at times the Ancient Mariner's slain albatross out of Coleridge's poem, and at others the inert form of young Bird Girl. He woke often, a startled cry stopped in his throat, the smothering weight of the slaughtered bird of his nightmare hampering his breathing, its blood soaking through his shirt, making a gruesome band round his rib cage. This wetness was, he recognized on shaking himself properly awake, the sweat of fear. And because the night sky was coal-black without the least glint of starlight, and his every joint pained him, that pressure of doom upon his chest seemed to him the inescapable fate of all the world's innocent creatures. The blood-stained, snowy white breast. Harpoon-struck. Arrow-struck.

Although he is overjoyed to learn the girl spoke during the night to Chandelier, he still worries about the lingering effects of the poison. She is such a delicate-looking child. He yearns to pray. But because he has never been a conventionally religious man, he lacks the strict forms. He has done true obeisance only to the spirit of that place he cherishes most on earth: his beloved Antarctica of the Emerald Heart. So each time he wakes, it is her spirit he invokes: his Great Queen of the Southern Pole. He peers through the dark, to the spot near the fire where Chandelier sits, his thin frame taut as a bow, watching over the wounded girl. Harry whispers: "Is all well, boy?" And through the dark, catches the murmured "yes" he yearns to hear.

Now, as the light of a new day breaks, and the pressure on his bladder grows intolerable, Harry realizes anew just how much he has come to rely upon the boy. Most particularly in the mornings, when the pain in his limbs rankles and his vision fogs, Harry finds Chandelier's aid indispensable: the strong, young, supple body that bends so fluidly to help an old man to his feet; the willing hand cupped at his elbow as a gentle guide and reassurance; the sharp eyes that help him steer through underbrush and tangled branches to some place private enough where he can empty his bladder without indignity.

Harry loathes the ignoble disguise of old age, and daily enumerates its most humiliating aspects to himself as a mantra that keeps his anger fierce, and his will primed.

> *I hobble (on the best of days).*
> *I limp (on the worst).*
> *I stink.*
> *I dribble.*
> *I drool.*
> *My eyes exude gum like the amber sap of a fir tree.*
> *I am sometimes beset by tremors.*
> *I do not recognize my own flesh, which has grown thin and spotted.*
> *It hurts to piss.*

My spirit is not at home in this fumbling carapace.
I did not think it would be like this.
It hurts to piss.
I am not this.
I am not this.

Once, he had a young body, lean and hard. On land, he was a runner. He had been a fighter too. He had to be. He abhorred sensualism. He did not eat the flesh of animals. His stomach turned at the sight of charred steaks, and plates piled high with pink-tipped ribs. Throughout his life, Harry had remained true to his own moral imperatives. He thought it wrong to slaughter beasts in order that he could eat. His vegetarianism is likely one of the chief reasons he is still alive. His years make him an oddity these days. He is eighty-eight. There are few in this apocalyptic time who make it to fifty.

In the City, the most pitiless of the young had found his seamed face an affront. (Was there ever a time when to be old warranted respect? Was even to imagine such a time an old man's folly?) In the urban streets, he had crossed paths with the Vigilantes for Beauty. They were succinct, these glossy, perfect children. He would grant them that. "Your ugliness offends me old man," their leader said. He had prodded Harry's chest with an iron bar.

"It would please me to snuff you out," the vigilante captain said. "You're grotesque. Useless as a two-legged dog."

"Snuff away," replied Old Harry. And there was the worst of it, his recognition that he would welcome immolation at the hands of this cruel and beauteous youth. Indeed, that he would welcome death at anyone's hand.

Even the young man's gasoline can was an objet d'art. Against a background of black lacquer, dogs with sinuous bodies and long narrow heads sank their teeth into each other's flanks. These dogs, Harry noted as the young man waved the can in front of his face, had all their legs.

Harry closed his eyes and gritted those teeth he had left, readying himself for the pain. The first touch of flame, he speculated, might well stop his heart. He waited for the stench of the flung gas; the sound of the struck match. Which did not come. When he opened his eyes, the young vigilantes had gone.

At that instant, Harry realized just how pathological was the City's influence, and how his own will had sickened, exposed to this heartlessness. He had come to the City to seek a pension. He knew he was deserving. He had done long and faithful service, even if his employers had constantly ignored his findings. But by the time his savings ran out and he arrived in the City, he could not locate his former employers at all. Did such a department in such a ministry still exist? Was there indeed a government of any kind? And if there was not, then what agency was it that erected the sky-screens? Who was it that operated the omnipresent mechanical eyes that scrutinized every public toilet and alleyway, and the underground parking lots where hundreds slept nightly? Harry had taken shelter in one of these concrete bunkers where the concept of privacy was as archaic as the virtue of kindness. The stench of these places was unspeakable, but what could one expect with no running water and no means to dispose of human waste but purloined buckets?

The irony was that he had come to the City in an effort to preserve his dignity. With a pension, he could purchase false teeth to replace those he had lost. He would be able to bite again into the tart-sweet flesh of apples, and chew properly the coarse-grained bread he loved. He wanted to purchase a cane, a sturdy companion with a hook carved to fit his hand and a stout rubber tip. He had reached that time in his life when he would soon require three legs in order to make his way through the world. The devastating confrontation with the Vigilantes for Beauty decided him. He would use what strength and mental acuity he had left to walk and keep on walking. He wanted to perambulate, to perform a plain and decent human act. This would help him exorcise the worst of the City's malign influence, which had so undermined his spirit he had welcomed the chance to die. He could still walk, albeit slowly, and with pain as his constant taskmaster. He would make a decent progress toward the bracing north, and perhaps see again a silvery stand of birch.

Harry had no illusions about his failing body. He knew he would never dance again. Dancing had once been his delight. He had whirled and waltzed alone on the ice floor of the continent that had drawn him like the most magnetic of lovers. He had danced beneath the miraculous hoops of the ice bows, balanced on one leg, his arms stretched above his head, palms touching, fingers pointed, as he swayed in worshipful silence, before the sun pillars. He had leapt upon the ice in a frenzied primordial joy under a sunset that resembled molten metal and churning fire. He was extinguished. He was purified. He was born again and again in that crucible of sheerest, virgin cold.

He had tried sex and found it vastly wanting. He had "swung both ways" as they used to say (Was there anyone else left alive, he wondered, who remembered that foolish phrase?). But with neither man nor woman had he felt anything approaching the ecstasy that bound him to the Earth's southern pole. There are times when Harry is parachuted back into sacred memories so vivid, and with such astonishing rapidity, that he seems to inhabit again his own youthful body. Just as now, he stands amazed, and almost dizzy, feeling again his young body's roaring hot blood, every muscle primed for purpose. He recognizes the situation immediately.

It was 3:00 AM in Ushuaia, Tierra del Fuego. He was a twenty-four-year-old world wanderer, recently arrived on a merchant vessel. He was also blind drunk, and this was the last time he would ever to drink to excess. Although he did not know it then, as he swayed in a back alley, fumbling with his fly, desperate to pee — his life's epiphany was on its way. Mere days separated him from his first encounter with the incomparable White Queen who was to seize his soul.

Every one of those days in the Land of Fire brought its own dire trials. Later, these seemed to him both right and fitting. He had to prove himself worthy. Fate had prepared a plot for him, and like the initiates in ancient rituals, he must undergo gruelling tests of body, intellect, and spirit. If he passed, he would glimpse the holy of holies. And if he failed . . . But Harry had not failed. And the trials to test his fitness had been gruelling indeed. First, as he rocked in that dark alley over a steaming puddle of his own urine, he was set upon by thugs. Harry was young and strong. But he was also terribly drunk. He was alone, and there were three of them.

He was badly beaten, a rib and his left cheekbone cracked, and dark bruises laid upon his flesh that took on the most surprising shapes — the outlines of animals' heads and of the world's land masses. The White Queen's lineaments dominated his upper left thigh. Looking down at himself, he saw the pipe-like peninsula veering southwest that made the plum discolouration unmistakably Antarctica.

There were other trials before he could make the fateful trip south.

After the beating, he stumbled to an exposed stretch of beach where he lay in a stupor, perilously dehydrated by the excess of alcohol he had pushed through his system. By the time his rescuer appeared, Harry was already in danger, his concussion compounded by the disorientation of hangover.

She was swathed head-to-toe in old white flannel sheeting. Only her eyes were visible through a slit in the cloth woven round her face. He thought at first she was Death come to claim him, a kindly, white-figured Death who hid her ravaged features out of courtesy.

Certainly Harry felt ready to die. He had been in the clutches of delirium, where a swarm of devils trod and pricked his flesh, seeking ever-new and tender spots to press their searing brands. When he felt her cool compress on his parched lips, and became aware of her white form shading him from the sun, the emotions that heaved in his chest so overawed him that he came close to passing out again. First came the surge of hope, so fierce it was electrifying, and his tongue tried to move in his mouth, but could not. His entire being seemed to rise up in answer to her pity, her tender ministrations, and the consoling clucking sound she made as she knelt closer to tend to him. Her compassion washed over him and made him want to weep, not for himself, but because her succour restored his faith in humankind, and in some unquenchable spark of goodness that would endure no matter how brutish and callous the world might appear.

In her eyes, he believed he saw a most rare and beneficent light. Yet he was never actually able to see her full face. She kept it covered for his entire stay with her. He was probably only a few days in her white-washed room, with its rudimentary bed, table and chair, and the pallet on the floor where he lay, his bruised and battered flesh anointed with her salves. But he so thoroughly committed the room's dimensions, gradations of whiteness, and sloping shadows to heart, that it became a perfect eidolon of the healing sanctuary.

Harry fell in love with a woman who remained largely invisible to him. He could not even properly discern the shape of her nose, cheekbones and chin beneath the wrappings of thin cloth. He did see her hands, with their strange pigmentation, pale blotches against dun brown. Her eyes and eyebrows both had a dark lustre, and so in his semi-delusion, and later in moments of alert wakefulness, he imagined her stepping naked toward him out of the tumbled swathes of cloth, so consummately lovely that his loins were on fire, and his heart yearned to know and worship her. He plotted his love-making carefully. He would begin by kissing her feet; then attentively, sensually, cover every inch of her with kisses, and as their two bodies entwined, they would literally rise. Harry had believed in those days in levitation, just as fervently as he did in the insuperable powers of love. These were certainties he had inherited from his mother.

But he was never to be granted carnal knowledge of his saviour-nurse in Ushuaia. Harry was never to see her face, or her breasts, or even her naked feet. Once his flesh healed, and his vigour and equilibrium returned, he began to venture out after dark for brief rambles about the streets. But always, the locus of her white room and obscured beauty pulled him back, his heart brimming with an emotion that far surpassed mere gratitude, and his head buzzing with awkward phrases in his ragged Spanish. "*Te quiero. Te amo. Toda la vida.*" What were the magic words that would spring the hasp that had so far prevented their discovery, one of another? How was he to reach her?

The fact was they had never spoken. She tended him in utter silence. When needed, she gestured to show him her intent. It did not occur to him until his third night circling her sanctuary, that she might be mute. So young was he then, and so thoroughly besotted, he was convinced the heat of his passion could cure her, melt away whatever flaw had undone her voice. He rehearsed for himself, with growing delight, the flute-like sounds she would make when at last they were joined together. In his imagined hearing, her voice resembled birdsong, buoyant, unforced, and with a trill that drew from him a joyous laugh in response.

On the third night of his rambles, he found her door barred to him. At first, he thought it was a mistake. He knocked. He rattled the latch. He called to her through the square iron grille set high in her white-washed door. He called and called until one after the other, all the doors in the narrow street opened. Someone hissed. A rock caught him sharply between his shoulder blades, winding him. From inside the room, he heard her move: a drape of cloth whispering against the floor, a sigh so heavy it seemed to invade his own chest. He saw the flat of her piebald hand pressed against the grille; then she thrust her forefinger through, the tip of her nail narrowly missing his eye.

"*Vete*," she growled. "Go. *Allez. Ist genug.*"

Harry stood outside the door, chastened and chastised, a virile young man gone weak at the knees. Once again, Harry swayed in a Tierra del Fuego alley-way, this time because his heart was broken. He remembered childhood stories his mother had read him of people whose hearts cracked at the exact moment they experienced a crushing loss. This sound he had always imagined like the snap of dry tinder. He and his mother lived in the country, and one of his tasks as a boy was to gather kindling, and to break it so that it fit the belly of the stove. Now he felt it was he who was ready for the stove's belly. He stumbled off down the alley, looking back once to see if her finger was still thrust through the grille. He saw only a narrow, gloomy corridor, its separate doors barely distinguishable. This was an image he folded into memory, and reworked over the years, so that in his last glimpse of his saviour's street, her door stood out with a dazzling whiteness. Her threshold's ivory gleam was nothing less than an assurance of paradise.

Harry had no idea, as he stumbled over parched ground toward a hostel where he would decide his next move, that this was the crux of his own life's plot. He did not recognize then the significance of the trials he had just undergone, beaten, ill, broken-hearted, and how they had prepared him for his life's abiding passion.

Where was there for him to go next but south, to the ends of the earth? He was ignorant then: he pictured a continent bleak and unforgiving, in whose frigid glaciers he might see reflected the death of his own spirit. Spurned by the Tierra del Fuego healer and still grieving for his mother, he was a young man bent on self-annihilation, at least symbolically; on a mortification of the flesh in a land so long ice-locked, it had banished greenness.

These were his thoughts as he stood on the deck of the boat travelling south to an imagined glacial graveyard.

The appearance of the legendary bird was Harry's first sign he might be wrong. Its luminous whiteness, extraordinary wing span, and faultless sailing on the wind were all so sublime, it was the word "angel" leapt first to his mind. An angel, despite the hooked bill and the unfathomable eye which challenged him to recognize its primordial power. "I have seen God," the bird seemed to say to him. "I have been here since the first days of Creation."

Harry, who was mesmerized, did not doubt it. He knew a portent when he saw one. And so it was the albatross, emblazoned on the polar air, which ushered Harry into a transfiguring passion of the kind many people yearn for, but few find. From that welcoming omen, he progressed step by step through a land and seascape that filled his eye, smote his heart, and made him anew. He recognized he was blessed to have discovered his life's truth so early. He was one of those who are born to love a landscape far more than they ever could another person. The spell of the Great White

Queen was an inescapable bondage, and if in her service he sometimes experienced anguish and physical pain, he bore them willingly, for they were his fate and the making of him. After that first journey south, he could no longer conceive of who he was without her.

The first lung-full of her air hit his blood stream with a revivifying rush.

Within days of his arrival, he contracted himself to one of the scientific crews who were resident year-round in Antarctica. Twenty years later, he had himself become a specialist in the bitter business of mapping his Beloved's decline. But he long continued to nourish the hope that she would survive, for her glories were as infinite as her dangers. Harry never forgot that beneath her gleaming surface lay fissures that had swallowed down far better men than he.

He recognized he was fortunate. The Great Queen treated him more kindly than she did others. Unlike some of his colleagues, Harry's fillings never fell out once exposed to the frigid air; his wounds healed speedily where others' did not; and he was in no danger of the emotional wreckage that each year reduced several of their company to the proverbial "toast." There was nothing to be done for those unravelled by the rigours of the polar dark and barrens but send them home.

Harry was legendary for his staying power and ability to rise above the fractiousness that inevitably beset the base in the gruelling months of endless winter darkness. He was able to navigate successfully the schisms, cliques, and shifting pragmatic alliances. With rare exceptions, everyone liked and trusted Harry. On the other hand, his colleagues gave him lots of room. They instinctively recognized his need for solitude.

Thus he was seldom plagued by midnight chatterers, or the self-proclaimed party animals forever seeking some new way to "blow off steam." When Harry closeted himself away or ventured out to walk alone in the freezing blackness, some of his colleagues assumed he was working on a book, or a pet theory. The more romantic among them speculated that he nursed a broken heart. Only his immediate superiors guessed the truth: that Harry was so in thrall to the glacial White Queen, she had become the reason for his existence.

In extremis, he thinks. I was happiest at the farthest reach of the world. The last place to be mapped and explored. The last to be polluted. The first to disintegrate visibly. In extremis. Once, the ice of Antarctica was two miles thick. But a hole in the sky triggered a melt of her immaculate emerald-hearted ice.

Harry saw the ice go. At first, he was fired with zeal. His reports to his superiors contained warnings as dire as any Old Testament prophet's. He watched the Southern Ocean rise and feared for the fate of the world. He found himself caught in Noah's horrific dilemma. He perceived the Inundation was inevitable, but no one was listening. Gradually, his zeal turned to anger and then his anger to anguish. In extremis. His Beloved was disappearing and there was no way he could stop it happening. Increasingly, Harry could peer down into vast rents in her glittering surface and see her mystery crudely exposed.

Yet the more her drab rock heart was revealed, the more he loved the continent that had consumed over two thirds of his life. His passion was now inextricable from his grief. He had been in the grip of this thorny paradox once before, hypnotized by the inexorable power of beauty in decay. This was when he wandered round the murky maze of crumbling Venice, just a few years before the pressure of the rising Adriatic became too much and the city's rotting foundation at last gave way. Harry was still a young man then, and his fascination with the fragile, sodden city perplexed him deeply. By the time he visited Venice, the city's art treasures had been removed for safekeeping. It was always *aqua alta*. Harry walked the wooden trestles set above the flowing streets and saw everywhere the rude red brick exposed, the exquisite creamy façades of salmon, ochre, and olive fallen away in great patches, and black mould creeping up to the roof tiles. Was he privileged or cursed, he wondered, to see one of the most fabled cities on Earth in the throes of death, blighted and covered with sores? He was both, he realized, for there was no escaping either the adoration or the dread such an imminent death inspired.

When, so many years later, he witnessed his Queen of Continents wasting away, the adoration and the dismay were intensified to such a pitch, Harry felt that impossible thing: his heart moved in his mouth. And the words he spoke aloud shocked him, for he had not understood until that moment the full extent of his passion. Once spoken, these words become an incantation without which he could not begin his day. It was as if they were now written into his cells. Clone him and his twin would rise up in the morning and speak them. *Salve Regina. Exsulto stellam maris.*

His daily incantation summons an imaginary light that conceals the gaping wounds of Antarctica; an elusive balm that restores for one instant at dawn her primitive blinding-white glory, her immaculate being.

Harry guesses that Chandelier is able to see this worshipful light spilling off his lips each morning in company with the rising sun. The boy is insightful, trustworthy and kind, all most uncommon virtues in this dark time.

He thinks of Lola, and how willingly she yielded up what life she had left for the young Bird Girl's sake. Harry wonders if he is capable of such selflessness, if he would sacrifice himself to save Chandelier. He believes he would. But how can he say with certainty until the instant the demand was made? He hopes he would. Leave it at that. For he dearly loves the boy.

It is like the plot of an ancient drama, he thinks. The one dies that the other might live. And here am I, the old man of the piece, moving stiffly over a patch of ground, seeking a private place to piss. At last, he feels he has gone far enough. There is more fumbling, and more pain and some waiting which he could have done without. It does hurt him to urinate, but the relief is wonderful nonetheless. As wonderful as it had ever been.

Harry flexes his joints as best he can to ready himself for his journey back to their camp spot. With his bladder blessedly emptied, he is newly alert to the possibility that other dregs of humankind like the poison-archer might still be tracking them. Evil never comes singly, or such has been his experience. They must get out of this coniferous forest with its thickly swaying branches that wreck perspective. There were simply too many places a deranged individual could hide and launch an assault before you had time to clutch your most tender parts.

He yearns for a vista where the land is open to the sky and the view uninterrupted to the farthest point on the horizon. In Antarctica, the conduct of pure light through clear air allowed you to see extraordinarily far into the distance. You walked and you walked, but the object toward which you were headed seemed to get no closer. Many of his colleagues found this phenomenon frustrating and duplicitous. But for Harry, it was evidence of a benign infinity.

For a moment, he is immersed again in his memories. His young, solitary self whirls in an ecstatic dance upon a gleaming ice-field. Thus Harry fails to watch carefully where he is going, and trips on a clutch of tangled crawling vine. He pitches forward, only saving himself from falling headlong by grasping a stout overhead branch. But in that wrenching movement, his shinbone strikes a rock-hard obstruction. It is the unexpectedness of the accident, as much as the pain, that make him howl.

What he has hit is a box, he sees, a cursed box made of what looks like cedar. Harry lowers himself gingerly to the ground, and touches the tender spot on his leg, feeling for a fatal break or splinter. For what recourse would an old man with a broken leg have but to ask the Outpacer to strangle him quickly, with a length of Lucia's rabbit snare perhaps? He could not lay the burden of his infirmity on them.

He is relieved to find that his bone seems intact, with the exception of a small lump rising on the taut skin, and a soreness that would spread into one of the blue-black bruises he had so often sported in his youth. So why do his eyes tear at the solicitude of the boy and Lucia and the Outpacer as they circle him with their urgent questions, and Lucia gently examines his injury? Is he surprised he is loved?

He stands on his good leg, assisted by Chandelier, and watches as Lucia and the Outpacer tug the offending box from out of the hollow where it lies, half obscured by the root and thick vine that sent him tumbling. Are they all hoping for a hoard of dried foods, he wonders: apricots, slices of apple and pear, wrinkled raisins whose goodness would enliven their blood?

The hasp closing the box swings back easily, as does the lid itself. Both Harry and Chandelier start as Lucia cries out in alarm.

For an instant, craning forward to peer into the box, Harry sees the same ghastly sight that has upset Lucia. Staring up at him from beneath a layer of gauzy fabric are three decapitated heads, the mouths stretched wide open as if in some last plea for mercy. He blinks and sees the truth: that these heads are in fact masks. The Outpacer picks one up from beneath its flimsy veiling. Harry now sees clearly its high glaze, the dark cavity of the gaping mouth, the black, elongated eyes and pronounced bulbous forehead.

This is not a face one warms to, he thinks. Yet he recognizes its power. He knows that the sounds issuing from that cavernous mouth with its reddened lips would likely transfigure a man's life; or at the very least, make him twist away in fear.

"Papier mâché," Lucia says. Her initial repulsion has apparently shifted to curiosity, as she touches one of the masks delicately on forehead, cheek, and chin. "How many are there?" she asks.

The Outpacer takes out the top three masks, two female and one male, all with shining black hair and lustrous eyes. Underneath, he finds a slatted shelf. This he lifts out to reveal three more masks also swathed in gauze. Two of these have male faces: one young with a sleek beard; the other grizzled, and with drooping eyelids. The third mask of this set is a woman with exceptionally wide cheekbones and a broad sculpted nose. Like the first three masks, this group all have the same wide-stretched mouths; the same bulging foreheads.

There is a third shelf in the box, and lifting it, the Outpacer uncovers two pairs of wings, made of white linen and wire. A fine hand, applying an iridescent blue paint, has created the illusion of profuse, overlapping feathers.

Lucia claps her hands as the Outpacer opens and folds the wings to mimic the progress of a butterfly.

"Will they divert Bird Girl, do you think?" The Outpacer folds the wings away and restores the masks to their original order. He hoists the chest to take back to their camp site, while Lucia and Chandelier help Harry whose leg is beginning to throb badly. Harry takes a paradoxical comfort from the fact he can still feel pain. He is far from dead yet.

When they get back, they see a pitiful sight. Bird Girl sits on the ground, hugging herself and rocking back and forth. She bites at her knuckles. She rocks and sobs and sometimes plucks at the flesh of her forearms.

"She will not be comforted," says Candace, who sits opposite the distraught girl. "She must go through it," Candace adds. "There is no other way."

This strikes Harry as the wisest thing he has ever heard Candace say. Yet he wishes desperately he had something to offer the girl to help her through her grieving.

He recalls how his mother had always baked fruit pies for funeral gatherings. As a boy, he had often wondered about this strange urge to feed those who were mourning. Only now, in his eighty-eighth year, as he watches the stricken girl rocking herself upon the earth, does he comprehend at last the significance of his mother's midnight labour, kneading and rolling out the pastry, and dabbing the flawless pie tops with milk. Finally, he understands that her baking had been an act of communion; that her gift of the tart and the sweet and the wheat-based crust was an affirmation of life's goodness.

Oh taste and be! He hears his mother's voice.

If he were a conjuror, Harry knows just what he would produce out of thin air for Bird Girl: a tray of chocolates, both white and dark, in fantastical shapes to make her smile.

"Taste and be," he would say, as he enticed her away from her agony with his solemn gift of sweetness. "Taste and be. And then gather up her spirit into your keeping."

Chapter Fourteen
Cravings

WHEN WAS IT, HARRY WONDERS, THAT he lost his craving for fine food? Like his sexual urge, it seemed to have disappeared altogether. But he certainly feels no less human in consequence. These days he eats enough to keep going. It sometimes surprises him what meagre nourishment he requires. He sees this as a great advantage. Even with what the gifted forager brings in, food is scarce. The five others are young, with sharp physical needs and desires. His tiny daily repast barely cuts into their supply. So where exactly is he drawing his energy? Harry believes he feeds on his memories of the two places he loved most in his life. And on hope, as well.

Often, his hope centres on a bird. Harry is not particular. It need not be a bird with a melodious song, or indeed any song at all. A croak, a caw, a cacophonous blast from a stretched throat, he would rejoice at any such sound as long as its maker was a bird. This is his dearest wish: that before he dies, he might once again see and hear a bird. It is not just a selfish wish, for Harry is certain that the bird's return will signal the world's redemption.

This certainty is rooted in primeval awe. When he was a young boy, a heron passed so low over his head he was momentarily enveloped by its shadow. Was the initial chill in his blood an atavistic fear he might be preyed upon and eaten? But all his anxiety dissolved as soon as he looked up at the angular silvery grey form sailing over his head. The bird folded itself sideways and landed in the stream beside him, with such a slow and elegant stateliness it seemed it was lowered lovingly, by some unseen power, on wires beaten thin as gold. He watched the heron make its way through the water, mesmerized by its measured cross-wise step. He did not think he blinked, yet suddenly the bird disappeared, as if it had passed through a door imperceptible to any human eye.

"Secret" and "mysterious" were the words that came to him. Years later, shaken to the marrow by his first sight of the monumental albatross, he had added the word "holy." Harry was certain — absolutely certain — that the spirit of creation moved in birds. Which was all the more reason to mourn the species after species he had seen disappear in his own lifetime.

So the hope of their return lives on in Harry, nourishing him as he nourishes it. What better food could there be, he often asks himself, for an ancient man in a cursed world? He realizes this hope that now flourishes in him is a force reborn. For many years, he had thought his capacity for hope was just as extinct as the many species he mourned. Harry knew it was Chandelier who had wrought this change. He looks at the boy and is amazed by the vigour of the child's selfless love. He does sometimes worry that he is undeserving of the devotion of such a rare and luminous boy. But what Chandelier gives, he gives freely, and Harry daily rejoices that fate has brought them together in his final frail years.

Since leaving the ruins of the Egg, Chandelier has himself discovered just how fluid is love's power. With Harry, his deep affection is sometimes a son's, sometimes a father's, and sometimes an acolyte's. With Bird Girl, he is becoming both brother and dear companion. With Miriam he had been son and lover in one, a bond that he nevertheless knew to be faultless. But at the core of their passion he sensed an unsettling power, like the live, quivering energy that jolts him if he mistakenly touches Snake when his guide is deep in thought. Chandelier understands this dangerous facet of the bond he had with Miriam through his nerves, rather than his mind. It was somehow a love too intense to endure, or be endured.

There is not a day when he does not think of Miriam, often with a sharp-toothed desire that perturbs him. Because he has not yet learned to masturbate, he is sometimes in pain. He has found a way to turn his thoughts from the demands of his sore need, and this is to focus on how Miriam mothered him. In particular, he concentrates on recalling the foods she prepared for him, with all the wonderful tastes he had not known existed. For like Harry's restricted fare in Antarctica, Chandelier's diet in the Egg had relied heavily on products freeze-dried and frozen. His father was uneasy about foods that might be genetically corrupted, and chose the nutritional elements of his family's diet carefully. On the other hand, their meals were strictly functional, with little to distinguish one substance on their plates from another. Food was fuel,

Chandelier's father maintained. He had long ago turned his back on anything resembling Epicureanism.

Miriam could not have been more opposite. All her life, she had derived the greatest pleasure from sampling the diverse foods and cuisines that were still available in a badly fractured world. During her life in the City, she had spent many happy hours preparing meals to make her friends smile and believe again in innocent pleasures. This was why one of her chief delights in living with the Silk People was their pair of goats. She rejoiced in these animals' robust health, their sprightliness and silkiness, their natural hauteur and their lustrous eyes. Miriam learned, through much trial and error, to make rounds of creamy cheese from their milk. This delicacy was shared among the Silk People, and the sharing itself had become ritualized, with a chant of thanks to Miriam for her patient labour, and to the goats for being what they were.

Miriam had fed Chandelier morsels of her precious cheese in her efforts to reclaim him from the trauma that made him freeze, burn, and shake by turns. She drew on the full range of her sensuous store to save him: the heat of her body, the warmth of her voice and breath, the prodding touch of her tongue, and the enticing tastes of as many different foods as she could conjure up. And at last, it was the sliver of ripe goat's cheese on his tongue that brought him back from the brink. He opened his eyes in surprise and Miriam's hand flew to her heart for she saw that he was saved.

Chandelier remembers still the delicious shiver along his spine, the way the buds on his tongue contracted, and how his mouth — or was it his entire body? — yielded to the creaminess, tartness, and sweetness. He heard a wild cry in his blood. Here was a whole realm of human experience of which he had been ignorant. And at that instant, inside Miriam's tent of parachute silk, he thought he glimpsed his father's shadow.

Chandelier had an inkling then of the boundless, dazzling and various world of which he had been deprived — a world that made his soul dance with joy. He did understand that his father had kept him apart from this world in order to protect him. It had been a deprivation founded in love. Just as it was love that prompted Miriam to feed him a morsel of goat's cheese, an enticement that showed him the way out of his wretchedness and near-madness. Love had saved him, and the taste of love had saved him, and never afterward could he separate the two.

Candace too, believes that food does not truly nourish the body unless love goes into its preparation, and the serving and the eating, and the thanks for all of these. She means by this the love of community; not the lesser, inevitably corrupting, personal love. She has planned in great detail the foods on which her ideal community would thrive. At the centre — of the table and of every meal — was bread. Round, wholesome granary loaves. Never, ever baguettes, whose shape she has always found offensive.

At night, when she is most aware of her constant hunger, she takes comfort in picturing herself at the head of a long table, covered by the fine linen cloth that lies folded now at the bottom of her pack. She will break off portions of the perfect bread with just-scrubbed hands, and distribute the pieces clockwise. She sees the glowing faces of the members of her fellowship — a word she treasures, which she has carried over from another time and kept safe. This vision generates a contentment that helps keep her warm as she lies curled at night on the hard ground. Her limbs relax as she recites to herself the various stages of the bread-making in which every community member would share: the vigorous kneading, the hopeful rising, the careful baking, the blessed eating. In the bread's dense, moist texture, she would taste both optimism and love. "Scrumptious" is the word she hugs to herself just before sleep comes. Scrumptious.

This is not a word that the Outpacer would ever utter except ironically. Food has always ranked rather low on his scale of sensuous pleasures. When he eats, he eats sparingly. He cannot abide gluttons. The tastes he favours tend to be dramatic: like the explosion of red-hot chillies producing a fire in his mouth that verges on pain. He yearns some evenings for a slim-necked bottle of pepper sauce from the Pleasure Zone. He could so easily have slipped one into the capacious pocket of his monk's robe when he was leaving the City. Then he could experience that simple joy of a few drops of flame upon his tongue. This was his familiar, beloved haunt: the land of pleasure-pain.

Or is that really what he yearns for? He wonders now if he wanted that fire in his mouth to restore his innocence, burn away all that he had been and done that was corrupt so that he could love at last, as other, far more virtuous beings loved. As Chandelier appears to love Bird Girl, selflessly and without taint.

Bird Girl had grown up in a household where everyone ate only what was wholesome. The New Amazons forbade self-indulgence of any kind. Food strengthened muscles, bones and blood, nerves and brain. Although she bristled at their expectation she would become a full-fledged Amazonian fighting machine, Bird Girl tried to keep to their dietary strictures. She ate frugally.

Intellectually, on the other hand, she knew herself to be greedy. She was ravenous for other realities, insights, and perspectives. Outside The New Amazons' warehouse fortress, a multiplicity of worlds beckoned. She wanted to see and taste and touch them all. And because she was young and eminently desirable, she found few doors in the City barred to her. Some of these doors she later dearly wished she had never entered. But others gave her access to the realms of learning she had dreamed of so long.

After the fee was paid and the deed was done, she had some clients — most often foreign — who chose to pay for her company for another hour or so because she was so frankly appreciative of their erudition and cultured sensibility. Bird Girl had gleaned a lot simply by putting on her round-eyed, little girl all-agog face. She had acquired, for example, a short history of porcelain; and learned about the symbolism of white jade, the handling of rogue elephants, and the search for the elusive thylacine. She heard poems in languages where she understood not a word, but whose sounds made her contemplative or happy nonetheless.

And there had been a man — an older, slender, Chinese man — who had covered her nakedness with an embroidered scarlet silk gown, and slipped jewelled silk slippers on her feet. He made her a vegetarian meal, working rapidly and gracefully, and set it before her and watched her eat. She could summon up every detail still: the crispness of lotus root and water chestnut, the dense goodness of the bean curd flavoured with ginger, pepper, sesame oil, and soy. And best of all were the lily buds and black mushrooms, with their yielding fleshiness and mysterious taste and scent of earth.

She exclaimed in delight — the food seemed to her so perfect. It struck her that respect and wonder had gone into its making, and so she ate slowly, aware that this was somehow an act of worship. Her Chinese client told her the dish was called "Buddha's Delight." He described for her the island of P'u-t'o, a nature sanctuary under the protection of the Goddess of Mercy. On this island in the China Sea, no life had ever been taken, he said, not even that of the smallest fish. P'u-t'o was home to the fantastic barking deer and the monks who lived according to the precepts of the goddess. They were compassionate, vegetarian, enlightened, and pacific.

Did such a place truly exist, she asked him. He assured her it did. The proof, he said, was in this dish he had prepared for her, in the tastes and textures she savoured. She wanted so much to believe him.

Consonance. Purity. Mercy. Yes, she thought she had been able to taste all these things. She hopes, always, that one day she might do so again.

Lucia's food craving has more to do with the making than the eating. She yearns to stand again over a simple, solid stove, gripping a wooden spoon as she stirs and watches the live, rolling essence of polenta on the boil. It could be a dangerous process, when the mixture in the pot turned volcanic, heaving, peaking, and spitting. One had to take great care.

Making polenta also required a muscular arm and much patience. Strength went into the stirring as the mixture grew gradually thicker. Getting the right consistency took time. But when at last the ideal blend was achieved, the corn meal and boiling water, butter and Parmesan transformed themselves into a substance that resembled molten gold. It flowed from the pot, ready for its metamorphosis into squares or rounds or heaped mounds.

As a child, Lucia found the entire process thrilling, but she had loved especially that final stage of shaping and moulding what was fluid and golden into perfect forms. Whether this fascination was the origin of her desire to work with clay, she was uncertain. Yet she did not doubt that from these simple components of bubbling water, yellow grain, labour and patience, there emerged a food both sensuous and wholesome. Polenta was part of her heritage. It sustained life and helped to keep it holy.

More and more these days, she yearns for this kind of sustenance to replenish her sense of well-being, for she is deeply troubled. She is plagued too, by what she sees as a sore moral failing: her duties as principal forager are starting to weigh heavily upon her.

Chapter Fifteen
Lucia Consoles a Sinner

WE HAVE SO MUCH FOR WHICH to thank good fortune. *O buona Fortuna*. Bird Girl has regained her strength. Her breast wound is knitting together well, although she will always have a scar. Grimoire, her heinous tracker, lies dead in the black water of the cave's abyss. By the workings of chance, and the doctor's help and advice, we all survived the fire-storm and the poisoned gas.

I wake some mornings and taste a different air, cold, blue-spangled.

What I cannot control is the circling of my thoughts, which drain my energy and make me sometimes irritable with the others. I go round and round this same conundrum that obsesses me: this folly I committed and the stain it has left upon my spirit.

Why did it happen? This is the question I ask myself a hundred times a day, although I know the answer perfectly well.

It happened because he had the face of a god, and hands like an angel-artist, with long, slender fingers.

It happened because I was stone turned to water.

He closed in on me in the wood. I was on my knees, gathering moss for my next menstrual cycle. I stood to stretch and ease the cramp in my thighs and back. Thus he surprised me, with my arms high above my head, and my back arched.

On his padded feet, with their soiled matted fur, he had approached me with an animal's stealth. I, who am never taken unawares, was for once absolutely undone. I understood then what it actually means to be petrified by fear. I was shackled by fear, every muscle frozen with the exception of my frantic heart. I recognized that I was under a spell; that doom had overtaken me despite my best efforts to outrun it. For here he was in all his corrupt and stinking flesh — one of the Rat-Men I had managed to elude in the City. The wry, useless thought came to me that I had escaped death-by-plague in the metropolis only to have it find me hundreds of miles away in a dismal forest. I struggled to scream so that I could warn the others, but no sound came.

I knew the Rat-Man's weapon would be a syringe, the tip encrusted with the blood of recent victims. Once the needle plunged into my skin, the best I could hope for was a speedy death, and that my polluted corpse would not infect my companions. As he came closer, his ugliness froze my blood, as well as my muscle and bone. Had I been able, I would have flinched away from the unspeakable head on human shoulders: the narrow, thrusting snout and the slit eyes set too close together and too near the coarse tongue visible through pronged teeth. I wanted to weep and send a great lamentation heavenward. I had loved beauty so. Why must I have this loathsome hybrid as my last sight on earth?

The graceful legs and elegant hands made the monstrous creation even more abominable. I was in anguish not just because of my approaching death and my inability to alert the others, but also at witnessing this absolute eclipse of hope for the world. I believed I was looking at the future: a repugnant experiment that had succeeded only too well. I had not thought it possible that the maggot of evil could glut itself any further. Yet here the proof stood before me.

I strove to ready myself for the death that now seemed imminent. I concentrated hard, for what I wanted above all was that my last thoughts be consecrated to those things in which I had been most blessed: my art, my family, ancestral images of umber Tuscan hills and orderly medieval towns, and the language of the great Dante that so often verged on music. *Per una selva oscura.*

I will die here, I thought, in a dark wood. My life ends where Dante's journey began. The rat's head came so close I could see the pores around its nostrils. The monster waved its exquisite hands; then folded them together, the fingertips touching in a classic attitude of prayer. I found this gesture so defiled I had to shut my eyes. I could no longer bear to look at this desecration of the human form with its heartless pantomime of faith. I closed my eyes and willed myself to picture the glazed red roofs of an ancient Italian hill-top town. These roofs, with their half-cylindrical tiles, seemed to undulate under my gaze. Here was the wave — the flawless, enduring red-glazed wave — that would carry me from this begrimed, corrupt world of mortal flesh to Keats's realm of ethereal things and rarefied truth and beauty.

Did I murmur aloud some words in Italian as a kind of benediction to myself? Even now, I am uncertain. I steeled myself to look again at the monster. I knew I must show courage in these final moments of my unwinding fate.

The instant I opened my eyes, the miracle occurred.

The Rat-Man tugged and plucked at the fur on its neck and the entire head fell away. The revealed face was of such extraordinary beauty, I gasped. Now I recall that sound with acute shame for it seems with that instinctual reaction I unconsciously invited all that happened afterwards.

Yet the transformation I witnessed was so astounding, it was impossible for me to keep silent. It was like seeing the heart of a myth enacted — a myth that was also the highest truth. How seamlessly the story unfolded: the ugly rodent turned into a young man glowing with health, his dark eyes and hair lustrous as polished jet. His lips were full; his smile beguiling. I saw a promise of paradise in those eyes and in that mouth. In another age, I might have fallen to my knees worshipping. Now I sighed and moaned — a sweet moan born partly of relief.

Did he misinterpret that sound?

"*Donna mi prega*," he whispered. And again: "*Donna mi prega*."

I was not aware that I had asked anything at all. But by that point, it was already too late for thought.

How exactly did it happen? Why do I feel compelled to go over this repeatedly, movement by movement? Why am I drawn to relive, scene by scene, the shameless spectacle of myself in the throes of desire? Is it because I still desire him, despite my distress at what I have done?

He told me his name was Guido Santarcangelo.

His beautiful mouth sought out the throbbing pulse at the base of my throat. The touch of his lips was a tease and a torture to me. I was recalled to the narrow bed of my adolescence, where I lay in chaste longing, waiting for the zephyr to part the thin curtains, and move over my body with a gentleness that made me flush and tremble.

Did I moan? "*Donna me prega*," he whispered. I revelled in his warm breath in my ear, and those luscious sounds born of my ancestral blood — "*Bella. Bella donna. Donna me prega.*"

My mouth opened to his. My back arced toward him so that my blouse brushed the taut cloth of his shirt. I did what my body bid, following where it led. But was this action wanton or pure? Am I wanton? But I must not vacillate. I know the answer.

"Enter me." Did I say this aloud?

"*Donna me prega.*"

"Enter me." Yes, I said this. I urged him on.

We undid my blouse so that my breasts were fully exposed to his hands and his mouth. I was overcome by the tumult of my own desire. I felt both torrential and verdant, as if petals flowed from my lips and from my fingers and toes. A single thought filled my mind: I had discovered a new meaning for the word "god."

While his hands cupped and stroked my breasts, his lips and tongue played over my belly and then down, as I helped him to draw down my long skirt. His hands and tongue sought out that part of me I had thought no man would ever touch. The play of his tongue on my flesh took me to the verge of ecstasy. I cannot deny that this was so. His tongue thrust deeper. My mind was a whirl of marvellous shapes: fluid sculptured forms made and yet to be, and always foremost, his beautiful face that rivalled the most sublime of Donatello's. I felt I stood on the balcony of a high tower in a hill-top town, looking out toward a glittering sea. I heard a song that was the coursing of my own blood, and of his. Surely this music came from the blood of our ancestors, making their claim?

I saw the perfect, black-haired child.

I cried out sharply, for his fingers had discovered my hymen.

The pain brought me to my senses. I was filled with self-disgust. What was I was doing behaving like a slut? I did not know this man and I stood naked before him, with his fingers inside me. I had fallen as low as the performers on the sky-screens, with lust driving me, and only lust.

"Stop," I told him. "Stop!" But my panic and self-disgust made me go further and I dug my nails so deeply into the flesh of his forearm that I drew blood.

He winced, pulled away and looked at me with hatred. Or so I thought.

"*Mi scusi*," he said. But truly I did not believe he was sorry. His words sounded hollow to me.

He began to dress rapidly. I could see his hands were shaking.

"*Mi scusi. Mi scusi*," he repeated.

He began telling me of danger, of a ball of poison gas in the sky that threatened us even as he spoke; of how it was imperative he get back to his duties. I wondered if he might be more than a little mad. But he was so insistent I began to believe him.

"You must hurry. I am going now to warn your friends. This danger I tell of you is real. Believe me! You must flee this place. Promise me you will do this."

I watched him race away from me through the wood; saw how he stumbled briefly as he pulled the hideous rat face over his own. Never before had I felt so sullen of body and spirit. I cleaned myself perfunctorily with a clump of moss because his probing fingers had made me bleed a little, and dressed as quickly as I could. I felt I put on clothes of shame. And I cried out in anguish.

I was amazed at what I had done. I had come so close to throwing away my chastity. I had *urged* a stranger to penetrate me. *Enter me.* I shuddered at the thought of my utter immodesty.

When I saw him again at the stone house, I could not meet his eye. My shame made me sluggish and despairing. I seemed not to know myself at all. For one unforgivable instant, I considered staying behind, letting the ball of poison gas find and exterminate me. It was an instant only, and I expelled the thought as craven and unworthy. I shook myself and stretched, striving to reclaim the body that was mine, and mine alone.

Once we were again on the road, in flight from the poison gas and the killing red rain, I tried to recover my habitual resolute purpose. I tried as well, not to think at all. I welcomed the familiar sensations of being foot-sore, the honest ache in my thighs and in my back; even the way in which thirst prickled like a thing alive in my throat. Our steady pace, the comforting reality of my body moving through space, the willing bearing of burdens (sometimes Lola, and always, containers of water and my own personal pack) helped to calm me.

I concentrated on images of the place I hoped one day to find: an environment untainted, with an abundant source of fine clay, where I could work and live in good faith with human and animal companions. I tried not to dwell on Guido Santarcangelo or to demean myself for what I had done. Regret was pointless, and a drain on my energy and spirit.

I turned my attention to Lola, who had begun to utter little cries in her sleep as she rode upon Bird Girl's back. I stroked the old woman's hand as we walked, and this effort to ensure Lola's comfort also helped restore me to myself. In this way I managed to walk a good half-mile, without a single thought of Guido Santarcangelo, or how my wantonness might undermine my strength and my daily duties to the others.

Then the dreadful thing happened. I saw Bird Girl fall, and the arrow lodged in her breast.

After the firestorm, even through the rawness of Bird Girl's grieving, I managed to fend off my own morbid thoughts. My worst lapse was when we took refuge in the dank cave with its dark cleft of heaving water. I looked down into that underground river and saw my sinfulness mirrored there. I faltered badly at that point, thinking myself sordid and tainted. It is still a struggle, but so far I have succeeded in keeping my consternation to myself. When images intrude — too bright, too lush, and definitely too hot — of all I did in that clearing, I counter them with my memories of dawn-work at my wheel.

In these recollections of my dearest task, I find the balm I need for my troubled spirit: the chaste sensation of handling the cool, moist clay; the thrill of sensing the pulse of yearning in the sleek, spiralling stuff upon the wheel. Some day, when I come at last to a place where the soil yields me a fine, workable clay, I will try to sculpt Lola's sacrifice. Yes, even the final terrifying rictus. Fleeting, subtle forms come to me, whose achievement I know will elude me time and again. I long ago learned to accept the likelihood of repeated failure. What matters most is the rich blessing of a state I sometimes enter where I am no longer myself, but a channel for an unseen force, potent and good.

Through the passion of sculpting, I know it is possible to slip the confines of self and fly; then return, stronger and purified, ready to work the deepest seams of solitude and honest labour. By contrast, my one experience of sexual passion left me feeling weak, grimy, and compromised. I soared briefly, yes. But the descent was abrupt and painful.

A single nasty thought continues to hammer in my brain: that I have transgressed against myself and ruined my own wholeness by inviting a man to enter me. Why had I cheapened myself in this way after all those years of caution?

This is what blind, eruptive passion does. I find myself thinking often now of the victims of Pompeii, and the hot lava that smothered them and moulded them, making their agony immortal. Some of these victims were found in brothels, although I was not told this as a child. The old aunts of course had postcards depicting the dead at Pompeii and my stomach would lurch whenever the images of those lava-caked victims appeared. I experienced a similar queasiness when I first saw the masks in the theatre box. I dislike their high glaze, their heartless eyes, and the brittleness of their manufacture. I find their bulging foreheads unnerving. But it is their cavernous black mouths that repel me most. Is it because these openings (are these beings singing, howling, or wailing?) remind me of my own dark cleft where Guido thrust his fingers?

The fact is that I still hate to look at these masks. Whenever Bird Girl takes hers out, I have to turn my face away.

Bird Girl's wound has healed well enough for us to move on. She is insisting that we take the theatre box and its contents with us. I keep trying to make her see sense; that the box is far too cumbersome and too heavy; that we would all soon weary of carrying it. As Bird Girl frowns and stamps her foot, I realize that I am the one who is weary. It is only then it strikes me how uncharacteristically bone-tired I am, yet simultaneously restless.

"But we must take everything. We just have to," Bird Girl pleas. Harry, Chandelier, and Candace all look at me in silence.

"Let's mind-weave," Candace says. My teeth clench at this saccharine phrase. I imagine her simpering, yet cannot bear to look at her. "Surely," she urges, "we can come to a compromise?"

I am concerned that the others are all thinking me intransigent, and insensitive to Bird Girl's needs.

"Yes," I say, as graciously as I can manage, "a compromise." And so we agree that Bird Girl and Chandelier will take the diaphanous wings to which they have become so attached for their pantomimes, and that we will each carry one of the masks.

"Six of us. Six masks," Bird Girl reiterates. "Six and six. And how light they are," she adds, plucking up one of the female masks and waving it about, before holding it up to her face.

I have to avert my gaze from the austere, haughty features, but the mask's censorious, heavy-lidded eyes pursue me nonetheless. I force myself to return the stare of this other face that seems to float in front of Bird Girl's own. I make myself study the cunning moulding of the papier mâché visage, the boldly realistic colouring, the crowning mass of coiled ebony hair, thick and shining, the pale bronzed-gold complexion which in a more cruel light, might appear jaundiced. It is a heartless face. A face, I am sure, that would have smiled to see the arrow pierce Bird Girl's breast. But could the muscles of that mouth ever move, even in the mask-maker's imagination? Or must it always be frozen in that black and gaping O?

I cannot help my reaction. My instinct tells me that these theatre masks harbour some unearthly and perhaps unsavoury secret. Yet what could I do but acquiesce to the girl's urging? It is true the mask is light-weight enough. The object adds no great extra burden, once stored in my pack. As we get ready to depart, I am careful to put my woman's mask in a large pocket separate from the one in which I kept the poet's life mask. I do not want them touching, or even proximate. I take care as well, to ensure the eyes in the harshly gleaming face stared outward, rather than at my back.

When I have finished, I see Bird Girl looking at me quizzically.

"Are you all right, Lucia?"

"Of course."

Bird Girl's brow furrows; then she turns to join Chandelier who is helping Harry massage his legs, in preparation for our journey onward.

Had I sounded impatient or churlish? I am ashamed of this new shortness of temper that sometimes infiltrates my words, and of my disinclination to forage for as long and as far afield as usual. The guilt is like a thorn lodged in my brain. I keep thinking I have harmed myself irreparably; that I am no longer what I was.

I hoped our continued trek northward would help to steady me and come to terms with my own failing. But after four days' steady walking, I am still in turmoil. By the time we set up camp tonight, my thoughts were once again a storm I am endeavouring to settle.

I try seeking comfort from memorized words of Keats's letters that I love in particular. "My solitude is sublime. The roaring of the wind is my wife and the Stars through the window pane are my children." Yet these words, which I have cherished for so many years, no longer bring me comfort because I have squandered my own precious solitude. I have abandoned myself to lust and am no longer worthy of the poet's idea of the sublime. The glinting stars I see above me seem fixed upon me in judgement.

At this thought fear takes hold of me, feeding on my every cell. Sleep will not come now. I have no choice, despite the dangers of the night-forest, but to get up and walk. I know I am far more likely to shake loose the needling remorse if I am moving through the surrounding dark. There is a moon, sometimes hidden and sometimes fully revealed, and I take this to be a good sign. As I walk, always keeping our camp-fire in sight, I almost immediately feel my hope renewed. I begin to make plans of building a home of blocks of clay, a kind of protective shell for myself. I picture a dwelling shaped like a beehive, with rounded windows for looking out and letting the pellucid blue air in.

I keep treading in a rough circle, with our campfire as its centre. My right hand is near the knife strapped to my thigh, and I make my way cautiously and quietly. When an odd bleating sound comes out of the dark, I am thus able to stop, and set my foot down again soundlessly.

I stand still, my body all attention, and take out my knife.

The bleating comes again, then a groan apparently wrenched out of deepest misery, and then a sob. There follows a sizzling sound, as if someone has laid a brand upon the night air. And then again: the pathetic bleating, the groan, the sob.

I recognize the voice that utters these sounds. But they so obviously belong to some private ground of pain, I am reluctant to intrude.

Then I smell the iron scent of blood. This smell, together with the human bleating and the sizzling upon the air, all come together in a picture I find unendurable. I have to intercede.

When I come upon him, I am appalled by what I see. The moon has emerged to reveal his nakedness. His burlap gown lies heaped at his feet. His mouth is twisted in agony, ruining his lean, wolfish beauty. The shadows under his eyes look like indelible stains left by years of bleeding or weeping. In his right hand he holds the viper-slim whip, twined with what look like stinging nettle and burrs.

It is harrowing to look at what he has done to his body. Yet I know I must. I cannot begin to guess the number of wounds he has inflicted on himself. Stripes, gashes, lacerations — some festering and some scabbed over and reopened by the lash — and blood running black in the moonlight. Never had I imagined that this was the secret the Outpacer hid beneath his robe. I wince to think of the burlap rubbing against his ulcerated flesh. It is all intolerable, as intolerable as if he had been flaying himself alive.

What he has done makes me think of Titian's painting of the flaying of Marsyas. The doomed man hung upside-down, while intently busy satyrs peeled off his flesh in strips. A dog lapped at a pool of blood at his head. Marsyas was being punished, Aunt Giulietta told me, by the god Apollo. As a child, this picture had revolted me. It had seemed to belong more to Dante's Hell than to the work of the sensuous Venetian painter.

The sickening thought comes to me that the Outpacer might be his own satyr. Was it possible he enjoyed this torture of himself?

He has not moved since my approach. He still grips the whip, which lies inert along his right flank. I both sense and see his alertness. I am aware now of the acrid odour of sweat mixed with blood.

"Who is there?" he cries out.

In answer I move closer so that I stand only a few feet from him.

I see some of his tension drain away when he recognizes me. He makes no move to cover his genitals, and I see that he is not sexually aroused. I understand that by his quiet acceptance of my presence we have entered some new, indefinable bond.

"If anyone had to discover me at my business," he says, "I would prefer it be you."

I feel dizzied by his use of the word "business." Yet what words would adequately describe this scene and the activity at which I have discovered him? Surreal? Nightmarish? Primal?

I look at this naked man of uncommon strength, and at the rope-like cording of muscle on his forearms and thighs and calves. I see the dark cavity that hunger has made under his rib cage. I see the greying tendrils of his pubic hair. I see the slashes and scores and punctures and abrasions that seem to cover every inch of his skin, with the exception of his hands and feet and face. It is a vulpine face, with blue burning eyes.

I am glad that he has apparently never lashed his eyes or mouth.

He falls to his knees.

"Will you hear my confession?" he whispers. He is wringing his hands. A shudder passes through him; then another and another. His breath comes quickly. Too quickly, I think. I fear he might have a fit.

I sit down near him.

Again he shudders. And again.

"It is foul," he says. "What I have done . . . and not done."

"I will listen," I say. But I am afraid.

His mouth moves, but no sound comes. He twists his hands and pulls at the flesh between his fingers.

"*Repentire*," I tell him. The word rises up out of my childhood, and I am grateful. It has solemnity and music. It sounds like a bell.

He comes closer to me, moving slowly on his knees. I wait for the words he is about to speak.

Chapter Sixteen
The Outpacer's Confession

HE PUTS ON HIS ROBE TO cover his nakedness so that she will no longer be exposed to his ulcerated flesh. Which is ludicrous, he thinks, given the substance of what he is about to relate: a story that has set the worm of self-loathing burrowing in his blood, bone, and brain.

"I am afraid I will pollute you," he tells her.

She has her face turned away from him. Under the flood of chill moonlight, her profile strikes him as having a preternatural strength, like an image on an ancient coin of hammered silver.

She puts her finger to her lip; then touches his hand, lingering only a moment, light as a moth.

"Please," she says. "Go on."

The elements of his confession feel to him like slivers of glass. He fears each word will produce a gout of blood in his mouth. He had not realized it would be so physically hard to wrest the words from himself; that they would have the power to pierce his inner throat and slit his tongue. His lips already feel numb and bloodied.

And yet how else could it be when one tries to recount the doings of the Theatre of Cruelty? "Doings" seems the right word. Not "endeavour" or "craft" or the stern and noble "work."

Just doings. Evil doings.

"I must go slowly," he tells Lucia. "I will seem to digress perhaps. But I must give you a context. I have to explain . . . "

"Yes," she says. "I am listening. We have time, given my wakefulness. Much time," she reassures him.

It occurs to him that he knows exactly what he is going to say. Day after day in his life as the Outpacer, he has been mentally rehearsing his confession, and this prologue. Is this because he has been waiting for the right listener?

He begins: "When I lived in the City, I joined a study group in all innocence. Each week we met to discuss the work of a long-dead poet and theatre director. This man had a theory about a new kind of radical drama that would open our minds to a rare understanding of life and the cosmos. He called it the Theatre of Cruelty because it used extreme sounds and sights as means to break through to the unconscious of people attending the play.

"All this greatly appealed to the man I was. I thought it good intellectual sport. I hoped that by joining the group, I might recapture some of the pleasurable play and stretch of the mind I had enjoyed as a student.

"I should explain that when I first joined the group, I had become jaded and numbed by my own sexual excesses and drug-taking. I woke each morning with a dry mouth, trembling hands, and a drum tolling in my head the grim rhythms of self-disgust. This is the despicable man I was."

The moonlight streams down upon his hands, which twist repeatedly in his lap. He realizes he has been silent for some minutes, while Lucia sits waiting patiently. He swallows, and begins again.

"I attended several study sessions in preparation for my admission to the promised mise-en-scène, when we were to put the dramatist's theory into practice. I enjoyed these evenings, where we read aloud and discussed Artaud's difficult, oracular prose. My glimmerings of understanding brought me an intense pleasure. The illumination, however brief, seemed proof that I was not yet entirely jaded. I had a spirit still that could leap up and be jubilant when it perceived the seeds of light in dark matter.

"I honestly believed that never before had there been such a need for the prophet's direct and bloodied truth. In moments of painful lucidity, I saw the travesty that human culture had become. What did we have in the City except a relentless stream of meretricious images that dulled the senses and undermined the capacity for disciplined attention? If we can no longer appreciate what beauty is, how can we be human?

"I saw the proof of this in the glazed eyes of the street dwellers who stared up at the sky-screens. I saw it in the addicts of the virtual reality palaces, so locked into their sensation-drenched fantasy experiences they were oblivious to each other and to the world. To me, they were barely recognizable as human, with their wraparound viewing goggles and super-sensory gloves. Their limbs jerked spasmodically in reaction to the brutish scenes played out in their private panoramas. Or they drooled or ejaculated inside their protective full-body suits, with sanitary pockets.

"Forgive me," he pleads. "It must seem to you that I ramble pointlessly. But I need to tell you . . . " Again, he breaks off.

"Yes," she says. "I understand. We have much time."

He finds relief in her calm demeanour and evident sympathy. He continues.

"One day it dawned on me that the virtual reality palaces made infants of their captives; that every customer was just an open mouth, twitching anus, and throbbing sexual organ. As for what was on the screens, it actually pained me to watch the degenerate spawn of the once-glorious medium of the cinema. That radiant world was now as dead as the common house sparrow.

"I should tell you that I had inherited a substantial share in a visual production company. This was willed to me by my patroness, a woman who loved me. With that inheritance, I nurtured dreams of rescuing film from its precarious state. I wanted to restore the medium's vigour and grace, and its power to astonish and to engage the mind and heart in wonderful, salubrious ways.

"Do I sound pompous?" he asks.

Lucia only smiles.

"My share in the company was substantial, yes, but not substantial enough. Every one of my proposals was thwarted by my colleagues on the board — by a raised eyebrow, and the blunt suggestion that I familiarize myself with market demand. For my elucidation, or my punishment, as I saw it, I was made to view the documentary footage of audience reaction to the company's latest product.

"It was a lesson I did not want repeated. The more barbaric the scene, the louder the audience cheered. Naked fists, naked swords, naked genitals. Gleaming guns, gleaming cars, gleaming teeth. All these elements, both the naked and the gleaming, inevitably came into frantic collision one with the other. The audience was as avid for yet another bullet-ridden corpse as it was for close-ups of yawning orifices in the obligatory orgy scenes.

"I was dumbfounded by how absolutely squalid the entire exercise was. 'Holes,' pronounced the chairman of the board at the end of the screening. 'They like to see holes. Holes in flesh. Holes between women's legs. That's your audience. They're crude. They probably go home and play happily with their own shit.' Everyone around the table laughed, except me.

"Our customers are vulgar, and we give them what they want, I was told. 'They give us their filthy lucre. We make a gigantic profit. It pays,' sneered the chairman, who was corpulent and bald, 'for your expensive suits.'

"I knew that the other board members despised me, and called me Gigolo Boy and worse behind my back. They had won their place at the table through cunning manipulation, or cut-throat tactics. I had won mine because a dying woman loved me far better than I deserved.

"I resolved not to let them intimidate me. Yet I had to concede they were right about the market. I was deluding myself if I thought I could re-educate the public's sensibility, or cultivate a niche market, producing real films for the discerning few.

"It was not simply that I lacked the financial resources to make the kind of film I had dreamt of as a young man. I knew I also lacked the drive. I was not willing to forgo my own comforts in order to see an artistic project through to its end.

I was not willing to suffer and to burn. I was quite certain that was what it took to make art.

"After that blunt lesson in the boardroom, I gave up all my dreams of personal creativity. I slid into the sump of the unthinking voluptuary. In rare moments of terrifying clarity, I would ask myself if I was unconsciously punishing myself for abandoning my muse.

"Can you understand?" he asks her.

She nods.

"It was a simple matter for me to evade these questions," he tells her, "and yield to my habitual hedonistic imperative: another potent drink, another warm and willing nubile body, another new drug to fracture reality into slabs of colour and a swarm of scintillating particles that might or might not be dangerous to the touch.

"I only realized how estranged I had become from any human dignity when I happened one day to glance up, and see my own naked coupling on a sky-screen. I felt sick with disgust at myself, and shame felled me to my knees.

"How could I have allowed that degrading spectacle on the screen to come about? I had a fleeting vision of my dead mother's face, appalled by her son's depravity. I heard myself cry out words I had forgotten I knew — *Aidez-moi! Aidez-moi!*

"Who was it, I wonder, that I implored for help?

"Within moments, I managed to recover my composure. But the incident stayed with me, as did those strange words, and the anguish they revealed.

"When I learned a few days later of the group dedicated to the principles of the French dramatist and his Theatre of Cruelty, I saw this as a happy portent. '*Aidez-moi*,' I had implored the vast insensate universe, expecting no answer. Yet an answer had come — through this opportunity to delve into the writings of a maligned genius with an extraordinary fire in his head.

"I had hopes that this study group might stir my own desire to make something, to dream again productively, or at the very least, renew my intellectual vigour.

"It all began innocuously enough. At the first meeting I attended, the group examined Artaud's idea of the intellectual cries that came from the flesh. 'There is a mind in the flesh,' he wrote, 'that is as quick as lightning.'

"I listened. I experienced a mounting excitement. I saw salvation as a real possibility for the first time in many years. I thought it feasible I might still become the man I had once envisioned.

"I was as delighted as a child the evening that the Theatre of Cruelty group showed scenes from Abel Gance's *Napoleon* in which Artaud played Marat.

"Have you ever heard of this old silent film?" he asks her.

"No."

"For me," he explains, "it is a masterpiece that has the impact of a visionary experience. I sat through it rapt twice when I was a student, awed by its grandeur and miraculous conveyance of palpable human emotion. And without speech! Studying the close-ups of those extraordinary, mobile faces, I sometimes wondered if Gance and his actors were another order of being altogether.

"Do you think I am being facile?" he enquires of her anxiously.

"I do not want you to think," he presses her, "that I am being insincere. It is only that I feel compelled to tell you the prologue. I must set out for you the circumstances that led to my embroilment in this heinous deed. I must explain to you fully how I came to be there. Otherwise, if I was to describe only the crime itself, you would think me a monster."

"Yes," she assures him. "I know you are sincere."

He takes a deep breath.

"I was speaking of Abel Gance's masterpiece, of the film's sublime artistry and technological daring. I was spellbound when he tilted the on-screen images of the seething revolutionary mob, rocking them back and forth. Watching, you could not help but feel the fatal reverberation of the Terror to come. An upturned world, where the streets ran with blood.

"When I first saw those scenes as a young man, I did not expect to see a Reign of Terror take hold in my own lifetime.

"Did you ever feel," he asks, "that our culture was one that had murdered time? The social malaise, the vacuity, the obsession with surface polish, the ultimate shoddiness, these were all aspects of time's vengeance on us.

"We slaughtered each instant in the frantic onward rush for novel stimulation. We cut off our own heads, and did not understand this was happening because we dishonoured time. These were the kinds of insights that came to me after I joined the study group. I was greedy for more.

"So when Artaud's glowering, incandescent Marat appeared projected on a wall, I gave the flickering phantasm my unadulterated attention. The others in the group watched the ancient film to observe their prophet. I sat, my body taut and eager as it always is in the presence of great art, striving to absorb how this superlative thing was made.

"That night I slept more soundly than I had for years. On waking, I felt light-hearted, and new-made. It was not until my second sip of coffee that I identified this rare state of mind as hope. It was still possible, I thought. I might still make something worthy of the word 'art' before I died. Hope — which I had hungered for so long without realizing it — transfigured the future, which seemed suddenly more spacious, like a great hall filled with light.

"And then..."

Here, he has to break off in his telling. He is not at all certain he can continue.

"I was happy," he tells Lucia again. He grinds his knuckles into the earth.

"I cannot go on," he whispers. The taste of blood is in his mouth again.

"*Repentire*," she counsels him.

The single word, spoken in her habitual low tone, reverberates through his entire being.

"*Repentire*," she repeats.

He is staring down at his knotted fists. Then he raises his eyes to look at her profile, gilded by moonlight. Slowly, she turns her head so that she faces him. He sees in her eyes her sincerity and compassion, and is reassured. She reaches out to enclose his right hand in hers. Her skin is calloused, warm and dry. He has the sensation that the moonlight encircling them is like cool water. He could turn his face up to the sky and drink.

"Confront your dark truth," she says. "I will listen. I will help you bear it."

He shakes his head. "It is far worse than anything you can imagine."

"You do not know what I have imagined, or can imagine," she responds. "You do not know what I have seen."

"*Repentire.* I will not judge you."

He is moved by her generosity and by her resolute calm. He realizes how unlikely it is that he would ever again find such a listener, willing to hear him out in silence and not shrink away in disgust at his story.

Yes, he thinks, I must tell her everything. But first he withdraws his hand from her loose clasp. He cannot speak while she still touches him. He cannot bear to feel her cringe once he describes the events of that bestial night.

"I will not look at you," she says. "Will that be a help to you?"

He nods.

She turns her face away so that once again, he sees her strong profile. Slowly, and with a methodical grace, she begins to unbraid her hair. He is grateful for her sensitivity, for this intimate gesture suggesting a protective domestic space. And whether or not this was her intention, he finds it soothing watching her hands unwind the heavy, glossy plait. He glimpses — however fleetingly — the possibility he might yet find peace within himself.

"For the performance," he begins, "they had draped the walls of the meeting place in dull black. There were no seats. We were told to stand near the wall. Once the performance was under way, we could move about or join in the action as instinct prompted.

"As instinct prompted," he repeats. He feels these words might choke him. Already, he can smell his own fear.

He stops. He looks at the luxuriant mass of hair Lucia has unbound. He lets his eyes follow the glossy undulation, wave after wave, which she has freed from the confines of the plait. How silent the night is. This too, he tries to absorb.

Repentire, he tells himself. He thinks of the millions of human beings before him who had indeed repented when they heard this word. He wonders if they then found consolation. He does not think he will. He does not believe he is deserving of consolation.

But surely Lucia is right? He saw the pity and the censure in her eyes when she looked at his wounds. Mortifying his own flesh is a form of wickedness in itself. What use will he be to them if his wounds turn septic?

"There were twelve of us made up the audience," he continues. "I remember counting. I presumed the other four members in the group would be our performers. I was restless, excited. It was a long time since I had seen any theatre. My expectations were enormous. I anticipated what — ecstasy? A blinding insight that would regenerate my own creative source?

"Whatever it was I expected, it was hell they delivered.

"The room went black, as if all the light in the world had been sucked away. The idea came to me that we were inside the belly of a beast. There was a distant rumble. It seemed to come from my left, and then from under my feet.

"This rumbling gradually got louder. How can I describe it? The sound was inhuman, harrowing, doom-laden. I imagined the earth tearing itself apart, somehow consuming itself, and groaning all the while. The room began to shake. This may have been only an illusion, created by the amplified sound. Yet it seemed real enough. I found it difficult to keep my feet. I was swaying badly. The room was still pitch-black so that I had absolutely no depth perception. I had no idea where any of the others were. If anyone had spoken or cried out, it would have been impossible to hear them through that infernal noise.

"The rumbling became a roaring that was next to unbearable. The sound penetrated to the marrow of my bones. It filled my chest, my head, my mouth. My body trembled and I could not control it.

"I remember thinking that this was Artaud's cataclysm and what a cunning job they had made of it. I was trying hard to stay objective, and protect some kernel of rationality through this onslaught on my senses. Yet the greater part of my mind was colonized by a blind mounting panic. I had an urge — and this is no exaggeration — to cry out for my mother.

"And just at that point when I thought I might weep or tear my hair out or go mad, the noise and the shaking ceased. The silence and the stillness felt like great healing draughts of spring water. They left us in that blessed state for a minute or two.

"A dot of white light appeared, somewhere ahead of me. It grew gradually higher and wider until it assumed the shape of a classic spot-light beam. I focused greedily on this light, which restored both the dimensions of the room and my own place in it. I could just make out as well, the forms of the others who watched.

"In the inverted funnel of the spotlight, a young girl materialized. She looked no more than twelve or thirteen. They had dressed her in a flowing, white garment. She had extremely long, fine hair, the colour of corn silk. She was slight and delicate. Her face reminded me of a miniature orchid I saw once in the Pleasure Zone.

Here he has to stop again. He clenches his fists, and puts his forehead to the earth. He imagines clawing a hole for himself to escape the demand that he utter these vile-tasting words.

"*Repentire*," she counsels him.

"I cannot."

"*Repentire*."

"Her eyes were closed," he tries again, "and her arms slack. It was only afterwards I realized she must have been drugged. The light widened to reveal her 'guardians,' or so I supposed them to be. Four members of the Theatre of Cruelty — two men and two women — were on her either side. Their robes were black. They wore crowns made of feathers. I remember thinking these headdresses must be inspired by Artaud's interest in the Tarahumara Indians of Mexico, whom he had visited. A negligible thought. And a thoroughly innocent thought, given what was to follow.

"The four guardian figures had coated their lips in a red so dark it verged on black. They had filled in the area around their eyes with kohl so that from a distance, these smudges looked like empty sockets. Their garish makeup made the girl appear even more fragile and vulnerable by contrast. For a moment, their black-robed figures enveloped her so that only her face was visible. I thought of a petal floating on a boiling, sullen sea. Her face did seem to be floating. I supposed this was a trick of the light.

"She was such a pale wisp of a girl. Yet she glowed. Surrounded by their oppressive darkness, by their crude, glowering faces, she seemed to be the repository of something sacred: like a promise that must never be broken.

"I ought to have leapt forward at that point, and carried her away. But I did not know. I had no idea what they intended."

He can taste bile as well as blood in his mouth.

Repentire.

"The room was plunged once again into absolute darkness. A grating music began. It seemed to come from under my feet: sounds so discordant, I ground my teeth together.

"Next came a penetrating whistle, whose shrillness made me want to weep. I was crouching, with my fingers thrust into my ears. I recall wondering why on earth they were inflicting this punishment on us, and what it had to do with Artaud.

"The whistle ended as abruptly as it began, and there followed another of those blessed silences sweet as mother's milk. It was the last time in my life I was ever to experience that sensation of relief, and unadulterated sweetness. I am not being self-pitying here. I am relating the facts. After that night, I was corrupt. I tasted corruption, and it set an infection raging in me which is my living damnation.

"I must stop a moment," he tells Lucia. His throat is parched. The horror of what he must speak next is a swollen grub in his mouth. He takes as deep a breath as he can manage, and resumes.

"In the murk, a point of light appeared, so tiny that at first I thought I might be hallucinating. This light gradually expanded, in keeping with the swaying rhythm of what sounded like pan-pipes. When the light was as large as an ellipse, I saw what had been hidden from us in the dark — that they had laid the girl out on a sacrificial altar.

"Her flowing drapery and her long hair cascaded over the edge of the marble slab. Her left arm hung slack. I presumed she was acting, and I marvelled at her stillness and at her almost ethereal beauty in her milk-white robes. The scene was masterfully rendered. I understood — with my nerve endings, as much as with my intellect — that she was intended as a sacrifice for the gods.

"The shimmering quality of the light, her own luminous pallor, the translucency of her garments, all these conjoined to make her appear numinous. In that crucible of light and dark, newly emerged from an earth-shattering assault of thunder and piercing sound, I was ready to see her as holy.

"I wanted to give myself over totally to the in-dwelling power of the theatrical experience. I wanted its magic to transform me.

"I began to feel any obdurate rationality in myself giving way. I sensed the approach of Artaud's whirling vortex, the fount of creation and of freshness. I wanted to taste and partake of that young girl's holiness. I do not mean in any lascivious sense. I wanted to partake of her sacredness symbolically. My supreme wish was that nothing, and no one, ever be allowed to harm her.

"Even as this resolution formed in my mind, the four black figures ranged themselves behind the altar. My analytical faculty was at work again despite myself. I wondered why the simple dichotomy of light and dark still works in us to such great effect, and whether the director had consciously intended the row of black forms to resemble carrion crows. My thoughts flitted to the very idea of crows, and how they have stayed with us, even those of us who have never seen a live bird of any kind. I wondered where and why their image is lodged in me: how it is I can picture so clearly their glossy sleekness, their cross-wise step, their cocked-head clever aspect, their razor-sharp beaks pecking meticulously at dead flesh.

"I saw a knife blade flash against black cloth, above the sleeping girl. Another flash and another and another, so that all four figures stood with daggers pointing downward at her body.

"Foolishly, I thought that they were about to mime a ritual slaughter; that with a manipulation of light and shadow, a contrived convulsion of the walls, they would create an illusion to liberate the unconscious. It was Artaud, after all, who first coined the term 'virtual reality.' And so I stood there, intent and expectant, greedy for experience, believing that the act about to be staged was a 'virtual' act. This was artifice — of a much higher order than the pap played out in the virtual reality palaces — but artifice nonetheless.

"This was what I believed at that moment.

"All four, as if choreographed, plunged their daggers into the girl's chest. I heard her moan. I saw her eye open and roll upward. A quickening fear and revulsion filled me. Through the sound of her pain, I grasped this was no illusion. Her blood began to spout, staining her white garment, pooling thickly on the floor.

"I understood, far too late, that they were murdering a child for our entertainment; that their outrageous misreading of a dramatist's theory had spawned a murder.

"I lunged at them, in some vain effort to rescue the girl and get her to a doctor. Even then, it was probably already too late. She could not have survived those strikes.

"I lunged. And they struck back. I recoiled at a heavy blow to my head. Then nothing — until I came to in a corner, swaying over a pool of wetness. Had they pissed on me after they knocked me out? Had I pissed myself? It hardly mattered when I saw the scene before me. I wished then that I had never emerged to consciousness, or that they had dragged me outside and beaten me to a pulp in the street. Anything would have been preferable to the abomination I witnessed.

"They were tearing her corpse apart, limb by limb, joint by joint, using knives, hands, fingernails. They were all at it; not just the four actors in black. Fifteen members of the Theatre of Cruelty were joined in the frenzied sport of dismembering a young girl's corpse.

"And now I will tell you the worst, although perhaps you think there can be no worse. But there is . . . " Here his voice breaks altogether. When he manages to speak again, he sounds hoarse. The shards of glass are once again embedded in his throat.

"These are the hardest words I will speak to you. I did not turn away fast enough, and some contagion in this repellent sport began to infect me. I felt a sick urge rise in me, prompting me to join in, to feel what it was like to tear her soft warm flesh apart with my nails. It was like the curse of the Bacchae, when the mob is caught up in a bestial madness. This urge came from the most loathsome part of what I am. I wanted to succumb; to know what it was like to dip my fingers in her blood and dismember her flesh. I believe I almost did.

"My hands began to shake. I was appalled at my own thoughts. I cursed myself. And I ran from that place, retching and trembling and half-insane with self-hatred.

"I have done much wrong in my life. I have indulged myself. I have sometimes delighted in masochistic practice. I have abused the affection of many women who thought they loved me. I have been callous, callow, cowardly, and selfish.

"But never had I felt myself mired in evil until that night. What else could I do but flee that abominable place? Only a god could have put that poor child back together, and breathed life into her again. And who among us now believes in beneficent gods and miracles of resurrection?

"I began to run; to get as far away from that corner of hell as I could. I ran until I thought my lungs would explode. When at last I stopped, beside a stagnant pond in a ruined park, I vomited again and again into the reeking water. But I knew I could never empty myself of the contamination of that girl's death and dismemberment. I felt deranged by my guilt, despite the fact I had no prior idea what they intended by their bestial theatre. I had absorbed their corruption by the mere fact of being in attendance and the sick stimulation of my execrable desires. Then — as now — I felt a maggot at work in every cell of my body.

"For a time, I thought I might go mad, so intense was my self-loathing. The Theatre of Cruelty had infected my idea of humankind. I began to think of all humanity as an aberration. I considered suicide. What stopped me? — I like to think it was some residual hope. But most likely it was cowardice about what lay beyond.

"I learned that the abyss of despair is no mere metaphor. I swayed on its edge. I urged myself to commit self-murder like a man. I sound self-pitying, I suppose, despairing for my own condition, obsessing about the impact of the girl's gruesome murder on me, rather than thinking of her.

"I can only assure you that I could not separate the two. I wanted her restored. I wanted her to be redeemed: to see her life force and beauty and wholeness given back to her. I wanted to be redeemed myself, purified of the slime and sewage in which I had willingly immersed myself. I wanted the very time in which we live to be redeemed.

"Everything I wanted was impossible: a child's fantasy. Yet the despair was real enough. I stopped eating. I dismissed my staff. I lay in my bed, curled in on myself, yearning to be taken back into my mother's womb, or into the womb of the earth. I was atrophying. I could not rid myself of the image of the girl, as she had been, and as she was when torn apart by fiends. I loathed my brain and my opposable thumb and my upright gait: everything that supposedly made me human.

"I think I might have died; simply willed my body to shut down. But salvation came to me in the form of a song. Or if not salvation, then at least an impetus to bear the burden of being human; to live out my natural span, but in a vastly different manner than I had to that point.

"The song came to me first by way of its rhythm. I did not recognize what it was right away. The tune comforted and heartened me. I found myself rising from my bed, summoned by its resolute beat. It was as if the various notes composed a living being, urging me to get up and move, to be courageous. I washed my face for the first time in many days. I ate a little. I made coffee. And still the thump and the roll of the tune stayed with me, inspiriting me and buoying me up. I had no doubt this music had come to me as a gift.

"Then I remembered who it was had sung this song. It was the woman who loved me and encouraged and supported me. And all the while, she was herself dying, wasting away. Despite the drugs, she sometimes suffered intolerable pain. It was then she would sing this song; blast it out of her frail lungs, and stomp about the house like a child pretending to be a soldier.

"The song was one she had learned in girlhood. 'I am not a Christian,' she told me. 'But the truth in this song is eternal. It is about fearlessness. Fearlessness.' She would repeat the word, hugging herself. In singing, in stomping about, she willed herself onward, with renewed fortitude, through the pain.

"When I remembered this, I also remembered the words, and I too began to sing. Do you know them?" he asks Lucia. And he sings softly:

> *Who would true valour see,*
> *Let him come hither,*
> *One here will constant be,*
> *Come wind, come weather.*
> *There's no discouragement*
> *Shall make him once relent*
> *His first avowed intent,*
> *To be a pilgrim.*

Lucia shakes her head. "You sang this song when we were in the cave, I believe."

He nods.

"To be a pilgrim," he repeats. "I recognized that this was my salvation. I would take to the road. I would try, in some way, to make amends through a pilgrimage.

"I had not planned on the self-mortification," he adds. "This need to inflict pain on myself is prompted by the self-hatred. There is no more to tell." He bowed his head, as if waiting for her judgement.

"You did not murder the girl," she says. "You had no way of knowing what they intended."

"I was complicit. I felt the urge, the loathsome, barbaric urge to dismember a dead child."

"But you did not," she insists. "You resisted that evil. You are guilty of being duped, and of being present at the time an evil deed was committed. Probably every one of us these days is guilty of such things."

"When it came to the act itself, you controlled the monster within you. You must hold fast to that truth."

"Your strength brings us all great comfort," he tells her. "Did you know that?"

She surprises him by asking: "Will you hear my confession now?"

He is staggered when she tells him of her erotic encounter with the plague doctor. He experiences as well, another emotion he cannot quite define. It resembles, but is not quite, dismay. Under the curtain of chaste moonlight, he moves closer to her on his hands and knees. He wants to comfort her, to tell her how negligible her perceived fault is. But he understands how huge she feels her disgrace to be, and he will not belittle her judgement on herself, however disproportionately harsh it may seem to him.

"I did not love him," she says. "Without love, it would have been a soiled and brutish act."

She buries her face in her hands. He draws her head toward his naked chest where his wounds are deepest. He strokes her hair. He is surprised when she lifts her face and touches her lips to his.

"*Repentire*," she says. "Can you say this word to me? Can we say it to each other with our bodies?"

For a moment, he is uncertain of her meaning.

"And is there love here?" he asks her. "Are you sure of this?"

"Yes."

They come together more slowly and quietly than he has ever joined with a woman before. It strikes him that their lovemaking has some chaste quality in common with the moonlight.

As they make their way together in silence back to the camp-fire, he thinks: I am transformed. And not just because she has removed the nail from my breast and unburdened my thought. I am, he recognizes in astonishment, a man who dwells in love. I had not known before that love is a dwelling-place.

At daybreak, he forges ahead to break trail. He feels he is moving through some new element; that there is a different quality to the light, purged of haze, absolutely crystalline. What cinematic image would he use, he wonders, to convey this unaccustomed brightness in his blood and brain? The swift realization comes that it would be a close-up of Lucia's hands, loosening and then braiding her long hair, strand over strand. He recalls ancient tales about the strength of maidens' hair; how it could secure a ship to its anchor, or save a man from drowning.

As he forces his way through a dense wall of evergreen shrub, he sees a sight to gladden the heart of any pilgrim. Set on the plain below a range of mauve hills, seven tents of silk tremble in their confines and drink down the colours of the rising sun. He rubs his eyes. When he looks again, they are still there: the burnished tents of dawn that affirm he has been shriven.

Chapter Seventeen
Bird Girl Sees Eros at Work

WHEN BIRD GIRL FIRST GLIMPSES THE line of tents, she stops and stares in disbelief. They look sublime, like solidified tongues of flame that burn, yet do no harm. The great ball of rising sun stains their flimsy cloth in colours that Lola loved: the apricot, persimmon, plum, and burgundy of the sheaths and strapless gowns she had put on to inflame her many lovers.

Passionate, yoni-obsessed Lola would have clapped her hands in delight at the sight of this dazzling array of delta shapes. She would have made some suggestive remark about thrusting points and vaginas, then wriggled her skinny hips and let loose one of her raucous laughs. Candace would have plugged her ears. Bird Girl misses Lola keenly. She misses her sense of fun and life force, and the way she got up Candace's nose. Lola loved the richly spiced drink of her memories. She loved to laugh. She loved Bird Girl. Bird Girl found herself wishing Lola hadn't. The fact is she feels unworthy of the enormous gift Lola made her. *She sucked the poison into herself to give me back my life.* Bird Girl reminds herself of this several times a day.

Lucia's Masks

In the first days of her convalescence, Lola's death put such blackness inside Bird Girl that she could no longer see things in their rightful wholeness. The entire world looked dull and flat to her, even the faces and bodies of her travelling companions, and most certainly her own body. She felt that her powers to renew herself had all drained away through the gaping hole in her breast. The wound throbbed and pulled and made her set her teeth together. Hot pincers gripped her nerves, not just where the hole was, but throughout her chest and arms. Lucia tended her with balms and kindness. Bird Girl tried to tell Lucia her grief, but could not find words equal to the deadening ache of Lola's absence.

"Try to accept her gift with grace," Lucia told her.

Later Bird Girl thought that if she had brought a book of poetry with her, she might have found some grace and comfort there, some fitting lines to recite for Lola as a tribute. She tried to call to mind poems that had given her great pleasure: works tight and sleek that nevertheless held immensities. But nothing came.

All Bird Girl could hear was her mother's voice on the afternoon of their final searing encounter. Every word Epona hurled at her that day was ugly: *slut, tart, degenerate.* And because Bird Girl felt so unworthy of what Lola had done for her, she started to believe her mother had been right. She was an ungrateful little whore. She was dirt. Hadn't she called her mother "a maimed dyke?" When she remembered that, the wound in her breast pulled so hard, the tears ran down her face. Bird Girl's mother had no left breast. It had been cut off to stop the cancer killing her. What an appallingly wicked thing to say to one's mother, even if Epona had called her "a disgusting little tramp" and worse.

It all happened the day her mother destroyed one of her most cherished books. She came home to find the ancient, treasured paperback in shreds on the floor of her room in the Armoury. When she saw what Epona had done (and she knew it could be no one else) she felt invaded, plundered and bereft. At first, she could not speak at all. It was as if, through the book's destruction, her mother had robbed her of language altogether. If she had owned a pet and her mother had slit its belly open and dismembered it, Bird Girl did not think she could have hurt her more.

As Epona saw it, she was saving her daughter from infection. She was helping Bird Girl to keep her heart and mind and body free of taint. Bird Girl was free to read all the "improving" texts she wanted. That meant works on the dialectics of sexuality and histories of ancient matriarchal civilizations. The Armoury also had a plenitude of manuals on bike mechanics, the arts of self-defence, and weaponry use and maintenance. What Epona absolutely forbade were works of the imagination. "You'll rot your mind, my girl." She meant that literally. Bird Girl's mother had no patience with metaphors.

Epona was wary of all forms of art. She saw them as trickery, a kind of despicable window dressing to obscure society's multifarious evils. "Facts, my girl. We have to face up to and confront the facts." She would aim her index finger at Bird Girl's forehead. "You have to keep your brain-box clean. If you gum it up with this make-believe rubbish, you won't stay sharp enough to survive. Don't ever forget," Epona would punch the air, a gesture aimed at the evil world outside the Armoury, "don't ever forget what we're up against."

She meant the "pestilential City" that was The New Amazons' battleground, and the hydra-headed sex trade which was their particular target. As she grew older, Bird Girl gradually perceived how her mother's rigid ideology had killed off her natural affections. Epona would never let herself succumb to the power of melody in music, or in the written word. And she seemed to have nullified in herself that urgent curiosity, which was for Bird Girl a driving force in reading stories. What happens next? How will the character you care most about get out of this terrible fix?

Epona did not care, as Bird Girl knew to her cost, about unexpected plot twists or the suspense that can set the pulse racing — like the bone-chilling thrill when David Balfour mounts the stone stair in utter darkness in the spooky House of Shaws, sets down his foot, and discovers only a chill and windy void. In that instant, it dawns on the reader, as it does on David, that his clay-faced Uncle Ebenezer has sent him up this stair — not to bed — but to death. And with David, Bird Girl always groped her way down again "with a wonderful anger" in her heart that matched his own.

He was Bird Girl's first great literary love and the first character whose skin she slipped inside so perfectly, she was able to look at the world through his eyes. She too stared in awe at the wild and treacherous Moor of Rannoch, and at the handsome face of Alan Breck, Highland Jacobite and inveterate gambler. She admired David's self-possession and astute self-assessment, his honesty and articulate powers of description. She was jubilant as she ran with David and Alan through the heather, outwitting the Redcoats. She stood frozen, as did her cherished boy hero, when Alan urged him to leap over a thunderous river. "I bent low on my knees and flung myself forth," David said, "with that kind of anger of despair that has sometimes stood me in stead of courage."

When she first read that passage, Bird Girl thought these were the wisest and most useful words she had ever come across. She memorized them. In fact, she could probably have recited the entire book she read it so often and so hungrily. She was happy there, in the thick of David's adventures, as happy, she thought, as she had ever been in her life. It was Laura-of-the-Gashed-Cheek who gave Bird Girl *Kidnapped* on her ninth birthday. Bird Girl saw that her mother was not too pleased, but she let her keep the book. Doubtless Epona had given the text a quick scan to make sure the content was salutary. What she saw was an old-fashioned children's adventure story she judged to be harmless.

But in the years to come, Epona would systematically censor or destroy books in her daughter's possession she considered to be corrupting filth. In the beginning, Bird Girl did ardently try to appreciate her mother's point of view. She gathered words she thought best described Epona's character. She would hug this little collection of adjectives to herself in bed at night, trying to get closer to her mother. So she rhymed off to herself: *sturdy, resolute, adamantine, unswerving, fearless, mettlesome, incorruptible.* As she grew older, and the gulf between mother and daughter became evermore apparent, she added other, radically qualifying words to this list: *rigid, unsubtle, unbending, philistine, puritanical.*

It was the unbending Puritan in Epona who wrenched Colette's *The Vagabond* from under her daughter's mattress, opened it, saw the words, "voluptuous body," and deliberately cracked the book's spine so that it broke in two halves. Epona then shredded the pages, spotted with age and smelling of damp, which had managed to endure more than ninety years in a world now absolutely hostile to books.

Bird Girl still feels sick and furious whenever she thinks about this desecration. What her mother did that day was barbaric. Bird Girl had paid dearly for that little book with her own blood. That was the price demanded by the black marketeer who set up his street stall one day, and disappeared the next. He was a remarkably tall man, and as thin and straight as the stem of a wine glass. He wore a battered fedora pulled low on his brow. He had a sensual mouth and hands so huge and restless that at first she thought she might have to secure *The Vagabond* with some slickly delivered sexual favours. But he wanted blood.

He had observed how keen she was. It was the only book on his table, cleverly camouflaged by a heap of gauzy scarves. So Bird Girl's first glimpse of Colette's powdered face, with those penetrating eyes blazing like lanterns, was through the filmy mesh of swathes of Prussian blue and magenta. She checked first to make sure there were no EYE officials hanging about, then picked the book up, riffled through its tender pages, and saw phrases that made her quiver with desire to possess this story whole. She knew at once that she would adore the heroine, Renée Néré, who chose to perform half-naked on the music hall stages of France rather than marry a wealthy man who adored her.

She had to read more — right away. "Can I look at this behind your stall?" she asked.

He frowned and rubbed his nose, before beckoning Bird Girl behind his display of jumbled oddments and tawdry treasures. She sat on an upturned wooden box, obscured by the open door of his van, reading greedily here and there of how Renée chafed at the idea of a rose-smothered domesticity. What Renée wanted above all was to be amongst "the wanderers, the lords of the earth."

It was at that moment that the idea of taking to the road first struck Bird Girl. In Renée Néré, she immediately recognized an alter ego. Renée was besotted with looking, and with possessing the marvels of the earth through her eyes: rippling fields of gold and crimson, the sapphire sea, the silvery wings of white owls. Bird Girl knew she would probably never see a white owl, except perhaps stuffed, in a glass case. Yet sitting behind that junk stall, her whole self seemed to quicken in answer to a ghostly call. She did not know why it had never struck her before that writing was what she wanted most to do herself. But the realization came in that instant, prompted by the probing eyes of Colette's portrait on the book cover, and by her heroine's urgent need to look so intently at the world.

"Blood," the stall man in the battered hat whispered to her. She could hear he was getting impatient. "Two vials for the book. If you're clean." This meant Bird Girl had to show him the encoded card the EYE made everyone carry, registering your blood type, genetic weaknesses, and viral load, if any.

She produced her card and he studied it closely. What if his syringe was recycled? She wanted the book badly, but she didn't want to risk death for it. She was lucky. He was well-equipped.

From the back of his van he brought out a brand-new syringe in its sealed paper packet, straight from the manufacturer. The vials he removed from a leather case looked equally pristine. The blood business was apparently quite a productive sideline for him, but Bird Girl chose not to speculate about where hers might end up.

"Good colour," he said, as they both watched the dark-red fluid slide inside the tube. Bird Girl clenched her fist and thought of Renée Néré. When they were done, the stall keeper even offered her a clump of sterilized cotton to press against the puncture.

He shook her hand at the conclusion of their transaction, which surprised her. "Enjoy it, kid," he said. "These little bird books are precious few these days."

At first Bird Girl thought he had read the book himself and was referring to the passage about the twilit silvery owl. Then she saw he was tapping the little orange ellipse at the base of the book's spine. Inside the ellipse was the outline of a white-bodied bird, with stumpy rigid black wings and webbed feet. Its tiny black-and-white head pointed upward and to the left, so that one got the impression it was regarding something quizzically, at a distance. A questioning, solid, assertive little bird, with its stiff wings and wide-planted feet.

Bird Girl must have looked quizzical herself. "Penguin," explained the stall-owner. "Penguin paperbacks. Used to be millions of them. Good literature affordable to the masses. Gone now, most of them. Burned. Ploughed under. Shredded. Doomed. Like the bird, when you think of it."

"What happened to the bird?" she asked.

"Waddlers. Didn't fly. Antarctica. Ice melted. Too hot. Expired."

She wondered then if he spoke in those terse, truncated phrases because English wasn't his birth language. It struck her that perhaps his speech patterns had come to resemble the bric-a-brac on his table: a miscellany of objects, all of which could slip easily into a pocket.

She never saw him again. But she often thought of his odd, eloquent elegy for book and bird.

"Filthy self-indulgence," was how Epona described *The Vagabond*, the day she found it hidden under Bird Girl's mattress. Such a delicate little book to meet with such a destructive force. What a pathetic sight Bird Girl must have looked: on her knees, attempting to patch together countless fragments of old paper. As she saw it, her mother had mutilated a woman of warm and abundant charms, with an amazing gift for luscious imagery and astringent insights. In fact, Bird Girl regarded Renée as almost a sacred being, her personal Prometheus. She had put a fire in Bird Girl's head that made her want to wander the world, and to write about what she saw. Rest in peace, Renée Néré, whispered Bird Girl, as she gave up the futile task. She sat on her floor, and cried so much a wet patch spread across her lap.

She did not hear her mother come into the room; there was only her startled awareness of Epona's sleek, high-polished black boots, the right foot tapping. When she was a child, the sight of that tapping foot could turn her stomach. Bird Girl could not recall exactly when she had stopped fearing her mother's anger. On the other hand, she could never entirely let go of the awe her mother inspired in her. But this time, not even awe could hold her back. Bird Girl sprang to her feet and let her fury speak.

She hated having to remember the details. Sometimes when she pictured them facing each other — Epona with her shingled hair and body encased in black leather, her daughter in the mint julep see-through mini-dress with her zebra leggings — it seemed a pair of blind and questing primordial beings was speaking through them. Two of the ancient Titans perhaps, loose and restless in the universe and seeking a likely host, found it in the sore wound opened between the leader of The New Amazons and her only child.

The words that came out of their mouths were coarse and brutal and cursed, as they were cursed by speaking them.

"Trash," Epona said, as she ground the tender fragments of *The Vagabond* with her boot heel. "Trash that inspires you to dress like a slut."

She touched Bird Girl in a way she never had before, with absolute contempt, her fingernail flicking up the hem of her daughter's dress, and catching briefly on the close-knit fabric of her tights. Her mother might as well have spat in her face.

And so it began: their final battle made of words: mutilating words that left a wreckage so total no forgiveness or atonement was possible.

"Slut," her mother called her, "Degenerate. Disgrace."

"Freak," Bird Girl called her mother. "Heartless. Maimed dyke."

Such cruelty issued from their mouths, and who or what directed them? What abandoned tutelary spirit, maddened by long neglect? It was not that Bird Girl was trying to evade responsibility for the scurrilous words she consciously formed and spoke. Yet on that grim afternoon she and her mother had hardened into extremes of what they were, and all that lay between them was ripe for death.

When she had finally gone back seeking a rapprochement, the Armoury had mocked her with its emptiness. Perhaps she would never know who had stormed The New Amazons' stronghold, and whether her mother and her band of warriors were alive or dead. This ignorance of her mother's fate was also a curse.

In the self-reviling days of her convalescence, Bird Girl was haunted by images of her mother strung up like an animal in an abattoir. Her own unforgivable words would invade her, like sharpened hooks that tore at her breast wound. Her grieving then for Lola would send her nearly deranged. Lola had sacrificed herself, not realizing how despicable, degraded, and worthless Bird Girl actually was.

If it hadn't been for Chandelier, Bird Girl wonders if she might have tried to do away with herself. How could she ever have thought him a bit dense, albeit gentle-natured? She is still astounded by the treasure trove of knowledge he brought to comfort and distract her during the worst of her clawing grief and self-hatred. It was a marvel really, just how much Chandelier had packed into his small head. He was one of those rare people who could simply scan a page and have its entire content memorized. He knows rather more about reptiles than she's interested in hearing. But he has stored away as well, the plots of countless myths and dramas and novels — and glory of glories — some poetry.

During her recovery, the two of them evolved a game of tossing one another poetic words or snippets to see what ideas or odd filaments of thought they might attract. "Darkling" was one of those words. Bird Girl had learned it from the Fool in *King Lear*: *So, out went the candle, and we were left darkling.* She had concentrated on every word the Fool spoke in that play. She loved the way he stood back and commented with such barbed wit and compassion on the old king's disintegration, and on human greed, folly, and betrayal. Bird Girl always imagined the Fool as small and young and fluidly acrobatic. She also thought of him as brave and blithe. He gave people the bitter draught of truth to drink down, but made it palatable with humour. She often wished that Lear's Fool, or someone like him, could be one of their company. So she was pleased to discover something of his mercurial spirit in Chandelier as she came to know him better.

When she spoke her word "darkling," Chandelier tossed it back to her in triplicate. He knew a poem called "The Darkling Thrush," about a frail and aged bird who chose to "fling his soul upon the growing gloom" of a killing winter.

He knew "Darkling, I listen," from "Ode to a Nightingale." The young poet who wrote this praise-song to the bird was dying of a wasting lung disease, Chandelier told her. That was why he spoke of being "half in love with easeful Death." When the poet hears the nightingale pouring forth its soul in ecstasy, he recognizes there could be no more perfect moment for him to die. "Darkling, I listen." Bird Girl thought the poet used the word to enfold himself: like a protective cloak against the dank night air.

The third "darkling" Chandelier tossed her was grim and chill, like dirty water flung in one's face. She recognized their own situation right away in the lines he recited. This was *their* time, as they were now, even though Chandelier told her the poem had been written hundreds of years ago:

And we are here as on a darkling plain
Swept with confused alarms of struggle and flight,
Where ignorant armies clash by night.

It is all still the same, Bird Girl thinks: the struggle and flight, and the clash of ignorant armies. The only difference is the EYE, which watched everything from its grand remove, and orchestrated more than any of us could ever know. Although she detested the endless, dismal forest, at least it freed them from the EYE's eternal surveillance and control.

A picture comes to her of the six of them: she and Chandelier and Harry, Lucia, Candace, and the Outpacer in flight from the City, labouring to cross the poet's darkling plain. They look far, far away, recognizable only by their respective shapes silhouetted against a pale green sky. These little shadow-figures struggling onward look so minuscule from that distant perspective and so obviously weary that the understanding comes to her. They are "the darklings."

She thinks then, as she often does, of the smooth glazed features of the masks from the theatre box. She is puzzled still by their huge, protruding foreheads that look oddly wrong and sore — and yet right somehow — for their stern and oracular faces. She wonders what obscure function or secret lies behind their wide-open mouths and the bulges above their eyes, and whether it might help the darklings in their journey.

She was studying her own mask, searching its coldly enigmatic gaze, when the Outpacer rushed in with his news about the camp of silk tents. He'd done a quick reconnoitre, he told them breathlessly, and seen women in long skirts, children, and a tethered goat. "A goat," he repeated excitedly. "Do you see the significance? If they keep a goat, they're probably peaceable."

Candace, Harry, and Chandelier all looked at him stunned. It took Bird Girl a moment to realize this was because the Outpacer has let down his cowl. He had at last exposed his face to all of them. She did not immediately notice because since his hood fell away in Lola's bedroom she has continued to visualize his face even through the shadowy burlap.

"I am sorry," he told them, "to show myself to you so abruptly. But how else was it to be done?"

Even Candace, whose mouth still hung open, seemed to recognize this as a rhetorical question. Harry nodded and cleared his throat, a sound gruff enough to jar them all out of their stupor and into action. Bird Girl's skin was buzzing, as was her head. She presumed the others felt what she was feeling: curiosity shot through with apprehension; hopefulness tinged with foreboding. What if the encampment was not what it appeared? What if they were walking into an ambush?

But oh, how those storybook elements pulled at her. She desperately wanted to see for herself the silk tents, the children, the women in their long skirts, and the tethered goat. She had never seen a real goat, but she remembered reading somewhere that this animal was known as the Mother of Destiny. She could not recall why, or what civilization came up with this idea. Was she the only one of the six harbouring the notion that their destiny would change once they met these people in their colourful camp?

Everyone, even Harry, appeared uncommonly edgy. She guessed that the Outpacer's sudden emergence from his cowl had augmented the general tension. It wasn't just the surprise of seeing a human face with the requisite eyes, nose, mouth, chin, and cheekbones, where for months one had seen only a folded hood. The Outpacer had the kind of features, and particularly the kind of eyes, that never failed to hit you like a lightning bolt. Was this because he looked so much like a wolf? Magnetically predatory. As if he could strip you naked and sink his teeth into your haunches, and you would say "thank you very much" and worship him and let him do with you as he would. Here he was — gaunt, grimy, and looking more than a bit haggard. Yet he was still unmistakably resplendent. Their protector, whose naked face they were all immensely grateful to see at last.

When the Outpacer asked Candace to go with him as emissary to treat with the people of the silk tents, she blushed right down to the top of her décolletage. Candace happened to have on one of her lower-cut tops this morning, and Bird Girl noticed how remarkably pretty and vulnerable the pink flush made her look.

Candace recovered from her embarrassment quickly enough, declaring rather pompously that she should carry a white flag. Bird Girl was sure she saw the Outpacer's lips twitch. "By all means," he said, at which Candace began looking for a stick stout enough to bear the length of dazzling white fabric she has taken from her pack.

Bird Girl was bewildered as to why Candace has been carrying a large linen table cloth, through all their travails. What on earth can she have had in mind, bringing something so completely impractical? The cloth did, however, make a very impressive white flag which Candace waved about with some panache.

As the two returned from the parley, they could hear Candace exclaiming: "Heart-warming; a brilliant success!" She was definitely swaggering. She boomed out that the People of the Silk were offering them hospitality for a day or two. Bird Girl tried not to dwell on how smug Candace looked.

They then all set off together to meet the People of the Silk.

When they finally emerge clear of the last of the prickly brush Bird Girl takes her deepest breath for months, revelling in the sight of the lifting hills on the unbounded horizon. She feels absurdly light and dainty and joyous. As they come closer, so dazzled is she by the vision of the sun-stained, silken tents that she does not immediately register Chandelier's shout of joy. Perhaps it is because the sound he makes seems so much a part of everything she beholds.

She sees an older woman coming toward them a tall, statuesque woman with red-gold hair arranged in a braided circlet round her brow. She wears a full-length gown of sapphire blue that flows in rhythm with her slow and stately walk.

"Miriam!" Chandelier exclaims. When has he ever sounded so happy? She understands this must be the healing woman Chandelier told her about, the one who cared for him after the Egg exploded, and who gave him the earring from which he took his name.

A giant of a man thunders into view. He is dressed in a stained leather overall, and his massive arms are bare. His head is huge, as are his hands. His mouth is wide open and he is roaring. It is the Maker, Bird Girl realizes, and the fear that grips her is a claw round her throat. Chandelier told her the Maker hated him so much, the man had carved a threat-mark on his spine. And so her breath catches to see the hard fury in the giant's eye. But the most terrifying thing is the lance he bears, its steely tip aimed at Chandelier's heart.

What happens next is so extraordinary Bird Girl cannot at first absorb what she is seeing. Candace, who had been standing a little to her left, transforms herself into a missile. Bird Girl watches unbelieving as Candace hurls herself at the giant, tackles him on his left side, and brings him down.

The giant roars again as the lance falls from his hand. They all run to where Candace and the giant grapple on the ground; then watch amazed as the huge man gets up and with an exaggerated chivalry helps Candace to her feet.

Their eyes lock. They stand motionless, Candace staring up at him, and the giant looking down at her. Candace's face glows as ripely as her heaving breast. She speaks not a word. That is how Bird Girl knows for certain that Eros has undone her.

Bird Girl inwardly wishes Candace joy of this glowering hulk of a man with his shaggy hair and rank odour she can smell even at this distance. Nevertheless, she feels a rancorous pain in her chest. It takes her a moment to identify this malignant sensation as envy.

Chapter Eighteen
Candace Is Vanquished

SHE WAS STUNNED WHEN SHE SAW the huge, unkempt man bearing down on Chandelier with his lance. For a split-second she pictured the boy's unspeakable death, his slight body impaled on this crude weapon and his life's blood seeping out. She was not conscious of thinking after that. The next thing she knew she was flying at the giant, her sole goal to bring him down before he can strike.

It is the hot animal stink of him that casts the first spell. As she hurls herself against the wild man throwing him off balance, Candace is both magnetized and repulsed by his ripe stench. Unconsciously she catalogues the ingredients of his pungent odour, identifying long-ingrained dirt, sweat of a peculiar fruitiness, and the shrill tang of dried blood and hot metal. This sharp scent of iron or perhaps something deeper in him still — in the lining of his gut or the marrow of his bones — draws her to him inexorably so that she knows herself immediately to be the nail to his hammer, the molten substance on his forge. She senses, even at this distance, how his fierce heat would dissolve all trace of a woman's lingering sin and restore her innocence.

Long afterwards, when she has borne him one child, and then another and another, Candace would continue to relive with blushing pleasure her first visceral response to the Maker. "My Vulcan," she calls him; "my man," words she utters with a tender pride and absolute fealty.

In the instant he helps her to her feet, she sees in his eyes a rampant desire that matches her own. The transformation comes about with a startling swiftness: the hosts of butterflies in her belly are now aflutter everywhere, craving sweetness that only this man can give her. Until this moment, Candace had no idea what passion was. She is overwhelmed by the agonizing rush of joy and suffering that impels her toward Vulcan; the compulsion to know and lick every crease and pore in his flesh and to dread his absence above everything else in the world. She is left reeling by the sheer intensity of desire: how hot it is and how sharp, as if his lance has indeed pierced her through. Her knees buckle. In her mind's eye she sees her idealized community dissolve, and this mammoth, uncouth, magnificent man stands in its place, his legs wide-planted on the earth.

The Maker takes her hand and guides her to a private enclosure he regards as his own. Candace, dizzied by her pounding heart, is aware only of a dappled greenness, a yielding softness underfoot and a rustling of leaves that verges on music. Later she will see that the whispering leaves belong to poplars and that the soft floor on which the Maker strips her bare is moss. She is overwhelmed by the fluid delicacy with which he removes her clothes and the gentle touch of his fingers and lips. Somehow she understands that he is deliberately holding back; that he is making the revelation of her nakedness a sacred act. His every gesture has a gravity that betokens respect; even, she thinks, worship.

Once she is naked, he walks around her, marking out a perfect circle. "How beautiful you are," he whispers. His words conjure up a mystical veil round them, as he looks with such evident wonder at her heavy breasts, her wide hips, her Rubenesque buttocks. He bends to caress her rosy knees, and her small feet with their rosy nails. She is spellbound when he flings himself on his knees and presses his face to the dark-blond curls of her bush, his tongue warm and a little rough. She gasps and moans as he explores the shape and thickness of her labia and how he might best bring her pleasure.

He lifts her up, although it seems to her that she has flown up to his shoulders where she sits, her legs splayed, her vagina spread open to his mouth. His massive hands brace her back as she yields to an undertow of sensation so rapturous she wonders if she has departed the earth altogether. There is an instant in which she pictures what a shameless spectacle they would make for an onlooker: a naked woman hoisted on the shoulders of a giant, her thighs pressed tight against his face, his tongue pushing deep inside her, his right hand stroking her buttocks and tickling her cleft.

Picturing herself thus — spread open, greedy for the pleasure Vulcan lavishes upon her, Candace triggers her own climax. The idea comes to her that her lover has somehow conspired to shower her with gold. Then she is lost to herself. The old Candace is no more. She is reborn and emerges from her metamorphosis only half aware of the wild cries she uttered during her transformation.

Candace never knew that her cries of ecstasy rang out clearly in the camp of the People of the Silk. Nor would anyone ever tell her it was Harry who coughed loudly and long in a vain attempt to protect her privacy.

The couple's consummation is accomplished hastily, then lingeringly, upon their bed of moss. Afterwards, they wash each other in a stream that runs cool and clear between banks of bulrushes. Candace touches Vulcan's chest, spreading her fingers wide in the black wiry hair, delighted at how tiny her hand appears against his thatch. She strokes his face adoringly and the thick rod of his penis springs toward her again.

"Wife," he says to her, while they are still immersed in the water.

"Husband," she answers him.

When at last he leaves her, because he is the Maker and must attend to the day's chores, Candace sits on a while alone. Despite bathing, she can still smell him on her skin. She is bewildered by the immensity of her joy, and yet how light and liquid a thing it is. She understands she is home at last, in a place of profoundest sheltering and fruitfulness.

A song rises up within her, an aria she had forgotten she knew. Indeed, she has to heart only its melody and phonetic sounds, for the aria is in Italian and Candace does not understand the meaning of the words she sings. Unlike her speaking voice, which tends to be nasal, her singing voice is an unalloyed and unaffected soprano. At the camp, her travelling companions hear this angelic sound and shake their heads disbelievingly.

"Can it be?" The Outpacer speaks aloud the question every mind forms.

"Who would have thought it?" Harry asks twice.

When Candace finishes the aria, she sings it once again. Both Lucia and Harry, who understands Italian, ponder the strange words.

For Chandelier, the song stirs memories that he would prefer left quiescent. This aria had been a great favourite of his father's, and its miraculous form had often taken wing beneath the roof of the Egg.

The boy, whose heart is already sore at seeing Miriam, flinches as the music floods his mind with pictures he finds unbearable. He tries fruitlessly to push them away; throws himself to the ground and sobs bitterly. Harry, who sees Chandelier's plight from some distance, tries to go to the boy. But it is one of those cursed times when his legs refuse to obey his will. The old man strikes at his faltering limbs in frustration, and cries out to Bird Girl who is already running toward the prostrate boy.

To all this Candace remains oblivious, wrapped in the globe of her own happiness. She has already moved on.

Chapter Nineteen
Chandelier Sees Snake's Tongue

Ombra mai fù di vegetabile
Cara ed amabile soave più

THE BOY GRINDS HIS FACE IN the dirt. He cannot stop himself, so heavy and unendurable is his pain. This music recalls joyous moments he has urged himself repeatedly to forget: those most rare times of family contentment when he felt himself nourished, like a normal boy with normal parents, all three bound by love.

Under the aria's spell, his mother's tranquillity appeared as a great and unusual gift. For those few minutes the music lived in the ear and mind, they were a family united in hope and yearning for a better world. The song permeated the enclosure of the Egg and made it boundless. Chandelier saw all this and understood that he witnessed happiness, all the more to be treasured because of its evanescence. For this aria held an unfathomable mystery — that after it faded away, he could no longer recall it.

Until that morning, hearing Candace sing, Chandelier had forgotten the notes and how a liquid, lucent voice could shape itself to them and summon up a palpable joy. He had forgotten those interludes when the bonds of filial love had seemed real to him, and solid and secure. He thought at these times he could imagine his very cradling, and appreciate most fully the dream of benevolent nurture his father had intended the Egg to provide. Through the life of the aria that Candace sets shining upon the air, he sees his parents again as they had been; and in the bitter taste of earth in which he grinds his face, relives again his excruciating loss.

In the silence that follows her song the boy gets to his feet. He is unsteady still, his pale face streaked with dirt and tears. Bird Girl comes to him and he leans needfully on her shoulder. Chandelier begins to quake, convulsed by a swift and uncontrollable tremor rising from the soles of his feet. It is not just the aftershock of grief that seizes and shakes him, but his present dilemma. He feels — quite literally — as if he is being torn in two. Here is his beloved Miriam, bestowing on him that particular gentle regard he had thought never to see again. And there stands Harry, to whose soul the boy feels himself bound as dear companion. There is no doubt that Harry looks at him as lovingly as does Miriam, and with the same deeply evident concern.

Bird Girl's hand at his elbow steadies him. When Chandelier looks again at Miriam, he sees how much more lined and strained her face has become since they first met many months ago. It dawns on him that she is wearing the mantle of the Seamstress. Miriam is now the leader of the People of the Silk, he realizes. This is why she looks so weary, and why her hands are already taking on the rigid shape of claws. He is saddened that her painstaking stitching of rents in silk is taking such a toll. He knows the Seamstress must keep the fabric intact, because the cherished silk is inextricable from the group's identity and spirit. The Seamstress must also be the group's wise woman and counsellor. This made a heavy burden, and Chandelier perceives with a pang that Miriam will now age far more rapidly than he.

If anything, this intensifies his wish to bow down at her feet. He wants, above all else, for her to fold him in her loose robe and strong arms, and later, in the fastness of her fluttering tent, to take him inside her. He believes he has returned to Miriam (for what else could this be but a return?) stronger and nearer to manhood.

But Snake is writhing and twisting in his spine. The boy sees the flash of emerald scales upon the sapphire air. He flinches as the forked tongue lashes his ear. He does not want to hear Snake's cold-blooded truth. Snake makes him confront Harry's name, and the question that pounds in his heart's blood.

"Face it. Why do I have a forked tongue, boy?" Chandelier knows he cannot shirk answering. Snake is the severest of taskmasters.

Dilemma. Conundrum. He sees that the forked tongue signifies choice, and that he must choose.

He looks to where Miriam waits at the opening of her tent.

He looks to see Harry standing beside a slim tree of freckled brightness. He sees his old friend reach out to stroke the bark, as if he caressed the cheek of his beloved. Harry beckons to Chandelier, and his outstretched hand is an open cup.

At that instant, Harry loses his footing and Chandelier feels his own heart lurch, and then quieten, as the old man succeeds in righting himself. So attuned is the boy to the frailties of Harry's body that he hears, even at that distance, a small gasp of pain escape the old man's lips. He makes his decision in that instant, marvelling anew at how varied are the forms of love. He goes to receive Miriam's blessing. This takes the form of a simple kiss upon his brow. He knows the imprint of her mouth is the token of a passion he will never experience with her again. Then Chandelier goes to join Harry, who has made him the gift of his most holy thoughts and hallowed remembrances.

"Birch," says Harry.

It takes a second before Chandelier grasps that this is the name of the slender white tree with the silvery marks and bands.

"This means," says Harry, "that we are nearly home."

"Home?" The word tastes strange on the boy's tongue. Yet when he says it again, the sound delights him. Both his mind and body yearn for this mysterious place he has never really known. He plunges his hand deep in his pocket where his fingers tighten on the little green stone tablet that had been his father's. It comes to him at last what this object is, and why his father had valued it so highly.

"The key to our underground in the air," his father called it, as he tapped out his messages to the Arête with the tablet's little metal paddle. This object Chandelier had taken from the ruins of the Egg was a Morse key. Morse was an ancient code, the boy recalls, its alphabet made up of dots and dashes of sound. So old was this code that the EYE, and all who served the EYE, had long ago forgotten it ever existed.

Chandelier cannot contain his excitement. He must tell Harry of his discovery. "A Morse key," he explains to his old friend, "for transmitting messages in code."

"Is it, boy?" Harry peers at the object that Chandelier cupped in his hands as reverentially as if it were a crystal chalice wrought for a saint.

"You don't say," says Harry. "Well, I never heard of such a thing."

Chandelier is delighted. If Harry has no knowledge of the Morse technology, this means the code is ancient indeed. Very likely the EYE is still oblivious to a means of communication so archaic. He begins to wonder if he might find a way to contact the Arêté's underground in the air once they reach this place that Harry calls "home."

Chapter Twenty
Harry Meditates on the Ice

HARRY HAD SOMETIMES DOUBTED HE WOULD ever again touch a birch tree. Yet here it was, one of a pale and gracious company that rose from this blessed earth on which he stood. Blessed, because here he had witnessed the miracle of the boy's rescue from a lance about to pierce his young heart. And Chandelier's saviour, oh wonder of wonders, was Candace-the-Self-Obsessed, Candace the Chatterer, the constant bane of an old man's existence. This unlikely twist in the group's destiny reinforces Harry's conviction that they are nearing some deep-dwelling source after which they all thirst.

Who would have thought it? Who would have thought that Candace would be the one to stay the giant's hand and save his beloved boy? Who would have imagined the Garrulous One had the courage, the daring, the fire in her belly, and the generosity to carry out this reckless but essential deed? The sheer unexpectedness of her act restores his faith in the possibilities for humankind. Candace stood revealed in his eyes. He is not at all chagrined or ashamed at his former poor opinion of her character. Instead, he is delighted to have his own caustic appraisal overturned.

"Delight," he thinks, is the correct word. It holds the luminescence that happiness brings to the seen world. This is the innocent clarity of earth's and his own first days. The boy lives. Candace has tumbled into a sea of erotic bliss. The tents and faces of the People of the Silk glow in the keen, clear air. The bleat of the goat is like a song rising out of his boyhood.

He and his five travelling companions have emerged from the jagged forest intact, if not unscathed. Harry can smell the clean north. He is sure he can hear, not too far off, the lapping waves of the huge lake of unfathomable depth, which millennia ago, mammoth, roaring sheets of ice had carved out of the earth. This might well be the same ice, Harry thinks, on which thousands of years later, he stomped out his ebullient, half-delirious ritual dance beneath the golden sun dogs of the southern pole.

Gigantic sheets of ice had travelled the face of the earth, shaping and sculpting, opening veins for turbulent rivers, raising mountains that would inspire men to dream of the faces of the gods. Ice was the prime mover in all he now beheld: the moss, the yarrow, the dark-purple hills, and this birch, whose papery smoothness is still cause for wonder. Harry would not have been at all embarrassed to admit that his first love was a slim white birch. He had been a solitary boy and a dreamer. The young tree, with its fluid grace, readily metamorphosed into a girl, whom in his chaste imaginings he adored. As he grew older and the pall of winter sometimes dragged upon his spirit, it was the birch that had the power to lift his mind again. Against the dark backdrop of the stolid conifers, they were a company of supple dancers with arms outstretched. Birch trees seemed to him to be always giving of themselves, sending out into the world bright, fluttering ribbons of silver and pale bronze.

He touches the silky inner bark with a reverence that seems as natural as breath. He feels the thrill and thrum of life beneath his fingers. For a moment he is a boy again, enamoured of an ivory tree whose mysterious markings bear a message he is not yet ready to understand. Does he grasp this message now? It is more, he realizes, than the simple promise of water underground. These trees speak of persistence, of the radiant spirits of earth. They tell the passionate story of endurance. Harry sees that he has himself lived out this story, and that his love for these trees is undiminished. The Handel aria Candace sang has reminded him of the deep roots of his boyhood attachment.

"The music is sublime and the plot absolutely absurd." So a cultivated companion in Antarctica had first introduced Harry to Handel's *Xerxes*. This man was a composer on a travel grant seeking inspiration from the great continent's ethereal spaces and unearthly silence. He took pleasure in playing for Harry some of the recordings he had brought south with him. Harry still treasures the memory of those bountiful hours.

"The Persian king Xerxes is singing of his great passion for a plane tree." Thus the composer had paraphrased for Harry the perplexing words of the opera's most famous aria. "Ah well, I told you it was absurd, "the composer continued. "But there is basis in fact, apparently. Historical records claim that Xerxes was indeed sent into raptures at the sight of a particularly magnificent specimen of plane tree. And he behaved as any wealthy lover would and hung her branches with precious gems and set a guard to keep watch over her constantly, lest she come to harm.

"But only listen," he exhorted Harry, "and you will hear something rare indeed that transcends the apparent nonsense of the words."

Harry listened and the aria poured through him. He tasted fleetingly a poignant insight into exalted love and longing. Yet almost as soon this idea crystallized in his mind, it vanished, and he could not articulate what he had understood so clearly only seconds before.

Ombra mai fù di vegetabile
Cara ed amabile soave più

Whatever the nature of the fugitive insight, now so many decades gone, Harry still sees no absurdity whatsoever in the tale of the king and his beloved. In fact, he feels a deep bond with Xerxes. Just as now he feels a most surprising bond with Candace whose mellifluous rendering of the largo still stuns him, even in retrospect. That she should choose this particular song, and bestow it so angelically upon the air, crowned Harry's own contentment. The boy lived. This was the bracing north and they would head out soon, farther north still, nearer to the mighty lake where long ago artists had made their pilgrimage, seeking the holy secret of creation and paying it homage with paint on canvas.

Harry understands the deep need of humankind for these acts of ritual observance. He senses that Lucia also understands. She sits not far from him on a stool of simple and practical design, fashioned by the Maker. Her face, with its look of rapt attention, declares her passion for her work as she shapes a handful of moist and yielding clay newly dug from the stream bank.

She glances up, sees Harry watching her and smiles.

"I have made a curious snake," she says. "Would you like to see?"

Harry peers at the sinuous form on Lucia's palm, and involuntarily blinks, so remarkable is the illusion of taut, electric life. She has fashioned the snake curled round on itself to make a double circlet. With a twig? — or perhaps her fingernail — Lucia has scored the body so as to give the impression of iridescent, diamond-patterned scales. With its sleek head upraised, the snake seems to regard Harry intently through long, narrow eyes. It has tiny distinct nostrils and a mouth set in an ironic twist that suggests a bemused omnipotence.

"You can almost see its tongue flicker," Harry tells her.

Lucia laughs and looks pleased.

The next morning, under a bronze-green dawn, the group, minus Candace, prepares to leave the camp of the People of the Silk. The most painful farewell is Chandelier's leave-taking of Miriam. From this scene, Harry averts his gaze. Just as they are departing, his eyes meet Miriam's. He sees she grasps the truth that he has already perceived: ultimately her love would have smothered the boy. Such truths are hard to bear, their eyes say. We who have lived so long know these things.

Harry wonders briefly how matters will turn out between Miriam and Candace; then embraces his own happy deliverance. There is no doubt that Candace had preyed upon everyone's nerves. Yet he is also well aware that their shared irritation, whether at her loudness, her interference or her clumsy attempts to dominate, has served them well. Justified anger at Candace had helped to spur them on and bond them one to the other.

Now they are five, moving northward in a silence that is both expansive and nourishing. In the quiet, the world comes to him in ways Candace would have disrupted had she still been of their company. He revels in leaf flutter, the slide of shadow and the sway of light, the surging power of stripped rock; even in the pleasurable awareness of his own breathing and the movement of his blood enlivened by this northern air. He rejoices too, at the great span of space through which they move. No matter in what direction he looks, the horizon affirms the endless unfolding of the world. In his mind's eye he sees the high-peaked waves of the majestic lake beckoning them onward.

It seems as if they have wandered into a new season of earth, as well as of time. The sun no longer pains his flesh or his eyes. Is this possible, he wonders, or just an old man's foolish fancy?

Bird Girl runs on lightly ahead, the breeze ruffling her pale blond hair, and fanning out the purple skirt she wears over bright-blue leggings. Harry is reminded of the dazzling hummingbirds he had seen long ago in Costa Rica. As if in response to his thoughts, the girl's arms become wings, rising, falling, circling. She is transformed into a whirl of colour, and at the end of her performance, she utters a strange ecstatic cry.

Beside him, Chandelier laughs. Then the boy falls silent a moment, before asking Harry: "Is she not beautiful?"

Harry is uncertain whether the boy means Bird Girl or Miriam. But he is happy, in either case, to give his affirmation.

By early afternoon, they come to a beach of fine sand bordering a bay of the great lake. A soft wind rises, circling them, where they sit captivated by the glittering mass of the incoming waves. To the farthest extent of their vision the steel-blue water surges and falls, and surges and falls. Harry soon enough makes his own breath and heartbeat consonant with this rhythm. He feels at home in this place where the monumental labour of the shaping ice is still so evident.

Farther to the west, a sheer cliff face rings the bay. Harry imagines that every crevice in that obdurate rock must hold an echo of the thunder of its own creation. The rock remembers, he thinks, and this realization strikes him as itself an act of worship. It is good to sit upon the beach with his companions, eating and drinking a little from the generous provisions gifted to them by the People of the Silk. Soon, they must set off again. Only a few miles more, and they will come to the abandoned mining company settlement. Its simple buildings are apparently still serviceable and sturdy. The People of the Silk told them there is even a generator that might be resuscitated.

Harry is not much interested in the generator. But he looks forward to some insulation from the damp night air and soil, and to viewing the sky through a window cut into stout logs. He is more than ready for looking at the world again from within a snug enclosure. Is this an ancient human need insisting itself, he wonders, or just the weariness of his old bones?

A tortured groan breaks in upon his thoughts and his spine stiffens in fear. The irrational fancy comes to him that what he hears is the lamentation of his mother's ghost, mourning his own imminent death. He shakes himself, and turns round to see Bird Girl at the water's edge. She holds aloft one of the papier mâché masks from the theatre box on which he had banged his shin. He sees she is using the mask as a sound box, funnelling the breeze from the lake through the wide-stretched mouth in the shellacked face.

He struggles to quell a prickling anger, whose sharpness is all the more surprising given that he has never had anything but the most benign feelings for the young girl. What is it about the inhuman mouthings from the black hole in that artificial face which disturbs him so? Why does this sound, and the look of this object that Bird Girl still holds skyward, make his sparse flesh contract even more tightly on his bones?

He has found the masks offensive since he first saw them staring up at him from inside the wooden box. Their slippery gloss, unnatural yellow and green flesh tones, bulbous foreheads and yawning mouth cavities, all stir in him the deepest unease. He had only agreed to carry one because Bird Girl was so insistent. He tries, as far as possible, not to think of the heartless, rigid old man's face that accompanies him as he walks, stuffed at the bottom of his drawstring sack.

Bird Girl springs round and makes one of her little leaps forward. Harry thinks her eyes look uncharacteristically wild. She holds her woman's mask, with its black lacquered hair and heavily lidded eyes, up against her chest. For a second, Harry feels a genuine fear for her sanity. Or perhaps for his own, for from his perspective it does look as if she cradles a cleanly decapitated head, the wide-open mouth frozen in a last attempt to speak. He glances at Lucia and the Outpacer, who still sit upon the sand, and at Chandelier, who has been staring out at the waves. On all their faces, he sees a mirror of his own concern.

Chapter Twenty-One
Bird Girl and the Dance

BIRD GIRL HUGS THE MASK TIGHTLY to her chest. Never before has she felt so fully alert and alive. Is it because of this place at which they have finally arrived? There is some all-restoring sustenance coming from the dark solid rock whose roots she senses reaching deep into the earth, and from the steadying motion of the lake-like-a-sea, which is so huge she cannot see its opposite shore. The air tastes cool and cerulean on her tongue.

The landscape gives of itself so openly and cleanly she is sure it is bestowing these qualities on her thought. She is seized by the certainty that this is the place and time, exactly now, when all five of them can enact the ritual that has gradually been taking shape in her mind.

It was Chandelier who'd suggested that the six theatre masks had probably been used for a dramatic chorus, with all the actors speaking in unison, precisely, to the last syllable. Not just a shared voice and intonation, but a common breath and pulse. She was sure this was why she had felt compelled to bring the masks. They would all put them on, and after a little rehearsing, they would speak or chant together in a perfectly achieved harmony. She imagined them creating a temple of sound, with fluted columns that let in the light and air. It would be a holy place made of human voice and breath, and of an unforced and unbounded passion.

The yearning in her — to perform the ritual here and now — was sharper than any desire she had ever known; keener even than her desire to possess an entire library or to be reunited and reconciled with her mother. It crossed her mind that perhaps this was what it was like when gifted people felt impelled to create a work of art. Then she pushed this idea away as far too self-regarding for her purposes. The ritual was not *her* creation. They must build this temple of sound together: she and Chandelier and Harry and Lucia and the Outpacer. Her part was to explain to them why it was so necessary.

First, they must do this for Lola. Bird Girl knew she would never be at peace until she had fittingly acknowledged Lola's sacrifice, and helped to create a ceremony that was artistic, dignified, and worthy of the old lady's gift.

And second, they must do it for their own sake: as thanksgiving for having survived the forest's traps and trials and in recognition of the destiny they had forged as a group. She doubted that any one of them could have made it through alone. Each of them, even Candace, had added to and fortified the life-story they shared.

Sometimes she thought she glimpsed this story's actual plot, like a braid of silver water running through the welter of events and heavy, tangled emotions. There must be a way to catch it and reveal its actual shape: just the way the choruses in Greek tragedies had done it. Chandelier had told her how the actors in the chorus would stand on their own and comment on the essence of the action, so that the audience was made aware of the overarching truth of what was really happening on the stage. Those choruses would say things like: "Vengeance feeds on vengeance" or "Suffering maketh wisdom."

Bird Girl had thought about it carefully and decided that for their chorus a chanting of pure sound would be best. For one thing, she hadn't been able to come up with the right set of words that could contain everything she wanted the ritual to convey. She wanted grief and joy and thanksgiving. And yes, she wanted the words to hold the wisdom/suffering equation too, and to let that much-tested truth ring out like a bell. So she asked Chandelier to teach her all the Ancient Greek ritual cries he remembered from his reading of the tragedies. She had somehow managed to weave these cries into a supple song. It surprised her how well all the individual utterances cohered. She was sure she could teach these interwoven cries to the others very easily indeed. What concerned her was the process of wearing and speaking through the masks themselves. She had foolishly supposed it would be a simple matter of putting the mask on and pulling taut the two leather straps at the back that held the glazed face snugly in place.

But once she had it on, the panic set in almost immediately. Paradoxically, she felt she was smothering inside the featherweight mask. She was taken over by the irrational idea that some doom was about to descend on her; that she had eaten Socrates' seeds of hemlock and that her limbs were already growing cold. She only just managed to control the impulse to pull the mask off, and apply her mother's counsel on what to do when fear-filled panic threatened to unravel you. Bird Girl began to breathe strongly from her pelvic floor until she was calm enough to start chanting through the black cavern of the mask's mouth.

Abruptly, she was rocked back on her heels. Zeus, or some other thunder god, was amplifying these sounds she uttered, doubling and deepening them so that they resonated powerfully within the hollow bulging forehead of the mask. God-speak, she thought. The cavity was full of a divine sound now, a humming that originated in the electric currents of earth and sky, setting the flesh of her forehead a-tingle. Next, it was as if someone had tripped a switch. Every cell in her body was quickened and filled with a honey-gold light. She both saw and felt this fluid light, which was suddenly a winged being ascending within her. *This is ecstasy at last*, she thought. Then she thought no more, until the moment she ceased chanting. She took off the mask and shook her head in wonder at where she had been.

Just to be certain that what had happened was not an aberration, she waited an hour or so and tried it again. The result was the same: she experienced the strangling panic and cold doom when she first put on her mask; then when she disciplined herself to the deep breathing and steady chanting, she activated the sublime sound box again. The god-speak reverberated against her vulnerable human flesh. And off she sped, light-footed and wide-winged.

Now Bird Girl had to grapple with a thorny moral dilemma. Did she have the right to ask the others to endure the state of cold-doom panic the mask brought on at first: like being immured alive in a tomb, with iron bands about one's chest? In Harry's case especially, does she have to right to ask?

She guessed that the revelation of the mask's sound box secret would only work fully if it came as a surprise. She examined the question again and again and finally decided that the ritual would not have the correct fittingness and potency without the masks. What they would be making was a work of art, albeit invisible and fleeting. And the first stage in the making of art was often painful, was it not — a period of doubt and helplessness that must be endured with courage and faith? One waited in the thick darkness, trusting that the inrush of inspiration would come. Wasn't that what artists of all kinds did?

Bird Girl resolved to counsel the others well. She would encourage them and teach them how to cope with that first petrifying panic when they donned the masks. They would succeed in speaking with one voice. They would see through the same eyes. They would do this for Lola's sake . . . She makes one of her little balletic leaps toward them where they sit, each wrapped in their own thoughts, upon the wide crescent of the strand.

"This is the time and place," she announces. She looks directly at each of them in turn. "We need to have a performance, a ritual, something to mark all we have come through. And I want each of us to put on our masks.

"To hold what has happened in remembrance," she adds urgently. "To give it a shape. And for Lola. With Chandelier's help, I have worked out what we will chant. It will not take long, truly.

"Please," she implores. And again: "Please."

They all look at her quizzically. She senses their reluctance, but knows she must persuade them at all costs. This is, and must be, the moment.

"I will coach you," she tells them, "in the sounds we will make with the masks on. These are ritual cries Chandelier taught me, which he remembers from the ancient Greek plays he studied in his father's library.

"I have thought carefully about this," she reassures them. "I am certain these are the sounds the masks demand. They are simple sounds, but powerful. This is the place, ruled by wind and light and rock and water, where they must be loosed again into the world.

"*Evoi, evan, alali, io, ia, iache, papapape.*"

They humour her and comply, practising the cries until she is satisfied. When they flag or grew restive, Bird Girl chides them lovingly, praises their efforts and inspires them anew to try to make "a living temple of sound."

"Raise the temple higher," she encourages them. "Raise it." Under her tutelage, the five transform the series of ritual cries into a chorus that is both sculptured and fluidly alive. Bird Girl is amazed at the visceral joy she experiences at hearing Harry's tenor blend with the Outpacer's bass, Lucia's contralto, Chandelier's countertenor, and her own soprano. She sees from their beaming faces, their uplifted arms, how pleased they all are with what they have made. The light reflected from the lake swings around and beneath them in a magnificent loop.

"We are ready," Bird Girl tells them, "to put on our masks."

She sees Harry and then Lucia frown. "But why," Lucia asks. "We've managed to produce this splendid, soaring sound together. Why must we confine our voices inside those hard, ugly masks?"

"You will see why," Bird Girl responds with all the assurance she can muster. "Please trust me on this."

⁓

Harry struggles to overcome his reluctance and perceives a similar slowness in Lucia, the Outpacer, and Chandelier as they take their masks out of their packs.

Bird Girl has put on her woman's mask with its broad, wide cheekbones, hypnotic black eyes, and chasm mouth. Already she is not herself, but some hybrid that makes Harry's flesh prickle. He feels more uneasy still when he puts on his old man's mask with its grey-white beard and sagging eyelids. Despite the lightness of the papier mâché, the mask seems to him a heavy, choking thing once it encloses his face. Abruptly, a blind panic mounts in him. He feels he is being smothered. He cannot breathe. The sensation behind the mask is akin to death. Images of the frozen faces of Admiral Scott and Birdie Bowers flash upon his mind's eye. He puts up his hand with the intention of plucking the mask from his face. He is a very old man who must protect what breath he has left. Bird Girl's childish game strikes him now as not only absurd, but dangerous. For one poisonous instant, he hates her and her foolish demands.

"Breathe." It is her voice he hears, booming from inside her woman's mask. "Breathe deeply and produce your sound from the pelvis. As deep as you can."

How ridiculous, he thinks. *From the pelvis.* But he obeys, and lets his arm drop. Glancing round, he sees through the eye-holes of the mask that Lucia, the Outpacer, and Chandelier are all following suit; he guesses that they too have experienced the same mortifying panic and the urge to tear these polished faces from off their own flesh. The girl in her gleaming wise-woman's mask continues to urge them on. They begin again the sequence of ritual cries they had perfected.

From the pelvis. Harry seeks the source of breath and sound from deep within, and strives over and over to keep at bay the fear of smothering death. He utters his sounds they have so carefully rehearsed. He joins in the chorus. Gradually he becomes aware of an extraordinary force filling the cavity of the mask's bulbous forehead. So powerful is the resonance of his own voice and breath in this hollow that he is initially stunned. Whatever is happening is electric. Then, just as unexpectedly, the reverberation triggers an ecstasy, and a current of joy passes through him. He feels clean and light, as if his body were somehow boundless.

When he looks out again through the eyes of his mask, he cannot at first believe what he sees. Bird Girl has taken off the glazed face, and she is dancing a kind of stately pavane with a great blue heron, whose long toes mark out perfect time upon the sand.

Harry plucks off the mask and rubs his eyes. When he looks again, the great bird is still there, dancing with the young woman. For an instant, as it turns, Harry and the heron exchange a glance.

See, I am returned, its eye seems to say. *What had been lost is found again.*

Harry continues to watch the slow, circling dance of bird and girl in rapt amazement, his mouth agape in an uncanny mimicry of the mask he holds before his chest. He looks at his companions and sees it is the same with them.

⁓

At first, Bird Girl is aware only of a flutter of blue. Then she sees the narrow head, topped by the black plume, the gleaming scimitar-like beak and the golden eyes with their unfathomable ebony pupils.

She takes off her mask and sees mere feet away from her the proud angular heron whose beauty makes her want to weep. He is as tall as she. His spindly legs strike her as absurdly delicate, but she notes their obvious strength as he makes an elegant side-step and inclines his head toward her. He bends his head again, and takes another sideways step. She understands then that he is asking her to dance with him, to mark out a graceful circle upon the sand.

Four times round they go, in keeping with a rhythm she recognizes as from the chant, which still moves through the air although they are all silent. She watches and keeps pace with each slow step and the high lift of the heron's knee, suspended for a moment. It is a dance performed in discrete parts, and it dawns on her that what the heron is doing is stitching one dimension to another with his delicate, elegant movement — not just space to time, but also the invisible to the visible.

On the completion of their fourth turn, the heron lowers his head, takes two steps back toward the lake. Then he turns, lifts high his great wide wings and rises up and off over the water. They all watch silently until he breasts the cliff to their left and disappears.

Harry is the first to bend down and touch with reverence one of the imprints of the heron's toes upon the sand. Then each of the others does this in turn, as if this gesture too is now part of the ritual they have performed upon the beach.

"A harbinger," says the Outpacer.

"A miracle," says Lucia.

"I did not think I would live to see this day," says Harry.

Bird Girl smiles widely at Chandelier and blows him a kiss. "I am happy here," she says.

Epilogue

I KNOW, MY BELOVED DAUGHTER, THAT you are as yet too young understand my words. But these are things I wish to tell you now, so that you can begin to absorb them as readily as you do the clear light and air of our northern home.

Since we came here, I often think of what happened when I put on the theatre mask at Bird Girl's insistence. At first I panicked badly. Wearing the mask was like being entombed alive. I felt the muscles of my face and my lungs begin to harden. I wanted to pull the wretched thing off before it succeeded in sucking all my breath from me and turning me to stone. I was terrified that the mask would kill me where I stood.

What stopped my hand was the example of Keats's courage through the ordeal of the making of his life mask. I thought of the many hours he had suffered with the thick plaster encasing his face, and how he was able to draw only the most meagre of breaths through the two tiny straws. He had undergone this gruelling procedure at the request of his artist friend. For my sake too, and the thousands of others like me over the generations who treasured the actual likeness of a great poet on one particular day in his twenty-fourth year.

If Keats could endure this sense of suffocation and near-death for Benjamin Haydon's sake, I chided myself, then I could do the same for Bird Girl who was so desperate to pay homage to Lola's memory.

"Breathe and produce your sound from the pelvis," I heard Bird Girl urge us. I strove to follow her counsel, and almost immediately wearing the mask became more bearable. Once we joined again in chorus to utter those strange ritual cries we had practised, I forgot about the mask altogether. It was as if we five now all shared a common breath. I had the sense of a greater company of beings speaking with us, perhaps even countless beings.

Then the first mystery showed itself. My speech-breath filling the bulbous forehead cavity revivified the ancient science of the mask. It was a sound box, designed thousands of years ago, to trigger a state of ecstasy in the wearer. The thrumming resonance in the cavity made every nerve and cell in my body vibrate. It was a shock, like an actual electrification of my entire being. I was opened, head to toe. There was a fountain of golden light inside me. I seemed to look out of other eyes, perhaps even out of the eyes of the original maker of these masks with their vast ritual power.

I knew I had been purified. I walked upon a terrace of stars. I ceased, I think, to be Lucia. A warm and sensuous wind bore me upward. Amidst the rushing stars, I saw faces, including my parents', as they were when they were young and unburdened. I saw the poet, seated beside an open window, listening to the nightingale sing upon the heath. I saw the long, lean face and body of the Outpacer as we lay together at your making. It was then I saw the glistening Egg come spinning out of the night. The state of ecstasy, as I now know, is preceded by a blinding flash. I could not look at him for long: the majestic, winged being who stepped forth from the Egg. His face and body were of such radiance, I had to close my eyes. When I opened them again, I saw Bird Girl dancing with the heron.

Bird Girl believes the heron was drawn to the tremulous quiver of our bodies and voices as we chanted inside our masks. She thinks the bird recognized our human desire to rise above what we are, and that he came to us in fellowship. There is no doubt he and Bird Girl made sublime partners. As they circled one another in the formal dance he defined, I was magnetized by his godly self-containment and awkward grace. I noticed that the bird kept a good distance between them so as not to hurt Bird Girl with his sharp beak. I also remember thinking: this cannot be happening. This dance Bird Girl is performing with the blue heron is a hallucination that will leave me desolate. But I had only to glance at the others, at their astonished eyes and open mouths, to be reassured. We all partook in this extraordinary privilege.

It was the heron who gave the sign the dance was done, with a slight inclination of his sleek neck. Then he turned to face the great lake, leant forward, spread wide his wings, and soared away over the water. We watched until he disappeared from view; then turned our gaze to the marks his feet had left upon the sand. Each of us bent down to touch the indentations his long toes made. Then we looked and saw in each other the same bracing joy that follows on an epiphany.

Bird Girl tells us that when she could bear it, she would look into the heron's fiercely glittering eye. There she seemed to see the whole of time, and the worlds within worlds that are creation, passing through their eternal cycles of doom and splendour. The dance was the miracle, she believes, that made us "darklings" light at last.

We tell each other this story often, oh my daughter, because Bird Girl's dance with the heron ushered in our time here and married us to this place.

Our new home is a group of sturdy cabins built long ago by prospectors and later used by an artists' colony. That first night there was a full moon, a dazzling milky white that made the lowly cabins look unearthly, even numinous. There were cabins enough that we each had one of our own. I made a simple bed of dry leaves under the small, square window through which I could see the moon. In the ethereal lunar glow I went over again all I had seen in the grip of the mask's power: the terrace of stars, my youthful parents, Keats and his nightingale, and the glorious, winged god who emerged from the flawless ivory oval of the Egg.

It was soon thereafter that Chandelier told us all the story of how Eros was contained in the World Egg, begotten by Night and made immaculate and polished by the wind. When the Egg cracked, it was the light of the first dawn. Then the god flew out bearing the seeds of all things, and that was the beginning of our cosmos. So we all have our beginnings in Love. Chandelier's father told him that this cosmogony belonged to the ancient Greek mystery religion of the Orphics. They cultivated rituals of purification and sought the state of *ekstasis* — the stepping out of the body we had all experienced when we chanted through the masks.

Lucia's Masks

Part of the mystery for me is whether I shared the thought-image of the World Egg with Chandelier when we performed our ritual chorus, or if it was the sound-box secret of the mask itself gave birth to the vision. But I know with full certainty that you were born of love, Speranza. Of this I have no doubt. Nor does your father.

We are nourished by many stories here in our new home. Bird Girl and Chandelier, in particular, have a great store of myths, tales, and stirring narratives. Every day Chandelier recites from his compendious, unfaltering memory, and Bird Girl writes down a poem, or a chapter of a novel in the massive log books left behind by the mining company. We are building a library here. These days, we each find great solace in our work.

We are all makers of some sort. We are becoming a part of this wild place, with its rock and mighty lake and green and lilac morning skies. We are being knitted into its monumental story.

Out of the clay of the soil, I made sun-baked bricks and built a little house shaped like the dome of Santa Maria del Fiori. The arched doorway and ovoid windows of my dome-shaped home let in a light of incomparable softness. It was here I gave birth to you, my dearest daughter. On the lintel above the door, I wrote in the soft clay "*Speranza mi fe.*" Hope made me.

This is what I have learned above all on my journey, Speranza: that hope must be added to each day and given shape through our singular acts of faith, and our unfailing attention to truth and beauty.

We add to our hope in many ways. Harry, Outpacer, and Chandelier together managed to resuscitate the ancient generator left by our predecessors. We use it sparingly, in part to operate the short-wave radio they also unearthed, which bears the proud Italian name Marconi. With the help of the radio, Chandelier, who paid close attention to all of his father's business, has managed to contact "the underground in the air" known as the Arête. This is the worldwide lifeline network that broadcasts any resurgence of art and ceremony, and the re-emergence of species. We believe the Arête is still safe from surveillance because the EYE is ignorant of the Morse code Chandelier is using for transmission. In fact, the EYE has probably forgotten that short-wave radio frequencies even exist.

We have sent the Arête news of the heron. We hear of wonderful things through the air-underground, including the rebirth of birdsong in many places throughout the world. Last week came news of sightings of the robin redbreast and the wren. We have ourselves now witnessed the return to the lake of the eider, the plover, and the tern.

I am greatly blessed as well in your health and beauty, my child, and I find myself often wishing my sister Sophia could see you, and you her. When you are older, I will tell you about Sophia and your grandparents, and the ancestral spirits who kept our family strong through a dark time.

I will teach you too, the stories that nourish the soul of our community: of Harry's enduring love for breathtaking places that have disappeared from the face of the earth; of Bird Girl's search for books and of her indomitable mother's crusade; of your father's dream of reviving the former splendour of the cinema; of how the garrulous Candace found love most unexpectedly. And why Chandelier's father created a protective Egg, where his son built up a vast knowledge he now generously shares with us all. In these ways the dream of the World Egg persists, and we feed on the truth of its founding myth as we would on honeycomb and other delicacies I sometimes find on my daily foraging.

These are skills I will also teach you when you are older.

Chandelier has just come to give me news gleaned through the Arêté I never expected to hear. Guido Santarcangelo of the confraternity known as the Rat-Men is seeking the whereabouts of a woman called Lucia, last seen near a stone house in Outland Tract 17 on the day the fireball struck.

"Do you want to reply?" he asks me.

I hold you closer. Your breath is warm on my neck. Your tiny hand grips my finger tightly even though you sleep. I stare out over the massive lake as if searching for a sign while Chandelier waits patiently. I realize that it is time to forgive myself for what I did with Guido. And he will surely want to know that the Outpacer and I have a daughter, with such a name.

"Please tell Guido Santarcangelo that I am well," I say, "and that I have a daughter, who is healthy and who is named Speranza."

I hear Chandelier's foot shift in the sand as he readies himself to speed back.

For the briefest possible moment, I relive my own amazement at Guido's revealed beauty when he pulled off the hideous rat's mask. This is our constant work, I realize — casting out the monster in ourselves and striving to be compassionate and selfless, even though we fail again and again and again. We must cast the monster out, over and over, as ceaselessly as the waves surge in toward me where I stand.

Come, Speranza. We will go and watch Chandelier send the message coded in those dots and dashes of sound that always make you laugh in delight. We will ask him to tell us exactly when he is spelling out your name in Morse. We will think of your name speeding along the invisible radio waves of the world; then silently give thanks for everything he rescued from the ruins of his father's house.

Acknowledgements

An earlier version of Chapter Four, "Their Feet," appeared in *The Malahat Review*.

I would like to thank Random House, Inc. for permission to reprint lines from Wallace Stevens's "A Rabbit as King of the Ghosts" (Copyright © 1967, 1969, 1971 by Holly Stevens).

In the writing of this book, and throughout the submission process, I was helped by the unfailing encouragement of Susan Tilley, Rhona Goodspeed, Catherine Joyce, Tom and Marilyn Henighan, Jacqueline MacIntyre, and Robert Woodbridge.

I am grateful to Sam Hiyate and Ali McDonald of The Rights Factory for their expert guidance on shaping the novel's story in its early days.

I would like to express my thanks as well, to Séan Virgo for his empathetic email companionship in the book's final stages, and the happy discovery of our shared admiration for Russell Hoban's *Riddley Walker*.

Books I found particularly helpful were Sara Wheeler's *Terra Incognita: Travels in Antarctica*; Francis Spufford's *I May Be Some Time: Ice and the English Imagination*; and Andrew Motion's biography of John Keats. An article by John Windsor in *The Independent on Sunday* of May 12, 1996 drew my attention to Thanos Vovolis's reproductions of the masks used in ancient Greek drama, and his discovery of their "sound-box" potential.

I am deeply indebted to the poet Robert Duncan, whose "Passages 14 — Chords" in *Bending the Bow* introduced me to the myth of the World Egg.

Wendy MacIntyre lives in Ottawa where she works as a freelance writer and editor. She has published scholarly essays and short fiction in journals in Canada, the United States, and Britain, including in the *University of Windsor Review* and the *Malahat Review*. Her novels are *Mairi* (Oolichan Books), *The Applecross Spell* (XYZ Publishing), and *Apart* (Groundwood Books), a young adult novel which was named one of the ten best picks for young adult fiction for 2007 by the Ontario Library Association .